SECOND SUMMER OF WAR

For Melanie,

Cheryl Cooper

Nov. 24, 2016

⊸ *Seasons of War* ⊷

SECOND SUMMER WAR

of

a novel

CHERYL COOPER

DUNDURN
TORONTO

Editor: Cheryl Hawley
Design: Courtney Horner
Printer: Webcom

Library and Archives Canada Cataloguing in Publication

Cooper, Cheryl, 1958-, author
         Second summer of war : seasons of war / by Cheryl Cooper.

"A J. Patrick Boyer book".
Issued in print and electronic formats.
ISBN 978-1-4597-0775-7

        I. Title.

PS8605.O655S43 2014   C813'.6   C2013-902960-5
                             C2013-902961-3

1   2   3   4   5   18   17   16   15   14

We acknowledge the support of the **Canada Council for the Arts** and the **Ontario Arts Council** for our publishing program. We also acknowledge the financial support of the **Government of Canada** through the **Canada Book Fund** and **Livres Canada Books**, and the **Government of Ontario** through the **Ontario Book Publishing Tax Credit** and the **Ontario Media Development Corporation**.

Care has been taken to trace the ownership of copyright material used in this book. The author and the publisher welcome any information enabling them to rectify any references or credits in subsequent editions.

                                                                        J. Kirk Howard, President

Printed and bound in Canada.

Visit us at
Dundurn.com
@dundurnpress
Facebook.com/dundurnpress
Pinterest.com/dundurnpress

Dundurn
3 Church Street, Suite 500
Toronto, Ontario, Canada
M5E 1M2

Gazelle Book Services Limited
White Cross Mills
High Town, Lancaster, England
LA1 4XS

Dundurn
2250 Military Road
Tonawanda, NY
U.S.A. 14150

For my three men —
Randy, Evan, and Brodie
— who helped me harness the wind

Prologue

Somehow she knew the way. Even though the night was concealed in a graveyard gloom, and she had been forbidden to explore the lower decks of the ship, she knew where she would find him. And he ... she prayed ... would be waiting for her.

With a lantern in one hand, her other pressing the thin material of her nightgown against her shivering body, Emily slowly picked her way through a labyrinth of greasy hammocks, rounded with the sleeping forms of the sailors. The sea was rough this night, the wind was a choir of melancholic wails, and snarls of thunder occasionally disturbed the creaking rhythm of the ship, but no activity, no human calls or commands, resonated overhead on the weather decks. No other creature seemed awake at this late hour except for the ship — her old timbers cursing and shuddering as the relentless waves thrashed her again and again. Emily wanted to believe that the sleepers, and the wood planks beneath her bare feet, belonged to the Isabelle, *but something knocked along the halls of her mind, some biting recollection that it could not be possible, for that great old ship, whose hull had been beaten and burned, lay rotting in the murky depths of the Atlantic.*

Locating the ladder to the orlop, she descended its slippery rungs, holding the lantern before her to light her way. The reek of unwashed bodies overwhelmed the salty air, and here, in the ship's bowels, the atmosphere was more hellish — a far cry from the peacefulness that slumbered above. Lying abandoned and for-gotten between empty wine casks and barrels of weevil-infested provisions were old men: blind, emaciated, half-naked, scratching furiously at limbs that were no longer there. Their noses were in various stages of decay, their skin a mess of red blotches, and they suffered cruelly, pleading with her to bring them a drink of water. Among them lay the young lieutenant, Octavius Lindsay, crumpled and still against the damp wall, an oozing depression where the side of his head should have been, his black eyes locked on her in a death stare.

Despite the sinister scenes, Emily pushed on — her feet unsteady on the warm blood that slithered like a serpent around the deck — more determined than ever to find him. There, up ahead, beyond the mire of human misery, was the surgeon's operating table. Hunched over it was a slim, shadowy figure, struggling, in the dim illumination of an oil lamp, to amputate the leg of a young boy who cried out most mournfully for his mother.

Leander.

Emily opened her mouth to call out to him, but could not summon her voice. Instead, a low, almost preternatural laugh erupted next to her. Spread out upon an oak bench was the corpulent form of a woman, mending a grubby shirt. When her laughter ceased she began humming a tune, as if she found strange delight in the pervasive suffering. Though Emily could not see the wom-an's features, she knew it was Meg Kettle.

"Ya daft girl," Meg hissed, jerking a fat thumb in the direction of the operating table. "Ave ya come lookin' fer yer precious Doctor Braden? Why, that ain't him. I told yas before ... yer doctor's lyin' on the ocean floor."

Emily groped behind her for the ladder that would take her away from Meg's rising cackle and the pain of her words, but as she mounted the first rung, the ladder — like the noses of the wretched sailors — collapsed in decay and disappeared altogether. Trapped, reeling in despair, she froze in horror as something unseen stirred in the shadows at her back. A gurgling groan followed the ominous sound of heavy, shifting chains. With a quivering hand, Emily turned and lifted the lantern, knowing all too well whose countenance would appear in the circle of light.

Trevelyan gazed at her a long while with the empty eyes of a tormented soul, and then, without warning, he lurched forward, seized her ankle with his scarred hands, and pulled her down into his dreadful darkness.

1

Wednesday, August 4, 1813

6:30 a.m.
(Morning Watch, Five Bells)
Aboard HMS *Amethyst*
In the Bay of Fundy

TEN-YEAR-OLD MAGPIE, the little sailmaker, stood stock-still alongside the starboard rail, wishing the beats of his heart would quit banging on his eardrums. He was certain of what he had seen. Had no one else noticed it then, gliding past them silently like a gigantic alligator, studying the movements of its prey before going in for the kill?

With a darting glance around him, Magpie could see that the weather decks were mainly empty; most of the men had not yet been called from their cots, or if they had arisen before the bosun's mate hollered, *"Up all hammocks ahoy,"* they were surely dressing below and contemplating their morning sustenance of cheese, oatmeal, buttered biscuit, and beer. The few who milled about above deck seemed — though sleepy-eyed and dragging their feet — to be completely absorbed in their chores, and the Officer of the Watch was nowhere in sight. Magpie was so shocked by the tranquillity of the *Amethyst* that he wondered if what he had seen had simply been a remnant of the frightful dream that had shaken him awake at this early hour.

Readjusting his new green eye-patch, Magpie again squinted into the fog bank that swirled around the hull and masts of the *Amethyst* like the wispy gauze of a woman's evening gown, his little sweaty hands instinctively fingering the blades of the magnificent dirks — the ones the privateersman, Prosper Burgo, had given him — which he had hooked upon the length of rope tied at his waist to hold up his trousers. He gave them a reassuring pat. Should the *Amethyst* be so ill-fated as to be attacked by ruffian boarders this morning, he'd be ready. In the meantime, it was imperative ... he had to alert someone. Leaving the rail, he forthwith ran into Mr. Austen, the former commander of HMS *Isabelle*.

"Magpie! Whatever are you doing up so early? Surely you're not mending sails at this hour?"

"Oh, sir," said Magpie breathlessly, "I couldn't sleep. I had one o' them bad dreams. Trevelyan had come sailin' back in his *Serendipity*, and he was aimin' to kill all o' us."

Fly Austen looked down at him with an expression in his eyes that Magpie longed to believe was affection. "And tell me, in this dream of yours, did you save me again, as you once did, by plunging your dirks into Trevelyan's thighs?"

Magpie peeked up shyly at the man for whom he harboured such great respect. "I woke up first afore Trevelyan started the killin'," he said. "But ya gotta know, sir, if need be ... I would do it agin fer ya."

Mr. Austen gave Magpie a warm smile. "But if it was only a dream, why is your breathing still laboured, and why are you trembling as if Trevelyan himself were standing behind you with a pistol directed at your head?"

"Oh! Sir! I think we need to clear the deck and beat to quarters."

"I beg your pardon?"

Magpie pointed into the gloomy fog. "Just now, somethin' ... somethin' went glidin' past us."

Mr. Austen swung around toward the rail, a note of alarm creeping into his voice. "Are you quite certain?"

"Aye, sir ... it came so close."

"What exactly, Magpie?"

"A ship, sir."

"Could it have been a fishing vessel? We *are* sailing in popular fishing waters."

"I seen its hull, and its gunports."

"Gunports?"

Magpie nodded his curly head.

"One deck of them or two?"

"Could only see one, sir, on account of this low-lyin' fog."

"And were the gunports opened or closed?"

"Closed ... I think ... sir."

"Were you able to determine its nationality?"

"Nay, sir, I didn't see no masts nor shrouds. I didn't see no distinguishin' colours or pennants."

Hastily Mr. Austen removed his bicorne hat, closed his eyes, and angled his head over the railing, as if he were listening to the sough of the fresh winds that ruffled his dark, wavy hair.

"What are ya hearin', sir?"

Fly called out to the men working on the weather decks for silence, and then he put his finger to his lips and looked down at Magpie. "I'm wondering if it's possible to hear the beating of their sails."

Pleased to have an excuse to lay down their brooms, barrels, and ropes, the sailors abandoned their posts and prowled to the rail alongside Mr. Austen. Among them, Magpie spied Morgan Evans. Once the carpenter's mate on the *Isabelle*, he had recently been given a promotion, and was presently the *Amethyst*'s head carpenter. A woolly thrum cap had replaced the knitted sock he once wore upon his head of shaggy hair, so that the men could easily spot him in the crowd. Morgan stood before Mr. Austen, bouncing from one foot to the other as he always did when his nerves had got the better of him. "Shall I fetch Captain Prickett, sir?"

"Aye, Mr. Evans. And perhaps you could also ask the bosun to awaken the men, and Biscuit to douse his breakfast fires, though he'll grumble like the devil."

Mr. Austen's quietly spoken requests confirmed Magpie's worst suspicions. His legs suddenly lost their strength, as if someone had thumped his knees with a mallet, and he had to lean against the ship's side for support. The Amethysts had not seen action for a month, not since the day they had confronted Trevelyan and his ship, the USS *Serendipity*, off the coast of South Carolina. Since then, there had been several sightings of enemy flotillas and American warships, but always the chase had ended in a lucky escape.

In no time at all, the bosun had raised the dead with his cry, the drummer had beat the men to quarters, and soon the decks were swarming with officers and marines and ordinary sailors, all questioning — as they assumed their stations — what it was that had been sighted in the fog. Captain Prickett emerged from his great cabin and stomped about the quarterdeck, buttoning his waistcoat — with great difficulty — over his abundant belly, and barking orders at his dazed men:

"Reduce to fighting sail. Double reef the topsails. Where the hell is the cursed bosun? The canvas is *his* responsibility! And where is the master to tell me where the devil we are? Mr. Piper! Clean up this mess at once, and clear for action. Jim Beef … if that's a can of grog I see in your hand, I suggest you dispense with it right away. Nay, man, not in your mouth. Over the side, if you please. I'll not have you falling down drunk at your post."

Close on Prickett's heavy heels was First Lieutenant Lord Bridlington, his white hands clasped as if in prayer, shuffling his feet and continually biting his lower lip. "Mr. Austen, can you be quite certain it's an enemy warship? The boy, Magpie, cannot be trusted. He only has one eye!"

"We cannot take *any* chances, Mr. Bridlington."

"Mr. Austen's right, Bridlington, we must prepare for the worst," said Prickett, throwing back his shoulders, which only resulted in his belly becoming more conspicuous.

"But these mists! We cannot see a thing. What will we be shooting at?"

"We won't take the first shot, Mr. Bridlington," said Mr. Austen, restoring his bicorne hat to his head, "in the event they prove to be a friend, not a foe. We'll wait to see from what direction their fire comes … if it comes at all."

Lord Bridlington withered away with a cry, and tried to hide himself behind Captain Prickett, as if he hoped that — were shots to be fired — his corpulent superior would take the hits for him.

Despite all the turbulence around him, Magpie still cowered against the starboard rail, but soon spotted Morgan Evans, newly returned from conveying all of his messages, and most likely having had a hard time of it trying to convince Biscuit to smother the fires on his Brodie stove. "Magpie! Get yourself below. It's too dangerous for you to linger here. Go and help Dr. Braden prepare his surgery table. He'll appreciate your company."

"I can't move, sir. It's like Jacko's gone and pasted me feet with some o' his shoemaker's glue and I'm part o' the deck."

"I'll carry you then."

"Oh, no, everyone'll be givin' me a turrible hecklin' if ya do that, sir."

"You've got to get a move on."

"Could ya let me lean on ya, sir, just 'til me legs work agin?"

Morgan offered him a supporting arm and together they forged their way through the congested quarterdeck, skirting the gun crews hunched over their long guns and carronades, and headed toward the fore ladder that would take them down to Dr. Braden's hospital. All the while, Magpie could sense an eerie calm overspreading the *Amethyst*. The men had taken their positions, and their eyes closely observed the rising mists on the ship's starboard side, their necks taut and extended as if hoping to be the first to glimpse the ghost ship. Magpie gazed up at the barefooted topmen, balancing on the yardarms — relieved he was not among them — and the men's sweaty faces, particularly those pinched with trepidation, were soon branded onto his memory. With care, he released the dirks from his belt and carried them upright before him.

The fore ladder was a mere step beyond them when Magpie saw it again; this time slinking alongside the larboard rail, on the opposite side of the ship from where most everyone stood watch.

And this time … its gunports were opened.

Magpie's brain had barely registered the ominous object when he was suddenly blinded by a cloudburst of red. The deafening explosion that followed rattled his teeth and jarred his bones. In a flash, Morgan's strong hands were on Magpie's head, shoving it down hard between his ankles, sending him and his heavy dirks tripping down the ladder.

7:30 a.m.
(Morning Watch, Seven Bells)

THE *AMETHYST* ANSWERED the mystery ship with a booming broadside, the powerful recoiling of the guns shaking every inch of the deck.

Magpie lay paralyzed in fear on the hospital floor, scarcely aware that someone in spectacles, rolled up sleeves, and dark breeches, was standing over him with an expression of concern etched upon his brow.

"Am I still livin'?" he squeaked, when he finally recognized the face peering down at him.

"You appear to be," said Dr. Leander Braden, reaching down to pull him to his feet, "although your unorthodox entrance into my hospital with those portentous dirks *could* have killed you." He led Magpie to a stool next to his operating table, and set him down upon it.

More alert now, Magpie looked around him in alarm. "Where's Mr. Evans?"

"Most likely he's in the hold, filling holes with oakum and pitch, so we stay afloat."

"He told me to come help ya with yer prep'rations." But Magpie could see that Dr. Braden had already laid out his frightening instruments of surgery upon a bloodstained square of cloth, which covered what was normally his writing desk. He didn't like the look of the doctor's inauspicious collection of knives — especially that big amputating saw — nor the peculiarity of the bone nippers and forceps: they acutely reminded him of the day he'd been laid out upon that table, Dr. Braden using some of those very instruments to remove his shattered eye.

A picture of twitching apprehension perched upon his stool, Magpie hooked the dirks onto his hempen belt, and listened to the now familiar tumult of war that thundered all around them. A choking black smoke wafted around his head, its acrid odour mixed with the foul smell of human fear, filling his nostrils. Above and below deck, there was so much shouting going on amongst the Amethysts, he could not decipher a single word spoken.

"It's not Trevelyan agin, is it, sir?" he asked, barely able to put voice to his thoughts.

Dr. Braden removed his round spectacles and tucked them into a breast pocket of the black apron he wore over his linen shirt, and then gave Magpie a reassuring smile. "You won't ever have to fear Thomas Trevelyan again. By now, he'll be back in England, and before long he'll be tried, found guilty, and executed."

"But 'til then, ya don't think he'll try harmin' Emily, do ya, sir?"

"The Duke of Clarence and his men will make certain she's kept safe from him."

"Are ya missin' her, sir?"

Dr. Braden raised an eyebrow, as if he had not expected to be asked such a question, but he could not conceal the sadness that subsequently crept into his blue eyes. There was a sharp intake of breath before he replied. "Since her leave-taking … my hospital has not been quite the same."

Not certain how to interpret his answer, Magpie dug around in his trouser pocket, produced a folded scrap of canvas, and unravelled it to reveal its secret contents: a gold-framed miniature of a young woman wearing a blue-velvet spencer jacket, pearls in her pale gold hair, and a mischievous smile upon her lips. He held it out to Dr. Braden. "Sir, I bin carryin' it fer a while now. Why, it means everythin' to me since I lost me blanket — the special one what Mrs. Jordan gave me when I were a climbin' boy and workin' fer Mr. Hardy in London."

Dr. Braden's face flushed as he took the miniature from Magpie and lowered his gaze upon Emeline Louisa Georgina Marie, the granddaughter of King George III; the only child of the Duke of Wessex.

"Well, sir, I bin thinkin' … maybe ya'll be needin' it now."

For a long time, Dr. Braden did not stir, but when at last he spoke again, his voice sounded strangely hoarse. "No … no, you keep it, Magpie." He quickly handed the miniature back to Magpie, and turned away to fuss with the instruments already lying in their organized line upon his table. Carefully returning Emily's picture in its bit of canvas to his warm pocket, Magpie wondered what he could say or do to cheer up the doctor, but at that moment a strident flock of men trudged down the fore ladder and into the sanctuary of the hospital. Led by Osmund Brockley, Dr. Braden's assistant, the group had volunteered — nay, felt it their duty — to leave their comrades behind upon the weather decks to contend with the hail of enemy grapeshot and musket balls while they carried the whimpering wounded down to safety, each one of them in turn delivering an accounting of the various afflictions which required ministration.

"Mr. Piper's got a mess o' splinters stickin' outta his legs, Doctor."

"Mr. Beef took it on the head, sir. A riggin' block knocked 'im silly."

"This one's gun jumped back on him and squashed his foot."

"We got a few bad burns here, sir."

"Young Sam went and regurgitated his vittles all over the ship's bell."

The last of the men to enter the hospital did not have escorts at his side. He was able to make his own way down the slippery rungs, although his face was as white as sea foam; there were beads of perspiration upon his forehead, and a large bloodstain on his starched and ruffled shirt.

In a voice as calm as a ship drifting in the doldrums, Dr. Braden first instructed the volunteers where to lay or leave the wounded, and then he addressed the straggler. "Lord Bridlington! What's happened to you?"

A stupefied Bridlington stared at his left hand. "A bit of grapeshot ... from nowhere ... it took with it one of my fingers," he stammered, looking quite as if he would faint dead away.

Realizing the first lieutenant's injury was not life threatening, Dr. Braden concentrated on Mr. Piper, who convulsed in pain upon the blood-soaked table, and spelled out directions to Osmund Brockley — who stood there with a vacant expression upon his countenance, licking his lips with his oversized tongue.

"Please pay attention, Mr. Brockley," said Leander sternly, "and do not make me rue the day I lost the skilful Joe Norlan to another Royal Navy ship."

Magpie led Lord Bridlington to the stool he had just vacated, and fetched him a drink of water and a cloth bandage to wrap around his hand, but while doing so he could not help his welling resentment toward these men — wounded or not — as they would now command Dr. Braden's undivided attention. Still, despite the agony of the injured and the bad smells, he wanted to stay and help if he could. Knowing the presence of sand on the floor was necessary to keep a ship's surgeon and his knife steady, he hurried to scoop up a large cupful from the sand bucket and scatter it around Dr. Braden's feet. When he was done, and had stood back to observe his efforts, he thought his chest would burst with elation, for not only had Dr. Braden been aware of his little initiative before he set to work on Mr. Piper, he smiled down at him and said, "Perhaps, Magpie ... every so often ... you would do me a kindness and show me her face."

9:00 a.m.
(Forenoon Watch, Two Bells)

LEANDER BRADEN COULD not comprehend why the guns had ceased firing when — it seemed to him — they had only just begun.

Having changed his shirt and, against his better judgement, left his few patients in the incapable hands of Osmund Brockley, he headed above deck for an explanation. In no time at all he had spotted the distinguishing blue bicornes of Fly Austen and Captain Prickett as they stood in consultation beside the ship's wheel. But even from a distance, Leander could see there was something in the manner in which the two men addressed one another that suggested all was not well.

As the sun had now completely burned off the morning mists, the mystery ship and its snowy-white sails were clearly visible, at two points off the larboard bow, too far away for the *Amethyst*'s guns to have further effect. The crew had been ordered to "stand down" and the activity on the weather decks had returned to normalcy. Even Meg Kettle, the laundress, had ventured from the safety of the orlop and come on deck to hang a few shirts and stockings on the rigging to dry — though it was not her usual wash day. She went about her tasks as she always did, swinging her prodigious hips provocatively, and openly flirting in between grumbling tirades on the subject of her aching back. If it were not for the sailors with their brooms and brushes, clearing the decks of splintered oak and little puddles of blood, and the foremast having been unburdened of its top half, one would hardly guess the day had had such an inauspicious beginning.

The Scottish cook, known only as Biscuit on account of his artistry in the baking of sea biscuits — his *pinch of sugar and shot of rum* placing them in good standing amongst the men who consumed them on a daily basis — buzzed around the quarterdeck, dispensing refreshments from a silver tray and jokey words to all of the officers who lingered there. His unkempt orange hair waved wildly about in the fresh winds, and his shirt was opened at the neck to proudly display his thick thatch of chest hairs. The moment he saw Leander approaching, he sprang forward to offer up a steaming mug of coffee.

"Ach, sir, ya look weary," he said in welcome, his skewed eye rolling about in a most disturbing fashion. "This here's fer yer pains."

"Thank you, Biscuit." Leander gratefully accepted the proffered mug and downed the hot contents in two gulps before fixing his attention on the fleeing vessel. "Do we know who our enemy was?" he asked Fly Austen.

There was no mistaking the hint of sarcasm in Fly's tone. "A bold Yankee privateer with no more than fourteen guns and a crew of approximately forty, who, it is more than likely sure, mistook us for a merchantman."

"Ha! And when that blighted fog finally lifted," continued Captain Prickett, crossing his arms atop his belly, "and they had had an opportunity to observe our size and power, they ran off like a frightened rabbit. Why, in their haste to escape, we could see them dumping their guns over the side of their brig."

"Either that or their leader was a paroled officer," Fly added gravely, "and knew, should the day not end in his favour, we would hang him."

Biscuit, ever ready with a quip (his impertinence rarely checked by any of the captains he had ever served — Captain Prickett included), had his own explanation for the privateer's hasty retreat. "Or they done reminded one another o' the prison hulks we got moored in the Thames and our disease-ridden prison here on Melville Island."

Captain Prickett released a long sigh. "Aye, and here the lads were raring for a bit of hand-to-hand combat."

Fly's jaw tightened. "There's still time to pursue them, sir. The winds are stiff and in our favour. Perhaps the lads may still have their fight."

Appearing not to have heard Mr. Austen's comment, Prickett helped himself to a sweet from Biscuit's tray, chewed hard upon it, and assumed the aspect of one deep in meditation. Undaunted, Fly pressed his point. "It would bring the people of Halifax such pleasure to see us bring one in, even a small, inferior one. Aside from perhaps the *Shannon*'s victory over the *Chesapeake*, our record at sea has not been impressive, and these privateers are wreaking havoc on our trade. They must be stopped."

Captain Prickett seemed determined to remain cheerful. "But, Mr. Austen, how quickly you forget our own splendid victory in bringing down Trevelyan and his *Serendipity*. We may travel a great distance on that sweet triumph for months to come."

Leander could see that Fly's hands had formed fists. "Sir, with respect, that was six weeks ago, and as for it being *our* victory ... have you forgotten the crucial role played by Prosper Burgo and his Remarkables?"

"Mr. Austen, do not delude yourself into thinking that Mr. Burgo and his ruffians could ever have brought Trevelyan down if it had not been for our presence and the threat of our superior gun power." Prickett gazed up at the blue sky. "Nay, I do not recommend further fighting on this fine morning; besides, that damned privateer blew away a portion of our foremast with those first feeble shots of hers."

"But that is of little inconvenience. We could quickly replace what was lost with a jury-rigged mast, and then we ..."

"Tut, tut, Mr. Austen," interjected Prickett. "I'll not have you being disagreeable, especially when Biscuit here has such exquisite plans for our breakfast feast!"

Fly's nostrils flared as he took a second to gather his composure, and then he swung toward Leander with an obvious desire to change the subject. "Doctor! Tell us, my good man, what is the butcher's bill?"

"Six wounded. No deaths, thank God."

"Any serious wounds?"

"Jim Beef may require trepanning, as there is a swelling on his brain, but the others are fine." Leander paused as Biscuit refilled his mug, and then glanced at Captain Prickett. "I'm afraid your first lieutenant, Mr. Bridlington, though he lost only one finger, is quite certain he'll soon be meeting his maker."

"That milksop!" barked Prickett. "I've a mind to leave him in Halifax when we dock. He's not fit for the hearty life on a man-o'-war. I'll recommend he take the first ship back to England, and take up the merchandising of women's hosiery."

"We're heading back to port?"

Prickett clapped Leander on the back, dangerously close to the spot where Trevelyan's bullet had entered his left shoulder. "Aye! I think we could all use two, perhaps three weeks in port to refit, collect fresh provisions, and find ourselves a sturdy new foremast."

Fly's eyebrows shot upward in disbelief, but this time he said nothing, allowing Prickett the courtesy of continuing.

"I say we all deserve a respite from our cares on the Atlantic, especially you, Doctor, for I have long been aware of a melancholy hanging around you like an over-starched neckcloth. Therefore, let us reward ourselves! A tavern stocked with ale, an excellent meal, and the delights of a brothel may do us all a world of good."

2

Wednesday, August 4

Early Morning
Aboard HMS *Impregnable*

EMILY BOLTED UPRIGHT in her cot.

Her hands clutched at her pounding chest as she fought to draw deep breaths and purge the hideous images of her dream. *He* would not harm her again ... her Uncle Clarence had promised her. *He* was in the bowels of the *Impregnable*, beneath the waterline on the orlop deck, his feet clapped in irons, with ten marines in attendance, their bayonets fixed upon him, ready to run him through should he so much as utter a single word.

Then why was it Captain Thomas Trevelyan continued to appear, night after night, in her dreams, like a repulsive sea creature intent on dragging her down into the blackness of his world? Would she not be free of him until a London tribunal proclaimed his guilt, and she had witnessed his execution, his pathetic remains tossed into an unmarked paupers' pit on the outskirts of the city?

Emily squeezed her eyes shut, forced the air into her lungs, and wished she were still safe in the hospital on the *Isabelle*, within reach of Dr. Braden as he cared for his patients on the other side of her canvas curtain. If only she could call his name and he would come to her, bearing a soothing elixir, and stay with her until her heartbeats had resumed their normal rhythm. But it was not to be. She was now travelling on her Uncle

Clarence's flagship, HMS *Impregnable*, within days of raising England, and Leander now sailed with the crew of HMS *Amethyst*, in the company of Fly Austen and Morgan Evans and little Magpie, hundreds of miles away, fighting a war with the United States. A month back, in what seemed like a lifetime ago, Emily and Leander had exchanged their farewells, and she wondered — as she did every day — if he were safe on the sea, and whether the thought of her gave him as much pain as thoughts of him gave her. But this morning, Emily would not submit to tears; she had already dwelled too long in the disagreeable company of sorrow and remorse. While she waited for the constriction around her heart to ease, and her trembling to cease, she refused to revisit her disquieting dream, choosing instead to recall the curves of Leander's face, his sea-blue eyes, and his last words to her before they parted. And the very instant she felt at peace again, she quit her bed and threw open the heavy gunport on the day.

It was early; dawn was nothing more than a glimmer of red on the far eastern horizon. Unlike the stormy seas of her nightmare, the ocean was calm, the breeze was fresh, and sitting low in the vast, brightening sky was the moon's ghost. Plying the waters near the *Impregnable* was the comforting presence of two brigs, part of her Uncle Clarence's convoy. Were she able to gaze out the ports on the ship's larboard side, she knew she would find two more sailing escorts there. They were all prepared, if need be, to engage in battle with an American or French frigate, or give chase to a pompous privateer. Their presence was a mighty deterrent to potential enemies, and in Emily's present state of mind she required calm. She could not bear to hear the guns of war booming now; she hoped she would never have to hear their thunder again.

On the weather decks above, the men of the Morning Watch went about their duties. The ship's bell rang four times, a whistle trilled, commands were barked, barrels rumbled along the deck, and, periodically, the good-natured voices of the men were raised.

"If you please, Mr. Scattergood, what is our present speed?"

"Five knots, sir."

"Up the mizzen with you, man. What are you waiting for?"

"Sir, I'm afeared of heights."

"Look lively, Mr. Clamp! Why, ye're a veritable sluggard this mornin'."

"With respect, sir, I won't have no vigour til I've had me breakfast."

"'Tis the voice of a sluggard — I heard him complain: 'You have waked me too soon, I must slumber again.'"

At that moment someone said something amusing, igniting peals of laughter that echoed round the ship. Emboldened by the stirring sounds of life and the shining sea, Emily gathered up her long hair in a red scarf and quickly dressed, pulling on the flimsy linen trousers and checked shirt that, at her request, had been secretly presented to her by the obliging ship's purser when she first boarded the *Impregnable*. Their quality and fit could not compare to that of the dear blue jacket and cream-coloured pantaloons little Magpie had once sewn for her with such care and attention to detail, but like so many other things she had once cherished, they too were gone, lost to the indomitable waves. She could not think of those days now, for if she were to submit to their poignant remembrance, she would never summon the fortitude to face the terrors that awaited her arrival in London.

Secure in her sailor's disguise, she slipped quietly from her cabin.

7:00 a.m.
(Morning Watch, Six Bells)

MIDSHIPMAN GUS WALBY, who was nearing his thirteenth birthday, hopped along the quarterdeck of HMS *Impregnable* in his ill-fitting uniform with the aid of a crutch. It had been seven weeks since his ruinous fall from the *Isabelle*'s mizzenmast on that dreadful, decisive day when Thomas Trevelyan had set out to destroy Captain Moreland's crew and his proud ship. Gus had broken both of his arms and his right leg that day, but in the past four weeks his arms had much improved, thanks in part to the admiral, the Duke of Clarence, who had insisted he rest up during their ocean crossing and take on only the lightest of nautical duties, and to Emily, who had frequently provided him with amiable company and had read to him multiple chapters of *Pride and Prejudice*, the book Mr. Austen had presented to her in Bermuda before she had departed for England.

But Gus's leg was not healing as quickly, and he feared for his future as an officer of the Royal Navy. How could he ever be promoted from midshipman to lieutenant with a crippled leg? Emily had shrugged off his concerns, arguing that in all her nearly nineteen years she had either been acquainted with or had knowledge of several naval captains who had had various limbs missing — she had even known one whose prodigious belly had wreaked havoc on his waistcoats — but their encumbrances had in no way diminished their effectiveness in leading men. Why then, she had asked, should a simple limp and a temporary dependency upon a crutch obstruct *his* ability in the future to command one of the king's ships? "Now mind you, Mr. Walby, I *would* be most concerned that promotion would forever elude you," Emily had added as an afterthought, a smile curling her lips, "if you possessed … a disease of the mind."

Gus tried not to think about his future; advancement and longevity in the Royal Navy were the least of his worries. Though he would not admit it, even to Emily, he was apprehensive about returning to England. How would he ever endure the endless hours while he convalesced? How long would he have to wait until he was well enough to resume his post? And if he were to return to the sea one day, might he be fortunate enough to sail once again with Mr. Austen, Dr. Braden, Morgan Evans, Magpie, and all those for whom he cared? However, deep in his breast, Gus hid the heaviest concern of all, one that pressed on his mind like a perpetual headache. His parents were both dead, his guardian uncle away at sea, who would be there to meet him?

Attempting to banish his gnawing anxieties, Gus gave his blond head a shake; besides, he had to pull himself together for he had an important errand to run. He was carrying a message for Emily. The only problem was, she was not to be found in her cabin — or, as she referred to it, her *little private box*, having once quipped, "Surely, Mr. Walby, my room has the same dimensions as one of the Duchess of Devonshire's hat boxes."

From experience, Gus was well aware that Emily did not take kindly to sitting alone in her quarters for any length of time. When they had sailed together on the *Isabelle*, she had been known to steal off, dressed in sailor's slops, to forbidden areas of the ship. She had once been found in the men's mess, swilling a mug of beer in the unsuitable society of Biscuit, the cook, and Jacko, the ship's shoemaker. Another time she had ventured down to the sail room on the orlop with disastrous consequences. For Gus it was not easy negotiating the ladders down to the lower decks with a crutch stuck in his armpit, and he was hopeful he would find her nearby on the weather decks.

He hobbled along the starboard gangway, careful as always not to bump into any of the working men and risk jeopardizing his agonizingly slow recovery. As he crept by the seamen they saluted him, and while he did his best to acknowledge those who made polite inquiries — "Are you well this morning, Mr. Walby?" "Is your leg better today, sir?" — he searched the length of the foremast for Emily. Just as he expected, there she was, sitting a hundred feet up on the foretop, her unbound hair flying behind her like the ship's pennants that billowed above the topgallant sails. Dressed in trousers and an oversized checked shirt, one might mistake her for a malingering sailor who preferred the warmth of the morning sun to his duty of unfurling the fore topsail; one would hardly suspect she was a granddaughter of King George III.

Relief flooded Gus when, having spotted him, Emily waved from her lofty perch and cried out, "Mr. Walby," saving him the embarrassment of having to call out to her. Early on in their voyage, the Duke of Clarence had overheard him address her as *"Em"* and the result was a spitting verbal reprimand: *"From this day forward, Mr. Walby, you are to address my niece as Your Royal Highness. And if I should hear you be so indecently familiar with her again, I will not hesitate to lash you to the crosstrees for the night."* Gus was in no doubt that the duke would carry out the punishment — the trouble was that it was not an easy task remembering to style Emily thus, especially when he was so used to addressing her otherwise.

Without delay, Emily jumped up and began her descent, leaving Gus scrambling to recruit two strong-armed sailors to stand watch beside him in the event she faltered on the shrouds and fell. But Emily clambered down the ropes with the speed and expertise of a seasoned seaman — with no indication of the troubled ankle she had broken weeks earlier while escaping Trevelyan's ship — and landed safely on the deck before him, her face a healthy glow of exertion, her dark eyes flashing. She straightened her shoulders and raised her right fist to her forehead in a respectful salute.

"And how may I assist you, Mr. Walby? Do you require me to swab the decks, sir? Scrub your soiled shirts? Clean out the goat pens? Toss a bucket of severed limbs overboard?"

With so many men working close by and, as always, unable to mask their interest in Emily, Gus, though he desired to, could not possibly return her lightheartedness. "The admiral … your Uncle Clarence … wishes to breakfast with you this morning," he said solemnly, "in his cabin … alone."

Emily angled her head in disbelief. "Imagine that! After all these weeks, my uncle actually wishes to spend time with me? Why, I was beginning to think he had completely forgotten that I was aboard and lodged in quarters four feet from his."

The two fell in together and slowly made their way aft, toward the *Impregnable*'s stern, where the duke maintained his comparatively spacious quarters.

"Perhaps he's been much occupied of late," offered Gus.

Emily scoffed. "Yes, yes, I believe so. Preparing for imaginary sea battles and drinking port with his senior officers, and contemplating a revival of his prospects of marriage to any and all available young women of wealth and position upon his return to London."

"Aren't you fond of your uncle?" asked Gus warily.

Emily's eyes softened. "Not really, but at one time I was … very much so. He and Aunt Dora and their many children were so kind to me when my father died. Seems so long ago now." She sighed. "There is good in him yet, though I detest how he's become so dependent upon his brother, the Prince Regent, and all of his royal advisers."

Gus tried to cheer her up. "I will never forget you telling me the story of how your uncle saved Magpie from a most wretched employer, and took it upon himself to take the little fellow off the streets of London, feed him, outfit him, and send him to sea."

At the mention of Magpie's name, a pained expression crossed Emily's lovely face, and in reply she could only manage a hollow "Yes." Abruptly she strayed toward the starboard rail and, once there, peered into the blue distance, as if expecting the English coastline to materialize in the vast emptiness. Watching her, with the wind tearing at her hair and clothes, Gus couldn't help wondering how often her mind returned to her recent past, back to the well-trodden decks of the *Isabelle*, and to the dear crewmembers with whom she had experienced so much. Gus yearned to give voice to his own turbulent emotions, to share his most precious memories of their time together on the *Isabelle*, especially those that included Dr. Braden and Magpie, and Jane Austen's magical book, *Sense and Sensibility*, but he did not dare disturb her reverie; moreover, an ascending lump in his throat threatened the appearance of tears, and he could not tolerate a ribbing from the men who eyed them with their blatant curiosity high on the yardarms, and from all corners of the weather decks.

Long minutes passed before Emily pushed away from the rail, in a way that suggested she had had to conjure up the strength to do so, and in silence they walked along the gangway, passing by the *Impregnable*'s petty officers, marines, stewards, carpenters, gunners, ordinary sailors, and landmen, all of whom seemed intent on interrupting their chores and conversations to watch her, or awkwardly bow their heads in respect. But she seemed incognizant to all the attention, and did not speak again until they had arrived at the small door to her cabin.

"I suppose my uncle insisted I come to his breakfast table appropriately attired in gown and tiara."

Gus lowered his voice. "His Royal Highness's exact words were: '*She's not to appear in those damnable trousers.*'" He attempted a smile, but was surprised when tears glistened in *her* eyes and, though she tried, she had difficulty fixing her gaze on him.

"When do you think we shall have our first glimpse of England?"

"If these winds prevail, perhaps as early as tomorrow."

"I don't want to go back home."

"But why not?" asked Gus, knowing the entire country would be heralding her safe return, including dozens of family members.

There was a catch in her throat as she said, "Because I ... I fear it."

Gus wished he could offer her comfort, and racked his brain for a few words of encouragement, but at that precise moment, a loud voice boomed from the neighbouring cabin, as if one of the ship's cannons had suddenly fired, startling him and causing the crutch to wobble under his arm. Was the Duke of Clarence about to fill his doorway with his portly figure, demanding an explanation as to why his breakfast was being delayed? Gus did not relish the thought of spending a night of punishment on the mizzen crosstrees. He looked up at Emily.

"You'd better hurry."

Giving him a quick nod, Emily turned away and disappeared into her *little box*. Gus stood transfixed a moment longer, hardly daring to breathe in the event the Duke of Clarence's sonorous notes should rise up again. Thankfully, they did not. Perhaps then it was only a servant — already within the confines of the great cabin — upon whom the duke was heaping his morning displeasure. Gus relaxed and stared sadly at Emily's canvas door.

"If it makes you feel any better," he whispered, "I fear it too … Em."

8:00 A.M.
(Morning Watch, Eight Bells)

EMILY'S UNCLE CLARENCE was well into his meal by the time she had changed into her blue-and-white-striped morning dress — the only gown in her possession — pulled her hair together in an untidy chignon, and arrived at his sun-filled cabin. Flourishing doughy fingers, he invited her to sit at the empty place setting across from him at the round oak table, and continued to munch away on toast lathered with butter and marmalade.

"I have dismissed my steward so that we may be alone, my dear, so I will ask that you serve yourself," said the duke, his full mouth, once Emily had seated herself and arranged a linen napkin upon her lap. "As you can see there's plenty of boiled duck and onions … oh, and bacon, and I thought you might like fruit fritters with whipped cream, so I asked Mr. Belcher to prepare them especially for you. How fortunate we were to meet those merchantmen coming from England with fresh provisions! Nothing quite like fruit fritters. Now, there is tea, but perhaps you would prefer coffee or a cup of chocolate?"

Emily recalled her customary shipboard fare prior to the time she had embarked upon the *Impregnable* for the journey home. On those lost ships, there sometimes had been little beyond a thin gruel or jellied soup. "No thank you, Uncle, tea is fine," she said, reaching for the vibrantly patterned bone china teapot. "I'm afraid I have no appetite for boiled duck and bacon this morning."

"You have grown monstrously thin since I last saw you at Bushy House. Why, your FitzClarence cousins shall never recognize you. But we'll change all that when we get you home. A few fine suppers at Carlton House should do the trick."

Emily studied her uncle as she sipped her tea; he seemed quite content to consume the breakfast feast on his own, reaching now for a rasher of bacon. "You're not sending me to Carlton House to live with the Prince Regent, are you, Uncle?"

"God damn, Emeline, my brother is far too busy ruling England for our dear father — on account of his most unfortunate illness — to have the added worry of *you* living under his roof."

"Would you allow me to stay with my Seaton cousins in Dorset? I should like to see how Frederick is faring."

Her uncle's eyes rounded in horror. "Wot? Your mother's relation who led you astray, who forced you to take that ruinous journey across the ocean on the ill-fated *Amelia*? Certainly not!"

"I wanted to go, Uncle."

"I'll not have it."

"Please, Uncle, please don't send me to Windsor. I should go mad with no companionship beyond my ill-tempered grandmother and my poor, unmarried aunts. The dimensions and diversions of a vault would be preferable to living there."

"Oh, well, I cannot have you living there either. It's too far from London, and, furthermore, your presence there would be too much stimulation for my mother."

Having expected to be sent directly to her grandparents' home at Windsor Castle and locked up in one of its cold chambers, Emily frowned in surprise, but did not dare question him; instead, she pleaded. "I should like to live with my FitzClarence cousins at Bushy House."

Her uncle shook his head in despair, as if he, and not his elder brother, carried the weight of England upon his shoulders. "You'll find Bushy much altered since your days there, Emeline. It's not the happy place it once was. I've ... I've locked up Dora's private apartments, and so many of the children are scattered, away at school, in the army, that sort of thing."

Emily felt a stab of disappointment, and found herself sinking very low. It still upset her to think that her uncle had separated with the most excellent Dora Jordan, the woman with whom he had lived in domestic bliss for twenty years. "Do you think Aunt Dora would allow me to live with her in Cadogan Place?"

Again he shook his head. "Oh, no, that would never do. The Regent would not allow it. Besides, Dora has many troubles, many troubles of her own — too many to take on the added anxiety and expense of you." He gave a nervous chuckle. "But you'll have the opportunity to see her on the stage; she still performs at the new Drury Lane. No, Emeline, I have devised *other* plans for you." He paused a moment to drain the contents of the teapot into his cup. "As you know, two days ago I ordered our escorting sloop to speed ahead home with my letters. It is my hope that, upon our arrival in Portsmouth, I'll have news from my couriers, and will then be able to tell you the name of the family with whom you shall be residing."

Emily's eyes widened. "You would have me live with strangers then?"

"My dear, you have been in the company of strangers — lewd hell-hounds and sinners — for the past few months. I cannot imagine you shall have any trouble at all adjusting to this new arrangement."

"I don't understand."

Her uncle set his heavily lidded blue eyes upon her, and assumed a hardened expression. "You are somewhat of an embarrassment to the family ... in your ... in your —" he groped a moment for the right word, "— your unmanageability."

"You think me unmanageable?"

"Yes, my dear, in the worst way. Let us recapitulate." The duke clapped his hands upon the table, and cleared his throat. "Without informing your *royal* family, you sailed from Portsmouth in April aboard HMS *Amelia* with your cousin, Frederick Seaton, who ... you should know ... will be soundly disciplined for your kidnapping once he has fully recovered his senses ..."

Emily was quick to cry out in protest, but her uncle cut her off and pressed on.

"The *Amelia* was subsequently attacked, you were taken prisoner by one Thomas Trevelyan, who, I have been informed, kept you confined in his great cabin for three or four weeks — without any form of chaperone, I might add — until such time as his ship, the USS *Serendipity*, encountered HMS *Isabelle*. During a tremendous battle, while grapeshot and splinters filled the air, you escaped through Trevelyan's broken windows, injuring your right ankle most grievously and taking a bullet in your right shoulder. You were then rescued by the Isabelles, and spent the next two weeks, in the close company of the aforementioned hell-hounds, in the ship's hospital which was administered by a Dr. Leander Braden, who ... I understand ... had a salacious interest in you."

Emily shot forward in her chair. "Uncle, that is completely false and unjust. First of all, I was *not* kidnapped by my cousin; secondly, at no time did Dr. Braden ever ..."

The duke raised his hand to silence her, and though his gesture was stern his voice was not unkind. "My dear, I am far from finished. Permit me to continue." He ripped a chunk of meat from the roasted duck carcass, stuffed it into his mouth, and slumped back upon the cushioned seat of his armchair. "While on the *Isabelle*, you caused the late Captain James Moreland much consternation as you developed a taste for laudanum, and had a penchant for climbing the shrouds and drinking ale with the sweaty, bare-shirted sailors, and while wandering the ship you incited the arousal of a some poor, young, unnamed sailor who attempted to …"

Now it was Emily's turn to raise a hand. "Stop! Please, Uncle! Please stop this madness! I do not know who has been feeding you this information, but your version of my life over the past several weeks has been unfairly prejudiced by your sources. I told you all when we first greeted one another in Bermuda. Have you now forgotten?"

"Ah, but Emeline, I've heard a great deal more these past few weeks on the sea."

"And why would you believe what *they* have to say over what I've already explained to you, especially when you have always been one to listen to and consider another's point of view?"

His fleshy cheeks flushed red. "Because *you* are a woman."

"What does that have to do with anything?" gasped Emily.

"Women tend to be fanciful, and, therefore, often don't know their own mind."

"I happen to be well-acquainted with mine."

"Do you really, my dear?" He raised his voice an octave. "Furthermore, you have not been in this world long enough to have a true understanding of the nature of men … especially those who ply their trade on the sea."

"That's ridiculous."

"Then, Emeline, tell me this: how the devil did you ever get yourself mixed up with this Thomas Trevelyan? And here I always thought you possessed sound judgement in all aspects of your life. What will the Prince Regent say when he learns his beloved niece is married to one of the greatest traitors England has ever known?"

Emily exhaled in frustration. "I am married to Trevelyan in name only. Rightly or wrongly, he assumed that being married to a granddaughter of King George would absolve him of the crimes he committed against England,

and enable him to collect the fortune and titles which once belonged to his step-father, Charles DeChastain. I told you before, Uncle, I only acquiesced and went through with the ceremony to prevent Trevelyan from harming those I —" she hesitated to steady her voice, "— so that he wouldn't harm the English prisoners he kept confined in the gaol of his ship."

Her uncle fixed his round stare on the bowl of fruit fritters. "Hogwash! We both know Trevelyan was carrying no prisoners in his hold! I am most disappointed in you, Emeline. The fact remains, *you* married the man, therefore, I can think of only one solution for you." Whether or not it was punishment for her to have to wait until he had popped a fritter into his mouth and savoured its exquisite qualities before he continued, Emily could not tell. "Given your unfortunate circumstances, the best we can do for you is secure an annulment, and subsequently search the Continent for an insignificant prince — perhaps an elderly widower — who has fallen upon hard times, and would therefore be overjoyed to win the favour of an English princess ... so long as I can convince the Regent to provide you with a small dowry."

Emily's mouth fell open, her blood boiled in her ears; again she tried to protest, but as she did her uncle abruptly pushed himself away from the table and reached for his admiral's hat. It seemed he had more pressing matters at hand, and that, as far as he was concerned, their unpleasant interview had reached its end. Helplessly, she watched as her uncle lumbered across the cabin floor and rattled the door open. His squat, bulky frame filled the small doorway, and he lingered there a moment before pronouncing his parting thought.

"Here we thought the Regent's daughter, Princess Charlotte, was a handful, showing her legs in public, preferring horses to literature, throwing tantrums, and keeping the company of Whigs. My dear," he said with a cluck of his tongue, "she truly pales in comparison to *you*."

3

Saturday, August 7

Noon
(Forenoon Watch, Eight Bells)
Aboard HMS *Impregnable*
Portsmouth, England

EMILY LOOKED UP from the pages of *Pride and Prejudice* and listened to HMS *Impregnable* quiver and gripe as her crew toiled to dock her in Portsmouth Harbour.

Earlier in the day she had stood at her open gunport, sipping lukewarm tea, and watched, for what seemed like hours, as the ship sailed past the chalk downlands of the Isle of Wight, and into the town of Portsmouth — its dockyards and collection of taverns, inns, and churches rather dreary and unwelcoming under leaden skies that threatened rain. She had marvelled as the senior officers on the weather decks had squabbled — in a manner not unlike a haggling group of women at a fish market — over their navigational charts and their opinions regarding the dangers that lay in the waters of the Solent. There was so much to consider that Emily was quite happy to leave the anxieties of seamanship to others, though she was not certain she had complete faith in their abilities. The men argued about the position of various rocks and sandbars and channels; some wished to adhere to the routes laid out upon the charts, knowing they had been plotted with consideration given to leeway and the tidal stream; others wanted to rely on visual clues — namely lining up the landmark transits of Gosport Chapel to the west and the Blockhouse to the east — in order to maintain the deepest water. One man carried on about keeping a sharp lookout for the red buoy that marked the sunken remains of the *Royal George*, and the white one that marked the submerged *Boyne*; another had much to say on the subject of misplaced buoys. Her admiral uncle, the Duke of Clarence, was among the contentious officers, his voice rising up, shrill at times, bemoaning the absence of an experienced pilot to steer them safely in and around *all* lurking impediments.

Soon Emily had tired of gazing out over the mundane vistas, for they did not fill her with any kind of joy; they only served as a painful reminder that her time on the sea had finally come to an end. Leaving the gunport, she had tried to occupy herself and her mind by inspecting the corners of her cabin to make certain she had collected all of her belongings — the paltry few she did possess — and had packed them away in the small chest the purser was kind enough to forage for her. She had then changed into the blue-and-white-striped morning gown — the one Magpie had especially sewn on the occasion of her Bermuda reunion with Uncle Clarence back in early July. Having slept in curling rags in an effort to smarten up her long hair — neglected for so long in either a straight queue or concealed beneath a scarf — she arranged the gown's matching bandeau upon her head, hoping it would quite impress the well-born ladies of Portsmouth and London, and keep them from gossiping about the style in which she dressed her hair. Boredom and cheerless thoughts had followed, at which time she had reached for the solace of the novel written by Jane Austen, Fly Austen's youngest sister.

But now, as she lifted her chin to listen, her ears detected a sound — nay, a racket — that rose in a deafening crescendo, surpassing that made by the mooring grumbles of the ship. She was about to make an investigative return to her open gunport when Gus Walby stuck his head into her doorway.

"Em, please come. You must see this!" In his agitated state, he hopped about on his crutch and playfully pulled her out of her cabin, out into the cool, windy day, where he led her to the spot near the rail where the admiral — beaming from ear to ear in his polished and pressed blue uniform — stood with his senior officers. Hanging back, Emily endeavoured to make sense of it all, while Gus's shining eyes observed her closely, awaiting her reaction.

On the wharves below, a sea of people rolled like a colossal wave toward their ship. Waving their arms about and roaring with excitement, men, women, and children of all ages, from all circles of society — some dressed in finery, others in rags — rushed to find a place to stand, as close as possible to the docked *Impregnable*. Emily was aghast. Never before had she seen so many gathered together in one location. It was as though a much anticipated country fair had just opened, and those who had waited patiently outside the restraining gates had all broken into a run to be the first to see the attractions.

"But I don't understand," she said to both Gus and her uncle. "Surely the people of Portsmouth are quite used to seeing a ship."

"Oh, my dear, they have no interest in the *Impregnable*," said her Uncle Clarence, a twinkle in his blue eyes.

"Oh! Is there a sea serpent clinging to her hull then?"

"No, Em, I —" Gus quickly broke off, and corrected himself. "I … I meant to say Your Royal Highness." Fortunately for him, the Duke of Clarence's present high spirits precluded any form of admonishment.

Emily still struggled to comprehend the extraordinary scene before her. "Has the Prince Regent come in a silk-lined coach and six to welcome you home, Uncle?"

A bit of sunshine left her uncle's smile. "Good God, Emeline, my brother has little time for me these days; besides, he's far too busy to come all the way to Portsmouth just to drink tea with us."

"Keep me in the dark no longer, and tell me why there's such a crowd here?"

"Isn't it obvious, my dear?"

"I can only guess that you and your escorting ships have been away at sea for a very long time, Uncle, and these people are family members come to welcome their loved ones home."

"Now you are approaching the truth." The duke firmly took hold of Emily's arm and steered her toward the rail, thrusting her into the clear sight of the stimulated throng of humanity beneath them. In her gown and bandeau, it was easy to identify Emily amongst the many male faces that lined the ship's side. A thunderous outpouring of *huzzahs*, whistles, and applause rattled Emily's eardrums, and, further adding to her discomfort, her uncle leaned in close to shout into her ear, "You see, Emeline, they've come to see and welcome *you* home."

Emily was completely astounded. "But why? I'm of no consequence."

"But you are, and curiosity has got the better of them!"

"Curiosity?"

"Word has spread very fast — most likely on account of my messengers sent on ahead of our ship. It's not an everyday occurrence that the ordinary people see a granddaughter of the king, who has lived among men on a congested ship, taken a bullet in the back, and married a most traitorous and contemptuous sea captain. Why, you've become a veritable spectacle." The duke paused in expectation, as if he thought his niece would soon burst into a fit of unmitigated delight, but when she remained speechless he chirped, "So, come along, my dear, let us give the people joy, and parade down the ramp arm-in-arm, allowing all to see the kidnapped princess, and her loving uncle, her brave saviour who sailed with a flotilla of ships to rescue her from the war-ravaged seas."

Emily wriggled out of her uncle's arm-lock and gave him an icy stare. "I will *not* parade down the ramp in front of all these people as if I'm some kind of prized horseflesh."

Her uncle's head shot back in disbelief; however, his recovery was a speedy one, and, not to be deterred from enjoying the occasion, he brushed away invisible bits of fluff from the gold braiding on his full-dress uniform. "Very well, when you are ready to leave, have Mr. Walby help you off the ship — if he's able to, although I daresay, *you* may have to carry him off! There's to be no dilly-dallying, for I've arranged for a barouche to transport us to the inn." He signalled to his officers to follow suit, and he led them down the ramp on his squat, unsteady sea legs, periodically acknowledging the people with an enthusiastic wave or a nod of his flushed countenance.

Emily sidled away from the rail on her own wobbly legs, and sought the comfort of an overturned bucket, away from the attentions of the clamorous crowd. Unable to match her uncle's ebullience she suddenly felt very tired, and desired — of all things — to return to the peace and quiet of her little cot, but she was too weary to even move. Her brown eyes dropped to the deck planks in a frozen stare, though she was conscious of the crewmen, leaving the *Impregnable* one-by-one, carrying their belongings in ditty bags strung across their shoulders, and balancing their hair-trunks and chests in or under their arms. Wordlessly, Mr. Walby, dressed in his cream-coloured pantaloons and blue jacket, leaning on his crutch, stood at her side. Glancing up at him, Emily could see evidence of his having been aggrieved by her uncle's insensitive remark in his young features.

"I've not been off a ship in months, Gus. I cannot even walk properly. Were I to attempt that ramp this minute, I'd surely topple over and end up smashed upon the pavement or stones, or whatever covers the ground down there, in front of all those people." Emily released a sardonic laugh. "A *veritable spectacle* indeed!"

"You shall not fall, Em," he said, attempting to sound strong. "I will help you down."

"I know you will, Gus."

The air around Portsmouth seemed to thicken and grow chillier, causing Emily to shiver. She looked skyward at the dark, racing clouds, wondering if they were planning to release a torrent of rain upon the town and its dockyards. Without any kind of warning, a drum rolled, its beats both startling and disturbing, and the words *"make way"* rang loud and clear. Instantaneously, a strange hush filtered through the crowds assembled on the wharves, and although they could no longer see her — hidden from sight on her bucket — Emily could see that each and every person had stopped moving, as if her Uncle Clarence had taken up a speaking trumpet, and ordered them all to *"be silent and stand at attention."* Those closest to the ship wore expressions of apprehension upon their upturned faces; some of the children, their mouths agape, had reached for the security of their mother's skirts, while the mothers, in turn, clung to their husbands' arms.

A few feet from the place where Emily rested, four red-coated marines appeared through the hatchway, gripping their muskets, eyes before them, backs erect, faces grim. Thereafter came the clanking, grinding noise of someone — his feet bound in chains — making his gruelling way, step-by-step, up the ladder rungs. Emily's heart quickened as she recalled the suffocating blackness of her nightmare. Captain Thomas Trevelyan — the man she had not laid eyes upon for six weeks, but whose diabolical shape constantly surfaced in her dreams — came slowly into her line of vision: first his hatless head, his straw-coloured hair long, matted, and unclean; then his torn and soiled shirt, his hands tied at his back; and finally his long legs, heavily bandaged around the thighs with old dressings. The marines might have allowed him freedom from his irons as he made his last journey up from the ship's hold, but they did not — there could be no opportunity for escape — and so a length of chain still loosely imprisoned his bleeding, ulcerated feet.

Feeling ill, Emily's first thought was to flee to her cabin, but she could not induce her limbs to mobilize. Her eyes stared, absorbing every terrifying part of him as he materialized bit by bit upon the deck — like a spider creeping out of a cavernous hole. The crowd stirred, exhaling a drawn-out exclamation of horror, but there followed neither boos nor hisses nor hoots of condemnation, only a watchful silence.

At first his eyes fought with the glare of daylight, but the minute Trevelyan lifted his heavily shadowed face in defiance, they beheld her. Ravaged by weeks of imprisonment, his uniform jacket and boots stripped from his body, he still stood tall, insurmountable; his spirits seemingly unbroken, his hatred still hot. He paused in his labourious march, ignoring the marine's bayonet that repeatedly jabbed into his back, and allowed his gaze to slowly rove over her. Emily expected to see a flicker of loathing cross his face, or a narrowing of the eyes, perhaps a sneer of the lips. But his face remained void of all emotion. His cracked and swollen lips moved, and he uttered nothing more than a single word.

"Pity."

It was not a plea for sympathy; it was spoken with regret.

There was no interest on his part in awaiting any kind of rejoinder she might have tripping upon her tongue. He moved on, dragging himself forward on the path marked by the marines. Emily watched him go, and suddenly she understood why the crowds had come to Portsmouth on this day. As her blood ran cold in her veins, she knew she had not seen the last of him.

9:00 p.m.
The George Hotel, Portsmouth

Safely ensconced within the private parlour of the George Hotel, the best inn Portsmouth had to offer, Emily nestled into the comfort of a velvet-lined chair, her hands clasped around a steaming cup of tea, and gazed into the crackling flames of a fire that one of the George's servants was kind enough to build for her.

It was chilly this August evening, for the rain had arrived the minute she got up the nerve to quit the *Impregnable* — only once Trevelyan had been carted away and was long out of sight — and had scrambled into the hired barouche alongside Gus and her Uncle Clarence. It was a relief to see the downpour; it had served to scatter the crowds, pressing around their carriage with their probing eyes and grasping hands. Her uncle's good-humoured smiles and chuckles were testimony to his enjoyment of all the attention, and Gus — high colour in his young face — had seemed to as well, but since it was *her* they were trying to touch, and *her* who received the queerest of looks, Emily had not shared her companions' enthusiasm, and wished to make a speedy withdrawal to the hotel. The crewmen of the *Isabelle*, the *Amethyst*, the *Impregnable*, and even the USS *Serendipity* had been known to stare at her, sometimes they had openly gawked, and she had understood that a woman was a rarity on a warship; however, the overwhelming majority of them had always maintained a respectable distance.

Across the immense rosewood table that gleamed in the glow of sterling silver candelabra, and was neatly arranged with three place-settings of fine china and crystal, sat Gus in a chair of his own, his crutch propped up beside it. His face looked so small sitting amongst the plump cushions, his complexion so pale — a stark contrast to the wine-red colour of the velvet upholstery. Both Emily and Gus had been summoned from their respective rooms on the second floor almost an hour ago, and been informed that supper would be served in the parlour, but thus far only a tray of tea and wine had arrived. The Duke of Clarence was to join them, having left them the instant they had descended upon the hotel, and set off to make *"his inquiries"* about the town. To while away the hours until his return, Emily and Gus had napped and walked the perimeter of their chambers, exercising their legs on firm ground, but neither had ventured to take a stroll about the town. The rain had been a deterrent, but then so were the crowds of curiosity-seekers who, upon hearing word that Princess Emeline Louisa was lodging at the George, had descended upon the hotel, the children pressing their noses and fingertips against the window panes of the first floor apartments.

In the time since they had convened in the parlour, Gus had said very little, most likely because the servant who had lit the hearth-fire, and brought them their tray, had — until a few minutes ago — plunked herself down on a stool in the corner and set her inquisitive eyes upon them. It had so annoyed Emily, who had wondered if the girl was hoping to see the two of them perform a juggling act with the fine china, that she kindly asked her to prepare for them another pot of tea. Only too pleased to be of service, the girl had propelled herself from her seat and dashed out of the room. Emily quickly seized the opportunity to address her taciturn companion.

"Are you hungry, Gus?"

"I am. I had no breakfast this morning."

"Why not?"

"Your uncle asked me to write two missives for him, and when I was done, the cook's kitchen was closed so I didn't get my ration of porridge and ale." He gave her a weary smile.

"I am hoping that same *irresponsible* man will soon return, for I would like nothing better than a bowl of soup right about now."

Gus's eyes absently studied his hands on his lap. "I suppose we'll be travelling to Winchester tomorrow, and I'll be left with *my* uncle."

Emily compressed her lips in reply.

"What if he's still away at sea?"

"Does your uncle have a wife?"

"No, just a housekeeper."

Emily sat forward in her chair, her eyes brimming with compassion, and gently placed her open palms upon the table. "Gus, you do know ... if I could ... I would take you with me. I may be the king's granddaughter, but I do not have independence of any kind. My will is smothered by the will of my family, and financially I've not two shillings to my name. I'm as poor as the lowly sailors who toiled on the *Isabelle*."

"Oh, but I would never have suggested that you —"

"But if I could," Emily interjected, "I would buy us a house in the country, and we could live there together as brother and sister."

Her remark was rewarded with a visible uplift in Gus's spirits. "I should like that, Em. And will you be returning to Windsor Castle?"

Emily let loose a sarcastic yelp. "Nay! Apparently I'm not particularly welcome at any of the homes belonging to my relatives. I am too *unmanageable* for their tastes, and so, I'm to live in London with a family of complete strangers."

Gus shook his head in wonder. "That doesn't seem right."

"No, it does not; however, I managed quite well living amongst the Isabelles, and, before Morgan Evans pulled me from the sea and brought me on board, I had not been acquainted with any one of you. But then you saw how quickly we all became … how you all became such good friends of mine —" Emily, her voice faltering, her emotions so close to the edge, turned away to stare into the flames. It was some time before she was able to look again at Gus, and not in the least bit surprised was she to find he had been closely watching her. Why even a boy of twelve years could guess the turbulent state of her thoughts and feelings! She felt her face grow warm, and went to great lengths to avoid his eyes.

Gus opened his lips, and hesitated before saying, "May I be so bold as to inquire — I've long wanted to ask you —" But he left off, his question unspoken. Perhaps he was wrestling with his better judgement; perhaps it was the sudden appearance of tears in her eyes.

"You're wondering if I am missing Dr. Braden." She heaved a long sigh, and turned once again toward the fire. "He is always present in my mind, lingering just beyond my reach, but lingering nevertheless, like a patch of blue sky on a rainy day, or an inspiring speech before going into battle, or a … a soothing voice when one is frightened by the dark. Sometimes I wonder if it all was nothing more than a dream, but then I see you, Gus —" her eyes found his "— and I am reassured that it did all happen, and I know that Leander Braden really does exist on this earth. You are my final connection to that time, to that frightening, magnificent adventure of mine … and to *him* … and when you leave tomorrow, you'll take with you my tangible proof that I did experience … if only for a little while … the freedom of another life."

Enveloped in the comfort of the crackling fire, their faces flushed with the warmth of the tea, the two fell silent, leaving one another to their own memories. When the parlour door screamed open, slamming into the opposite wall — and surely leaving a deep depression in the plaster — they were both dragged back to the present with a violent start.

Into the room swept the Duke of Clarence, smartly attired in fawn-coloured breeches, high-top boots, and a pickle-green waistcoat, though his plump figure could not do them justice. At his round chin was an elaborately tied neckcloth, and his voluminous Carrick coat straddled one arm. He stood there a moment, his coat spilling raindrops upon the rug, beholding them with eyes full of expectation, quite as if he were sitting in the royal box at the Drury Theatre, waiting to see the young Dora Jordan perform her famous role of *Rosalind* in her yellow knee breeches. Emily and Gus sat up straighter in their chairs, wondering what was about.

The duke bowed dramatically before them, and announced, "Emeline, Mr. Walby ... *dinner* is served." Then he stepped to one side to allow the entire kitchen staff, and every one of the George's servants (there were so many of them, Emily suspected some of them had been summoned from neighbouring inns) to parade into the parlour with the dinner feast. One-by-one they placed their dish or bowl or platter upon the rosewood table with a formal flourish, naming the dish they carried:

"Filet of lamb."

"Grilled sea bass."

"Braised chicken in lemon sauce."

"Roast of beef in butter sauce."

"Savoury meat stuffed vol-au-vents."

"Asparagus tips."

"Candied carrots."

"Potatoes ... *au gratin*," the latter words being pronounced "O grey-tin."

The last dish to be set before them was a puréed pea soup with croutons, the aroma and consistency of which would surely put Biscuit's oft-served jellied pea soup *muck* to shame. Next there came the desserts, which were placed with equal fanfare upon the parlour's commodious sideboard for later.

"Apple meringue."

"Vanilla soufflé."

"Egg custard."

"Rum and apricot cake."

"Strawberries and pears."

"Spiced nuts and raisins."

Emily watched the grand proceeding quietly from her chair, her lips parted in bewilderment. Why the only missing item was the trumpeter and his festive salute, although she did have a moment's worry that he was still to follow. She smiled warmly at each and every one of the eager servants, and then shot her uncle an admonishing glare. "Sir, I do not understand. There are only three places set here upon this table; yet you have ordered enough food to feed every man and boy who travelled with us across the ocean on the *Impregnable*. Shall they soon be joining us?"

"Good God, Emeline, you can be very droll at times. They shall not! This is a trifling, nothing more! Why we could never have enticed the Regent to Portsmouth with a mere nibble of an incentive such as this. Nay, the meal is for *our* pleasure alone."

He bustled out the disappointed servants, who surely had hoped to watch Emily stuff the food into her mouth — each one scurrying to bow or curtsy or cry out gleefully, "Please enjoy, ma'am" as they headed toward the doorway. Uncle Clarence closed the door upon them, tossed his damp Carrick upon a sofa, and plopped down upon the chair reserved for him. "No need for servants," he said, reaching for the platter of lemon-sauced chicken. "Dig in ... help yourselves."

"All this food! Uncle, what've you done to the cook? Surely you've killed her with exhaustion."

"Not at all, my dear, for she had half the town assisting her. And the best part of all ... it will cost us nothing. Everything — the food, the accommodation — is extended to us compliments of the townsfolk." Uncle Clarence abruptly dropped the chicken, threw back his chair, leaped up, and marched across the room toward the heavy draperies that hid a large, street-facing bow window. Drawing them aside, he pointed toward the scene beyond. A tight gathering of people started in excitement when the object restricting them from an interior view of the hotel was stripped away, and they recognized Emily sitting at the table. At once, they began waving at her and tapping upon the panes; some even blew her kisses. For the most part, the crowd consisted of children — poor children — and Emily could see that many of them held flowers or ribbons in their hands.

"Please don't tell me they've been standing there ever since we arrived," said Emily in consternation.

"They have been, my dear, simply to catch a glimpse of you!"

"They must be cold and starving, and here we sit by a fire with a feast for hundreds."

"The proprietor was kind enough to allow them to stay so long as they were quiet, did not break the windows, and didn't trample his flower gardens." Uncle Clarence bowed before the crowd, and then, as quickly as he had parted them, he shut the draperies upon the hopeful faces and returned to his supper. Piling high his plate with an assortment of savoury dishes, he inhaled the aromas, emitted a sigh of contentment, and got right down to the business of eating. While he smacked his lips, Emily spooned out some soup for herself, and Gus sampled the beef and asparagus.

"Now then," he said, assuming an air of gravity. "For the morning I have arranged a coach and four, although — goodness! — I had a terrible time with the post-boys, who did not seem to care that we're not carrying mail, and fought monstrously over who should be selected to accompany us on our journey. I had wanted footmen, but the post-boys were so endearingly insistent. Mr. Walby, we shall stop first in Winchester. Your uncle is not at home; it is believed he's in the West Indies, but his sister has agreed to take you in."

"Aunt Sophia?" There was pure terror in Gus's voice.

"Yes, yes, that's the one, and upon your arrival, I've arranged for a doctor to see to you. He's old and retired, but highly regarded."

Gus sank further into his chair.

"Then, my dear," said Uncle Clarence, angling his head in Emily's direction, "we shall away to London."

"And where will you be dropping *me* off?"

"Oh, it is a surprise, and you'll thank me for it."

At this point, Emily could not have cared less if her uncle had arranged for her to lodge in a den with a pack of wolves, but the distress evident in Gus's face was discomfiting. "Could we not stay here another day or two, Uncle, at least until we've regained our land legs."

"Absolutely not! I must be back in London in time to be fitted up for a new suit of clothes, so that I may attend the Regent's birthday party on August twelfth." He poured a glass of red wine for himself and contentedly raised it to his lips. "Now eat up, and then we will to bed, for we depart in the Morning Watch at eight bells."

4

Sunday, August 8

8:00 a.m.
(Morning Watch, Eight Bells)
Aboard HMS *Amethyst*
Halifax, Nova Scotia

UPON WAKING AND discovering a warm, pleasant day beyond the cramped, stuffy quarters of his hospital, Leander Braden had made his way to the bench on the poop deck's stern, there to eat his breakfast of cheese and biscuit, and to read in the peace and quiet before resuming his duties. But this morning he was restless and distracted, so much so that after he had downed his light meal, he found he could not concentrate on Thomas Campbell's poem "The Pleasures of Hope," completing only a stanza or two before the inclination arose in him to set down the book and once more look out for his friend, Fly Austen.

Fly had promised to return to the ship early Sunday morning, before muster and church service on deck. He had been gone since Friday noon when they had come sailing into the Halifax Harbour and accompanied Captain Prickett ashore in the launch almost the minute the *Amethyst*'s anchor had been dropped into the depths, leaving Lord Bridlington in charge, who insisted he stay with the doctor so that his battle wound might be cleansed and re-bandaged on an hourly basis. There was little doubt in Leander's mind that Prickett would be gone for days, enjoying the sumptuous hospitality of the Admiralty in addition to the more rustic, but convivial, hospitality of the taverns and brothels — thoughts of the latter having sustained the man's spirits in the days before their arrival in port — and happily wallowing in the Haligonians' praise for his part in bringing down Thomas Trevelyan's ship. But Leander knew his friend, and firmly believed Fly would return when he said he would. Besides, though he would admit it to no one, he was hopeful that Fly would bring with him news of Emily.

Snatching the spyglass from the deep pocket of his new bottle-green coat, Leander placed it to his eye and scoured the waters around the King's Naval Yard. The *Amethyst* lay anchored in the middle of the harbour in the company of six other ships-of-the-line, and HMS *Centurion*, now a hulk put to good use as a hospital and receiving ship, but there were no small boats travelling the distance between them and the shore. From his vantage point, Leander could see plenty of activity afoot in the yard: two small frigates were being constructed, the banging of the shipwrights' hammers echoing over the water; a careened ship had a team of men stripping the barnacles from its hull; large kettles of pitch were being boiled; new masts were being hauled from the sail loft; a wall of stone was being erected; meat was being purchased in the victualling yard; a cluster of men stood chatting near the door of the blacksmith's shop; and naval supplies were being transported to and from the various storehouses.

Leander turned his glass upon the Commissioner's House, a three-storey architectural beauty with a sloping roof and large, harbour-facing windows which stood out from the rest of the low, flat nondescript wooden buildings and warehouses built around it. He was more than likely sure it was Fly's location, for H.R.H. Prince Edward, Duke of Kent, had been known to stay there during his time in Halifax as commander-in-chief, and Captain Broke of HMS *Shannon* had been taken there to recuperate after his ship's battle with the USS *Chesapeake*. Unfortunately, at this early hour, there was no one about except for a washerwoman hanging out the laundry.

Much to Leander's chagrin, another attempt to read was thwarted by the appearance of the *Amethyst*'s own washerwoman, Meg Kettle, whose bulk he could see waddling up the ladder with her large basket. She was cursing and chuntering away to herself, and intent on invading his quiet domain in order to string up a few freshly laundered hammocks in the rigging of the mizzenmast. Laundry was rarely done on a Sunday — Mondays and Fridays being the more traditional days — but regardless of the day chosen for the task it was commonplace to hang it to dry in the fo'c'sle rigging. The problem was, with Captain Prickett away from the ship and the Amethysts still working on replacing the broken foremast, Mrs. Kettle was marching — as was her way — to her own rules, indulging in her own caprices.

Leander glanced up at the grumbling, grey-haired woman, whose hips were as broad as the ship's beam, snapped his book shut once and for all, and addressed her in a cool manner.

"Are you unwell this morning, Mrs. Kettle, or just out-of-sorts?"

"I ain't never well, Doctor," she grunted, "on account o' the babe in me belly, and the rotten work ya gives me to do. I were treated with more respect on Trevelyan's ship."

"And that surprises you?"

Mrs. Kettle ignored his remark. "Still can't keep down me vittles in the mornin'."

"Were you late getting to bed last night?"

"I'm late to bed ev'ry night, Doctor. Ya would knows that if ya was to leave behind yer books and doctorin', and come have a wee bit o' fun with us."

"I've warned you before about the imprudence of drinking each evening in your condition. Perhaps if you were to entirely leave off your rations of grog, and avoid rum and ale when you are dancing with the men on deck, you might feel better."

Mrs. Kettle's eyes widened. "What other pleasures do I 'ave in this life, Doctor?"

Leander raised one of his auburn eyebrows to convey his disbelief.

Gathering up her mud-coloured calico skirt, Mrs. Kettle spun about and began fastening the wet hammocks to the rigging with fat wooden pegs. "It's Prosper Burgo what puts me in a temper. Here I was thinkin' maybe I'd found fer meself a decent man — a father fer me child what's comin' — and the scoundrel goes and runs off."

"I believe the man is just trying to make a living. He's not assigned to the *Amethyst*. He has a very good ship of his own."

"He could 'ave asked me to go with him, now couldn't he? Nay! The scoundrel ran off; he won't be back."

Leander mulled over how best to put his next theory into words. "Perhaps Mr. Burgo was discomfited by your *other* pleasures."

Mrs. Kettle, arms akimbo, her sausage fingers drumming her ever-thickening waist, rounded on him. "And how else am I supposed ta earn me money? I git paid a pittance fer slavin' on this ship, cleanin' the lads' stockings and dirty drawers. If I were to leave off lyin' with the men, I might as well drown meself."

"Yes, please," whispered Leander to the wind.

"Ya think maybe I'm not good enough fer Prosper?" she cried, jabbing a finger at him. "Is that what yer sayin'?"

"I did not *say* such a thing, nor *think* such a thought."

"Ya think yer so superior on account o' that princess what fancied ya fer a week or two." Mrs. Kettle quickly finished up with her hammocks, and groaned as she bent over to scoop up her basket from the deck. She then planted her feet on the ship's planks to aim her last dart at Leander. "Ya ain't no better than me, Doctor. Why the minute that harlot lands in London, she'll 'ave the Quality vyin' fer her — men with heaps o' money and fancy titles — and afore long she'll be forgettin about ya. Why, ya might as well 'ave gone down with the *Isabelle*."

A dozen rejoinders burned in Leander's brain before he made his reply. "Thank you for that, Mrs. Kettle. You know it puzzles me greatly that Mr. Burgo would ever have run off in the night and left you behind when you are so generous in manner … so affable a woman."

Mrs. Kettle jerked her head backward in surprise, and was a long time in responding. "Well," she snarled, kicking at the deck with the toe of her boot, "there ain't no sense in ya dreamin' 'bout somethin' ya can't 'ave." With a toss of her chin, Mrs. Kettle marched across the poop deck, leaving Leander believing his day would have got off to a much better start if he had stayed in bed to eat his cheese and biscuit. Languidly he lifted the spyglass to his eye, and gave a silent word of thanks when the *Amethyst*'s launch immediately popped into view.

Fly was on his way at last.

Noon
(Forenoon Watch, Eight Bells)

HOURS LATER LEANDER finally had his opportunity to speak to Fly in private. Upon his arrival back to the *Amethyst*, there was much he had to discuss with Lord Bridlington, and then of course he had to be present for both muster and the Sunday church service. Leander was writing a letter at his desk in the hospital when Fly, carrying a paper-wrapped parcel in his hands, came stomping down the ladder with a big grin on his face.

"Mr. Austen, I would kindly remind you that my patients require a bit of peace and quiet down here," said Leander, folding up his letter and returning his friend's smile.

"Aye! My apologies." Fly glanced around the small space to find only one of the hospital hammocks filled. "Is Jim Beef still in a bad way?"

"No, he's come through the swelling on his brain nicely, and periodically is conscious, though when awake he claims to be Davy Jones and enjoys pronouncing doom on the lot of us."

"I understand he was a Tom o' Bedlam from the Bethlem Hospital before he was deemed a *curable* and impressed upon the *Amethyst*. It is more than likely sure he thought of himself as Davy Jones many years ago."

Leander chuckled as he pulled up a chair for Fly. "Come sit and tell me of the amusements in Halifax, and all the manner of debauchery you have indulged in over the past few days. In your absence, my life has been dull; my company the fretful Mr. Bridlington — you'd think the man had lost *all* of his limbs — and the ill-natured Mrs Kettle. If it weren't for little Magpie, I believe I would've thrown myself into one of my hammocks, and happily joined Mr. Beef in his madness."

Fly's gaze fell upon Leander's letter. "Ah, I see you are busy writing again."

Hastily, Leander stuffed the folded parchment into his sloped writing box (the one Morgan Evans had recently knocked together for him) that sat atop his desk and turned the key in its tiny lock. "You are changing the subject on me. I asked about Halifax."

Fly plunked his parcel down upon the desk, flipped the chair around backward, and straddled it. "And if your red face is any indication, I'm guessing it's addressed to the enigmatic Emeline."

"Actually," Leander began, hoping to keep his flush in check, "I'm writing a love letter to Mrs. Kettle. I thought, now that Prosper Burgo has left us and he is seemingly out of the way, I should unburden the longing in my bosom to the woman. My only worry is that the long-absent Mr. Kettle may one day surface."

Much to Leander's discomfort, Fly — his facial features twisted in a stultifying grin — stared him down.

"I ... I only hope," he stammered, "that *she* has made it safely to England by now." Fly's stare grew brighter and more unsettling. "And, I confess, I would like to know if she still ... if she still thinks of me occasionally."

Fly leaned forward to punch Leander on his upper arm. "While I do believe she's now safely in London — for only the most foolhardy would have attempted to attack Clarence and his flotilla — I rather doubt she still thinks of you. Knowing she may never see you again, Emily has most likely decided to make the most of her marriage to Thomas Trevelyan. Hmmm ... unless ... have you told her that you have now managed to put aside five shillings for your future?"

Leander shook his head in wonder. "You are quite astute at savaging a poor man's confidence, Mr. Austen."

Fly laughed and began wrestling with the string holding his paper-wrapped parcel together. "You do know, old friend, I'm not *all* brute. Let me show you what I have here, and then I'll tell you something that may lift up the corners of your sad mouth."

Heartened, Leander watched as Fly peeled back the paper layers to reveal a feast of food. "I've been spoiled these past days at the Commissioner's House; therefore, I could not countenance returning to Biscuit's cooking, and a meal that might include his lobscouse or fried goat — though I do hope he has brought in fresh vegetables and soft bread, and perhaps some unsalted beef for the men from shore. So, before quitting Halifax, I did a bit of shopping as well as a bit of pilfering —"

"Hopefully not in the victualling yard," interjected Leander, hungrily eyeing the spread of fresh rolls, cold chicken, boiled eggs, ripe strawberries, and apple pastries.

"Certainly not! Nay! I was able to charm a good lady into opening up her bakeshop early for the rolls and pastries; the rest I stuffed into my pockets while breakfasting in the company of Captain Prickett, a few vice-admirals and members of local gentry. It's amazing really the strawberries aren't mashed to a pulp."

Leander grimaced. "In your pockets?"

"I jest, old friend, eat up."

Producing two clean cloths, which would serve as napkins, from a cupboard at his back, Leander tossed one at Fly, and then the two men set about to eat the cold chicken and eggs with their hands.

"Your news, Fly," Leander soon said, trying to quell the eagerness in his voice. "Don't keep me waiting any longer."

"Right then! The truth is … I bring both good and bad news," said Fly, wiping his fingers on his cloth. "I'll begin with the good. Prickett has presented his resignation from the Royal Navy to the Admiralty, citing his age, and complaints of rheumatism and fluttering nerves. I shall soon be assuming command of the *Amethyst*."

"Congratulations! I know how difficult it's been for you to stand by while Prickett and Bridlington pretend to lead the Amethysts."

"I have been waiting for another command for a long time now. And … we've been given fresh orders. Running into that American privateer in the fog a few days back was exceptional. Business has dried up in these parts, for our merchantmen rarely sail unescorted nowadays. The result? Our enemy has now found new hunting grounds. As so many of our ships are blockading the French in their harbours, or over here doing the same thing to the American warships, our enemy privateers are having great success in striking where we are *not* — in the waters around Britain."

Leander looked at Fly blankly. "You're telling me that we shall be securing the shores of England from American privateers, preying on our trading ships?"

"Aye, we shall be!"

Leander leaned back against the bony spindles of his chair, looking somewhat dejected. "I am happy for your new command and for your new orders, but I must ask … knowing we are simply taking our fight into new waters … that I will continue my days on this ship, sewing up heads and lopping off limbs … how *did* you think this news might cause me to smile?"

Fly began tapping the smooth, rounded curve on the back of his chair. "My new command and new orders can wait; I've been called back to London for two reasons: firstly, to attend an inquiry regarding the loss of the *Isabelle* —"

"Yes, why is it," interjected Leander, "a court-martial has not yet been called to settle the affair?"

"For the simple reason that, in order to do so, there must be present at least five captains or admirals in the court, and preferably more, especially when Britain suffered such a great loss."

"And the second reason?"

"To testify at Trevelyan's trial. A date has not yet been set for it; however, Whitehall wants me in the city, to stand there prepared when the time comes."

Still not satisfied, Leander furrowed his brow.

"And you, my friend, having been a witness to the destruction of Captain Moreland's *Isabelle*, and subsequently been kidnapped by Trevelyan … along with the king's granddaughter —" Fly paused to give his friend a long, significant look. "*You* are going with me."

5

Sunday, August 8

3:00 p.m.
The outskirts of Winchester

WHEN THE COACH HALTED Emily's head collided with the window's frame, instantly awakening her. Sleepily she gazed about, trying to recollect the day and her whereabouts. Uncle Clarence sat next to her on one of the coach's two olive-green velvet seats, fussing with his cane and brushing dust from his cream pantaloons in anticipation of his disembarkation.

"Now, Mr. Walby, look sharp," he said in an exasperatingly boisterous tone, shifting his bottom forward onto the edge of the seat. "We shan't be dallying here at your aunt's place for long. There're many miles between Winchester and London."

Across from them, Gus sat alone. To see his face, one would suspect he was about to be buried alive in the next cemetery they happened upon. Adding to his frail, deflated appearance was the tight midshipman's uniform he wore. Having lost his own to the sinking of the *Isabelle*, he had inherited one that had once belonged to a young Impregnable who had been drowned at sea, but its white trousers and jacket sleeves rode well up above Gus's respective ankles and wrists. Emily could see, in the nervous blinking of his eyes and the compressing of his lips, his struggle to stay strong for the sake of the Duke of Clarence, for it would not do to break down in front of *him*. Trying to ease some of his anxiety, she gave him an encouraging smile, which he tried so very hard to return.

The exuberant post-boys scrambled down from their rumble seat on the back of the coach, arguing about which one of them was going to offer a helping hand to the princess. Jostling one another, they finally succeeded in swinging open the door and pulling down the steps. Uncle Clarence was the first one out, and he exclaimed relief as he stretched his legs, took in the fresh air, and looked about. It had been his intention that they get underway early from Portsmouth, but the townsfolk would not have it. Their delay in departure was the result of an invitation to take breakfast with a local wealthy family who provided them with a feast that had surpassed — in both presentation and variety — their supper at the George, and who had invited a number of their neighbours to join them — many of them having gaped at Emily through their quizzing glasses during the meal, leaving her suspecting that overnight she had acquired a second set of eyes.

Following the sumptuous breakfast, a few of the village ladies had pleaded with them to take tea and pastries with them. Where good food and festivity abounded, Uncle Clarence could not say no, while Emily confessed to being pleased with the arrangement. It had been her wish to meet some of the village children, especially those who had hung about the George for hours in the hopes of seeing her, and to whom she had gently instructed the hotel's servants to give the plentiful remains of her supper dishes. Moreover, the delay had served to postpone her inevitable separation from Gus. But she had not meant to sleep — could hardly believe she had been able to do so — during the bouncing, jolting coach ride to Winchester, and felt she owed Gus an apology for slumbering away their last moments together.

"I am sorry for my drowsiness. It's been months since I was forced to speak to so many people, and eat so many pastries."

"I slept most of the way too," admitted Gus, though there was something in the jumpy expression in his eyes which caused Emily to doubt he was telling her the truth.

Peering out through the open coach door, Emily could see a timber-framed, thatched cottage, set in a copse of mature beech and elm trees and surrounded by a fence badly in need of a fresh coat of paint. In the distance, beyond the stirring trees, were acres of green, sheep-dotted fields. Though somewhat rundown, it was a beautiful place, and she would happily have ended her journey here, had it not been for the severe-looking woman — presumably Gus's Aunt Sophia — who had emerged from the house with an unhappy baby in her arms, and who shrilly yelled at the three noisy children circling around her feet lest they *"trip her up."* It did not seem to excite the woman in the least that a member of the royal house was standing in her front yard, for she neither smiled nor curtsied nor invited Uncle Clarence in to drink tea. Despite her chilly reception, Emily's uncle chatted away merrily to the under-whelmed Aunt Sophia on the subject of her sturdy-looking children, and of his own *ten offspring* he had left at home.

Despite the fact that Emily had not sought their assistance, the young post-boys seized her hands and, with silly grins upon their faces, fairly lifted her out of the confining coach, setting her down somewhat roughly upon the narrow, hedged-in road that ran alongside the cottage fence. Then they dashed to help Gus, and in a flash had him safely delivered to her side, and propped up once more upon his crutch. Taking a deep breath, Emily fixed her eyes on the top of Gus's blond head, and felt her heart breaking.

"Promise me you'll take good care of yourself, Mr. Walby?"

"I will," said Gus, casting an uncertain glance in his aunt's direction.

"Once I know where I'm to be left I'll forward you my address."

He nodded wistfully.

"And will you write to me?"

"Every day, Em," he said in a strangled whisper.

Emily wanted so badly to leave him smiling. If only she could reassure him that the very instant Trevelyan was pronounced dead in his hang-man's noose, she would hire a coach, leave London, come straightaway to Winchester to collect him, and together they could journey back to Portsmouth to stow away on the first Royal Navy ship leaving for the war on the American coast. The unspoken words weighed heavily upon her tongue, but how cruel it would be to instill so much hope in Gus, when Emily herself was no more certain about the future than he was. She leaned against the gatepost to steady her failing legs.

"You go on and greet your Aunt Sophia," she said, giving his arm — the one gripping the crutch — a quick squeeze. She whispered a hurried goodbye, and then made for the coach, thankful that the post-boys were standing by to help her manage the steps.

"Oh, fine! And what kind o' help will ya be 'round here, hobblin' about on a stick?" Aunt Sophia's harsh words of greeting to her nephew sailed clear across the yard to strike Emily's ears. It was too much; she could not bear to hear more.

"Please ... please close the door for me," she called out to the post-boys, too anguished to do so herself. Away from all prying eyes, shut inside the hot, silk-lined, velvet-upholstered body of the coach, she allowed her tears to fall, and prayed her uncle would not linger long. The sooner they departed the better.

Regrettably, a peek beyond the coach window was not promising.

Gus, his Aunt Sophia, and the children had disappeared into the house; however, her Uncle Clarence was now exchanging pleasantries with a respectable-looking older gentleman who had come walking up the laneway from the direction of the village, holding onto a leather bag. Emily's first impulse was to cry out and wish them away, but curiosity stopped her. Brushing away the tears from her cheeks, she sat up straighter to observe their exchange.

The gentleman looked to be perhaps sixty-five. He was tall and slender, his posture upright, his hair grey and thinning, but neatly cut, and there was something in his manner of conversing with her uncle that hinted of intelligence and good breeding. Emily doubted he was Aunt Sophia's husband — if, in fact, the woman actually possessed one — so who was he? She noted with delight the way in which the gentleman planted his feet on the gravel laneway, and carried his head, tilting it forward to show keen interest in her uncle's speech, and was surprised to feel a twinge of excitement rising in her breast which ignited her imagination.

Thirty long years had suddenly passed — half a lifetime — and there, no more than a few feet away, stood Leander Braden. He was older, but still handsome and wise, and had spent years trying to find her, going from village to village on foot, making inquiries as to her possible whereabouts. He had come round this place before, but had come again straightaway, having heard in town news that the Duke of Clarence and his niece were travelling this way en route to London and would be stopping here. He had to know. Was it true? Was the niece with whom the duke travelled his own Emily? Surely ... any minute now ... her Uncle Clarence would clap the man on the back, wish him joy, and invite him to look no further than the coach that stood on the laneway. Slowly the gentleman would turn his head around and see her there in the window. His dear face would then break into a

*broad smile and his blue eyes — for surely he had blue eyes — would brighten with
elated incredulity, and he would come forward to greet her, one hand held out to …*

Though she desired him to do so, the older gentleman did not glance
her way; Emily was never given an opportunity to look upon the full contours of his features, nor confirm the hue of his eyes. Perhaps it was just
as well. As the conversation ended abruptly with the gentleman bowing
before Uncle Clarence, and moving on up the grass pathway to Aunt
Sophia's front door, she tried to laugh off her whimsical reverie. But she
could not, for a cloud of longing clung to her, as if she had been awakened
prematurely from a rare and wonderful dream.

The minute Uncle Clarence had reinstated himself in the coach, sitting
opposite her this time, upon the seat still warm and reminiscent of Gus
Walby's recent occupation, Emily desired nothing more than to return to
sleep. She waited for her uncle to reach for his cane and rap its carved ivory
head against the wall of the coach to signal to the coachman, and as they
lurched away from Aunt Sophia's house and started down the road to London
— Emily refusing a last glance toward the windows, lest she should find the
lone figure of Gus Walby standing there — she made her hopeful inquiries.

"Who was that man, Uncle?"

"Why he's the doctor I arranged to come and look in after Mr. Walby.
Decent of him to come straightaway."

"A doctor!" Emily drew in breath. "And his name —?"

"Why I haven't the faintest notion," he said, peeling off his brown
leather gloves. "He didn't say, and I didn't think to ask."

9:00 p.m.
Hartwood Hall

IT WAS UNCLE CLARENCE'S intention to dump Emily off hastily and uncere-
moniously at the north-facing entrance of Hartwood Hall, claiming he had
an evening engagement he desired to keep in the city, though his arrival
there would be quite late. Throughout the last leg of their journey — from
London to Hampstead — it had been raining heavily, and he was eager to
be off again, as the roads were poor and muddy, and it would take him close
to two hours to reach his destination.

Emily was incredulous. "This is rather untoward, Uncle. Have you no interest in giving me an introduction to the good people of the house? Do you mean to leave me off here like a child in a basket with the hope they will heap pity on me and take me in?"

Her uncle burst into a chuckle. "They're not even at home, Emeline, and shan't be returning for a day or two. The minute the servants open the doors — ah, there they are now! I can see them gathering with their umbrellas and candles — you will have the best surprise, and will understand why I chose to leave you *here*."

"I am feeling ridiculous!"

"Oh, ho, no need for that, my dear. Now then you do have the addresses of your family members, as well as that of your friend Mr. Walby?"

"I do," said Emily, trying, like the barrel of a musket, to lock her enlarged eyes on his.

"And when we next meet out in London society, I do not wish to see you draped in that gown again. I've grown frightfully tired of it in our travels together."

Emily smoothed the folds of her blue-and-white-striped morning dress. "In that case you shall be disappointed, Uncle, for a very special person sewed this gown together for me, and I intend to wear it often."

Her uncle snorted. "God damn, do not forget who you are! It'll not do to have the Regent's niece and the king's granddaughter traipse around in an inferior, homespun gown, nor, for that matter, sailors' trousers, for that is what I surmise you have packed away in that chest of yours."

"That may well be true, but you forget, Uncle, I have little beyond what I'm presently wearing. The clothes with which I departed England four months ago have now settled upon the sea's bottom within the wreck of the *Amelia*."

He looked pleased with himself. "I've seen to all that! Clothes and little accessories you shall soon have, for the Regent has kindly seen to providing you with a gift of five hundred pounds."

"That is more than generous of him, Uncle, but now that I'm not living under my grandfather's roof, I don't need the Regent's charity. I should like to *earn* my keep. Perhaps the women who work here in the kitchen would happily employ me to wash the china and crystal."

"God Almighty, Emeline! No need for that sort of nonsense."

"As this little reticule I am now clutching, given to me by the good ladies of Portsmouth, hasn't a shilling in it, perhaps you would keep the Regent's money, and be so kind as to loan me just enough so that I may buy a loaf of bread while I await my first bit of pay."

Uncle Clarence patted Emily's hand. "Not to worry, set your mind at ease; it has all been taken care of for you, my dear."

"Then would you be so kind as to explain it all to me, Uncle?"

"No time for that. Rest assured!"

"You haven't even informed me as to how long I might be here."

"A few weeks … perhaps a few months."

"Months!"

"These sorts of trials take time, Emeline," he said, curtly. "Now … now here is the housekeeper waiting patiently for you at the coach door. Hurry, hurry, the unfortunate woman is getting wet. Give your old uncle a kiss and be off."

Their goodbyes were exchanged in such an expeditious manner, her uncle almost pushing her out the door and into the rain, that Emily was left wondering if he was embarrassed about being seen in her *unmanageable* company. The post-boys fetched her small clothing chest from the roof of the coach, handed it off to one of the waiting servants, and in an equally hurried way bowed and wished her "Godspeed." In no time at all the coach was off again. Emily watched it trundling away, the clip-clop of the retreating horses growing fainter and fainter, until the wet, shadowy world of gusty trees and endless acres of black parkland had swallowed it whole. Feeling quite lost and in a daze, Emily felt the heavy arm of the faceless housekeeper wrap tightly around her shoulders and quickly steer her toward the light and warmth of Hartwood Hall, which loomed before her like three ships-of-the-line with their lanterns ablaze, sailing abreast on the darkened sea.

And yet … the *Isabelle*, her crew, and Leander Braden had never felt so far away.

6

Monday, August 9

As Fly Austen swept into the great cabin, apologizing for his tardiness and having missed supper, Biscuit uncorked another bottle of Madeira and presented the latecomer with a glass, before refilling those belonging to Captain Prickett, Lord Bridlington, and Leander Braden.

"Ach, Mr. Austen, and ya missed one o' me specialties tonight," he chirped as Fly took his place at the round table, sampling his wine as he lowered himself into his chair.

"And what was it I missed, Biscuit?"

Biscuit's odd eye rolled in his head, while he winked his normal one. "On a hint from the doctor, who told me ya was fanatical fer it, I cooked up a shank o' fried goat!"

The men all laughed when Fly glared at Leander. "Had I received intelligence in advance of the delicacy you planned to serve us for our supper, I'd never have bothered to investigate the desertion of our men."

Captain Prickett sat back leisurely in his chair, his wine glass propped up upon his prodigious belly. "And how many have we lost while sitting here in Halifax Harbour, Mr. Austen?"

"Four landmen and two sailors," answered Fly, somewhat perplexed at Prickett's devil-may-care attitude.

"Their names?"

Fly reached into his uniform jacket to produce a slip of paper, upon which the names of the missing men were recorded, and handed it over to Prickett who pursed his lips in concentration as he perused the list.

"A weakling, a scoundrel, three troublemakers, and one saphead," pronounced Prickett, carelessly flipping the paper onto the oak table. "In addition to ourselves, Mr. Austen, I granted leave to no one but Biscuit and my purser, so they could round up fresh provisions in the victualling yard, and to Morgan Evans, and a few men of his choosing, who went in search of a new foremast. Did you learn how these men were able to leave the ship?"

"They swam to shore."

"They swam! Why there's hardly one amongst us that can swim!"

"I believe they took along a barrel or two to aid them."

Prickett harrumphed. "Well the lot of them are dolts. They won't be missed."

"With your permission, I'll send a few trustworthy men ashore to track them down, as I understand you'd like to weigh anchor tomorrow morning."

"Do not bother yourself, Mr. Austen. We're better off without them."

"But we're so short of able-bodied men."

"If you'd told me that Dr. Braden had left us abruptly —" he paused to acknowledge Leander with a bow of his head, "I might consider going after *him*, but these men are an insult to the service; in fact, I'm rather pleased they're gone. Nothing to be done now but write an *R* beside their names in the ship's muster book."

"An *R*?" asked Leander, looking to his naval companions for an answer.

"It stands for *Run*, Doctor," replied Prickett.

Fly and Leander exchanged looks before returning to their wine. While Bridlington brooded — perhaps hoping no one would pin the blame on him, as he had been left in charge — Fly switched the subject. "Captain, upon your return from shore this afternoon, you said you'd received updated orders. Are we still returning to England?"

"We are, but now we shall have company."

"Will we be travelling in a convoy?"

"No, thank goodness!

Fly narrowed his dark eyes. "But I understood the Admiralty demanded all Royal Navy ships travel in groups these days."

"You understood correctly, Mr. Austen, but I detest having to stay all together, especially when crossing the Atlantic in all manner of weather, with ships that travel at various speeds, and with captains who are invariably suffering from drunkenness or pompous egoism." Prickett shifted his bulk toward his first lieutenant. "Bridlington, remember the annoyance of escorting those two merchantmen back in June?"

The first lieutenant's answer was high-toned. "Aye, sir!"

"Why the minute we were shot at, they took off like frightened women! Nay! There shall be no convoy." Prickett extended his glass toward Biscuit so that he could refill it. "We've been instructed to stick like tar to a government mail packet, HM *Lady Jane*."

"A packet? And what will she be carrying?" asked Fly.

"In addition to eight guns and a crew of thirty-six, she will be carrying several important dispatches, private goods, a dozen or so passengers, and *gold* bullion."

"A tempting target for Yankee privateers?" offered Leander.

"Precisely, Doctor, thus the reason we're to escort her home. These packets have had a hell of a time fighting off enemy privateers of late."

"With us about, no one would dare attack her," said Bridlington, contemplating his bandaged hand.

"No one except perhaps Prosper Burgo and his unruly Remarkables," smiled Fly.

"Thank goodness they are on *our* side," Leander smiled back.

They raised their near-empty glasses and cried in unison: "To our ships at sea."

"And may God steer us and the *Lady Jane* safely home," added Captain Prickett. He slurped up the last of his wine, and set his relaxed gaze upon Leander. "On second thought, Doctor, should you like to get ashore for an evening before we set sail, I shall grant you leave. I did promise you earlier, and have not yet kept my word. You could visit a grog-shop or two, mingle with the fair ladies awhile — you will find them *most* accommodating company — and keep an eye out for our missing Amethysts."

"But, sir," yelped Bridlington, "what if my hand should start bleeding again and the doctor's not here to tend to it?"

Prickett's gaze slid around the table before settling upon Bridlington's ashen face. "I'll seize one of the doctor's colossal knives, cut off your entire hand in one swift blow, and be done with your incessant snivelling once and for all!"

Lord Bridlington cast his wandering eyes toward the cabin's ceiling, and loudly exhaled to display his indignation.

Prickett snorted and repeated his suggestion to Leander. "It'll do you good to get off the ship for a while, Doctor."

"Thank you, Captain, but seeing as you may have to amputate Mr. Bridlington's hand, I'd better stay to make certain you do a decent job of it."

"Suit yourself, man," said Prickett, who then leaned in companionably close to Leander and gave him a wink. "But, tell me, on those nights when visitors did come from shore ... did you not take advantage of ... well, you know ... of any opportunities?"

Leander calmly maintained eye contact with Prickett. "I was very much occupied with the dozen or so men who suffered bad falls apparently brought on while doing cartwheels and handstands on the deck for the benefit of the female visitors."

Bridlington, trying to salvage his dignity, jumped back into the conversation. "I daresay I should've liked it if that Jim Beef had deserted with the lot of those weaklings! He's become most irksome."

"How so?" barked Prickett, looking about to see where Biscuit and the wine bottle had gone.

"Last night, around midnight, I found him perched in the rigging, proclaiming to be Davy Jones, saying that the *Amethyst* was a floating coffin and that we were all heading to our doom. Can't you do something about him, Doctor?"

"I can heal a man physically, Lord Bridlington," said Leander, "but just as you cannot harness the wind whilst your ship sits in the doldrums, I cannot harness a man's mind."

Prickett punched Bridlington in the arm. "But we *are*, man."

Bridlington pulled back and twisted his skinny neck to stare at his captain. "We are *what*, sir?"

"Sooner or later, we *are* heading to our doom."

9:00 p.m.
(First Watch, Two Bells)

As TWILIGHT SETTLED upon the hills of Halifax and her harbour, the lights in her scattered homes and on the anchored ships gleamed like stars that had fallen to earth, and the air that whispered around the *Amethyst* was fresh and clean on this August night. Magpie sat upon a dilapidated box by the bowsprit on the fo'c'sle deck, his unattended mending upon his lap, his tall *Isabelle* hat upon his dark curls, and smiled to himself as he listened to the rich, deep-toned voice of Morgan Evans who was singing to a cluster of men seeking entertainment before retiring to their hammocks.

> *But should thou false or fickle prove*
> *To Jack who loves thee dear*
> *No more upon my native shore*
> *Can I with joy appear*
> *But restless as the briny main*
> *Must heartless heave the log*
> *Shall trim the sails and try to drown*
> *My sorrows in cans of grog.*

Unable to find a second available box for himself, Dr. Braden sat beside Magpie on the deck planks and rested his back against the square, clunky carriage of a bow-chaser. He had managed to affix the handle of the lantern he carried onto a protruding piece of the large gun, so that its flame flickered by his shoulder, enabling him to read his slim volume of poetry. Magpie had never before heard the name Robert Burns of Scotland, although Dr. Braden admitted to having a great appreciation of his poetical works. A few yards from where the two relaxed, the sailors tapped their toes, clapped their hands, and at times raised their voices in song with Morgan. Amongst them was Meg Kettle, swinging her hips about in dizzying circles, occasionally lifting her coarse skirt to show the grog-mellowed sailors a bit — or in her case a lot — of leg. It seemed to Magpie that the laundress had quite forgotten her heartbreak in losing Prosper Burgo, and was tickled to be the centre of attention once again, now that Captain Prickett had announced their leaving Halifax at first tide, insisting the men be early to bed and alert for their departure, and thus stemming the nightly flow of female shore visitors to the *Amethyst*.

Magpie swung around eagerly to look at Dr. Braden. "Are ya gonna write to her, sir, to tell her yer comin'?"

Leander lowered his book, a distant smile playing upon his lips. "I would like that of all things, but no, I think it's best we surprise her."

"And where is it ya send yer letters, sir? Do ya just write: *To Princess Emeline Louisa Georgina Marie in London*?"

"No!" laughed Dr. Braden. "Although they would most likely still find their way to her. No! Before she left she gave me her uncle's address at Bushy House, and assured me any letters would be safely delivered to her."

"And, sir, do ya ... do ya really want me comin' with ya?" Magpie asked, his heart rate accelerating.

Dr. Braden placed his book on the deck, pulled his long legs up to his chest, and hooked his arms around his knees. "I don't believe Emily would want to see *me* unless I had *you* at my side."

"Very kind o' ya to say, sir."

"In fact, if I were to show up at her door alone, I believe she would instruct me to turn around again and not return until I had *you* with me."

"But are ya quite sure they'll be allowin' me off the *Amethyst*?"

"I am your doctor, you are my patient, and since you suffered a tremendous injury to your eye, it is my duty to see you have the very best attention. Therefore, while we're in London, we shall have you examined by the very best physicians."

Magpie absently fingered the green patch which covered the hole where his eye once was. "I've already seen the very best, sir."

Dr. Braden smiled in gratitude.

"And ... and do ya think we kin go to one o' them fancy restaurants in London, sir, and buy us some supper?"

"Naturally! We've worked hard enough to be rewarded with a few shillings of pay before we leave the *Amethyst*. We'll do just that."

Magpie was thrilled to the core. "I'll do the orderin', sir, and we kin sup on roast o' pork an' potatoes, a kind o' mint sauce, *soft* biscuits, cheese, and baked bread puddin'."

"Is that not the meal the Duke of Clarence presented you with when you were cleaning his chimney long ago?"

Magpie nodded proudly.

"Well then, perhaps good fortune will fall into our laps, and you and I will be invited to dine with the duke and Emily at Bushy House!"

Magpie's one eye shone as warmly as the lights of Halifax. "That would be just grand, sir."

Suddenly Osmund Brockley rose up before them, his oversized tongue dangling on his lower lip. "I've been searchin' for ya, Doctor," he said. "Could ya look in on a poor lubber what's complainin' of abdominal pains, sir? He's moanin' somethin' fierce." Excusing himself, Leander jumped up and headed off with Osmund, leaving Magpie on his own to enjoy the music.

Morgan was singing a sad song now — an old Welsh melody, he'd told his audience. Under normal circumstances the song's words would have caused a lump to form in Magpie's throat, but he was too excited about the prospect of seeing Emily again — even if they first had to sail for several weeks to cross the Atlantic. Wouldn't she be surprised to see them! He folded his arms across his thin chest and daydreamed about their reunion, imagining her reaction when she threw open the castle door to find Dr. Braden and him standing there. As Morgan was nearing the end of his song, Magpie contemplated the comfort of his hammock, and the continuation of his dreams with his head on his pillow. He grabbed his mending and was just about to quit his box when someone called out to him.

"You there! Little sailmaker!"

At first Magpie thought it was Osmund Brockley, that the man hadn't followed Dr. Braden to the hospital after all, but in looking all around him he could see no sign of Osmund anywhere. Moreover, there was no one standing nearby on the fo'c'sle, nor anyone hanging above his head on the foremast yards who might have owned the voice. The revellers, who had gathered for entertainment, were all drifting toward the ladder that would lead them down to their beds. He thought to call out to Morgan, but unable to spot his friend's woolly thrum cap in the crowd, he despaired that *he* had already disappeared below deck. Thinking he had imagined the voice, Magpie sprang up and was about to the follow the men when it called out a second time.

"You there ... the boy they call Magpie."

Wheeling about, Magpie caught sight of a shadowy figure roosting upon the bowsprit. Purple twilight glowed all around him, hiding the man's face, but Magpie could see long hair blowing in the breeze, and an unravelling of long skinny arms and legs that reminded him of a prodigious spider.

"Ya won't be havin' no supper in no fancy restaurant."

Magpie blinked in confusion. Whatever did the man mean? Perhaps he believed the Admiralty would never release an insignificant sailmaker from his duties on the *Amethyst* to allow him to go into London. Well then, Magpie would protest, and inform this strange man that Dr. Braden was an influential physician who would see to the arrangements. But the shadowy figure held Magpie transfixed, and rather than explaining it all to him — when really it was *not* his affair in the first place — Magpie simply asked him, "Why not?"

Slowly the dark spectre rose up to a standing position on the bowsprit, one skinny arm holding onto a rigging block for balance. Magpie still had no idea who the man was; he could not see his face beyond a nose as large as a pelican's beak, and he did not recognize the grim voice that finally answered his question.

"'Cause I sees ya clingin' to a dead man on the sea."

Magpie considered crying out, *"Identify yerself,"* but there was something chilling, an element of foreboding in the man's words which caused Magpie's own to die on his lips. Convinced a giant web was about to be tossed upon his head, trapping him to the bowsprit, Magpie spun about, tripping over his dilapidated box, temporarily losing his *Isabelle* hat, and scrambled to catch up to the retreating revellers and the safety of their numbers.

7

Tuesday, August 10

9:00 a.m.
Hartwood Hall

GLENNA McCUBBIN RAPPED upon Emily's door and entered her corner bedchamber. As suspected, the girl was still fast asleep in the commodious canopied bed, which she had declared — upon seeing it Sunday night — could easily accommodate a gundeck full of sailors. Glenna scurried around the vast room as fast as her arthritic ankles would take her, throwing open curtains onto the day. It was still raining and dismal outside, which disappointed her greatly, for she had hoped to impress Emily with the views overlooking Hartwood's south lawns and the city of London beyond. But there was such a thick mist rolling around the parkland, one could barely see the trees and gardens below, let alone the rising chimneypots and jumble of edifices in the distance.

"Glenna? Are you there?" The drowsy voice had come from the bed.

"I am, Pet! When ya didna come down fer yer breakfast, I worried ya'd perished in the night, tho' I'm shocked to find ya still abed," Glenna said, wrestling with a set of gold-tasselled curtains. "Why, I let ya sleep all o' yesterday! Did ya become a lazybones then on the sea without yer old Glenna about?"

Emily struggled to sit up, and smiled at the woman she had known her entire life. "Glenna McCubbin! Is it *really* you? I was so tired, so bewildered when I arrived here, I was quite certain I was dreaming."

Glenna and her plain, brown, rustling skirts came rushing toward the bed, where she plunked her rounded rump down upon the mattress near Emily and reached out to give her hand an affectionate squeeze. "Bet ya figured ya'd never see yer old nurse again! But here I am, havin' survived the wreck o' the *Amelia*, and me heart still beatin', tho' I do despair fer the rest o' me!" She stood up quickly, and wavered a bit on her feet. "But no time fer it now. I'm the housekeeper 'round here, and mighty lucky to have the job — bless yer Uncle Clarence — so I've come to tell ya to git outta bed."

Emily moaned. "May I sleep late just one more morning, Glenna? I haven't slept in a bed like this for months, and it's raining outside, and the owners of this fine house are not even at home."

"Nay! Up ya git! That's all bin changed. They surprised me by turnin' up here fifteen minutes ago, demandin' we heat up breakfast as they've had none, and very anxious to meet the Princess Emeline Louisa."

Emily bolted upright, horror seizing her sleepy face. "But I'm a mess, and I've nothing to wear except for a pair of trousers!"

Glenna jerked her lacy-capped head toward an immense wardrobe near the bedroom door, where Emily's blue-and-white-striped dress hung upon a wooden hanger. "Whilst ya was sleepin', I cleaned and pressed yer gown fer ya, and yer underclothes, and found fer ya some satin slippers and silk stockings that'll surely fit. Just splash a bit o' cold water on yer face — there's water in the pitcher — and pin up yer hair, and I'll come back fer ya in fifteen minutes."

"But Glenna…!"

"What now, Pet?" the older woman asked, huffing in Emily's doorway.

"I don't even know the name of the kind gentleman and lady who have graciously extended to me their hospitality."

"What? Yer Uncle Clarence didna think to tell ya?"

"He did not!"

"Fancy that! Why ya've come to the blessed home of a duke and duchess!" she winked. "Now be quick with ya."

Before Emily could question her further, Glenna had disappeared down the first floor corridor, leaving her alone in her gloomy room amidst antique furnishings to marvel at the scenes of ornate pagodas and curious boats and ships depicted upon her Chinoiserie wallpaper.

Listening to the rain pattering upon the windowpanes, she wondered if she was in for a surprise.

9:30 a.m.

GLENNA LEFT EMILY standing diffidently in the doorway of the breakfast room on the ground floor of Hartwood Hall. On a more congenial day, the tall sash windows that looked out over undulating trimmed lawns and flower gardens would have delighted her, but this morning everything had a grey cast to it: the outside views, the pastoral wallpaper, the steaming feast laid out upon the sideboard, her mood, even the four individuals who sat stiffly around the long, linen-clad table. Emily took a deep breath, certain she was far too weary to be thrown to the wolves so early in the morning. If only jovial Uncle Clarence could have stayed long enough to manage the formalities of this first meeting.

There was a brief respite before anyone spotted her, allowing Emily time to observe at least two of the four family members. At the head of the table, wearing a black waistcoat and jacket, sat the man Emily reasoned to be the owner of the house. Never in her eighteen years had she laid eyes upon such an exceedingly large gentleman. He looked as if he had not quit his armchair — which surely was custom-made for him — in many months, and if he should be inspired to move, he would require assistance from the entire household staff. He wore a white, powdered wig on his big head, and his prominent nose resembled a ripe pear, but though his eyes and shape reminded Emily of a frog, his pockmarked face was not an unkind one.

At the opposite end of the table sat his duchess, swathed in black like her husband, in a long-sleeved, high-collared dress that seemed inappropriate for the warmth of August. She was a tall, angular woman who carried her head high and wore her ink-black curls lacquered to her forehead and cheeks. Emily could tell the woman had once been handsome, but the deep lines that ran from her nostrils to the corners of her mouth gave her a hardened, uncompromising expression. A young man and girl sitting on the side of the table nearest Emily were presumably two of the duke and duchess's children; however, with their backs to her, she had only a glimpse of them. The son was dark-haired, perhaps in his mid-twenties, and the daughter a sallow-complexioned, fiery red-haired creature who reminded Emily — though she had never actually seen one before — of an other-worldly pixie or sprite.

The instant the family caught sight of her, the high-ceilinged room filled with the abrasive noise of chair legs making contact with the wooden floor as they all rose to greet her — the duke struggling a bit to raise himself up. Solemnly, they bowed their heads, and Emily bowed hers in return, but afterward they all stood there in silence, giving one another darting looks while the rain knocked upon the tall windows and the steaming food on the sideboard cooled. Finally, the young man, as if sensing his parents' uneasiness, came forward. He was older than she had first suspected, perhaps closer to thirty. His large eyes were coal-black, heavy-lidded, and close set, and he wore his dark brown hair forward in a cropped, dishevelled style. His nose was wide, though nowhere near the proportions of his father's, and as he approached her, Emily could not decide whether to proclaim him a good-looking man. She was, however, thankful for his friendly smile.

"Good morning, Your Royal Highness. I am sorry ... were you standing there long?"

"No, not at all."

"We *do* have a butler. He shouldn't have left you there unannounced."

At the risk of stirring up trouble for Glenna, Emily refrained from informing the man that the housekeeper had guided her to the breakfast room.

"Welcome to Hartwood Hall," he continued. "I trust you found everything to your satisfaction upon your arrival."

"I did, thank you." Emily looked first at the duke, and then at his wife. "I cannot thank you enough for opening your home to me."

They bowed a second time, and the silence resumed.

"Excuse me but I ... I wondered," began Emily, hating herself for feeling nervous, but hating the silence even more, "would it be an imposition if I were to ask you *not* to address me as Your Royal Highness. I should very much like it if you would call me Emeline, or ... or just Emily if you wish."

The duchess rolled a stupefied glance down the long table at her husband, while the son quickly replied, "Of course ... so long as you call me Somerton, and my little sister here," — gesturing toward the red-haired sprite who was busy giving Emily a hollow stare — "is Fleda."

Emily smiled at Fleda, but the girl's stare only grew more intense. The duke dropped into his chair, and when his bountiful flesh had been comfortably unfurled upon his seat he surprised Emily by crying out, "Splendid! I am Adolphus, and if it pleases you, you may call me Uncle Adolphus, although I know you already have an uncle by that name."

Emily did not miss the dramatic scowl that crossed the face of the duchess. "Thank you, sir, I do, although whenever I see him, which is rarely, I call him Uncle Cambridge."

"Splendid! Then there shall be no confusion. As your Uncle Clarence and I are old friends — practically family — this arrangement will be all most pleasant."

Somerton offered her his arm, and escorted her to the place of honour on his father's right. It was only when Emily was finally seated with the rainy morning at her back that the duchess made an effort to speak.

"This is most unbefitting ... Emeline," she said, slowly turning her head about, her chin elevated, to look everywhere but at her guest. "However, if it is your *fervent* wish ... I am Helena." Her voice was thin and crackly, as if she required a good clearing of the throat.

Adolphus clapped his huge hands to summon the servants. Five of them scurried into the room to prepare plates of herring, poached eggs, ham slices, grilled tomatoes, and mushrooms from the chafing dishes on the sideboard, and once they had served the food to the family they scattered themselves around the room and stood quietly, awaiting further orders. Normally breakfast was the meal during which one helped himself to the sideboard selections, but Emily suspected the duke did not take much exercise and preferred to be waited upon. With the delicious smells of her breakfast teasing her nose, and her cup filled with creamy coffee, Emily sat alone on her side of the table, taking small bites of her food as she expected at any moment to be interrogated. There was much she thought of asking the four who sat around her, periodically casting a furtive glance in her direction (except for Fleda who continued staring while she chewed on toast), but she knew enough to wait for their inquiries.

"I am sorry for the weather," said Helena, gazing with indifference out the tall windows, "but we do have a well-stocked library you may wish to peruse. Perhaps you'll find a lady's novel or two upon the dusty shelves with which to *amuse* yourself."

It was on Emily's lips to reply that she would actually prefer to search Hartwood's dusty shelves for medical textbooks, but as she had no interest in having to explain herself — for she had a feeling it would surely cause the duchess's eyelids to flutter in disbelief — she simply thanked the woman and reached for the warmth of her coffee cup.

"I shall ask Glenna to show you around the house after breakfast," said Adolphus, spooning salt upon his eggs. "I'm certain you'd like to spend time with your old nursemaid."

Emily gave the duke an appreciative smile, despite the fact that her nose was suddenly assaulted by a rank odour which obviously emanated from the man's grotesquely large body, and that, regrettably, overpowered the pleasant aromas of her meal. "Thank you, yes, I'd like that. Glenna and I have much catching up to do."

Helena lay her silverware down with a clatter upon her plate. "But, Dolly," she whined to her husband, "I've asked Glenna to prepare the menus for the ball this weekend. The woman is far too busy to be taking people on tours around the house."

Emily could see that Somerton was preparing to speak, and she wondered if he would volunteer to be her guide, but to her surprise, the glowering sprite beat him to it. "Glenna is too fat," said Fleda impassively, "and will surely get very red in the face if she climbs all the stairs. *I* will show Emily around."

Helena delicately picked up her knife and fork once again. "First of all, young lady, it is *Emeline*, not *Emily*. Secondly, do not forget that your lessons shall begin shortly."

"But I already know far more than Mademoiselle!" said Fleda, setting her pale-green eyes on Emily in a way that suggested she hoped to make an impression on her.

"Then you shall concentrate your efforts on the pianoforte," returned her mother dryly. "I do *not* need an intelligent daughter."

As if to ward off a family squabble, Somerton hastily introduced a fresh subject. "In your honour, Emeline, we're throwing a ball this weekend, and have invited all of our friends to attend."

Adolphus signalled to one of the servants to bring forward the basket of rolls, and then he added, "Thus our delay in returning to Hartwood, for we were riding about the countryside, dispensing our invitations, and so long in doing so we were caught in the rain and forced to spend the night at a friend's house."

Emily screamed silently before making her reply. "Oh, please, do not trouble yourselves on my behalf. I'll be more than content to keep to my room while I'm here."

Somerton allowed his dark gaze to linger on her face. "That'll never do, especially when all of England wishes to *dance* with you."

"And all will be most anxious to hear of your adventure on the Atlantic," said Adolphus, peering down his pear nose at her.

At the far end of the table, the crackling voice of the duchess rose up. "Besides, Emeline, we are all most anxious to take part in society again. We have been in mourning these past three weeks, and have not been able to accept any invitations from our friends. I cannot count the number of dinner parties we have missed as a result."

Of course, thought Emily, who until this moment had not realized that all four of her breakfast companions were draped in black — another indication her mind was as thick as the fog that lurked around Hartwood Hall. And yet, she was aghast to think her Uncle Clarence had left her here, amidst a newly grieving family.

"One of my brothers," said Fleda quietly.

"Oh!" gasped Emily, glancing in turn at each family member — none of whom appeared to be disquieted — before extending her sympathies. "I am terribly sorry for your loss."

Helena's ice-blue eyes met hers, and in a tone bereft of emotion she said, "I have several sons, Emeline, and he was *not* one of my favourites. Now then ... if you have a special dish or dessert you'd like us to serve at the ball, please say so, and we'll include it on the menu."

Noon
Hartwood Hall

At noon Glenna came looking for Emily and Fleda, and upon discovering the two on the second-floor landing, peering through the big oval window that afforded a panoramic, if somewhat grey-shrouded, view of London, she relayed the duchess's strict instructions that Lady Fleda was to return at once to the schoolroom as Mademoiselle was not to be kept waiting a moment longer to begin morning lessons.

"Her Grace ain't happy," said Glenna, breathing heavily from climbing two long flights of stairs. "'Tis best ya hurry along."

Fleda pulled a face at the housekeeper, but did not budge an inch. "I don't want to. There isn't a *thing* Mademoiselle can teach me! She's as dumb as a tree stump."

"I thought your mother was hoping you'd practise the pianoforte today," said Emily, hearing some of her rebellious self in the girl.

"What purpose does the pianoforte serve?" Fleda asked gravely.

Emily gave her a puckish smile. "Why you'll be able to entertain us with your magnificent melodies at the ball."

Fleda's green eyes narrowed as she puckered her thin, bloodless lips.

"Ya'll git yerself a husband that way, by impressin' him. All men o' quality want a refined lass fer their wife."

"I'm eleven years old, Glenna," protested Fleda. "I don't want a stupid husband."

"Ya say that now," said Glenna, wobbling toward the staircase down, "but when ya get to be Emily's age, ya'll be wantin' one."

Fleda waited until Glenna's bouncing lace cap had vanished from sight, and then she upturned her pale, unsmiling face. "Mother told me you already have a husband, and that he's to be hanged for crimes against England."

Emily held Fleda's gaze a moment, but made no reply beyond a slight incline of her eyebrows. Lifting her skirts, she headed toward the stairs, hoping Fleda would follow her down and make no further references to the subject. And as soon as the unhappy Mademoiselle had her reluctant student in her clutches, Emily devised plans to return to her room to rest and fortify her resources before the next interview with the duke and his family. But to her dismay, she discovered Somerton waiting for her in the small antechamber next to the schoolroom.

"Unless you've seen enough of Hartwood for one day," he said, pushing away from the wall against which he had been leaning his head, "I've come to continue your tour."

Removing from her mouth the hand that had been concealing a yawn, Emily banished her disappointment and tried to inject enthusiasm into her voice. "How very kind of you! Let's see … we've already toured the orangery, and all of the principal rooms, and peeked into all of the bed-chambers, dressing rooms, servants quarters … we've even done the attics; however, I believe there's a portrait gallery somewhere on the premises that your sister neglected to show me." Emily left off at telling him of Fleda's admission that she abhorred the paintings of her ancestors, or, as she had been wont to describe them, "those creepy old men and women in their ridiculous clothes, whose dead eyes follow your every move."

Somerton looked hopeful. "Would you like to meet my family?"

"Are all of you hanging in stately frames, glowering down on us small beings who look in wonder upon your sumptuous, painted images?"

"We are!" he said, lifting one dark eyebrow. "As a matter of fact, we're all there, every one of us, back to the very first Duke of Belmont. And you're in luck — no more stairs to climb — for the gallery is right here … in the music room."

Somerton invited her to follow him through a colonnaded archway and into a rectangular room on the north front side of Hartwood Hall, which must surely have equalled the size of the *Isabelle*. An elegant, rounded window flanked by curtains of green-and-crimson-striped damask dominated the far wall and overlooked the courtyard beyond the main entrance, where Emily had been dropped off on Sunday evening. Arranged in an orderly semicircle around the window was a collection of musical instruments, including a chamber organ, a square harpsichord, a cello, two violins, a harp, and the dreaded pianoforte. The walls were painted a pond green to complement the gilt frames of the portraiture, and nestled around the room's main feature — an elaborate chimneypiece and overmantel mirror — were sofas and chairs in coverings that matched the window hangings.

"On the night of the ball, *this* will be the principal dancing room," explained Somerton, looking around him with satisfaction. "Do *you* play an instrument?"

"I love music, but I do not play."

He raised his eyebrows. "How were you ever able to avoid instruction while growing up?"

"My teachers gave up," Emily replied, admiring the cornice of sculptured harps. "I was far more interested in climbing fences and jumping off barn roofs into stacks of hay."

Somerton's glance wavered, as if he were not certain of her sincerity. "Have you an interest in learning now?"

"And be held a prisoner of Mademoiselle?"

He laughed. "Are you perhaps fond of balls?"

An old memory of dancing a cotillion with partners whose hands were clammy, and whose clumsy feet frequently tripped up hers, drifted through Emily's recollection. "I am, so long as the company in attendance is well versed in the intricate steps of the dance selections," she replied playfully, "and therefore able to forgive both my forgetfulness and shaky sea legs."

Emily noticed a slight narrowing of Somerton's eyes, and as she made for the wall opposite the chimneypiece to study the portraits of the present inhabitants of Hartwood, she felt their dark gaze examining *her* from the loose knot of pale-gold hair on her head to the tips of her white satin slippers. When his examination was complete he followed her, and held up his hand to acknowledge the first of the formidable portraits. "This is my brother, Wetherell, the Marquess of Monroe. He's the eldest."

"I thought you were the eldest," said Emily, surprised to see such a remarkable resemblance between Wetherell and his thick-featured father, right down to the outdated, powdered wig upon his head.

"No, I'm the second eldest. It's Wetherell who will one day inherit Hartwood, though he doesn't care much for the management of its affairs. Furthermore, he doesn't get on with my father, and prefers his residence in London. I doubt you'll even see him during your stay with us."

"Do you assist your father in overseeing the estate?"

"I do. I'm the only one of my brothers living here at present."

Somerton wandered down the line of portraits, telling her something about each of his brothers: their names and professions, their foibles and interests, as well as those of their wives and mistresses. Emily did her best to listen, but she was so tired she found it impossible to assimilate all of the information and worried — should Somerton decide to test her — that she would fail miserably in recalling which one was George and which one was Henry, and which ones had chosen careers in law, or politics, or the army. By the time they reached the last of the portraits, Emily felt an overwhelming desire to lie down.

"This is the youngest ... second youngest if you consider my sister, Fleda."

Emily assessed the countenance of this final brother. His complexion was not a smooth one; though the artist might have softened it somewhat with his professional brush strokes, the cheeks were pale and hollow, and his thin, dark hair was combed flat upon his head. Outfitted in the uniform of a Royal Navy lieutenant, his stance seemed self-conscious, and his coal-black stare communicated a profound unhappiness. A sick feeling began to stir in Emily's stomach as words spoken long ago echoed in her ears.

Perhaps you have made the acquaintance of my family ... my father being the Duke of Belmont.

I wanted a career in law, you know.

Why, then, did you choose the navy?

For the simple reason that the choosing *was done for me.*

Beyond the walls of the music room the rain fell harder and the wind intensified, wailing as it searched for a way inside the house. Shivering, Emily felt the rise and fall of a ship on a stormy sea, thought she heard the sound of sails snapping, and remembered the chaotic atmosphere in the bottom of the sinking *Serendipity*, a pistol emerging from a bloodstained uniform jacket, and the head that was subsequently pulverized by a bullet. Somerton was standing close to her — too close — curiously observing her face as she mentally counted the portraits on the wall. The final tally came as no surprise.

I am my father's eighth son.

Emily could think of nothing but ending the tour. Facing Somerton, she endeavoured to smile. "I thank you for generously taking the time to show me this lovely room, and telling me something of your family."

His eyes probed hers. "But I've not yet told you anything of my youngest brother."

"I — I can see he chose a profession in the navy," said Emily, thinking she might be ill; perhaps if she were able to splash some cold water on her face. Hadn't Glenna set out a water pitcher on the commode in her room first thing this morning?

Somerton nodded, his eyes still locked on hers. "He did."

"And as I know something of the Royal Navy, I can see he was an officer."

"Yes ... a first lieutenant," he said expectantly, perhaps waiting for her to add something more. When she did not, he pressed on. "And the last we heard of him, he was serving under Captain James Moreland of HMS *Isabelle*."

Fighting to maintain an attitude of indifference, Emily quietly replied, "I'm sorry to hear of it."

In the silence that ensued, a glint of suspicion crept into Somerton's eyes. Emily lifted her chin to gaze upon the youngest brother's white hands, solemnly folded upon the hilt of a sword, and then slowly she backed away from her host. "Will you please excuse me? I'm feeling rather unwell, and should like to lie down for a while."

Somerton's stare softened. "Yes … yes, of course … by all means. I'm sure your journey has left you weary." He straightened up, then bowed toward her. Emily bowed too, and wheeled about, hurrying as decently as was possible to arrive in the antechamber, and therefore pass from Somerton's sight. She paused for a moment, leaning against one of the chamber's columns, to breathe deeply the oppressive air of the house, and collect her wits.

She could not have borne to hear him utter the name of his dead brother, despite the fact that she knew it … all too well.

8

Tuesday, August 10

HAVING LOCATED HIS dilapidated box from the previous evening, Magpie had carried it — along with his neglected mending — to the poop deck where he relaxed in the sunshine near the stern, watching the sailors replace the new spanker sail that he had just finished sewing. His work filled him with pride, and he loved watching his fresh lengths of canvas being secured to their ropes and pulleys, always hopeful the men doing the work might shout out praise for his fine craftsmanship. But Magpie had another excuse for wanting to leave his sail room on the dank orlop. Last night he hadn't slept well, for he had fully expected that dark spectre to come knocking on his door, hover near his hammock, and breathe more haunting pronouncements into his ear. Surely whoever it was would not appear during daylight hours, when so many moved about the decks. Surely he was a night creature that only surfaced when the sun had set.

Forgetting his terrors for a time, Magpie peered into the distance beyond the *Amethyst's* frothy wake. No longer could he discern the hills of Halifax on the western horizon; the whole coast of Nova Scotia was fast receding in size, looking more like a thin slice of phantom shore than the vast expanse of terrain he knew it to be. Already missing the security of land, he hoped to soon glimpse Sable Island, for it wouldn't be long now until they were engulfed in miles of empty waves. Magpie found some comfort in seeing the little mail packet, the *Lady Jane,* sailing safely in their shadow — like a child in its mother's arms — even though she had already proven herself a spirited child, and had been ordered to slow down, her diminutive size capable of travelling much faster than the ponderous *Amethyst* of seventy-four guns, three masts, and five hundred men. It would be nice to have company on their Atlantic voyage.

Magpie heaved a sigh as he studied the large holes in his stockings. If Dr. Braden and he were going to be invited to dine with Emily and the Duke of Clarence at Bushy House, he would have to attempt to salvage his threadbare bits of wool with some momentous mending. He reached into his pocket for the folded scrap of canvas that safeguarded Emily's miniature, and polished her golden frame until she gleamed in the afternoon sun. Then, holding her high, he pretended that her brown, smiling eyes could actually behold him.

"I'm comin' to see ya, Em, and I'm bringin' Dr. Braden with me. We'll be a while 'cause we gots a big ocean to cross, and I'm worryin' ya won't be allowed to see me on account o' me poor clothes, but I'm still comin' be what it may."

A shadow suddenly fell across Magpie, unnerving him at once, for in his mind it must be the spectre come to pounce on him and drag him to his cobwebby lair, but when he raised his head and blinked into the sunshine, he was relieved to see a much rounder figure than the lanky one that had chilled him to the bone last night. It was Meg Kettle who stood before him, her heavy arms folded upon her heavy bosom, her face percolating with ridicule.

"Well, if it ain't Maggot Pie, the one-eyed monster!" she said, bursting into a gusty laugh. "'Ave ya gone mad then? Sittin' here, speakin' to a painted picture?"

Magpie hastily returned Emily to his pocket. "Ain't none o' yer business who I'm speakin' to."

"Imagine … makin' love to a picture!" she hissed in a low voice only Magpie could hear.

"Ah, push off."

"Why, I ain't never seen such a sight! Yer as daft as the Doctor."

Magpie's face grew hot with humiliation.

"D'ya think yer goin' to be allowed into the castle o' King George to see 'er?" she asked, her voice rife with sarcasm.

"I might be," was his diffident reply.

"Ya forget yerself, little Maggot. Ya ain't no more valuable than a lump o' mud in the Thames River."

A scorching anger boiled in Magpie's chest. How would she like it if he gave her shins a good trouncing? "Ya ... ya better watch yerself, Meg Kettle," he stammered.

"And why should I be watchin' meself?"

"'If ya can't figure it out, then *yer* the daft one!"

Meg's hands found her broad hips. "Are ya plannin' ... in the dead o' night ... to give me a Jonah's lift into the sea?" She laughed again. "Why yer so scrawny ya couldn't throw *yourself* overboard."

If he lingered a moment longer in her odious presence, Magpie knew he would utter things he would later come to regret. He hopped up off his box. "Ya better watch yerself, 'cause —"

Meg's eyes disappeared into loose folds of skin, and her neck jerked backward, setting her jowls in motion like that of a farmyard turkey. "'Cause why?"

Bunching his threadbare stockings up in his fist, Magpie backed away from the laundress. "I knows all what ya done. 'Cause I seen ya with Mr. Octavius Lindsay on the *Isabelle* ... doin' yer plottin' together. Yer a traitor!"

The second his brave words had tripped from his tongue, he bolted from the laundress and her tottering shadow, across the poop and down the ladder to the safety of the quarterdeck. Had he loitered to witness the effect of his intimidation, he would have been richly rewarded for Meg Kettle was utterly dumbstruck.

8:30 p.m.

(First Watch, One Bell)

AFTER AN EXHAUSTIVE SEARCH, Fly found Leander leaning over the taffrail on the ship's stern, his slim fingers clasped around a mug of coffee, gazing dreamily out over the water toward the lights of the *Lady Jane*.

"I've spent the better part of a Watch combing the ship for you. I checked the middy's berth and the sail room on the orlop, thinking you might be punishing the young ones with reading lessons, and then I scoured the galley, wardroom, and hospital, of course, on the upper deck. And here I find you draped over the taffrail like a penniless poet contemplating a plunge into the sea to end his sufferings."

Leander filled his lungs with the fresh evening air. "My reason for being drawn to this corner of the ship is not as drastic as all that. I'm listening to the music coming from our sailing mate. Someone on the *Lady Jane* is playing a violin, and playing it quite well."

Fly slumped down upon the stern bench. "Come away from your romantic musings and cheer me up!"

"And why is it you need cheering up, old man?"

"Old man?" frowned Fly. "You have the audacity to filch my name for *you*?"

"Oh, no! You often refer to me as old *fellow*."

"Oh, I see! Well you are an old fellow … younger than me in age perhaps, but far more mature in your deportment." Fly exhaled in mock disgust. "I still say you should have taken Prickett up on his suggestion of shore leave in Halifax. I should like to have observed your behaviour in a dancing hall."

Leander raised his auburn eyebrows. "I would have been completely beyond myself."

"Aye! And had a lusty wench made amorous overtures toward you, I'm quite certain you would have stuttered, and grown flustered, and known not how to proceed."

Leander looked askance at Fly. "It's astounding I call you friend when you are so frequently like a millstone, grinding the poor grains of me to dust."

"Cheer up, old fellow … I need *you* to lift my spirits this evening. Shall we drink something stronger than coffee, or shall you be called upon shortly to perform intricate surgeries and therefore have need of your faculties?" Not bothering to await Leander's reply, Fly searched the deck for someone he could order about. "Ah, Biscuit, I believe you're hiding there in the gathering gloom."

Biscuit's head with its thick shock of orange hair appeared between the newels of the poop deck's railing. "I'm smokin' a cigar with me lads, sir. Not often I git the chance to do so."

"If that is indeed true, mind you don't burn down the ship," growled Fly.

"No worry in that, sir. What kin I git fer ya?"

"Bring Doctor Braden and me some of Captain Prickett's best red wine."

"Right away, sir, the minute I've had me last puff."

When Fly had completed his transaction with Biscuit, and had relaxed his weary body against the stern bench, Leander sat down beside him. "I cannot understand why you require a bit of cheering up, when, in my estimation, *you* have nothing to grumble about. It's been some weeks since you encountered the enemy and suffered the loss of men. The incident with that skittish American privateer a few days back was nothing more than a bit of morning agitation, like finding a snake in one's bed upon waking. And as recently as two days ago, you were the toast of the Halifax nobility."

Fly pulled off his hat to give his head a good scratch. "It's Prickett; he's become most aggravating."

"How so ... beyond his habit of spitting in one's face at the supper table?"

"The instant we raise Portsmouth, the man is happily relinquishing command of the *Amethyst*, and yet he forgets we're weeks away from a safe harbour."

"Are you saying the man has forgotten we're still fighting a war?" asked Leander.

"Precisely!"

"Is there too much banqueting and frivolity on this ship for your tastes?"

"Aye! I believe so! Prickett and I cannot agree on anything, which is fine so long as our voyage is an uneventful one and we face no American — or French — warships in the next while."

"But I thought, when Prickett rescued you after the sinking of the *Isabelle*, he happily sought your advice on all matters; that he, in fact, had *you* commanding the ship."

"Only when it came to the drubbing of the enemy. He was totally unprepared to face Trevelyan, and therefore allowed me to make the decisions pursuant to the chase. But now, when there's no immediate threat, I find myself powerless, standing helplessly by while Prickett thinks of nothing but the reward that will await him when he presents the *Lady Jane* unmolested to the Admiralty, and the honours which will surely — though undeservedly — be heaped upon him for his role in nabbing Trevelyan."

"Then tell me, if the *Amethyst* were yours to command, what would you do differently?"

"For starters, I'd focus less on my stomach and the prospect of riches, and more on discipline! The men … they've grown soft. At the very least, gun cleaning and drills *must* form part of their work day."

"I believe you once had the Amethysts practising their gun skills."

"Aye, but the minute the *Serendipity* was sunk, and Trevelyan taken prisoner, Prickett no longer desired to *waste* his stores of ammunition." Fly suddenly jumped up to yell at the unseen smokers below the poop deck. "Puff your last, Biscuit, and bring us our wine! I've waited long enough."

There was a scurry and shuffle of feet as the reluctant Biscuit did his bidding. Fly resumed his seat, sighing heavily as he did so. "You see, even our Scottish cook is slow to carry out orders!"

The two friends peered into the diminishing light on the seas around them and were lulled into a reverie. A few stars dotted the night sky, and off the *Amethyst*'s larboard side, just behind them, they could see the glow of the *Lady Jane*'s lanterns and hear the haunting strains of her unknown violinist.

When Fly spoke again, his voice was sombre. "This night is calm, yet I feel unease."

Leander set his coffee mug down at his feet. "Then speak to Prickett in the morning when he's at breakfast, and at his best. Tell him of your concerns."

Fly released a lighthearted snuffle, and then faced his friend in earnest. "I should like for you to see your Emily again, old fellow. It's my duty to get you safely home."

"And you shall," smiled Leander. "Now, banish your unease, and let us … let us get drunk."

Fly blinked in disbelief. "This cannot be! Is it the grave, pensive Dr. Braden I hear speaking?"

"Quite so!" Leander stood up and reached down to pull Fly to his feet. "And since Biscuit is far too slow in bringing us our wine, let us go fetch it for ourselves."

9

Thursday, August 12

11:00 a.m.
Outskirts of Winchester

GUS WALBY LIMPED DOWN the laneway as fast as his crutch would enable him, determined to be out of sight before his Aunt Sophia even realized he was gone. He had fled the cottage just minutes before she had raised that shrill, awful voice of hers to boom her midday orders — so reminiscent of the *Isabelle*'s firing cannons — to fetch the milk and prepare the sandwiches for the children and the two labourers who tended her sheep in the fields. Although he knew that upon his return she would unleash a nasty reprimand and send him upstairs to his lumpy cot under the eaves without any dinner, Gus was far too excited to hang about and do her bidding.

The doctor had promised to visit again on Thursday, *"around the hour of eleven"* he had said, as he planned to travel by horseback this time. He had further promised to stop by the posting inn in Winchester for any letters addressed to *Mr. Augustus Walby*. It had been four days now. Surely today there would be a note from Emily.

Having reached a bend in the laneway, where the road widened and fell away into a valley and the trees were as thick and shady as the beech and elm around Aunt Sophia's home — and he was most assuredly out of earshot should *she* begin hollering — Gus rested upon a low stone wall, and there he ate his apple (stolen from his aunt's heavily guarded kitchen basket) and affirmed that his pocket still held his three pence. He'd never sent a letter to anyone before, but he did know he had to have money to pay the postmaster in the event one should be sent to him. It was cheaper — and quicker — to send a letter from one address to another in London, but then Winchester was quite a few miles outside of the city. He hoped he had enough.

The better part of a half-hour had passed away when Gus felt a few large droplets on his head and sensed the world darkening. Peering up through the canopy of tree branches, he could see sombre clouds gathering over the countryside. Then at long last he heard a horse cantering up the road, and although the man sitting astride a chestnut mare was concealed in a traveller's cape and broad-brimmed hat, Gus knew it was the doctor. Tucking his crutch under his arm, Gus raised himself up off the wall and hurried to meet him, his body quivering with anticipation, his face all smiles.

"Mr. Walby!" the doctor called out upon spying him. "I see you are taking my advice and getting some fresh air."

Gus nodded. "I am, sir!"

"And have you been exercising your leg?"

"I have been … every day!" Gus wanted so badly to tell the doctor his aunt possessed a knack for inventing chores, and refused him rest of any kind until the sun had left the sky, but he could only think of the possibility of a letter from Emily.

"That's important, Mr. Walby, if we're going to see you back with your seafaring friends as soon as possible." He leaned back in his saddle to look up at the patch of leaden sky between the agitated trees. "But perhaps it might have been wiser if you'd stayed in the house today."

"I wanted to come and meet you, sir."

The doctor nodded, but continued his study of the sky and absently said, "Those clouds have followed me all the way from Steventon."

The three pence — now enclosed in Gus's fist — were burning the palm of his hand. "Did you have a good trip, sir?"

"I did indeed, having managed to keep my horse, my leather bag, and myself dry." Sliding down from his saddle, the doctor joined Gus on the laneway, keeping his sights upon their destination up the road. "But I suggest we hurry back to your aunt's or we shall soon be drenched."

Gus couldn't wait a second longer; he gazed up hopefully at the long-legged gentleman who walked beside him, whose face was partially obscured by his wide brim. "And … and, sir, were you able to stop in the village?"

The doctor caught his breath in hesitation, and when he finally looked down at Gus there was a sympathetic cast in his old eyes. Gus's stomach dropped as if he had ingested a stone.

"I did, Mr. Walby, but —" he shook his head ever so slightly, just as the rain came. Quickly he peeled off his broad-brimmed hat and placed it on Gus's head. "Now we must hurry."

Inwardly Gus heaved a huge sigh, thankful that the pelting rain and hat concealed his great disappointment. He had *such* things to tell Emily, but he had no idea where to address a letter to her. An eternity would pass before the doctor's next visit, and the days in between would be endlessly long, full of chores and exhausting games with the children. And what if there was still no word from her the next time? Dreadful thoughts, as dark as the ominous clouds overhead, suddenly raced through his mind. Had some misfortune befallen Emily on the road to London? Had King George locked her up forever within the forbidding walls of Windsor Castle?

Or … or had she simply forgotten her favourite midshipman — the now crippled and worthless Augustus Walby?

Noon
Hartwood Hall

EMILY OPENED HER EYES and was startled to find Glenna's round, glistening face in hers, examining her as if she were a fresh cadaver.

"Are ya finally awake, Pet? Are ya feelin' better?" Glenna sank down on the bed beside her and, picking up one of her hands, began caressing Emily's old scars. "Ya've been sleepin' fer two days now, and His Grace was worryin' about yer health, and wonderin' if he should be cancellin' the ball on Saturday eve."

Emily wriggled her way up onto her pillows, discouraged to find that unpleasant jittery feeling still present in her stomach. "I do feel better, Glenna," she lied, "but I *do* wish I could ask the family to cancel. I've no desire for dancing and society."

"Lud! I've never met the lass who didna live fer a ball."

"You've met one now."

Glenna waved off her indifference, wriggled her bottom about on the mattress as if finding for herself a comfortable position, and then gave Emily a devilish grin. "I bin itchin' to ask ya! What did ya think o' Mr. Lindsay when ya met him the other day?"

Hearing the name *Lindsay* made Emily wince. That haunting portrait in the music room — the one of the youngest son with the desperate eyes, the last thing she'd seen of Hartwood House before retiring to her bed, pleading illness — cast a long shadow in her consciousness. She had told no one of her shock, not even Glenna.

"Do you mean Lord *Somerton* Lindsay?" asked Emily.

The older woman made a sucking sound of impatience with her tongue. "Well who else would I be meanin'?"

"Why I … I thought nothing of him."

"Ya didna think him a handsome man?"

"No! Not at all."

Glenna stared at her as if she'd uttered blasphemy. "I think yer lyin' to yer old Glenna. Did ya not notice his well-shaped head, and his well-formed hands, and … and the sturdy muscles in his calves?"

"He was wearing boots when I met him," Emily responded flatly.

"Well, when ya see him at the ball, wearin' his breeches and silk stockings, take a good long gawp at the man's legs."

"Perhaps it's only his calf-padding that has you so giddy."

"Calf-paddin'? Not our Somerton; he's no need fer such silly accessories."

"I do confess … I did notice … that Lord Somerton's eyes were —" Emily drew out her words to bait her old nurse, "that his eyes were *not* blue."

Glenna pulled a wry face. "Now what kind o' remark is that, Pet?"

"They're too dark, too probing," said Emily, adding under her breath, "A family trait, I believe?"

"Well, just ya wait 'til ya see the lasses fawnin' over him on Saturday."

Emily adjusted herself against her pillows. "Why him? I'd have thought they would save their *fawning* for the eldest son, the marquess. What's his first name again?"

"Wetherell?" Glenna threw back her head to chortle. "Nay, it's Somerton they all want. One day ya'll understand why."

"Well *the lasses* can fawn away. It'll provide me with entertainment when I am reclining on the sofa, eating lemon ice."

Glenna gave Emily's hand a playful slap. "What's happened to ya, Pet, since the night when the *Amelia* was burned, and we was parted? Where's yer pluck gotten to?"

"Everyone knows I'm a married woman."

"Pshaw! And everyone *knows* yer marriage is a sham, and those what don't soon will."

Emily held her eyes at half-mast, and spoke with exaggeration. "I must behave as such until my family is able to secure an annulment for me."

"The young men won't be waitin' 'round fer that to happen. They'll be lined up wantin' to dance with ya, married or no. Ya shouldna be waitin' 'round fer it neither! Why, Pet, ya can have any man ya desire."

Emily rolled her head away from Glenna, her eyes falling on the black, calf-leathered, gilt-banded volumes of *Pride and Prejudice*, lovingly arranged on her little bedside table. Then she glanced up to watch the sun shadows attempt to find an opening in her thick gold curtains, stirring up memories of her old bit of canvas on the *Isabelle*, and the man who waited beyond. "They'll have to find other partners, for I shall tell them all that my ankle is swollen."

"Nonsense!" snapped Glenna.

Emily strangled her surging emotions before turning again to her old nurse. "I don't want to stay here," she whispered.

Glenna swivelled her neck to gape at her. "I thought ya'd be happy to be with yer old Glenna. And once ya get to know the Duke and Lord Somerton —"

Emily grasped Glenna's arm. "Is there some way I can leave? I must write to Uncle Clarence and ask him to come get me. Fetch me some paper and a quill!"

"I will not. Ya won't be leavin' me sight agin."

"I cannot stay here!"

"Why ever not?"

"It's … it's not home. These people are strangers."

"Yer right lucky to be invited to Hartwood Hall."

"Show me the road, and I'll walk to London."

Glenna chortled. "Ya'd be nothin' but pap for the highwaymen what roam these parts. I wouldna advise it." She stiffened. "And where is it ya plan to go?"

Emily looked fiercely determined. "To sea ... back to the sea."

All the warmth drained from Glenna's face. She pursed her lips and set her double chin. Emily was so familiar with that disapproving countenance. "So long as there be breath in me bosom, ya'll *not* be returnin' to sea."

"You came with me once, Glenna."

"Ah, and ya forced me to come then — you and yer cousin, Frederick Seaton, sayin' it would be a vacation, nothin' more — and I ended up nearly drowned in the Atlantic, and seein' such terrors, and that ogre, Trevelyan, pushin' ya about so roughly. It all ripped me heart in two. Nay! There's to be no more talk o' leavin' here and walkin' to London, and nothin' more about the sea." Glenna stood up abruptly, the sudden movement making her unsteady on her feet. "Now, git yerself dressed. Her Grace desires to drink tea with ya in the music room."

"Oh, Lord, please no!" begged Emily, slumping back upon her feather pillows.

"Ya canna lie here in bed forever. Besides, Her Grace has *things* to discuss with ya." Glenna's tone was now teeming with hoarfrost. Swinging about on her arthritic heels, she sloped forward, and, with a determined stomp across the carpet, made for the bedroom door, surprising Emily — who figured the old woman would now punish her, as she had in the past, with a prolonged period of silence — when she came to a halt and twirled around to throw her a final frown. "Before I go, tell me somethin'. Earlier when ya was sleepin', I heard ya call out."

Emily raised her head off her pillows. "What did I say?"

"Were ya havin' a nightmare?"

"I ... I don't remember having one."

"Well, ya kept callin' out to someone."

"Who?"

"Someone named *Leander*," she said, narrowing her eyes, "and I don't suppose it was the mythical Leander ya were addressin' — the one what swum the Hellespont to be with his Hero."

1:00 p.m.
Hartwood Hall

The music room was bright with afternoon sunlight, making a more favourable impression upon Emily, who had first viewed it while it had been cloaked in a dank gloom. Helena Lindsay, however, had chosen to drink her tea far from the brilliance that filtered through the far wall's elegant window, preferring to be near the entrance to the room, in the cooler shadows beneath the portrait of her eighth son. Perhaps she hoped to make a fast exit, or be in a position to call for help if Emily became too *unmanageable*. She turned her thin face in Emily's direction, but did not rise from her chair; instead, she extended one slim, amber-bejewelled hand, inviting her to sit opposite her at the small, round mahogany table.

"Tea?"

"Yes, thank you," said Emily, lowering herself into the green-and-crimson-striped damask of the proffered chair, not daring to glance at the haunting portrait behind the duchess. She kept her eyes on the woman's slender fingers as she decorously lifted the silver pot and poured steaming tea into an exquisite china cup before handing it off to Emily.

"I trust you are feeling better, Emeline," Helena said in that peculiar voice of hers.

"I am, thank you," said Emily. "I didn't realize how exhausted I was, but then I've not slept in a real bed for months. Ship hammocks do not provide the same level of comfort."

"No, I should think not," said Helena with disinterest. She kept her lips attached to her cup for a significant moment before speaking again. "And shall we have the pleasure of your presence at the ball on Saturday, or shall you be keeping to your room?"

Feeling as if she were agreeing to a public beheading, Emily was slow to reply. "I would be honoured to join your family and friends."

"Good. My husband did mention a postponement of our soiree, but I wouldn't hear of it. I've ordered a gown of cream silk and matching turban, and look much forward to shedding these ghastly mourning weeds. If I have my way, I'll never again wear a gown of crepe or bombazine." The harsh lines on either side of Helena's mouth curved into a smug smile as she gazed out the large window.

Following the woman's eyes to the far end of the room, Emily caught a glimpse of red-haired Fleda running about in the back courtyard with a handsome, excitable dog. But there was no evidence of enjoyment on Helena's face as she watched her daughter at play, and soon she turned again to Emily.

"Glenna tells me you have no decent *habiliments*, and you most certainly cannot wear *that* to the ball," she simpered, her eyes flickering over Emily's blue-and-white-striped dress.

"I would think you'd prefer to see me dressed thus than attired for the evening in a pair of seaman's trousers and scarf," said Emily, her blood beginning to simmer.

Helena arched her dark eyebrows. "Its colours are not becoming; you look very yellow in it. I daresay the Prince Regent would be horrified to see you dressed in such an inferior rag; I know your Uncle Clarence was."

Emily took a deep breath. "As my uncle seemed in such a hurry to bring me here, he didn't consider stopping by Windsor to collect any of my belongings. As for the clothes I brought with me for the journey across the Atlantic … they were all lost on the *Amelia*. I am certain you can understand … it's not easy to acquire women's clothing while at sea."

"These ships you were on … could you not have insisted one of them stop in New York or Boston so that you could disembark and purchase clothing worthy of your social standing?"

"For the most part, I was travelling on Royal Navy ships."

Helena gave her a blank look. "Then what was the problem?"

Emily wrestled down her mounting impatience. "We avoided American ports, as our country is at war with the United States."

"Yes, but it's not a *real* war," Helena said, studying the pattern on her teacup. "Is it?"

The heart-stopping boom of cannons, musket fire, and men's piteous cries resounded in Emily's ears. The smells and horrors of Leander's hospital rose before her like a knife-wielding murderer. The shock of Octavius Lindsay lifting the gun to his head and …

"I'm afraid it is very real."

"How fascinating," she said with the enthusiasm of a dozing dog. "And all this time at sea, did you never once get off whichever ship you happened to be on?"

"While on Trevelyan's ship, we did make one stop ... in Charleston —"

"Charleston! And you couldn't find any shops in Charleston? And here I understood it to be quite the fashionable city."

"I was Trevelyan's prisoner. I was not allowed out of his sight, and therefore had no opportunity to go *shopping*."

"I see," said Helena through her teeth.

"My Uncle Clarence informed me of a generous allowance the Prince Regent has made available to me. Perhaps it was given to you for safekeeping?"

Helena responded with a graceful nod, but said nothing.

"If I could trouble you for ... a portion of it ... and for a carriage ride into London, perhaps I could buy a few necessary *habiliments* before the ball."

Helena regarded her with cold indifference. "As you are still a child, Emeline, and therefore likely to spend it on frivolous amusements, I've been instructed by your family to manage your allowance."

A silence dropped between them like the ghastly thud of a guillotine. The force of those words felt like a slap to the face, leaving Emily stifling the urge to return the blow. Fortunately, before she dumped the contents of the teapot upon Helena's lacquered curls, relief arrived in the form of a distraction as the world outside the music room enlivened with the noisy clatter of wheels on gravel. Both women eagerly sought the window, and watched as three large wagons entered the courtyard and came to a stop before Hartwood's north doors, there to be greeted by Fleda, her prancing dog, and a number of the household staff.

Helena set down her teacup in a manner that intimated the interview was at an end. "Ah, this will be the French chef I hired for the ball, and the first of the supplies. Now I must oversee to their unloading, and make certain they've brought us wax candles and the right cuts of meat for our guests." She rose from her chair; Emily following suit.

"Do not despair about your simple dress and lack of accessories at this time, Emeline. My maid has been busy these past days, making a most sumptuous gown for you." Helena studied Emily's head as if she were examining a poorly executed painting. "And on Saturday, once she's set my hair, she'll be exceedingly pleased to dress *yours*."

They exchanged bows, and Emily, her temples throbbing with pain, watched her drift from the music room and into the antechamber. Lost in a helpless stare long after Helena's footsteps had echoed away, Emily tightened her fists. Though her mind was a vexatious jumble, a slight movement near one of the chamber's columns caught her attention. At first she thought a member of the household staff had come to alert the duchess of the deliveries; however, the figure that emerged did so with a degree of surreptitiousness, leaving her wondering if perhaps she had spotted an eavesdropper. For a fleeting moment, as the figure dashed from the column and into the safety of Hartwood's endless halls, Emily's eyes met those of Lord Somerton.

10

Friday, August 13

Near Midnight
Aboard HMS *Amethyst*

MAGPIE'S EYE POPPED OPEN. In the blackness of the sail room on the *Amethyst's* orlop deck, he froze in his hammock, hardly daring to breathe, and listened to the night. What was it that had disturbed his sleep: a figment of a frightening dream, the wind whipping the ship's old timbers, or someone lurking beyond the door — a drunken sailor, perhaps — trying to feel their way to their bed in the blinding darkness?

Three decks up the quartermaster tolled the ship's bell eight times. Magpie had been late retiring on this night, thrilled to have been invited to play games with the young midshipmen in their lively berth, but he had no idea if the eight bells marked the end of the First Watch or the Middle Watch — if it was midnight or four in the morning. Then again, maybe it was dawn, later than Magpie had surmised, and one of the men simply had need of a new sail.

But his good sense told him otherwise.

There ... there it was again! That sound! A rattling of the door latch! Someone *was* attempting to get in. Magpie yanked his blanket to his nose, but his alarm prevented him from calling out, or scrambling for a weapon of some kind, or blocking the door with rolls of heavy canvas. If someone had come to do him harm, he was in a hapless predicament.

The door opened with a foreboding creak; a lantern's glow eerily illumined the sail room, sending Magpie into a cold sweat. Peering over his thin blanket, he watched helplessly as a longhaired sailor — hunched over on account of the orlop's low ceiling — ambled toward the corner where Magpie kept the sails stacked up against the wall. The man muttered to himself, queer, incoherent words, and — as if incited to a fit of rage — began vandalizing the canvas rolls, hurling them about, and tearing at the sturdy material with his teeth. Was he looking for something? Did he think he'd stumbled into the closet that housed Captain Prickett's wine and spirits? Was he under the misconception that Magpie had stolen his purse of coins and hidden it here in this room?

As suddenly as it had begun, the man's fit ceased, and he turned on his heels and trudged toward Magpie's hammock. For a brief second, the lantern cast light upon the sailor's countenance, revealing swollen, ugly features and a conspicuous nose. Magpie stiffened like a cadaver and squeezed his eye shut. Best to pretend he was sound asleep, though no silent coaxing could slow the awful hammering of his heart.

Hoisting the lantern high above the hammock, the man stood transfixed for an eternity, growling like a mad dog and releasing vapours of stinking breath that reeked of rotting meat. Magpie was so grateful for the blanket that enshrouded his nose. Holding his breath, bracing for the worst, he feared the man's hands would soon close on his throat and crush the life from him; instead he set the lantern down upon the floor and snatched the *Isabelle* hat from his pillow. Then laughter — surely a sound only a savage could create — filled the dimensions of the sail room, and the man — much to Magpie's relief, for he could again draw breath — shuffled away from his bed. With his eye still tightly shut, it was hard to discern his exact whereabouts as he delivered words that chilled Magpie to the bone.

"Time's comin' when ya won't be seein' outta the other eye neither."

Then Magpie heard no more.

Wild-eyed, he risked a peek over his blanket, fully expecting to find the man brandishing one of his sharp sail-making tools, or preparing to set the room afire, but he was gone; he'd vanished, as if he had slipped through the oak walls of the ship, taking the *Isabelle* hat with him.

Liberating all of his anxiety in one giant whoop, Magpie propelled himself from his hammock, his bare feet barely touching the floor. He seized the deserted lantern and dashed for the exit, beyond caring if the man — *the spectre* — lay in wait behind the door, intent on tearing him apart with his teeth. He *would* not ... he *could* not spend the remainder of the night in the sail room.

Saturday, August 14

7:30 a.m.
(Morning Watch, Seven Bells)

WITH A START, LEANDER straightened in his chair. While he yawned he looked with dismay at the ink-blotted, crumpled letter upon his hospital desk, which had spent the night under the weight of his crossed arms and sleeping head. What would Emily think if she were to receive such a letter? Surely she would believe an interloper had rescued it from the wastebasket, and it was, therefore, not meant for her consumption. He tucked it away in his writing box with myriad others neatly addressed to her, in care of the Duke of Clarence at Bushy House. What did it matter that not a single one had yet been dispatched to her? In all likelihood, he would be back in London before the Amethysts met with and entrusted their homeward-bound letters to the crew of a fast-sailing clipper, en route to England, and thus be able to hand deliver them himself. The prospect made him smile.

Standing up, he stretched out the knots in his back, gazing as he did so into the forepeak's narrowing, wishing — as he always did — that Emily's cot was hanging there as it had on the *Isabelle*, and she still slumbered there ... and that he could soon wake her to delight once again in her sleepy smile.

"Is that a sigh I'm hearin' from ya, Doctor?" asked Biscuit, lumbering into the hospital with the ponderous breakfast tray.

Leander took the tray from the cook, whose own breakfast leftovers were still wedged between his grey teeth, and plunked it down upon his desk. "It is!"

"Why, ya should be givin' thanks! No sails on the horizon, fresh winds, the *Lady Jane* is still sailin' within scope like a good lass."

"Yes," Leander said, lost in thought, "another long, uneventful day —"

"Is it eventful ya want? Now ya're not hopin' fer a battle, and yer hammocks to fill up with the dead and dyin', are ya?"

"I think you know me better than that."

Biscuit placed his roughened hands on his hips and winked his good eye. "I suppose yer recallin' the time when a lovely princess were keepin' ya company."

Leander poured milk into his morning tea and kept his face hidden from Biscuit, not caring to have the cook guess his feelings. "That seems a lifetime ago now," he replied quickly, handing Biscuit two wooden bowls of oatmeal. "Now, if you please, help me pass round the breakfast."

Although Biscuit was happy to oblige, the moment he set off on his task he let loose a deprecating snarl. "Ach, Doctor, ya might've warned me ya had a fifth patient, so's I knew how many oats to boil."

Leander swung around in time to see Magpie's curly head appear above the side of a hammock that he had assumed was empty. There was a worrying redness in the boy's one eye, and his face was swollen and blotchy. "Biscuit, would you see to a cup of chocolate for our newest patient?"

"Right away, sir," the cook chirped, departing at once for the galley.

Leander dispensed the breakfast bowls to his four other patients before checking in with Magpie. "And why didn't you wake me?" he asked, pretending to be cross.

"'Cause I felt sorry fer ya, sir, sleepin' at yer desk."

"Are you unwell?"

"Nay, but I —" Magpie paused to study the faces of the others in the hospital, as if he were looking for someone in particular. "Ya don't mind me comin' here, and pilferin' a hammock and all, do ya, sir?"

"You know I don't." Leander dragged his chair over to Magpie's bedside and sat down. "Now then, tell me what brings you here?"

Magpie opened his mouth to speak, but stopped short, and glanced around him again. The four patients, who previously had been occupied with the mechanics of silently spooning oatmeal into their mouths, had all lifted their chins to listen.

Recalling a time on the *Isabelle* when Octavius Lindsay had posed a threat to the boy, Leander leaned in closer. "Is there someone … someone bothering you?"

Magpie fixed his eye on Leander's face, and whispered, "I bin seein' and hearin' things."

"What kind of things?"

"He's bin comin' at night."

"Who?"

"The spectre."

"The spectre?"

"Last night he were in the sail room."

Leander relaxed his furrowed brow. "Did he hurt you?"

"Nay, but I almost fainted dead away with fear."

Biscuit hurried into the hospital with Magpie's cup of chocolate and handed it off to him. "Are ya okay, wee lad?"

Leander's tone was crisp. "Magpie's fine, thank you, Biscuit, but I should like time alone with him. Could you engage my google-eyed patients in conversation? Lead a sing-song if you must."

Biscuit grinned. "I'll tell 'em a few jokes, sir, to keep their ears off o' ya."

"Now then, Magpie," Leander said, returning to boy, "start at the beginning."

"The first time, I saw him on deck — at night, in Halifax ... all legs and arms he was, like a spider, and he said such things, strikin' terror in me somethin' fierce."

"And you've no idea who he was."

"I bin thinkin' he ain't real, sir."

Leander crossed his arms as he pondered that one. "First off, tell me about last night."

"He came into the sail room ... through the door ... holdin' a lantern, and he messed around with the sails, and stole me *Isabelle* hat from under me nose. And when he left ... well, I think he passed right through the side o' the ship."

"Are you quite certain of that?"

"I ain't certain 'o nothin', sir."

Being no closer to understanding Magpie's plight, Leander's lips curled in disgust upon hearing intrusive steps on the ladder and the simpering voice of Lord Bridlington.

"Doctor, come away from the sailmaker. You must attend me at once."

Leander could not resist a sardonic reply. "Did Captain Prickett make good on his promise and perform a botched amputation on you?"

The hospital inhabitants laughed, Biscuit the loudest of them all, for, having distracted the patients with his wit, he was already warmed up and in a jokey mood. Twisting his neck around, Leander was disheartened to find Meg Kettle straggling behind the first lieutenant. "What rabble is this? Oh, Mrs. Kettle! And to what do we owe the pleasure of your company? Do you need immediate attending as well?"

"I might be," she sneered, rolling her hips about provocatively. "But best ya come visit me tonight, so's we 'ave a bit o' privacy, eh, Doctor?"

An ensuing rumpus struck Leander's ears. He closed his eyes and rubbed his forehead in exasperation. Whispering an apology to Magpie, he stood up. "It's far too early in the morning for your side-splitting humour, Mrs. Kettle."

"And, Doctor," added Biscuit with gusto, "here ya was thinkin' the day would be dull."

"I thank you all for providing me with an auspicious start to my day, but I require quiet in here, and a clearing out. Goodbye, Biscuit! Mrs. Kettle, collect whatever laundry it is you've come to collect, and leave. Now then, Mr. Bridlington, how can I be of assistance?"

The men in their cots piped down, Biscuit reluctantly returned to his galley stove, and the first lieutenant started in on a litany of calamities relating to his lost finger. "I can neither write in the logbook nor raise a sword, Doctor, and I take no pleasure in my meals for I cannot cut my meat, and it is hellish buttoning one's jacket with one hand, and Captain Prickett becomes irritable and unreasonable whenever I ask him for assistance —"

While Leander examined Bridlington's offending hand, he noticed Mrs. Kettle hovering near the ladder. It seems she had not come to collect anything at all. Though she ignored the warning glance he darted in her direction, she withdrew a few steps and made an attempt to conceal herself behind a timber post. Then the sides of her mouth fell and she glared like a fiend at Magpie, and before disappearing into the cheerless recesses of the ship, she dragged her forefinger across her neck in a terrorizing, throat-slicing gesture.

11

Saturday, August 14

10:00 p.m.
Hartwood Hall

EMILY STOOD BY HER south-facing bedroom window, gazing down upon the frenzied scenes below. A hundred torches lit up the front lawns, and carriages of all sizes and descriptions jostled for space between the house and the gardens, so that the footmen, in their traditional powdered wigs and distinctive livery, could allow their guests to disembark without being crushed by a set of wheels or an agitated horse. If it were not for the women's finery — flowing gowns of white muslin, fluttering fans, feathered turbans, coifs of flowers, and jewels that sparkled in the torchlight — and the happy expressions evident upon their countenances, as well as those of their male chaperones — Emily would think she was witnessing a ship's crew dashing about on deck to gain their action stations before an enemy encounter. The murmur of impassioned voices filtering up from the lawns soon permeated the ground floor of Hartwood Hall, growing and swelling in volume until the house vibrated with a high-spirited energy. And, under its influence, Emily was relieved to find her lonely mood beginning to lift.

Tearing herself away from the window, she sought the full-length looking glass beside the wardrobe and scrutinized her appearance, while Fleda, in a dress of lemon-yellow muslin, her red hair arranged in loose ringlets and ribbons upon her head, looked on in flushed excitement from a chair arranged near the doorway.

Helena's choice of a gown for her came as quite a shock, Emily being convinced the duchess would connive to attire her in a drab dress of bombazine or crepe; instead, what had arrived at her bedchamber was a gown of mull silk, the colour of pink roses, with a tunic-length overdress and lace edging along the neckline, which, despite it being low-cut, retained a respectability, as Emily had refused to don the proffered wadding and whalebone to coerce her breasts upward to meet her chin. The short, puffed sleeves were adorned with nosegays of silk flowers, so too was her pale-gold hair that had been dressed in the Grecian style by Helena's giddy maid. To complete her full evening dress, Emily had been loaned white elbow gloves, pink silk slippers, and a string of fine pearls.

"It's been months since I've seen *this* sort of reflection in the mirror," she said, performing a pirouette.

"You remind me of a princess in one of my storybooks," Fleda said with a glimmer of admiration in her green eyes.

"Yet if I were strolling about on the ... on a ship, not one of the men would recognize me in such finery." Emily was careful not to mention the *Isabelle* by name, in the event Fleda questioned her about her brother, Octavius.

"Why not?"

"They were so accustomed to seeing me in trousers, and my hair falling down my back or wrapped in a neck scarf."

"But you're not on a ship," said Fleda solemnly. "You're here, where you belong, and you're dressed as you should be."

Emily gaped at the girl, astonished to hear such words voiced by an eleven-year-old. "Shall I have the pleasure of meeting some of your brothers this evening?"

"Not one of them could get away on such short notice."

"I was hoping to at least meet Wetherell."

"I don't think you'll ever meet him. Mother says he lives at Boodle's in St. James's Street in London — whatever Boodle's is — and doesn't like to leave his friends."

"Oh, I see," said Emily, avoiding Fleda's mystified expression, and any further discussion on the subject; it was not her place to explain the voluptuous character of the renowned men's club to the girl. "Now tell me, has your mother arranged for you to delight us all tonight by playing a musical piece on your pianoforte?"

She shook her ringlets. "Glenna says I must stay out of sight with Mademoiselle, and content myself with the pastries and iced creams. But I will watch you dance."

Emily smiled at her. "And will you rescue me if a man with a monstrous belly asks me to dance?"

"I'll soon be sent to bed, and the ball will go on until five in the morning, but I know Somerton will rescue you."

"Somerton?"

Fleda was about to say something more when someone crept up behind her and delivered a sharp rap upon the open door. To Emily's utter amazement the pineapple-shaped head of her Uncle Clarence appeared, and he entered the room, mopping his brow with a handkerchief.

"God damn, Emeline, you should've come down long before this. The guests are waiting for the first dance, and the master of ceremonies was instructed that you were to select and lead it." He continued into the centre of the room, stepping past Fleda, as if she were invisible. "Now, I've come to warn you … don't select a minuet, my dear, for they are quite passé these days. You might want to consider a cotillion."

"Greetings to you too, Uncle," said Emily, reaching out to shake his hand. "How lovely to see you again so soon. I had no idea you were coming here tonight."

"Wot? And miss a good party? And here I've barely recovered from the Prince Regent's birthday celebration of two days ago," he said, giving his stomach a friendly pat. "But I am a good sort, and would never turn down an invitation from my old friend Adolphus Lindsay."

Emily longed to berate him for his appalling behaviour the night he summarily dropped her off at Hartwood in the rain, but she could only laugh at his good humour. "Actually, Uncle, I was thinking … perhaps we might begin the ball with a waltz, and I'll ask the musicians to play the *Brighton Waltz*."

Uncle Clarence looked horrified. "You'll do no such thing, Emeline! I'll not have a man's hands on your waist."

Fleda giggled.

He stared down at the seated giggler, as if he were seeing her for the first time. "And who is this mite? Your serving girl?"

Fleda jumped from her chair and lifted her pointed chin in defiance. "No, sir! I'm Lady Fleda, the daughter of the Duke and Duchess of Belmont."

The Duke of Clarence's eyes rounded in surprise. "How d'ye do?" he said cheerfully, and then startled Fleda by grasping one of her small hands and kissing it before hastily flinging it away. "Well, well now! I didn't know my old friend had a daughter."

Emily frowned at her uncle. "How can you not have known?"

"Adolphus and I, when we do get together, don't talk about our children. We have important things to discuss such as politics and horses and the state of the Royal Navy. And I'll wager *he* could not name all of *my* sons and daughters!" He stamped his foot impatiently, unaware of the hollow cast that had crept into Fleda's eyes. "Now then, my dear," he continued, giving Emily's gown a once-over, "I am thankful you look decent, and not like a sea swabber; however, we must get a move on, for the guests will soon grow restless and storm the first floor — as the revolutionaries stormed the Bastille — to gather you up them-selves. Remember to smile sweetly; do not dance more than two times with any one man; maintain a good posture at all times; don't laugh too loudly — that is most vulgar — and for goodness sake don't drink too much punch." Firmly, he took hold of her upper arm and steered her toward the bedroom door.

Emily winked at Fleda, and said, "Dear Uncle, although it won't be easy for me, I shall try."

10:20 p.m.

THE RESOUNDING VOICE of the master of ceremonies alerted the guests as Emily and her uncle entered the music room.

"His Royal Highness, the Duke of Clarence and St. Andrews, and Her Royal Highness, Princess Emeline Louisa."

The laughter and hum of conversation subsided, allowing Emily to hear her heart thumping in her chest. In a rustling and scuffing of skirts and heels those who were sitting stood up, and those who were standing whirled about, all to scrutinize the newcomers with startling, unmasked attention from all directions, many from behind waving fans and through quizzing glasses. Beside her, pinching her arm in his grasp, Emily's uncle preened, beaming broadly at the fair ladies who had their enticing décolletage on full display, as they made their way to the far end of the room where the band members — resplendent in their blue and red uniforms — were awaiting their instruction. Emily did her best to return the guests' ingratiating smiles, but as she knew no one beyond the Lindsay family — Helena, all elation in her new cream silk, and Adolphus ensconced on the sofa with a bumper of punch in one fist and a cold veal pie in the other, and frequently expressing his satisfaction by calling out *"Splendid"* — by the time she reached the band, she could recall only a blur of white faces and a panoply of ostrich feathers, starched collars, lace caps and ruffles, and colourful costumes.

Her uncle leaned in toward her. "Now, Emeline, I think it best that I do the choosing of the music and steps for this most important first dance. A longways country dance would be most appropriate." He straightened before the bandleader, and called out, "'Wakefield Hunt.'"

Much to his perceptible satisfaction, Uncle Clarence's ears were met with a roar of approval from the guests, which he gratefully acknowledged with a graceful bow. A number of couples scrambled to take their places in the set, hoping to be the ones that would find themselves standing next to the royals, and as the first notes of music filled the room, Emily found herself staring not into the contented countenance of her uncle, but into the expectant eyes of Lord Somerton.

"You … you look quite different," he stammered, standing before her, attired in a cutaway coat of sky-blue velvet and matching satin knee breeches. Emily thought him dressed more for the king's court than for a private country ball, and could not resist snatching a peek at his shapely calves.

"As do you, sir."

"If you don't want to dance with me, I'll go quietly away. It was … it was your uncle's idea."

"Oh!" said Emily, somewhat chagrined, looking about her and spotting that meddler, her uncle, further down the dance line, having claimed the hand of a stout older woman with a happy disposition and a silk turban adorned with nodding ostrich plumes.

"It was a toss-up between me and Mr. Gribble," Somerton grinned, causing Emily to stop short.

"Mr. Gribble?"

Somerton leaned toward her to speak sotto voce, as there were many appreciative ears nearby. "He plans to press you to dance and stay near to him the entire evening. Be forewarned: I believe he intends to propose marriage and whisk you away to his country seat."

"Perhaps Mr. Gribble has not heard that I'm already married."

Somerton's reply was swift. "You must know that that'll not stop the men from trying, especially since your husband is locked away in Newgate Prison, and therefore not here to challenge your suitors to a duel."

"Is that where my husband is? Have they not hanged him yet?" Emily was pleased to see Somerton mentally calculating whether he should laugh or look alarmed.

The dance began. Stepping toward one another, they clasped hands briefly before twirling about and returning to the line formation.

"Perhaps my *suitors* should be informed that I'm a poor royal, and have nothing to my name."

"Do you think then that all men look upon you as nothing more than a valuable prize?"

It was a question that could not preclude a raw reminder of Thomas Trevelyan.

"Yes! They must all see me as a ship full of the king's gold and treasure — to be boarded and taken, but only against my will."

"It may well be true that some would look upon you in that light, but you must know not all of our sex is cut —" Somerton could only complete his thought once they had performed a number of intricate steps "— from the same length of canvas."

The expression in his eyes made Emily feel suddenly ill at ease, and she was grateful when they parted for a time and she was able to smile comfortably as she took up the hands of several new partners. Though deep concentration was a necessary evil — her recollection of the dance steps being quite rusty — certain faces amongst the admirers and observers scattered about the room now stood out. In front of the chimneypiece stood a cluster of young women who had evidently given careful consideration to their evening dress; they were all pearls and ribbons, their intricate hairstyles most likely achieved only upon great exertion by their harassed maids. Their eyes, having previously been locked upon the Duke of Belmont's second eldest son, caught Emily unawares, and while she could not decide if it was the result of a digestive disorder or disdain for the royal princess in their midst, their rouged countenances were twisted in scowls and aimed at her.

Before long Somerton was again at her side, though they did not speak until the dance had come to an end and the flushed dancers and onlookers alike had raised their hands to applaud the skilful musicians.

"You made no comment upon my last remark."

Emily lifted her face to his in question.

"That ... we men are *not* all the same."

"There was no need to argue you on that point."

"And why not?" he asked, taken aback, as if he had fully expected to have to defend the honour of the male gender.

Emily's lips curled enigmatically. "Because ... I happen to know they are not."

They did not converse at all during the second dance, a slow minuet — though Emily could feel Somerton's inquisitive eyes on her — and when it was done she bowed, thanked him, and left him to the pretty smiles of the décolleté crowd that now swooned with trepidation near the chimneypiece.

Midnight

WITH A PROMISE TO dance with him again later, Emily pried herself from the clammy clutches of the moustached Mr. Gribble and fled the music room in search of sustenance. Every part of her ached, for not once had she sat down or even had a chance to catch her breath. Surely climbing the shrouds of a ship was a much easier task than making polite chatter, fending off impertinent inquiries, and dancing with unsavoury partners. It had just been announced by the master of ceremonies that a buffet was being served to the guests in the dining room under *"His Grace's newly installed gas-fired chandeliers,"* and Emily, hoping to be one of the first to arrive, hurried there.

Upon entering the glittering chamber, she was chagrined to find it already jammed with hungry guests, as noisy as those she had left behind in the music room, and all of the chairs set at the long dining table occupied. Thinking it best she return later, she was about to retrace her steps when her arm was snatched up by Mrs. Jiggins, the stout woman with the ostrich-plumed turban who had been Uncle Clarence's first dance partner, and — with ceremony — she was led to one end of the table. The woman's happy disposition had, evidently, been made even happier as the hours of the evening wore on.

"Sit here, Your Royal Highness," she gushed, pawing Emily as a servant boy rushed to bring her a chair. "We want to hear how you're getting on."

With an unrefined push from the overwrought woman, Emily was assisted into the chair, and upon looking up found two endless lines of curious faces fixed upon her, their eyes sparkling like the chandeliers above their heads, their florid faces smiling, all of them gregarious in their deportment.

"Was it so terrible being shot in the leg?" Mrs. Jiggins asked, taking her place next to Emily and laying her bejewelled hand upon Emily's forearm.

"Actually, I was shot in the shoulder."

"Ohhh!" gasped the crowd.

"And were you standing on one of the ship's yards at the time of your shooting?" asked one of the gentlemen seated nearby, who appeared to be less inebriated than the others.

"No, I was swimming in the ocean at the time."

Another upsurging gasp issued forth from the onlookers. "Whatever were you doing swimming in the ocean?"

"I was trying to decide if I could safely swim away from the American ship and toward the British ship," was Emily's levelled reply.

Those around her shook their decorated heads in consternation.

"And what were these two ships doing? Were they exchanging news and niceties?" asked Mrs. Jiggins, who had made it clear to the diners — with little hand gestures and nods of her silk turban — that she would lead the conversation.

Emily was careful, lest her eyes should widen in disbelief. "No, I'm afraid they were exchanging *broadsides*."

"Whatever is a broadside?" asked a thin voice from the lower end of the dining table.

"The shooting off of cannons and long guns, my dear," answered someone.

"Goodness me!" came Mrs. Jiggins's breathy reaction. She motioned to a hovering servant to bring a selection of pastries to Emily. "Why would you ever choose to take a swim while two ships were shooting off their cannons at one another?"

Emily tried to invoke a measure of patience in her reply. "I wasn't taking a swim for pleasure. I had escaped from the American ship as she battled one of our Royal Navy ships."

A drunken voice rose up from amongst the heads. "Americans? I thought we were fighting the French."

"Oh, we are, but apparently we've now taken up a second quarrel with the Americans," said Mrs. Jiggins, her ostrich plumes nodding with authority.

"As of when?"

"Last year, I think it was."

"Why did I never hear of it?"

"And whatever for?"

"I believe our disagreement is over the issue of taxation."

"On what? Our tea?"

"Ladies," pleaded the gentleman near Emily, "you're mistaking our present quarrel with one of the causes for the American War of Independence, and, you may recall, during those years *we* were the ones taxing *their* tea."

"Well, I cannot keep it all fixed in my mind."

"Pray, let us eat instead."

"Her Grace has certainly outdone herself by bringing in a French chef."

"Yes! These profiteroles are divine."

"And do taste the apple tarts!"

Mrs. Jiggins seemed indignant with her companions' preference for food over the recounting of great adventures, but, making a speedy recovery, she smiled congenially and leaned in toward Emily so that she might have a good view of her diamond necklace. "You must forgive them, Your Royal Highness; they don't understand war and politics as I do. Now, go ahead and enjoy your pastries." She gave Emily's hand a gentle pat. "And let us speak together *sotto voce*, for I'm quite in painful suspense to know how you managed on these ships in the company of lusty sailors. Had I been in your place, I'm certain I would've abandoned all virtuous notions, and, despite the stink and dirt, indulged daily in carnal recreation."

2:00 a.m.

Outside the night was warm, even at this late hour, though a cool respite from the flummery and overheated noise of Hartwood's ground floor, where the volume had reached a crescendo as the guests — so decorous in the beginning — unleashed their inhibitions with the aid of lively Scottish reels and plenty of drink. It had taken forever to pry herself away from the dining-room table and the insatiable attentions of Mrs. Jiggins, and upon wandering wearily back to the music room Emily could see that even her Uncle Clarence and the Duke of Belmont had overindulged; she was appalled to have found them napping on separate sofas. It was evident, however, that the duchess found this arrangement to her satisfaction. Having foregone the pleasures of the midnight buffet, she was still dancing, her normally reserved temperament having slipped to permit clapping in time to the music and occasional tweets of laughter.

Finding an empty bench under an enormous chestnut tree, Emily arranged her gown upon its wrought-iron configurations and gazed upon the far-off lights of London. Nearby stood the carriages and their attending footmen, belonging to the guests determined to stay until sunrise, when every drop of wine and every last morsel of the French chef's feast had been devoured. Emily wondered how difficult it would be to clamber atop one of the closed-in carriages, or slide into the seat of a barouche or curricle, and wait for the owner to — inadvertently or not — offer a ride to the city. To amuse herself, she pictured Glenna McCubbin bursting into her room to awaken her Sunday afternoon, and finding her bed empty, its former occupant miles away from the high walls of Hartwood.

It was a gaggle of giggling women, having abandoned propriety to run across the lawn in their flowing gowns, who cut short Emily's machinations. They dropped to the grass only yards from where she sat, hidden by the low-hanging branches of the chestnut. In the torchlight she recognized the young ladies as the ones who had shot daggers at her early in the evening when she had been partnered with Somerton for the first two dance selections. With mild amusement, Emily listened to their banter.

"Lord Somerton said I was the prettiest girl in the room."

"I daresay he told you you were the fattest in the room!"

"No, he did not! In comparison to his father, I'm a twig."

"Well, he said I was the most graceful dancer of all the ladies at the ball."

"Pish! According to Lord Somerton, my gown is the most exquisite one he's ever laid eyes upon."

"He won't be impressed when he sees it again, all rumpled and marked with grass stains."

Peals of drunken laughter ensued.

"I had been fretting so before the ball, worried that that pompous Princess Emeline Louisa would bewitch him." Emily's name had been scornfully enunciated. "But he never asked her for another dance after the first two, and I believe he only started off the dancing with her to please the Duke of Clarence."

"Certainly he never seemed to give her another thought afterward. He seemed so very contented with us."

"I'd so hoped to find that she resembled a horse, like her cousin Charlotte, the Prince Regent's daughter."

"It appears she's not as fond of food as Princess Charlotte is."

"They say she was half-starved at sea. That her captors fed her nothing but oiled rats."

"Well, you won't have to worry about Lord Somerton hoping to make a match with her."

"With Princess Charlotte?"

"For goodness sake, dear sister, do follow the thread of the conversation! Not with Charlotte, silly, with Princess Emeline, for *she* is already married."

"Yes, but I heard that when her husband is tried, he'll more than likely be found guilty and put to death, so then she'll be free to marry again."

"But Helena Lindsay would *never* allow her son to be married to such a notorious woman."

"Indeed! Not after the disappointment of her eldest son, the marquess."

"Lord Somerton deserves a woman of good breeding ... such as myself."

"You should be so lucky!"

"Princess Emeline, for all her beauty and royal connections, deserves nothing more than an English tar named Jack."

Their laughter rang clear across the dark, rolling lawns of Hartwood, echoing throughout the distant woods and turning the heads of the footmen who stood vigil by the carriages. But the girls soon tired of the subject, and, desperate to replenish their empty punch cups and seek more merriment, they scrambled to their feet, brushed themselves and their silk slippers off, and scampered toward the glittering hall.

"Ladies," one of them shouted as they ran, "let us determine, once and for all, which one of us is most favoured by the *breathtaking* Lord Somerton."

Emily turned away from the ridiculous girls to gaze upon the waning moon that navigated alone in the inky sky just above the London spires, shivering in the fresh breeze that incited the chestnut tree to whisper and stir around her. Strains of a familiar and poignant tune suddenly floated upon the night air. Lifting her head to listen, a lump slowly rose in her throat. It was Bach's haunting composition "Sheep May Safely Graze," a favourite of Magpie's. From where was the music coming? It was hard to imagine the musicians installed in the ballroom had decided to hush the happy crowds with the hymnal piece. Was it coming from a snug cottage or perhaps a tavern on the heath? Or was a little piper playing it somewhere on the sea?

Far too soon the lonely notes died away and, left to endure the more joyful, carefree sounds of the night, Emily was overcome with grief. Lying down upon the bench, its cold iron cutting into her exposed flesh, she cried herself to sleep.

12

Monday, August 16

MAGPIE RESTED HIS HEAD upon his upturned hand and stared down at his dinner of brown stew and pork, absent-mindedly watching the trickles of gravy charting a course around his square wooden plate.

"What's wrong with you, Magpie?" asked Morgan Evans, giving him a playful kick under their mess table. "You haven't touched your food."

"Ya should be chirpin'," added Biscuit, who had left his galley to sit down for a spell with his messmates. "Mealtimes are the best bits o' the day — our one delight."

"Fer me it's me twice-daily grog rations," said Jacko, smacking his blubbery lips.

"Ach," moaned Biscuit wistfully, "if only Captain Prickett's rum weren't so watered down, it might have the effect o' warmin' our bellies to be sure."

Morgan nudged Biscuit, hoping to unseat the cook. "What do you have to complain about? You've access to the stores of rum all day long, and take full advantage of it."

Repositioning his bottom upon the bench, Biscuit assumed a stately manner. "Mr. Evans, the day ya want to trade occupations with me, ya let me know."

Around the table, the men guffawed. "Ya can't even git the food right, Biscuit," said Jacko with a glower, pointing at his plate. "God help us if ya was responsible fer patchin' up the sides of the ship."

"We'd be certain to sink straightaway."

"Ha, ha, ho, ho!" was Biscuit's sarcastic response.

Morgan looked again at Magpie. "So, what's all this sullenness about?"

It was the spectre that had stolen Magpie's appetite in recent days, but he could not tell the men of his fearful experiences, for surely they would be merciless in their teasing. And though he was now safe at night, having gained sanctuary in the hospital in exchange for helping out Dr. Braden whenever he was free from his sail-making duties, he was still terrified of another sighting. In a quandary, Magpie fished for an answer to give his messmates.

"It's the rollin' of the ship. It's takin' me appetite away."

"That's never bothered you before," said Morgan, looking concerned. "I've never known you to be sickened by the waves."

Jacko chewed thoughtfully on a lump of pork. "I overheard Mr. Austen sayin' this morning he didn't like the look o' the sky. He thinks we're in fer a big one."

Recalling the spectre's words of doom, Magpie looked alarmed.

"Not to worry, Magpie." Morgan smiled. "The *Amethyst* is weatherly and solid as a rock. She's built to withstand a pummelling from wind and waves."

"He's right, lad," added Biscuit. "Few ships go down on account o' storms."

Magpie glanced first at Morgan, and then at the others sitting around the table. "What about the *Blenheim*? The Duke o' Clarence told me he lost his son William on that ship back in 1807 … that it vanished without a trace on account o' awful weather."

"No one knows that for sure," said Morgan. "It was just speculation that the *Blenheim* foundered in a heavy gale. There were some that'd seen her in port after the storm had passed."

"But the Duke o' Clarence told me she was last seen sendin' out distress signals in a big gale o' wind."

"Magpie, it *was* well-known that the *Blenheim* was in very poor condition."

Jacko frowned at Morgan. "Where did she go down?"

"Near Madagascar."

"Where's that, sir?" asked Magpie.

"The Indian Ocean, off the coast of Africa, and we're a long way from there," said Morgan, pitching a piece of biscuit at Magpie's chest.

Magpie flinched. He hated the thought of the Duke of Clarence's forlorn son drowning in such a foreign and frightening sea, so far from all that he had loved.

"No worries," continued Morgan, "especially with Mr. Austen on board. He saw us through the end of the *Isabelle*."

"It ain't him I'd be worryin' about," hooted Jacko, "it's them sorry lot o' Prickett and Bridlington. Depends on who's in charge ... who's makin' the calls."

Magpie was picturing himself clinging to a dead man when the plates and mugs on the table began sliding about. "Could the winds throw us on a lee shore? Could we be dashed on rocks like a crate o' eggs?"

"Little chance o' that! Ain't no shores nearby to be dashed upon!" said Biscuit, catching his sliding mug and raising it to his whiskery mouth.

"And nobody 'round to come to our aid if we are," said Jacko, chuckling.

"The *Lady Jane* —" yelped Magpie with a glimmer of optimism, "— wouldn't she help us?

"She'll go down afore us, I'll warrant," said Jacko, wiping his mouth with the back of his big hand. "It'll be ev'ry man and *Lady* fer themselves."

The men all laughed, leaving Magpie puzzled that not one of them seemed unstrung by all this talk of approaching storms and shipwrecks; in fact, Mr. Evans seemed to be in uncommonly high spirits. How could they feel this way, especially when the wind that howled around the *Amethyst* was arousing the hairs on his scalp, sounding as it did like every sailor that had ever perished in the Atlantic had gathered around them to weep?

"Now then, lad," grunted Biscuit, "ya best eat up me hearty pork stew to conserve yer strength, so's ya kin swim to England ... if need be."

2:00 p.m.
(Afternoon Watch, Four Bells)

THE AFTERNOON SKY was rapidly turning into night.

Fly Austen, his head down in the wind, pulled his way to Captain Prickett's cabin. To those sailors and assorted individuals he met along the way he roared orders — orders that should have been given some time ago, when the first cracks of thunder had rattled their ears and the lightning flashes revealed the ever-increasing swells of the sea.

"Take these chicken coops below! Lash the oars and pikes to the masts! Have the lifelines ready, fore and aft! Mrs. Kettle … take your infernal laundry down at once, and quit cursing like a costermonger."

"Ain't no one kin hear me with all o' this caterwaulin' wind," she shot back, ripping down a saturated shirt from the shrouds.

"Sir, what about the sails? Should we be takin' in some canvas?" asked the worried looking helmsman, Lewis McGilp, who, along with a second sailor, struggled to steer the ship.

Fly blinked through the sea spray to find the topgallants still flying, and hid his frustration. "I'll have a word with the captain and get back to you straightaway."

Captain Prickett was in his cot, which seemed to sway leisurely as the ship rolled, like a child's swing. On the floor were the remains of a cake that looked as if someone had gone at it with his hands.

"Sir, the gale is quite upon us now. May I suggest we take up the sails and try to ride it out?"

"What's that Austen?" asked a groggy Prickett.

"Sir, your attention is needed on the quarterdeck. The men want to know what your orders are regarding the sails."

Prickett tried to raise himself up in his cot, but found he could not, and fell back upon his bedclothes. Fly could see that his waistcoat was unbuttoned to allow his belly room to manoeuvre.

"Are you unwell, sir?"

Prickett chuckled. "I'm afraid I'm not able to leave my cot."

"Shall I call Dr. Braden for you?"

"Nay, don't bother the man. No need for it. I've just been overindulging. You know how I delight in Biscuit's spice cake. Then, of course, I had to wash it down with ale —" Prickett produced an empty mug from under his blanket.

"Your orders then, sir?" said Austen, trying to maintain civility.

"Do what needs to be done to see us through, Mr. Austen." Prickett licked his fingers before throwing his hand upon his forehead like an actor in a histrionic play. "In the meantime … I shall sleep off my indigestion."

2:30 p.m.
(Afternoon Watch, Five Bells)

THE DARK OCEAN ROSE and fell around the *Amethyst* like an endless terrain of desolate, bituminous hillocks and hollows.

Holding tightly to the boats fastened to the ship's waist, Fly, Leander, and Magpie stood, soaked to the bone, near the mainmast — which buckled and groaned in a most alarming manner — watching the men on the soaring yardarms scrambling to take in the sails. The ship pitched and heeled in the grey-crested swells that washed over the fo'c'sle every time she plunged headlong into the foaming sea, the water pouring out of her scuppers like fountains in St. James's Park.

Looking uncertain, Morgan Evans suddenly appeared before them to address Fly. "Sir, shall I search out Captain Prickett or report to you?"

"Captain Prickett is indisposed at the moment. What's the situation in the hold?"

"The water's coming in fast, sir. We're quickly filling the leaks, but the men working the pumps are faint with exhaustion."

"How much water in the bilge?"

"Three feet and rising, sir."

"I'll send down a fresh crew immediately, Mr. Evans. Now return to your men at once. Lord knows they need your guidance."

With a word of thanks and a salute, Morgan headed into the wind toward a hatchway and disappeared into the lurching hull of the *Amethyst*. Distressed by the amount of seawater cascading onto the lower decks, Fly yelled, "All hands! Batten down the hatches."

Lord Bridlington, the Officer of the Watch, approached, trying to stabilize himself with his healthy hand and keep his other one safe from further harm. "Oh, Mr. Austen, I'm afraid we've lost sight of the *Lady Jane*. What shall we do if she's been stove in and sunk?"

"I cannot worry about it at this moment."

"Then please pray that she'll be there, waiting for us on the horizon when this storm has passed, for I simply cannot bear to hear the captain's tirade on the subject. He'll surely blame me."

"My immediate concern is for *our* men. Round up a fresh crew to man the pumps. At once!"

Bridlington set off at a snail's pace, infuriating Fly, especially when the first lieutenant was struck down by the heavy sea and wasted precious time fussing over his maimed hand. But too many other anxieties were weighing on Fly, specifically the worry of the *Amethyst* rolling over on her beam-ends. "Stand ready by the guns! If need be, unlash them and throw them overboard. I'll not have us capsizing." Having dispensed with the necessary orders for the time being, he called out to Leander. "Have you come to stand with me at the mouth of Hell?"

Leander glanced up nervously at the great press of canvas. "I thought … should someone have the misfortune to fall … I'd stand here ready."

"I'll catch 'em fer ya, sir," shouted Magpie into the gale, feeling safe — as nowhere else — in the presence of Mr. Austen and Dr. Braden.

"Magpie, I'd breathe easier if you would remain in the hospital," said a disquieted Leander.

"Please, Doctor, I'd like to be stayin' up here with ya."

"Perhaps then, you could help Mrs. Kettle," suggested Fly, his eyes noting the laundress, wrestling with her baskets. "She'll never be done with it, and I fear the wind has already whisked away a good number of shirts."

"We can't have the lads naked, can we, sir?" chirped Magpie.

"We cannot."

"Fly!" yelled Leander. "Send Mrs. Kettle below. She's in no condition to be wandering the deck in a storm."

Fly nodded in agreement, and hollered, "Mrs. Kettle!" When she did not respond, he grabbed the speaking trumpet from the sailing master's hands, and bellowed, "Meg Kettle, get below now!"

With a scowl and a saucy word on her tongue, the laundress finally jerked her head in their direction, in time to meet a giant wave that flooded the decks, slapping her off her feet and sending her into a screaming collision with the mainmast. The gale tore at the contents of her laundry basket, scattering articles of clothing everywhere, some clogging the ship's scuppers, which served to drain water from the decks, most lost to the sea.

Magpie set off to collect what he could before they were washed away forever, his task taking him further and further away from Mr. Austen, who, having little faith in Lord Bridlington, had gone off to make certain men had been gathered for the pumps, and from Dr. Braden, who had immediately dropped to the deck to attend to Mrs. Kettle in her fuddled state. Near the bowsprit, his eye widened in horror; the fo'c'sle deck sloped toward the sea like a wooden ramp to Davy Jones's locker. Grasping the lifelines, Magpie tried to gather the lost clothes, but the wind made it hard work, and he hated the thunder for startling him and the flashes of lightning for illuminating such a fearful world.

Perched in the fore rigging was the spectre; his long arms locked around the strong ropes, his long hair flailing about him, the wind tugging at his unbuttoned shirt.

Spying Magpie, he bawled his gloomy pronouncements in a voice that rivalled the cracking thunder.

"Hold fast, ye wretched soul. The end o' life as ye know it has come. Woe and despair will escort us all to the grave."

Then he released a laugh — a deep, penetrating laugh that, with the cacophony of creaks and moans and howls and cries all around, made Magpie's blood freeze in his veins.

But their encounter was short-lived.

A wall of water whooshed up before Magpie and carried him down the deck, away from the spectre, snatching him up so quickly there was no time to call out for help or grab on to the safety of something lashed down. Its force was so tremendous Magpie could only think it was an ocean beast that had seized him, a colossal feline creature that had him by the scruff of the neck, intent on giving him a severe drubbing. Showing no quarter, it knocked him around like a toy before dragging him over the side of the tilting ship and sucking him into the roiling sea.

13

Monday, August 16

2:00 p.m.
Hartwood Hall

Emily gazed up at the dreary sky and felt light drops of rain on her nose. For two hours she had been walking the grounds of Hartwood, determined to regain her strength and vitality, depleted by months at sea — and further drained by the ball — and was not going to be deterred from her goal by the arrival of a little rain shower. Her first hour had been spent poking about the little bridges and glass-like ponds on the lower front lawns; her second around the service wing, the kitchen gardens, and colourful rhododendron bushes near the house; and now she was on the wooded driveway that led to Hartwood's gatehouse, hoping to explore the roads beyond the Duke of Belmont's land. There was no need to concern herself that the hem of her blue-and-white-striped morning dress was damp and encrusted with dirt, and the cooling breeze ruffling the heath was wreaking destruction upon her unbound hair, for it seemed there was no one around to be met. The whereabouts of the Lindsay family was a mystery and their staff — though she had periodically spied Glenna at the windows, watching her rambles — was all indoors, feverishly engaged in the restoration of Hartwood after the weekend festivities, or so they had been when she had first left the house. Wandering alone, Emily had revelled in her pensive freedom, so that when, from out of nowhere, swift-moving footsteps approached, she could not help feeling a surge of annoyance.

"Wait up!" cried Fleda, running along the driveway, her dog trotting along beside her.

"Where've you been?" asked Emily. She had not seen any members of the Lindsay family since the early hours of Sunday morning, when she had finally abandoned her cold bench under the chestnut tree to seek her warm bed; her last few meals taken alone at the dining room table with no other company than the silent servants.

"We have been visiting friends in the neighbourhood with your Uncle Clarence. Father didn't wish to awaken you on Sunday when we set out —" Fleda paused to roll her eyes. "I had to come back for my afternoon lessons with Mademoiselle, but everyone else is still away."

"When will they return?"

"When Father has had his fill of refreshments. He's always most interested in what people serve for tea and luncheon. And when your uncle is satisfied that he's asked everyone how they enjoyed the ball, and if they enjoyed meeting *you*."

It was Emily's turn to roll her eyes. "And what has their response been? Were they overjoyed to meet the *scandalous* woman who'd sailed the Atlantic with a flock of pirates?"

Fleda was surprisingly reverential in her response. "They cannot stop chattering about you. The women speak of nothing but your hair and your ball dress, which pleases Mother so, and the men … they are all clamouring for details of your sea adventure."

"Most likely they were unsatisfied with my replies to their questions on Saturday night." Emily couldn't resist a lighthearted laugh. "Although I did tell one of my dance partners that I'd single-handedly manned the cannons during a battle with the Americans, and another one that I'd walked across an iceberg."

"And did you?"

"No," Emily said wistfully. "And what of Somerton? When shall he be home?"

Fleda picked up a stick and tossed it into the darkening woods that flanked the serpentine driveway, her dog making a mad dash in search of it. "He plans to go on to town for a few days."

"Are you able to divulge the nature of his business in town?"

"He's been invited to stay with a family eager to have him marry one of their daughters."

Emily was reminded of the silly girls who had run across Hartwood's lawns at two in the morning. "And shall he?"

"Would you be upset if he did?"

"Of course not," Emily said quickly.

"Mother says their father doesn't have a large enough fortune for her tastes."

"How sad to dash their hopes," said Emily, feeling genuine sympathy for the unknown girls.

"She thinks Somerton deserves someone *much* better."

Emily bristled. "Does your mother have someone in mind?"

Fleda's green eyes unwaveringly met Emily's; her solemn face revealing nothing.

"If not ... I could always introduce Somerton to my cousin Charlotte, although I understand that, at the moment, she's being courted by the Orange and interested in a Slice."

Fleda's smooth forehead wrinkled like a freshly ploughed field. Seeing that she had successfully baffled the girl, Emily hurried on toward the formidable walls of stone that marked the entrance to the Hartwood estate. "Let us ask the keeper to unlock the gates, so that we may take a stroll to London."

"A stroll? It's almost two hours to London by coach."

"What an adventure we could have!"

Fleda looked uncertain. "Our gatekeeper won't open them for you."

"Why ever not?"

"I'm not allowed to go beyond this point."

Emily was undaunted. "Then I'll simply climb over them, and take that walk by myself."

Emily could see Fleda's mind working. "If you did so, they'd surely come after you."

"Who would?"

Fleda shrugged.

"Highwaymen on horseback, brandishing pistols perhaps?" said Emily, studying the dark grey stones in the wall, searching for one with a sufficient protrusion that could provide her with a leg-up.

"Let's go back," Fleda said sullenly. "It's going to pour rain soon."

The last thing Emily wanted to do was return to the house. In casting about for something to warrant a delay, she was cheered to see a large black-and-white bird perched atop the wall, its little glossy head set on an angle, its black eyes on her, looking as if it desired to be included in the ladies' conversation.

"Oh!" Emily gasped, advancing toward it slowly, pleased that it was not frightened away. "It's a magpie!"

"I *hate* magpies," said Fleda. "They're such noisy birds, and they steal things."

"They are intelligent."

"You'd better speak kindly to him, or you'll have bad luck."

"There's no need to," said Emily smiling, "for he's looking directly into my eyes. I think we are already friends."

"Glenna says if you see one sitting on its own, it means someone is going to die."

"Scottish lore!" scoffed Emily. "Actually, if I remember correctly, you only have to worry if you see a lone magpie near the window of your house."

"But my brother Octavius died," said Fleda quietly.

Emily could offer the girl little beyond a compassionate glance. "That happened some time ago."

The magpie skittered along the stones and then flew off, Emily watching the bird's journey into a maze of mountain ash branches until she could no longer see it.

"Did you know my brother?"

Emily set off reluctantly toward the house, wondering as she had from the first moment she set eyes on Octavius's portrait hanging in the music room how long it would be before the Lindsay family learned the true nature of her *acquaintance* with their lost son. "No, I did not *know* your brother."

"But Mother said you were on the *Isabelle*."

Aware of Fleda's eyes on her, Emily kept hers lowered on the gravel driveway. "There were four hundred men on the *Isabelle*. I was only acquainted with a handful of them."

Fleda stopped walking. Emily stopped too, and turned to give the girl a quizzical stare.

"I don't understand how you couldn't have known my brother."

Emily spoke gently. "I just told you. There were so many men, sailors, and landmen, and —"

"But he was an officer, a first lieutenant."

"I was confined to the ship's hospital, Fleda, and therefore had no opportunity to meet many of —"

"Did you know Captain Moreland?"

"I did."

"Captain Moreland was a family friend."

Emily remained silent when she noticed the slight quiver in Fleda's chin.

"I cannot believe he didn't introduce you to my brother. He should've been proud to have you make the acquaintance of Octavius."

"I am sorry I cannot tell you what you want to hear," Emily said helplessly.

Fleda's eyes narrowed in suspicion — Emily certain they could see directly into her soul — and then curtly the young girl spun about and stomped off. Breathing heavily from his forays into the woods, Fleda's dog hesitated, as if he were undecided whether to stay or go, but he soon bounded off to catch up to his mistress.

Emily stood there watching them go, past caring when the clouds could no longer contain the rain, and she was soon soaked to the skin. Again she pondered taking that road to London, and was certain she would have had it not been for the gatekeeper who scuttled from the sanctuary of his cottage in order to open the wrought iron gates to admit the Duke of Belmont's carriage.

2:30 p.m.
Hartwood Hall

GLENNA HELPED EMILY out of her sodden dress. "What a mess ya are! There's to be no more traipsin' 'round Hartwood in the rain. I'll not have it."

Emily had no will to retaliate. With apathy, she eyed the mess of boxes and bags heaped upon her bed and the three splendid new gowns hanging from its posts.

"What's all this?"

"Ya lucky lass! Ya'll find jewels there from Rundell and Bridge, and perfume and sweet-smellin' soap from Price and Gosnell. Oh, and there's shoes and hats from the shops on Bruton and Conduit Streets."

"Has Her Grace spent every pound the Regent kindly gave her for my custody on all of this?"

"Heavens no!" said Glenna. "He's been most generous fer sure, but Her Grace will guard every farthin' with her life, and purchase only what's necessary."

"I thought I might, at the very least, be allowed to go to London myself to shop."

"Why put yerself to inconvenience," asked Glenna, drying Emily with a towel, "when ev'ry shopkeeper is only too happy to ship their wares to ya here?"

Emily exhaled a lengthy sigh.

"Are ya not happy with the lot?"

"Of course I am, but there's no need for Her Grace to have gone to all this trouble for me."

"She didna do it all herself, ya know," winked Glenna. "I helped a wee bit with all the orderin'. But if ya don't find what ya need here, I'll take ya next door and show ya all o' the gifts left fer ya yesterday."

"Gifts? Oh, heavens, Glenna. Pray, what gifts?"

"The chamber next to yours is filled to the ceilin' with bonnets and parasols, fans and reticules and gloves and the like. Why a body can hardly squeeze between the lot!"

"But I've no need for such luxuries. Please ask Her Grace to distribute them amongst the servants of the house."

Glenna shoved her horrified face into Emily's. "I'll not insult the givers. Why they'll be wantin' to see ya wearin' their gift at the next ball."

"Not another ball!"

"The duke and duchess were so pleased with Saturday, they're plannin' another one, much to the neighbourhood's delight."

For the longest while, Emily said nothing and quietly submitted to Glenna's towel drying, which now seemed more of a drubbing. "Our men fighting on the sea, and — I suspect — our soldiers, have nothing at all. They're lucky if they own a decent pair of shoes or boots."

"It's none o' yer concern, Pet," said Glenna firmly. "Yer life's here in England as Princess Emeline, and it's only right ya dress proper."

"I shall not require a castle of clothes while I languish here at Hartwood."

"What's all this nonsense about languishin'?

"I have nothing to do here … no occupation."

Emily's old nurse grumbled as she tossed the damp towel onto a chair, and went to fetch one of the new chemises and silk corsets from the bed. "Nothin' to do, ya say? With all o' the parties and dances ya'll be goin' to? Why ya'll soon be receivin' an invitation every night o' the week."

"One cannot spend one's life doing nothing but seeking to be entertained."

Glenna shrugged off her comment as she helped Emily into her underclothes. "The Regent might even have ya down to Brighton fer Christmas."

Emily wheeled about. "Christmas! In Brighton? I've no interest in being a guest at his pavilion."

"Why it's an honour to be invited there."

"But his dining room's always so overheated, and his suppers go on forever, and his bands play so loudly, I'm always left with a headache."

"Ya'll do what yer told while yer stayin' here, Pet," scolded Glenna. "And if the Regent invites ya to Brighton, that's where ya'll be goin'."

Emily felt Glenna tighten the lacings on her short corset. "Do you not think I'll be long gone from Hartwood by Christmas?"

"If the trial is done at the Old Bailey, I suppose."

"But Uncle Clarence said that could be months away."

"'Twould be tomorrow if it weren't fer all o' the thieves and murderers and ravishers of women livin' amongst us."

"I feel — I feel I am no better off than I was while locked away on Trevelyan's ship."

Glenna made a clucking noise and straightened her old frame to frown. "I don't remember ya bein' a grumbler. With all this," she waved her arms at the fortress of bags and boxes upon the bed, "and ya still find somethin' to complain about."

"You really don't understand, do you?" said Emily sadly.

"I don't suppose there's anythin' to understand. Ya've grown ungrateful of late. Now quit yer grumblin' and put on one o' them new gowns." Glenna collected the towel and Emily's wet clothes, and wobbled toward the door. "I need ya down in the parlour, and to make haste."

"Why?"

"Yer uncle's returnin' to town soon and desires a quick word with ya first." She wavered in the doorway as if contemplating another reprimand. "Ya could do what Her Grace does ev'ry day o' the week."

"And what's that?"

"Write letters."

Emily faced Glenna. "Yes! Perhaps I should write to my grandmother, Queen Charlotte, begging her and my old aunts to come visit me?"

"Her Grace would be happy to be receivin' the royal highnesses here."

"And do you believe Her Grace would be overjoyed to join us as we spend the day playing backgammon and pressing flowers?"

The sarcastic note in Emily's voice did not escape Glenna; her hands found her hips and her lace cap shook formidably. "Nay! I was thinkin' ya could write to the one ya was callin' out to … the one ya never said nothin' to me about even when I asked ya. To yer Leander, the one — I'm suspectin' — what's caused all this unladylike change in ya."

The two levelled glances at one another, but it was Emily, mindful of the unsettling tick of the mantelshelf clock, who was the first to falter and look away.

2:45 p.m.
Hartwood Hall

MAKING HASTE PER Glenna's stern instructions, Emily pinned up her hair, slipped into the simplest of her new gowns — a scoop-necked muslin frock with mauve satin ribbons hugging the bodice and hem — and set off for the ground-floor parlour: a compact, cosy chamber sandwiched between the south-facing breakfast room and the magnificent book-lined library. She was hopeful of finding Uncle Clarence in a benevolent disposition, so that, if an opportunity arose, she could appeal to him — beg him if she had to — for a respite in town. Surely there could be no harm in such a simple request?

Rather than finding him alone while he awaited her presence, she found him nestled in a plush chair, swirling a glass of wine and deep in conversation with both the duke and duchess. As their voices were all suspiciously low, and not one of them had heard her approach, Emily ducked into the library to watch and listen.

"I've been told that the trial's to be set for early October to allow Mr. Austen time to return to England," said Uncle Clarence. "If he's received his summons and started back home, there's no telling of his exact whereabouts, and, naturally, one never knows how long these ocean crossings may take. If the winds are in his favour, we might expect him back in early September."

"Who is this Mr. Austen?" asked Adolphus, trying to sit forward in his chair.

"He was Captain Moreland's commander. A fine gentleman, I understand … so very capable. I should've carried him back to England with me on the *Impregnable*; however, I had no authority to do so, and his leadership was sorely needed on the American coast, as the Royal Navy continues to be destitute of good men."

"Would his sister, by chance, be the novelist Jane Austen?" asked Helena.

Uncle Clarence beamed. "She is indeed! In fact, I must tell you, on our journey home, Emeline was reading Miss Austen's latest offering, *Pride and Prejudice*, given to her as a parting gift by Mr. Austen. The Prince Regent is quite an admirer of the lady, you know."

From her library corner, her back resting against a shelf of old leather-bound volumes, Emily could not resist a smile. Hearing the name of Fly Austen pulled around her all the excitement of the sea.

"What I don't understand is all this delay," whined Helena. "I figured Trevelyan would've been hanged the moment he set foot on English soil."

"My dear, we're a civilized country, and the man must have a fair trial."

Helena gasped. "What? A traitor must have a fair trial?"

"One never knows what astonishing information may be revealed at a trial," said Adolphus. "Perhaps this man's not as insidious as we all believe."

"Dolly, how can you say such a thing, with all we've heard, all we have been told thus far?"

"That's just it," rejoined Adolphus. "Aside from the facts with which our dear Clarence has been able to supply us, outside accounts of Trevelyan's atrocities may well have been overblown."

"Really, Dolly, you do surprise me!" scolded Helena. "Let's not forget this man was directly responsible for the death of so many, including your eighth son."

"Quite right, quite right," muttered Adolphus, giving his throat a nervous clearing.

"Still, Helena," said Uncle Clarence, "every effort will be made to give the man a fair trial."

There was a brief silence, then Adolphus spoke again. "As you instructed, Clarence, we've been careful not to question your niece on her ordeal, although I fear many of the ball guests were clamouring for delicious details, and may have gone too far in their inquiries. But I do wonder … has she said anything to you about our Octavius?"

"Not a word," Uncle Clarence replied quietly. "It's more than likely she was not acquainted with your son. From what I've been told she was confined to the hospital on the *Isabelle*, and rarely allowed to leave it. But it will be necessary for her to take the stand, for I believe she's witnessed a great deal and has not told me the half of it."

After they refilled their glasses, Helena politely inquired if she could interest the gentleman in sampling an apple tart, one of the excellent few left over from the weekend feast.

"Emeline is well aware her story must be saved for the stand," resumed Uncle Clarence, smacking his lips. "I now expect the prosecuting lawyer to show up here within the next two weeks or so. I'll write to you of his coming, or, if I'm able, I shall bring him myself. He desires to begin gathering evidence, and to read the letter Captain Moreland composed before his death, which Emeline has in her safe possession. But, let me be clear, he must be able to meet with her in a private place. We cannot have the servants listening at the door."

The duke and duchess both murmured their agreement, and gave him their assurances that all would be arranged to his satisfaction.

"As to your other inquiry," continued Uncle Clarence, "the Prince Regent has informed me that he'll do what he can to rush Emeline's annulment through Parliament. Given the circumstances surrounding her liaison with Trevelyan, there should be no impediments, and then we shall be in a position to consider your proposal. The sooner we have her married — legally this time — the sooner we can rest up. Already the Regent and I have spent far too much time on her affairs, although we gladly do so out of respect for our late brother Wessex."

Emily tensed against the bookshelves, hardly daring to breathe.

"You will keep us informed of the progress of the annulment," said Helena.

"I most certainly will, and perhaps, when you hold your next ball, I'll have good news for you," said Uncle Clarence with fervour. "But before I speak my farewell to my niece and take my leave, I must impress upon you the necessity of keeping your eye on her. I was most distressed to see her out in the rain near the main gates."

"I'll see that that does *not* happen again," said Helena with conviction.

"It's a fear of mine," continued Uncle Clarence, "that she may try to escape."

A gruff laugh burst from Adolphus. "Where to? Why? How can she be anything but happy here at Hartwood?"

"It has come to my attention that, whilst on the *Isabelle*, she became exceedingly attached to one of the men. And though I doubt the complete authenticity of my source's recounting, I was told that Emeline planned to … had promised this particular man she'd come back for him the minute she could."

In the library, Emily's lips suppressed her fury.

"Who is this fortunate fellow with whom Emeline is besotted?" asked Adolphus.

"He was the *Isabelle*'s ship doctor, a man named Leander Braden."

Helena's response was rife with derision. "My word! A ship's doctor? I'm afraid, Clarence, your Emeline is a rather senseless girl."

"We'll beat it out of her," Adolphus piped in.

"Yes, when *we* are done with her," said Helena, "she'll have no more thoughts of returning to the sea to her little doctor."

14

Monday, August 16

3:00 p.m.
(Afternoon Watch, Six Bells)
HMS *Amethyst*

PRIOR TO THE HATCHES being secured with battens, Fly Austen and Morgan Evans pulled their way back up to the main decks, both men having seen with their own eyes and therefore been reassured that fresh hands had relieved the pump crews. From the yards, an ominous shriek rose up.

"Man overboard!"

Fly rushed to the starboard rail. "Where? Where is he?"

"I can see him, sir!" pointed Morgan. "Look out from the mainmast."

In no time at all some of the sailors, balancing perilously on the fore chains in order to provide ballast and keep the ship upright, scrambled over the bulwark and, needing no instructions, began hurling whatever they could lay their hands on in the direction of the hapless victim.

"Get anythin' what floats!"

"Careful now, or ya'll fall in yerself."

"Hurry! He can't last long."

"Who's the poor Jack?"

"Must be a landlubber!"

"Nay! 'Tis the little sailmaker! 'Tis Magpie!"

Winded, Fly reached Leander's side when the last words were communicated in dreadful shouts. It did not surprise him to see Leander scramble to his feet, immediately distracted from Meg Kettle, who lay groaning and sprawled out upon the sodden planks of the deck having taken — in her collision with the mainmast — an injury to her abdomen.

Blinking into the turbulent gloom of the sea, Leander gasped. "Not Magpie! Fly, please, tell me it's not Magpie." He did not await confirmation from his friend, instead he sprang into motion, leaving the task of transporting Mrs. Kettle to the hospital — *"With care if you please"* — to Morgan, who stood nearby begging to know how he could be of assistance, and shouted out at the men glued to the rail to keep their sights on Magpie's bobbing head. "Seize anything that's not nailed down. Should the mainmast fall throw it overboard too." Leander hurried aft with Fly — keenly aware of his intentions — close on his heels.

"Lee! Don't even think of going out there."

"I must."

"This is madness!" yelled Fly, trying to grab his arm.

"Aye! It is!" Leander yelled back, shrugging him off.

"It'll be the end of you both."

"We'll come back. The sea — I swear — she's not as furious as she was earlier."

"For God's sake, Lee, you're needed on this ship. Others can go. I'll instruct them —"

"No! This is for me to do."

Fly was finally able to break his friend's reckless stride by seizing his coat tails. "Dr. Braden, I — I forbid it!"

Leander swung around, and for a heated moment the two friends eyed one another in the battering rain. "I must go. I must at least try. Can you honestly tell me you would not enter a burning house to save your children?"

Unnerved by the wild expression in Leander's eyes and the ragged despair in his voice, Fly released his coat and backed off.

"Please ... I beg you ... just help me lower the skiff."

With churning resignation, Fly lifted the master's speaking trumpet to his lips and croaked a call for men to manoeuvre the dangling skiff from its davit on the ship's stern. He had just begun the terrible task of handpicking others to accompany Leander when Biscuit appeared at his side.

"As me rowin' skills is legendary, I'll go with the doctor!" Seeing Mr. Austen's astounded face, Biscuit added, "I ain't just an exalted cook, ya know!"

Leander reached out to give Biscuit a handshake of gratitude. "Bless you."

With the cook now barking the orders, the men — whipped by wind and waves — toiled to control the skiff that wildly swung about with every lurch of the *Amethyst*. All the while they struggled to preserve a toehold on the ship, lest they too became a victim of the sea. Those who were going jumped aboard, and slowly — far too slowly for Leander's gnawing anxiety — the skiff began its interminable descent into the swirling water.

Over the taffrail, a shaken, heartsick Fly called out to his friend. "If — if the boat should overturn, stay with it, or hold fast to an oar. I cannot afford to lose you."

The hysterical cries of the men at the starboard rail, still hurling encouragement and buoyant objects at Magpie, fell beyond earshot as Leander, Biscuit, and three volunteer sailors who were ready to take up the oars, disappeared below the *Amethyst*. Looking up at Fly, whose countenance was wreathed in worry, Leander replied, "And if I lost that little lad, I couldn't live with myself."

3:15 p.m.
In the Atlantic

First Lieutenant Bridlington hooked his arm around one of the lifelines stretched across the quarterdeck and began squawking. "What in hell are they doing? The fools! They'll all be drowned!"

Morgan Evans, who had returned from delivering Meg Kettle to the hospital and placing her in the *incapable* hands of the disconcerted Osmund Brockley, shouted above the howling wind, "That doesn't help the situation any ... sir."

Bridlington's eyes bulged from their sockets. "Mr. Evans, do not forget yourself and your — your uneducated station."

It took every ounce of his discipline for Morgan to ignore the officer's contempt. His eyes remained fixed upon Magpie — who appeared as inconsequential as a breadcrumb on the wardroom table — and on the progress of the skiff which, tossed upon those mountainous swells, seemed so helpless.

All the horror and pain of Mr. Alexander's drowning off the coast of North Carolina once again overwhelmed Morgan's agitated mind. That day, more than two months ago, when he and Mr. Alexander had fallen from the yards of the *Isabelle* in a hurricane, he had come so very close to drowning and it was impossible to forget those dreadful moments, panicking for air, the terrifying darkness of the water, and the awful awareness that life was about to end. The very thought that poor Magpie was being tortured thus made Morgan physically sick.

It was doubtful the boy could swim, but somehow ... somehow he was managing to stay afloat — one wave tearing him further away from the ship, another conveying him closer again. The Amethysts had thrown all kinds of objects into the sea — including several capstan pawls and pieces of a scuttlebutt that had been stoved in by the oppressive waves — praying fervently that one of them would be swept within reach of him. So far their efforts had failed.

Though he longed to go into hiding below deck to steady his nerves, Morgan fought the urge to do so, and demanded of his sore lungs to continue hollering support. "That's it, Magpie! Keep your arms up! Don't fight the waves — let them carry you. Dr. Braden's coming for you. He's coming for you, and he'll be there soon."

Meanwhile, at his back, Bridlington railed on, squawking like a chicken about to be cooked in a pot of boiling water. "Dr. Braden's a fool. Mr. Austen should never have allowed him to leave the ship. Doesn't he know we need the doctor's services? Who'll tend to my hand should he drown? It hasn't healed yet, you know. And yet, we've no use for that young sailmaker, especially since he only has one eye. The boy is ten years old! He has no parents, no living relatives, who then will ever miss a trifling *mite* such as —"

Morgan's eyes blazed murderously. Flouncing away from the starboard rail, his trembling fist shot out with the speed and force of fired grapeshot and smashed into Bridlington's face, sending the shocked lieutenant tripping and flailing backward before landing in a pathetic heap on the same spot whereupon Mrs. Kettle had previously been slumped in agony. Before Bridlington was even cognizant of his injuries, Morgan could see the ruin he had inflicted. Though the driving rain dashed away much of the gore, Bridlington's mouth was a blackened, blood-filled hole.

In his baffled state, the first lieutenant tried to grab the lifeline to pull him into a sitting position, and once he had managed to do so he sat gathering his wits, alternately hiding his wound with his arm and spitting out mouthfuls of blood. A horrified look leapt into his eyes when he realized more than blood was being spit out upon the deck.

"My teeth! You've broken my teeth!" His scream was garbled. "You're a fool, Mr. Evans, a damn fool. I'll have you punished most severely for this. I'll have you hanged, drawn, and quartered for this … this … this devilry!" He swivelled his messy face around to scan the buckling decks. "Mr. Austen? Mr. Austen! At once, Mr. Austen, order the doctor to return to the ship. I've been violated in a most atrocious manner."

The queasiness in Morgan's belly intensified. He began shaking. Flexing his painful hand — the one that had wreaked the damage — he dragged himself back to the sorrowful scenes beyond the railing.

Magpie's little head was no longer visible in that immense sea.

3:15 p.m.
In the Atlantic

ABOVE THE DIN OF the storm, and despite the salty water unremittingly oppressing his ears, Magpie was certain he could hear Mr. Evans calling out to him, though he hadn't a clue what he was saying. One minute Magpie found himself turned toward the *Amethyst*, full of hope, for he was cheered to see the men at the rail waving to him and hurling buckets and barrels at him with all their might, the very next he was spun around, facing an endless, nightmarish landscape of watery hills he had not the energy to scale. The ocean moved in such strange ways, surely its humps and rolls meant the lurking presence of great whales and saw-toothed sharks that would, any second now, swallow him whole or tear off his legs. The blackness beneath him, which boiled and frothed up like a cauldron of Biscuit's soup, contained terrifying secrets, and if it wasn't a shark that intended to swim off with his parts, he imagined the grey, grasping hands of drowned sailors, dragging him down into their dark place. Was this the same agony the Duke of Clarence's son had felt as his ship had foundered in the Indian Ocean, near the coast of Madagascar — that far-off place that struck such sinister fear in Magpie?

He kicked off his shoes, praying a meal of leather would satisfy the ocean beasts, and tried calming himself, allowing the waves to carry him where they would. He did not possess the strength to fight his way back to the ship, and if the blinding waves would only cease breaking over his one eye, he might be able to tell whether the boat coming toward him was filled with rescuers, or if the storm had simply knocked her free of the ship. But it was so hard to stay calm when he felt as if he were falling into a deep, cavernous hole where his mates would never ever find him.

Sputtering and fighting for air while the ocean thrashed him about, Magpie could only pray someone would soon deliver him from this ghastly evil. If he allowed himself to think of Emily, sitting in her London castle, receiving news that the little sailmaker was lying in a lonely grave on the ocean's mucky bottom, he was sure he would cry, and crying would only steal further from his waning store of strength.

"Magpie!"

The voice roused him. It was nearer. Rolling his head about, he was sure he could see faces through the sheets of seawater. But these faces were not on the ship; they seemed to be walking on the waves. How could that be?

"Magpie, if you can, swim to that length of timber. It's so close to you."

It sounded so very much like Dr. Braden.

"Ach, lad! Hold on, hold on!"

And was that Biscuit? Or was he dreaming? Had he already drowned perhaps, and these were the peaceful, familiar voices that would transport him from this world into the next? Would Emily suddenly appear and come forward to take him by the hand and lead him into that strange new land? Shivering, for the sea was growing colder by the minute, Magpie closed his eye and waited for her to come, thinking, if she did come to him now, maybe dying wasn't so bad after all.

Something began tugging on his shirt. Grasping hands! Were these the dreaded drowned sailors? Nay! The hands weren't pulling him downward, they were lifting him up. Muffled, frantic voices jostled in his waterlogged ears. But he felt disembodied, as if he were drifting away, and could not see what it was that had a precarious hold upon him. Something large brushed and bumped his back, wrenching him away from the hands. But then other hands seemed to be grabbing for him.

Again he was bumped, this time by a powerful moving force. He was certain he heard Dr. Braden cry out in dismay, "Dear God!" Up shot Magpie, carried forward and around and around. Was it a whirlpool? Magpie hardly cared. He could do nothing to save himself. On and on it kept pulling him, making him dizzy, until — at last — he felt a foundation beneath his legs, and came to an abrupt stop when his head struck an unyielding object.

And then he knew no more.

15

Wednesday, August 18

10:00 a.m.
Hartwood Hall

SMILING TO HERSELF, Emily closed her book, rose from the bench beneath the shady arms of the chestnut tree, and ambled toward the two-storey bricked edifice of the service wing that sprawled across the land to the northeast of Hartwood Hall, its earthy, purple-brown colouring inconspicuous next to the gleaming whiteness of the house. Feeling quite at home, Emily entered the high-ceilinged kitchen with its five sash windows — opened to admit any and all breezes — and with interest observed the activity that abounded within its roomy perimeter.

Dressed in starched white aprons and caps, a dozen servants were arranged around two massive square-topped tables in the middle of the stone floor, kneading dough or furiously beating on bowls while they gossiped with one another. On the right-hand wall stretched the black-iron range, stewing stoves, spits, and baking ovens, with their copper awnings that sent the excess heat and odours out the windows, all in use and steaming, and overseen by the perspiring cook, who barked instructional orders to her troop of assistants. Opposite the coal-fired ovens were deep porcelain sinks overflowing with soiled pots, pans, dishes, and utensils, and attended by two young scullery maids who laughed at a private joke as they went about their washing and drying. Noticing

Emily standing in their midst, they ceased their scouring, kneading, beating, and basting, stared at her open-mouthed a moment, and then quickly curtsied.

"Good morning to all of you," said Emily cheerfully. "Thank you so very much for the delicious breakfast."

Their glistening faces rippled with surprise and again they curtsied.

"Is there a special dinner planned for this evening? You all seem to be so busy."

It was the cook who finally found her tongue. "No, Yer Royal Highness, it's just an ordinary day fer all o' us."

All this effort, thought Emily, *for the few who sat, three times a day, around the breakfast and dining tables in the big house, far from the smells and heat and bustle of this quarter.* "I don't suppose I could help you, could I?"

They gave one another sidelong glances, knowing not how to answer her, and then looked to the cook for guidance, though she too seemed quite at a loss.

"I'm sorry," Emily said quickly, hoping to lessen their discomfort. "Perhaps one of you could tell me the whereabouts of Miss McCubbin?"

Before anyone could say a word, Glenna materialized from the adjoining laundry room, in her plain brown dress, her arms piled high with freshly folded sheets. Seeing Emily she stopped short, and with a quick flutter of one linen-bound hand signalled to her to follow her out of the kitchen and into the courtyard.

Reluctant to leave all the excitement, Emily gave the servants a wistful smile and pledged to pop round another time.

"The service wing is off limits to ya, Pet," asserted Glenna when they were safely beyond the eyes and ears of the kitchen staff.

"For heaven's sake, Glenna!"

"They'll all be cluckin' away in there now. They ain't never seen the duchess stop in fer a wee chit-chat."

"I was hoping one of the bakers could teach me to make bread and cakes. I remember as a child I was once allowed to knead the bread dough, though I was forbidden to mix the ingredients together."

"Are ya bein' facetious agin?"

Emily grabbed Glenna's arm. "I would truly love it!"

"'Tis no place fer King George's granddaughter," said Glenna, reinforcing her declaration with a stern bob of her head.

"Would it just be best for all if I kept to my room?"

"Might be a sight easier," sighed the old housekeeper, setting off on the south-facing path toward the house. Again she stopped short, this time to give Emily a sizing up. "And why is it ya have on *that* gown agin when ya have three new ones to yer name?"

Emily ran her hand along the sleeve of her cherished blue-and-white-striped dress, but remained tight-lipped.

"Before ya come to the luncheon table, be sure to change to satisfy Her Grace." Glenna trudged on. "Now, what is it ya need from me?"

"I wondered if the mail had come."

"It has."

"Was there anything for me?"

"Lud, Pet! I don't rifle the mail, I just hand it off to Her Grace." Glenna's eyes narrowed. "Ya weren't expectin' somethin' that quick from yer sea friends, were ya?"

"I was hoping to receive a note from Mr. Walby in Winchester."

"And would this Mr. Walby's given name be *Leander*?" asked Glenna, cocking her head to one side.

"No, his name is Augustus ... Gus Walby," she replied steadily, unwilling to oblige Glenna's itch for information. "He's the young midshipman who was badly injured on the *Isabelle* ... the one who came home with Uncle Clarence and me. I believe I mentioned him to you. Almost immediately upon my return to *consciousness* after landing in on your doorstep, I wrote to him to let him know my address. That was several days ago; I did think I would hear from him before now."

"Well, the mail ain't always very reliable. I'm sure ya'll hear from the lad soon enough." Alerted to approaching footsteps on the pathway, Glenna's face broke into smiles. "Since yer letter writin' ain't very successful, and I'll not have ya bakin' cakes with the servants, here now ... here's a bit o' entertainment fer ya."

The housekeeper hurried off with her laundry, leaving Emily alone to greet Somerton.

10:20 a.m.

OUTFITTED IN HIS RIDING GEAR, Somerton stood there awkwardly, his gaze at first unable to meet Emily's eyes. She wondered if his uncharacteristic diffidence had anything to do with the conversation she had overheard the other day between his parents and her uncle. Why they had been practically congratulating one another in their collusion to have her married again — *legally this time*, of course. The niggling memory of it caused Emily to be trifling in her manner.

"I didn't expect you home so soon."

"Oh! Why is that?"

"Fleda told me you were staying in town for a week."

"Ah! Well! It was best I didn't overstay my welcome."

"Were you unable to pick a bride from amongst your host's many daughters?"

Somerton reddened under the hot August sun. "Did Fleda tell you I was off in search of a bride?"

"She told me something to that effect!" Emily looked longingly in the direction of the wooded walk on the western acres of the parkland, shimmering on the meadow like a welcome desert oasis. "It's so humid out. Shall we?"

"I would like that," said Somerton, settling in at her side. "The truth is … I was going to suggest we go for a walk."

"You look as if you're preparing to take a ride this morning."

"I am, but it can wait 'til later."

As they entered the invigorating woods, Emily said, "And so … are you?"

Somerton appeared puzzled. "I am sorry … am I what, Emeline?"

"Seeking to find for yourself a bride?"

He took his time in replying. "Not at the moment, no."

"Well, when you are ready to begin your search, it might benefit you to know, while seeking a breath of fresh air in the early hours of Sunday morning, I overheard several young ladies squabbling over which one of them was most *worthy* of you." Emily leaned in toward him. "Bravo, Lord Somerton! It seems you have secured for yourself several admirers."

Somerton gave a nervous sort of laugh.

"Tell me, was there one in particular that you fancied above the others?

If so, do describe her to me, for I'm quite sure I can still recall all the young ladies who were in attendance at the ball."

His smile was guarded. "Is everyone so anxious to see me married off?"

"I've no idea. Are they?"

They strolled along in silence, Emily at ease as she admired the sun shadows that pierced the canopy of trees, hoping she might spot another magpie amongst the tangled branches, while Somerton, a particular stiffness in his stride, kept those dark, close-set eyes of his fixed upon the path. It was only once they had stopped to greet the ducks, paddling serenely on the glass surface of one of Hartwood's ponds — Emily wished she had a crust of bread to offer them — that he spoke again, only now on a new subject.

"The book you're carrying … what is it?"

She showed him its leather-bound front cover.

"*A System of Surgery?*" he cried.

"Written by the eminent practitioner, Benjamin Bell."

"Volume one!" he cried again.

"Were you expecting Mrs. Radcliffe's *Mysteries of Udolpho?*" she asked with enhanced formality.

"I was hardly expecting a book on surgery," spluttered Somerton.

Emily refused to be put off by his astonishment. "I was so pleased to find a number of medical books in your well-stocked library. Do you have a doctor in the family?"

"My grandfather had a great passion for medicine. It was a hobby of his." He frowned. "Are you planning to perform surgeries on us all while you're here?"

"I was hoping, should you fall from your horse or be shot accidentally while hunting for grouse, you might allow me to further my knowledge by practising upon you."

"You cannot be serious!"

"Oh, but I am! When I leave here, when the dark cloud of this looming trial has passed over, I plan to seek permission from my family to take up the study of medicine."

"You … you do mean midwifery, do you not?"

"No! I do not."

Somerton stole a glance at her. "Your family may have other plans for you."

"I am certain they do."

"And if they do not heed your wishes?"

"I shall strike out on my own."

"I've never heard of a woman doctor before." There was no enthusiasm whatsoever in his voice; in fact, Emily was certain she detected an undertone of agitation.

"If one does not already exist in England, then I shall be the first," she said, hugging the book to her breast.

"The knowledge you already possess ... I'm guessing it was acquired while you were at sea."

"It was."

"I believe you have seen things that no woman should ever have to see."

"Nor any man, but gangrenous limbs, brutal amputations, and festering gun wounds are common realities to some of your countrymen; at least, I know they are for those who serve England on the Atlantic."

"You actually witnessed amputations?"

"I did, and worse," she said quietly.

"I cannot imagine anything worse than an amputation."

Octavius Lindsay's last moments flashed before Emily's eyes.

Unaware of her abhorrent thoughts, Somerton paused beside a flourishing rhododendron bush and planted his boots in the gravel to observe her closely. "Wouldn't you like to have a family, Emeline?"

"I would, very much," she replied, stooping to smell the dusky-yellow flowers. "But not right now, and not with my present husband."

"Of course not," he concurred. "But don't you think your family will try to make an advantageous marriage for you once you're free from Trevelyan?"

"They shall try, I'm sure of it. I am not, however, going to be forced to marry Mr. Gribble." She arranged her features to convey mock horror. "Is my family, unbeknownst to me, hoping I will marry Mr. Gribble and be *whisked* away to his country seat?"

"Not to my knowledge," Somerton answered soberly, impervious to her jesting. "Although I do believe Mr. Gribble himself was hoping to secure your affections the other night."

"The man is in his sixties!"

"Yes, and he has quite an assembly of young children at home."

"Then he needs to hire a governess. The man has no business to come fishing for a young wife."

When Somerton seemed unwilling to prolong the topic of Mr. Gribble they resumed walking, the pathway through the woods now leading them back toward the house, which gleamed like a full moon against its backdrop of summer greenery. Emily studied his profile, only to find his mind seemingly hard at work.

"If you were to find a younger husband," he began slowly, "one who was well connected and could offer you protection and all the fruits of life, would you give up this notion ... this hope of yours to study medicine?"

"I would not," she said resolutely. "I do not require connections, nor to be protected, and as far as I am concerned I shall not find the *fruits of life* on a country estate nor in a fashionable townhouse in Mayfair."

Somerton's eyes widened. "It's only your youth, your idealism speaking, Emeline."

"Oh! Is it? Do tell."

"We all hope for a life that is not within our grasp when we are eighteen," he said, assuming a preachy tone. "You women all have such imaginations. Soon — you'll see — soon you'll be more concerned about your dinner guests, and how many children you have in the nursery, and the receiving of a new ball gown will throw you into an impassioned level of excitement." Somerton spoke so evenly, he could have no idea of the effect his words would have on her.

"Will it?" she hissed.

"I'm sure of it."

"The women with whom you are acquainted, are they all like-minded?"

"I would say so. You women are all the same. Quite uncomplicated, I find."

"Perhaps you should leave your estate more often, Lord Somerton."

"I beg your pardon?"

"I am younger than you, by at least ten years, I believe, and yet already experience has taught me that not all men are the same. Their thinking, their motives can be quite diverse. Why not say the same about the female sex?"

"I'm afraid my experience with your sex has not taught me otherwise."

"How long have *we* been acquainted?" asked Emily, an edge surfacing in her voice.

"A week or so."

"Can you really come to know a person in a single week?"

"No, I suppose not."

"Then, please, do not presume that parties and ball gowns will become the sum total of *my* existence."

She brushed past him to return to the place by the southwest corner of the house where they had begun their walk, and only when he had arrived there himself did she bother to square off with him one last time.

"Thank you for the exercise," she said tersely. "It was most refreshing."

His earlier diffidence having vanished, he glared down at her; the contemptuous expression flickering on his face so eerily similar to his youngest brother, it startled Emily. With a prim bow of his head he strode off toward the stables, but not before uttering a few final harshly-spoken words.

"Yes, and the conversation most enlightening, though I fear for you, Emeline. I fear you shall end up *bitterly* disappointed."

16

Thursday, August 19

11:00 a.m.
Winchester

GUS LAY STILL IN HIS lumpy cot and cocked his ears to the sounds that reached the mullioned window of his attic room. There was a clip-clop on the cobbles of the backyard, followed by children squealing with delight and a kindly voice conveying words of greeting. At last, the doctor had come! Gus had been so hopeful he would visit today, for a whole week had passed since his last visit and feeling poorly as Gus was, Aunt Sophia was rapidly losing patience with what she termed *his refusal* to help her round the farm. At the very least, he needed the doctor to confirm the validity of his illness.

Hearing the old man's slow footsteps approaching on the steep stairs, Gus anxiously studied the boundaries of his attic room. It was low ceilinged and so narrow there was space for nothing beyond his cot and a small chest of drawers. Where would the doctor sit as they visited? And was the money still laid out upon the top of the chest in the event he was carrying a surprise for him? Sitting up to reassure himself the three pence were still there — that Aunt Sophia or one of his little cousins had not already snatched them up — Gus was settling back under his frayed counterpane when the doctor's smiling face appeared in the doorway.

"What's all this, Mr. Walby?" he asked, setting his leather bag and broad-brimmed hat down upon the bare floor. "Your cousins told me you were not at all well."

"I haven't been well for the past two days, sir," said Gus. "I've been feeling achy all over, and I have a cough that hurts my chest, and I don't have much energy to help Aunt Sophia."

"I was most pleased with your progress a week back. What've you been up to since then?" he admonished with an inquiring frown. When Gus, uncertain of how much to tell him of Aunt Sophia's demands and expectations, did not answer right away, the doctor nodded his head and said, "Let me have a look at you."

Gus shifted over in his cot to make room for the doctor to sit down, which he did, immediately reaching for Gus's wrist.

"My goodness, Mr. Walby, your heart is pounding so rapidly I can barely count the beats." With the palm of his hand he felt Gus's neck and then his forehead. "You're a bit feverish. Then again, it is stiflingly hot up here."

"I'm anxious, sir."

"Why is that?"

Gus's words tumbled from his mouth. "Well, I was hoping maybe you had a letter for me."

The doctor compressed his lips. "I don't; I'm sorry."

Sadly, Gus gazed at the three pence upon his chest of drawers. Aunt Sophia would surely find them before he ever had a chance to give them to the doctor in exchange for the long-awaited letter. It was a wonder he'd been able to keep them away from her for so long.

"I don't understand, sir," Gus said, trying hard not to choke up. "She said ... she said she would write straightaway to let me know where she was."

"Perhaps she's been visiting with various members of her family, and therefore has not yet any permanence in address."

"I hadn't thought of that."

"I'm certain I shall find a letter awaiting you the next time I go to Winchester," he assured Gus.

"I do hope so. I've been so afraid that something awful has happened to her."

"With everything you've told me about your friend, Emily, I'm further certain she can take care of herself. The dangers on English roads are nothing compared to the dangers one must face on the sea."

"Do you worry about your son on the sea, sir?"

"Yes! Every day! But he's a grown man, and a most capable one."

"That he is, sir." Gus looked up admiringly at the doctor, who was so deep in thought and gentle with his poking and prodding. How fortunate he was to have the father of Leander Braden taking care of him. Emily had come so close to meeting the man that day the Duke of Clarence had brought them to this house. Would he ever have the chance to tell her of the coincidence? "Have you received any letters from your son, sir?"

"Not for a very long while. However, I do understand these things. My older brother was a sailor with a merchantman that sailed all over the world," he said proudly. "Three years after he was drowned off the coast of Bermuda, my family received word of it."

"Three years? How awful!"

"Apparently the ship carrying word of his merchantman going down was lost in a storm. It's a wonder my poor parents ever learned the fate of their eldest son at all." He paused to give Gus a pensive smile. "That is why I've been so grateful to hear what you've been able to tell me of *my* son, and to know that he survived the sinking of the *Isabelle* and his incarceration at the hands of Thomas Trevelyan. I will admit, knowing you had sailed with him was the reason I so readily agreed to take you on as a patient."

"Did the Duke of Clarence know your relationship to young Dr. Braden when he retained you, sir?

"I think not. The message came to me by other means. I just happened to be in Winchester when the word went out that Master Walby, recently of HMS *Isabelle*, was in need of medical services." The doctor placed his hands on his knees and stiffly stood up. "Now, I must go downstairs to speak with your Aunt Sophia."

"Am I going to die, sir?"

"Not today, Mr. Walby," he laughed, "but I believe that your symptoms may be relieved if we try bloodletting —"

"Not with leeches, please, sir, I couldn't stomach those horrid things."

"No, I'll try making a small cut in your arm, and then perhaps a poultice will help for your chest infection." Old Dr. Braden glanced at the open attic door. "I do wonder how it is you manage all the steps with that leg of yours."

"It hurts climbing up every night, sir, and it takes me a while, but I think it's helping to strengthen me."

"Good! Now, I'll need your Aunt's help in preparing the poultice and locating a bowl for me. And while I'm down there I think I'll have a chat with her about easing your workload."

"Oh, she won't like that. She already thinks I'm a burden to her, and not good for anything."

"Well," he said firmly, "if she has a problem with the arrangement I'll pack you up and take you back to Steventon with me."

Gus's pale face lit up. "Would you, sir?"

"I just might. Now, I'll be right back to fix you up." At the attic door he turned around to beam at Gus, in a way that suggested he had a wonderful secret to divulge. "Let's write a letter directly to the Duke of Clarence at Bushy House, and see if he will tell us where Emily is lodging."

"Oh, thank you, I would like that." Gus tried to sit up, thinking this was as good a time as any. "And sir? There's — there's something else I've been meaning to tell you about your son. And just in case you don't receive a letter from him for three years, I'd like to tell you now."

Old Dr. Braden looked drawn all of a sudden. "Do you have bad news for me?"

"Oh, no, sir, I think you will find it is the *best* of news."

There came a great sigh of relief. "Thank goodness," he said, returning swiftly to Gus's cot. "In that case, you must tell me now. The poultice can wait."

Gus snuggled back under his counterpane while old Dr. Braden settled in at the end of his bed, and as he started in on his story he happily imagined the look of shocked surprise that would surely seize the doctor's face when he informed him that his son loved a princess.

Noon
On a Prison Hulk in Portsmouth Harbour

THOMAS TREVELYAN SHUFFLED around the rotting fo'c'sle of what was once HMS *Illustrious*. Regardless of the fact that he now possessed a pair of shoes — or rather, thick pieces of wood strapped to his feet — the open wounds on his soles had not yet healed, and stabbing pains still aggravated his legs where, some weeks back, they had been assaulted by a miniature, dirk-wielding mongrel.

"Keep moving! That's it! And give praise to the Lord for the sliver of space that allows you fresh air and exercise. Anywhere else … anywhere else and your emaciated faces would be pasted to the walls, and your noses in one another's armpits," taunted the lieutenant-in-command, a slovenly fellow who rested his thick haunches on the old capstan as he bellowed his palaver. Trevelyan was convinced the hapless man had been sent here to oversee the hollow-eyed beings on this forsaken prison hulk as a form of punishment for some naval misdemeanour: having falsified the muster books, or committed an act of insubordination, or sodomized one of the ship's beasts — a goat perhaps. Despite his unkempt appearance the lieutenant was a sight better than the others who commanded the prisoners, among them a bloated master's mate, a one-armed cook, twelve old seamen, and four ragged boys. In addition there was a more formidable-looking guard of soldiers, thirty in all, who manned the sentry huts and the gallery built along the water's edge, but only because of the loaded muskets they carried.

As he plodded along, Trevelyan's hooded gaze drifted toward the smoking, dismantled hulks moored in a line in the Portsmouth Harbour, at the mouth of the Portchester River. He had been told that they housed prisoners of war, rounded up from vanquished merchantmen and warships over the endless years of fighting Napoleon and France. Grilles of thick cast iron covered gunports, and where white sails had once billowed tattered laundry now stirred in the light breeze. Blackened walls rose ever higher from the weather decks to accommodate a disarray of rough-hewn cabins and sheds, and to separate the prisoners from those assigned to watch over them. It was hard to imagine those forlorn hulks ever having proudly circumnavigated the globe for England. In comparison, those on HMS *Illustrious* were fortunate indeed, only recently had she become a prison ship, and as yet her hideous transformation was not complete. But with boatloads of new prisoners arriving daily, forced at gunpoint along the sea-level platforms constructed all around her and up her rickety steps, it was only a matter of time.

Twitch caught up to him. The man was always hanging around, though Trevelyan had no idea why, for none of the other prisoners had ever said a word to him and therefore seemed ignorant of his name and history. What little information Trevelyan had on Twitch had been supplied by the man himself: he had been born Asa Bumpus in New Bedford, been seized from an American privateer, and subsequently considered unfit for His Majesty's service. It was no wonder. His unfortunate frame convulsed whenever he spoke, as if he had developed the *itch* or had a most urgent need to visit the privy. Balancing on yardarms or heaving barrels upon his back would have proven impossible for the man, hence his transportation to this hellhole, anchored like a colossal wooden coffin in the harbour's mud.

Trevelyan gave Twitch an apathetic glance. "I see you've acquired a new hat."

"Won it gamblin' from some poor naked bastard, who had nothin' — no hammock, no blanket or bed — 'cept for this here tricorne," said Twitch, whose smile revealed two lines of broken teeth, the result of an old game of cards that had ended badly.

"You could have suggested he wear his hat on other parts of his body besides his head," said Trevelyan.

"He'll be naked fer awhile yet. It'll be months before they'll be givin' him another yellow round-about jacket and pantaloons."

Trevelyan was only too happy to have sold off his provision of prisoners' clothing — the coarse, tight-fitting, tawny-coloured inferior rags that distinguished those trapped in miserable captivity — within days of his arrival on the *Illustrious*. Most of the men, shuffling with him, were dressed thus, but not all; and what did it matter when it was plainly evident who was a prisoner and who was not?

"Perhaps you should cease your preying upon those who've no clothes with which to cover themselves up."

Twitch ignored Trevelyan's admonishment to parade before him, very nearly tripping him up. "Got me a new coat too. What d'ya think o' it?"

Stifling his annoyance, Trevelyan replied, "It doesn't fit you properly. It's much too big."

"Right! But ain't it fine? It's velvet to be sure." Twitch lifted up the hem of his coat and caressed the material as if it were the hand of a lady.

"It is far too hot to be wearing a coat of velvet."

"Just what the poor bastard I stole it from said to me."

"You stole it?"

"Aye! Heard him complainin' 'bout the heat, so I filched it last night whilst he slept. Overheard someone askin' him this mornin' where his coat had got to, and he said, *'What coat? I've never owned a coat in me life.'* I tell ya, the man's brain is out o' order. They say he's been livin' on prison hulks fer four years all told."

"That explains it," said Trevelyan dryly, taking sudden note of a group of official-looking men, outfitted in a variety of uniforms, boarding the hulk. They walked about on deck with an aggressive stride, presumably meant to intimidate, and shoved aside those prisoners who faltered in their way. When all eight of them had stepped on board, they sought out the insignificant lieutenant-in-command.

"Ya should try gamblin' with me some time," suggested Twitch.

"I prefer to keep my clothes, thank you."

"Come winter, think o' the pretty price this coat'll fetch."

"Come winter, I don't intend to be here."

Twitch guffawed, his unfortunate mouth thrown to one side of his face as he did so. "Right! Now, if ya was to take up gamblin', and wagered yer captain's breeches and shirt, ya might get yerself a decent supply o' tobacco and enough burgoo and turnip to fill yer belly, though it be a shame ya no longer have yer jacket."

Trevelyan did not answer straightaway, having been distracted by a new commotion and an order to *"make way."* The ship's company of boys was removing two skeletal corpses from the hulk, bound in their filthy hammocks, their eyes and mouths still open in a ghastly grimace. They should have been transported to the hospital ship in the harbour long ago; instead, their illnesses were ignored. As he followed the boys' weaving and bobbing through the prisoners, Trevelyan silently cursed his circumstances.

The slovenly lieutenant had told him he would soon be transported to Newgate, but that with its overcrowding and the daily influx of new prisoners there would be a delay. "Be thankful," he had jeered, "the sooner you get there, the sooner they'll hang you." *Surely*, thought Trevelyan, *there was some living relation of his who would soon learn of his whereabouts and send money, or see to his being paroled in a nearby town.* He was an officer, not a common seaman, and despite the list of offences mounted against him, he was — he believed — still eligible for parole. If he stayed here much longer, he would die. They were carrying out the dead at an alarming rate, not surprising when pestilence raged in every crevice of the hulk, and the air was so fetid below deck some had suffocated to death.

Finally, he responded to Twitch, no hint of his anxiety in his evenly spoken tone. "Sidle over to those men who just came aboard and find out what their business is with the lieutenant."

Without questioning his mission, Twitch set off, elbowing his way to the capstan, around which the newcomers stood in their discussions. Wincing in pain with every step, Trevelyan pressed on with his exercise, looking back over his shoulder at every opportunity to observe Twitch's progress. The simpleton had flattened his meagre body against the bulwark, behind the carriage of a dormant six-pounder broadside gun — the only gun still on the fo'c'sle deck — to do his eavesdropping. The official men, so absorbed in conversation, seemed oblivious to the pathetic humanity limping around them.

In no time at all, the eavesdropper returned.

"What's all that about?" demanded Trevelyan.

"They're plannin' to move a bunch o' us, split us up between the hulks, some to Chatham on the Medway; the French to Portchester Castle, and some to that new prison at Dartmoor."

"When?"

"All's they said was within the week."

Trevelyan acknowledged his findings with a nod. "Anything else?"

Twitch's crooked smile spread slowly across his face. "I believe yer one o' the ones they're movin'."

"Why is that?"

"They're sendin' some to Newgate in London!" he chuckled.

Trevelyan was careful not to show his alarm. Twitch obviously knew more about him than he had suspected. Did the others as well? They carried on around the deck, Twitch chattering about the number of prisoners that had perished during his brief captivity on the *Illustrious*, relishing his own graphic descriptions of their fatal maladies, while Trevelyan, his mind miles away and racing like the clouds overhead in the summer sky, eyed the simpleton's newly acquired velvet coat and tricorne.

17

Thursday, August 19

1:00 p.m.
(Afternoon Watch, Two Bells)
Aboard HMS *Amethyst*

WHEN HIS EYE OPENED upon the day, Magpie was relieved and grateful to find himself at home, in the warmth of the *Amethyst's* hospital. Mr. Austen was standing tall next to his hammock, the brass buttons on his uniform coat reflecting sunshine, and Osmund Brockley was hovering nearby, his tongue hanging out of his mouth as usual, his hands clasped around a bowl of steaming gruel. Magpie kept his eye fixed on the kindly face of Mr. Austen, determined not to dispense any notice at all to Meg Kettle, who filled the hammock next to him — probably shirking her chores and faking illness — her features all contorted in a sour expression as she mouthed the words "Maggot Pie!"

"How's the head?" asked Mr. Austen, blinking down at him.

Feeling tenderness near his left ear, Magpie's probing fingers landed on a bump the size of a quail's egg. "How'd I get this?"

"You don't remember?"

Magpie's face wore a frown until he caught his breath in remembrance. "I were in the sea, and gettin' tired and cold, and waitin' for Emily to come."

"EMILY?" cackled Meg with glee. "Yer a daft one, all right!"

"Hush!" cried Fly. "Mr. Brockley, fetch Mrs. Kettle her breakfast this instant; her tongue requires occupation." Fly relieved Osmund of his bowl of gruel and handed it to Magpie. "Now then, tell me why you were waiting for Emily?"

"I thought I were dyin', sir. I thought she might be comin' to take me to the other place."

"Well, you're very much alive, Magpie, and if we're to keep you that way, you must eat something. You've been lying here for a few days, and each time you came to we weren't able to get you to swallow more than a spoonful of soup." There was a melancholy cast in Mr. Austen's eyes that Magpie didn't like to see, and his smile was inordinately solicitous.

Magpie sat upright with his bowl. "How'd I get back on the ship, sir?"

Mr. Austen folded his arms across his chest. "Ah! Would you believe a leviathan wave? It swept you up and, like a barrel, rolled you right back to us. You landed in on the quarterdeck, whereupon you knocked your head about, but you returned to us safely, for which we are *all* most thankful."

In response to Mr. Austen's declaration there came a snarling sound from Mrs. Kettle's hammock, like a pack of dogs fighting over a chunk of meat, its owner trying but failing to exasperate Magpie, who was so happy to feel the gruel warming his empty stomach and to have the momentous presence of the commander at his bedside. Turning his back to Mrs. Kettle, Magpie silently thanked the stars for his safe return. On the deck above the hospital the air was infused with the steady banging of hammers and carefree voices. Sunshine poured in through the open gunports, and the *Amethyst* was travelling on a tranquil sea. Osmund Brockley, who was never one to work quietly, stepped lightly about on the floor planks and, once he had secured food for Mrs. Kettle, wordlessly tended to the bruised head of a third patient. In the centre of the hospital, sun shadows danced upon Dr. Braden's desk, empty except for the locked writing box, which Morgan Evans had knocked together for him in Halifax. Though Magpie felt a sense of well-being, free from the terrors of the stormy sea, something unpleasant began to prick at his waterlogged brain.

Mr. Austen stepped closer to his bed, clasping his hands behind his back. It gave Magpie a pain in the pit of his stomach to see Mr. Austen looking very drawn, like a sail deprived of its driving wind. He wondered if he was going to say something more to him, perhaps question him further on his experiences alone in the big ocean, but a step on the hospital ladder diverted the man's attention. It was Morgan, pulling the woolly thrum cap from his head, shifting nervously from foot to foot. Magpie beamed at him, so glad he was to see him, and yet Morgan did not, would not, look his way.

"Excuse me, sir, Captain Prickett wishes to speak with you. He asked that you come straightaway."

Spying Mr. Evans, Mrs. Kettle started in her hammock. "What's all this? Yer still about? I woulda thought ya'd been clapped in irons by now fer all yer mischief."

In bewilderment, Magpie's eye hopped from the carpenter to the commander and back again.

"I don't suppose," muttered Mr. Austen, raising his hand to silence the laundress, "you know what he wishes to see me about, do you, Mr. Evans?"

"I have an idea, sir, but I don't like to say," Morgan replied, his eyes never leaving Mr. Austen.

"I'll come. In the meantime, may I ask … could you stay a while with Magpie? Maybe take him above deck when he has eaten … if he feels strong enough to take some fresh air? I haven't yet had a chance to … I was about to, but —"

Morgan's reply was swift. "Aye, sir. I will, sir."

Without a parting word or glance, Mr. Austen hurried from the hospital. Magpie's heart pounded in his chest as he waited for Morgan to locate a stool and carry it to the side of his bed away from Mrs. Kettle.

"What's happened, sir?" he asked in a frightened whisper. "Why should ya be clapped in irons? And why … why is Mr. Austen so aggrieved?"

There were tears working in the corner of Morgan's eyes when he finally lifted them to Magpie. "When you were in the sea," he whispered, "five men set out in the skiff to get you. You came back, all on your own, but *they* couldn't reach the *Amethyst*, and *we* couldn't steer her toward them."

A stone dropped in Magpie. He remembered … those familiar voices that had called out to him over the howling wind, so close to where he was fighting for his life, and those strong, comforting hands grabbing for him … latching onto his shirt just as the wave came … the one that had wrenched him away …

He looked up at Morgan to await the final answer.

"I'm afraid … we lost them."

1:30 p.m.
(Afternoon Watch, Three Bells)

A SOBER-SOUNDING Captain Prickett invited Fly to enter the great cabin.

"Do come in, Mr. Austen. Sit yourself down and I'll have my servant get you a glass of refreshing wine. Goodness knows you could use it, seeing as your appearance reminds me of a fish caught on a hook."

Fly seated himself next to Bridlington, who lost no time in inviting attention to his facial injuries by fingering the bandages around his mouth. "You asked to see me?"

"That I did!" Prickett swivelled in his cushioned chair to give loud instructions to the hovering waif to fetch them wine and a dish of sweets, and then eyeballed Fly.

"Now then, two things, first of which is this sorry business involving Mr. Evans. It must be settled. What do you suggest as a form of punishment?"

"I will tell you with honesty," Fly said with a sorrowful shake of his head, "it is my *wish* we do nothing at all."

Bridlington nearly jumped out of his boots. "Mr. Austen! We cannot let this pass. Your chap assaulted me. Why I hardly have a tooth left in my head."

Allowing his glance to rove over Bridlington, who sat cross-legged and trout-faced in the comfort of his armchair, Fly felt a powerful temptation to inform the first lieutenant he would have done the same had he been in Mr. Evans's place. It was therefore necessary to restrain his thoughts before he again opened his mouth. "My apologies … I'm afraid I've no appetite for discipline, my mind being full of nothing beyond the loss of our five men."

"Put aside your soft feelings, Mr. Austen, and think clearly. Violence to a superior may result in death," admonished Prickett, so serious in his demeanour, such a far cry from the slobbering bump in his hammock that Fly had seen earlier in the week.

"And Mr. Evans has been allowed to wander at will these past days," Bridlington said, his speech an unfortunate sequence of lisps and whistles. "It's abominable that we've not taken any action against the man, and now the men are whispering that the *Amethyst* is managed by milksops."

"I've told you before, Bridlington, you *are* a milksop!" said Prickett, his reproach leaving his second-in-command muttering under his breath. "Naval law dictates a punishment must be exacted no later than twenty-four hours after the transgression. In any event, we *have* had our reasons for delay, but now Mr. Austen, I require your immediate counsel in the matter. How shall we proceed?"

Fly answered quickly. "Mr. Evans is one of our best men, industrious and loyal, and his skill as a carpenter is unparalleled. You've seen how well he's organized the men and patched up the damage done by the storm. I plead for leniency in his case."

Prickett rubbed his nose in circles as he considered the situation, while a red-faced Bridlington squealed, "Leniency? I'll settle for nothing less than a flogging."

Fly looked toward Prickett. "Might we take a moment to consider Lord Bridlington's ill-conceived remarks prior to Mr. Evans having struck him?"

"By all means! Bridlington, forthwith!" said Prickett. "What exactly did you say that caused Mr. Evans to erupt like a volcano?"

Bridlington's messy mouth dropped open, as if he were insulted to have to explain his actions. "I ... I merely said we needed the doctor back on board ... that it was outrageous for him to carry out such a foolhardy rescue."

"According to Mr. Evans, you said we had no need for a *trifling mite* such as Magpie."

"Mr. Austen! I said no such thing! Furthermore, I'm incensed that you'd take the word of a lowly carpenter over mine," cried Bridlington, flouncing in his chair.

"Gentlemen, I realize how dangerous it would be to overlook offences against us, and allow men to see a weakness in those of us who lead. Nevertheless, it would be reckless to forget the importance of every man on this ship. We are all valuable. If we concede that some are better than others, that some are worth saving and others are dispensable, God help us all if and when we meet with disaster — whether it be the enemy, another storm, a shipwreck — and those we deem to be inferior do not have our backs, or do not choose to take hold of our hand and pull us to safety. Mr. Evans's feelings toward young Magpie are strong indeed; it's a brotherly affection. And were it not for our young sailmaker, I wouldn't be here at all. You might recall he saved my life, in the face of the worst kind of adversity, and I've no doubt, Lord Bridlington, he would one day do the same for you. I am therefore severely prejudiced in this affair."

Bridlington swung toward Prickett, and pleaded, "Sir?"

The servant boy crept into the great cabin, bearing a tray, startled by the sound of Captain Prickett's bark. "'Bout time! We might have perished for want of food and drink. Set it down and out with you." Once the boy had done his bidding, Prickett tapped his fingers on the table. "Well, Austen, I'm leaving this one in your hands. You decide the punishment, but punishment there must be! I'll not have my men think of me as a bumbling sort, though I care not for their opinion of my first lieutenant."

Bridlington slipped into a muttering funk and said no more, which suited Fly, who hoped that neither man noticed the shaking of his hand as he reached for his glass of wine. "Thank you. I'll have an answer for you by day's end."

"Now, on to our second bit of unpleasantness," said Prickett with less gravity, his cares having been somewhat eased. "We cannot continue this futile searching."

"We have been searching but three days."

"Mr. Austen, I fear they've all drowned by now," said Prickett, taking up his glass of wine, his voice devoid of compassion. "We've criss-crossed the ocean in the vicinity where they were last seen and found nothing."

"Exactly! Aside from some of the items we heaved overboard for Magpie, we've found no debris, no bodies, nothing that would indicate disaster for either the *Lady Jane* or the skiff."

"With the *Lady Jane*, I agree, there'd be evidence floating about. But the skiff — be reasonable, Mr. Austen."

"A man can survive —"

"If the *Lady Jane* managed to get through that storm, she'll be well on her way to England and we *must* catch up to her. I have my orders!"

"Would you permit one more day, sir?"

The crease between Prickett's eyebrows deepened. "I will admit I'm quite desolate without Biscuit; however, I'll give my consent in the hopes we come upon the *Lady Jane*. Should we find nothing in four and twenty hours, we shall push on our way."

Fly's shoulders relaxed. "Thank you." Quitting the great cabin with alacrity, he was relieved to be away from its disagreeable occupants. He paused by the ship's wheel where he closed his eyes to replenish his flagging spirits in the warm sunshine. Hearing his name, he was surprised to find a barefooted Magpie standing diffidently near the larboard rail. His face was tear-stained, but he carried himself well, and his voice was full of resolve.

"Mr. Evans told me what happened, so I had to find ya straightaway."

Fly was at a loss to know how to console the boy.

"Could I borrow yer spyglass, sir?"

"For what purpose?"

"I'm goin' to scour the waves, sir. And I'm not leavin' the deck until I find Dr. Braden."

"Very well, Magpie! You shall have my spyglass, but only on one condition."

"Sir?"

Fly smiled in gratitude at the boy. "When I am able, you allow *me* to scour the seas in your company."

18

Friday, August 20

11:00 a.m.
Hartwood Hall

As Emily meandered over the south lawns near the house, she could see Helena standing in the west garden in a snowy-white dress, one hand shading her eyes from the sun, the other waving to her in a summons. At first Emily wondered if perhaps the prosecuting lawyer had arrived from London to question her, but then Helena's crackly voice rang out, meanly interrupting the birds' melodies in the chestnut trees, and the lazy hum of the summer heat.

"Come drink your tea, Emeline. Fleda and I are waiting."

The woman is always drinking tea, thought Emily crossly. She ambled up the undulating lawns, Benjamin Bell's *A System of Surgery* tucked under her arm, toward the garden where a little table had been set up under the shade of an ivy arbour, in amidst rows of trimmed shrubs and flower beds. Had the woman nothing better to do? Emily had no desire to sit awhile with the duchess and her red-haired daughter, who had not uttered a single word to her since Monday, when their walk together to the main gates of Hartwood had ended on a bitter note. At least she did not have to face Somerton. Following their stroll through the grounds two days ago, he had delayed his intended ride around the estate and immediately left for town — perhaps, this time, to prey upon the hospitality of a more prosperous family. Was there no friend, no ally to be found at Hartwood? Even Glenna, her old nurse, was irascible and overbearing, and too eager to point out the limitations to her freedom. Adolphus was more benevolent in his attentiveness toward her, but he slept away much of the day — most likely to allay the distress of digestion — and when he was not abed, he was off visiting his neighbours and tenants, sampling their luncheon and supper victuals.

"Good gracious, you're not reading *that* book again, are you?" mewled Helena, as Emily joined mother and daughter at the table.

"I am!" she said with a smile, setting down the precious volume by her feet. A glance at Fleda revealed the girl to be in a dudgeon, flinging bits of almond cake behind her chair to rid herself of her salivating dog, who only wanted to rest his head upon her lap.

"Why?" was Helena's terse rejoinder, as she signalled to the waiting servant to pour the tea.

"It's most informative, and as I fear I have grown dull of late it's a way to keep my mind sharp."

"I regularly receive the *Lady's Magazine* and *La Belle Assemblée*, and you may have them when I'm done *my* reading. I believe you might find their content more *useful* than those shocking medical volumes you tend to favour."

Fleda, deciding she had shunned her houseguest long enough, or perhaps incapable of withholding from her acquaintance what she perceived to be a deep, dark secret, finally glowered at Emily. "Somerton says you hope to study medicine."

"I do."

"How very interesting." Helena's voice was as dry as firewood. "Although, I think it is wise to leave the study of medicine to men; to those who can best withstand the sight of blood and entrails."

Emily reached for her tea, that she might shut her lips upon the gold rim of her cup and prevent her hands from forming fists. Unfortunately the hot drink did nothing more than give her a hot flush, causing her further irritation.

"And all this exercise that you do, Emeline, and in this heat! I swear you cover five miles a day."

"It has helped me regain my strength, and my land legs."

Helena inhaled sharply. "Firstly, a young woman of your breeding should take care not to broil her skin in the sun. I would therefore suggest, when taking exercise outdoors, you wear a bonnet. Secondly, you should limit the amount of time you spend walking; otherwise, you will surely gain unsightly muscle."

"I shall heed your wise counsel. Were anyone to notice I had muscles in my legs, I'd be quite appalled," said Emily with a cheerfulness of disposition.

"I am happy to hear it, for where you are concerned we don't need any further grist for the gossip mill."

Their first cup of tea was drained in silence, Emily aware of nothing aside from the sounds of clinking china and Fleda's snuffling dog as he lapped up his morsels of cake. Once their cups had been refilled, Helena stirred to life with a self-satisfied toss of her lacquered curls.

"Now for the reason I wanted to speak to you! His Grace and I are planning another ball, as our last one was such a triumphant affair; the talk of the neighbourhood, you know! I have every confidence the prospect will pull you from your lamentable state of dullness."

Emily's stomach fell away. "How wonderful! Have you set a date?"

"Not yet, for I want my son Wetherell to attend, and he will not respond to my letters to make known his availability."

Recollecting that both Somerton and Fleda had doubted she would ever have an opportunity to meet their eldest brother while at Hartwood, Emily said, "Perhaps some of your other sons will come in his stead."

"No, I must have Wetherell. It's high time he met the Princess Emeline Louisa."

For a moment Emily mused on the complexities of the duchess's remark. She did not care to meet the eldest son, whose portrait inferred he was a younger version of his wigged father, any more than she cared to suffer through another evening of frivolity at Hartwood, but an opportunity to irreproachably cause Helena discomfort presented itself, diverting her attention for a time. "I'd be more than happy to accompany you to *town*, and meet him there."

"That is out of the question."

"May I ask why?"

"He'll have to meet you here," replied Helena, sipping her tea.

"I was thinking it might be nice if you and I could shop in New Bond Street for accessories for the ball."

"You have all you will need right here at Hartwood."

Emily tried to sound convincing. "Oh, but I cannot be seen wearing the same pink silk gown!"

"Your new evening dress should suffice."

"Well then, perhaps your eldest son would be agreeable to join us in seeing a play at the New Drury Lane Theatre."

Helena was aghast. "A play?"

"Yes! I should so like to see my Aunt Dora perform again."

"I've never attended a play in my life."

"Oh! How sad."

"There are always vagabonds and rogues hanging about theatres, and I simply could not countenance the thought of them jostling *me* to get a good look at *you*."

While Emily wondered if she should laugh or cry, Fleda jumped into the discussion. "Wetherell doesn't like leaving his residence at Boodle's in St. James's Street."

A glow of mortification crawled up Helena's thin neck, and an explicit admonition for the girl to keep silent was meted out in the form of a piercing glare. Perhaps deciding that her glare was not ample enough punishment, she pounced upon her young daughter, striking an unfair blow. "Fleda, why did your maid not curl your hair this morning? I detest it when your hair is straight. You look like a drowned rabbit."

Fleda turned immediately toward Emily to blurt out, "Mademoiselle left this morning, and she's not coming back."

"I'm sorry to hear of it."

Helena dabbed at her forehead with a lacy handkerchief. "It could *not* have come at a worse time."

"Will you be advertising for a new governess?"

"With all I must bear, I cannot think of it now. I resent being burdened with such a task … such a dreadful process, having to interview all those pathetic girls to make certain they are suitable and possess some refinement, and now with all the arrangements I must make for the ball —"

"I'd be pleased to take over Fleda's instruction."

Helena blinked at Emily as if she had proposed an insurrection against the government.

"At least until you are able to replace Mademoiselle."

Her cold, blue stare intensified.

Emily persevered with eagerness, aware that Fleda was squirming with excitement on her chair. "It would provide me with an occupation while I await the trial, one I would relish, and devote myself to with the utmost attention and zeal."

"What an absurd idea! I cannot retain you as governess to Fleda."

"Why ever not?"

"King George's granddaughter … a governess?"

"Then give me the title of companion."

"Unthinkable!"

Emily filled her lungs, refusing to be put off her idea. "Very well, then! As I don't require a title of any sort, think of me as Fleda's sister, doing what any older sister would do: taking her instruction in hand."

Fleda was standing now. "Oh, Mother, please!" she cried.

Helena shut her eyes, the worries of the world etched upon her face. "Take your slobbering pet and leave the table at once!" she snapped.

Woefully hanging her head, Fleda pushed her chair back and marched across the garden, her innocent dog prancing at her side. There was a long, uncomfortable silence as Helena waited until her daughter was safely inside the house.

"Your uncles would never agree to such an arrangement."

"Why seek the approbation of my uncles at all if you and I were to agree to it?"

"I'm quite at a loss."

"In what way?"

"What could *you* possibly teach my daughter?"

The denigrating note in Helena's voice enraged Emily. "What would you like me to teach her?"

"You do not play the pianoforte, or any other instrument; you don't embroider, or do fancy needlework, or sing, or paint watercolours to my knowledge."

"Fleda's a clever girl. I'd concentrate on reading, geography, history, and arithmetic."

"Aside from reading, she has no need for such subjects."

"Very well, I do know a little French, and something of drawing."

"Compared to Mademoiselle, I fear your knowledge of French would be insufficient."

"Then I'll teach her how to ride a horse."

"Ah! And risk the two of you riding into London together?"

For a time Emily said nothing at all, so taken aback she was by the direction of the conversation. "Forgive me for the suggestion; I only thought it might be a way of helping out, to show my gratitude to your family for providing me such kindness and a roof over my head."

".Oh, come now, Emeline! Even if *I* were to agree to this arrangement, which I never would, you'd have to be supervised. It would be necessary for me to accompany you in the schoolroom every day; otherwise, I'd fear you filling Fleda's head with nonsense."

The contrived sweetness in Emily's voice gave way at last. "Pray, what nonsense?"

"The probability that you would end up instructing her on the ways of sailors, and how to shoot a pistol, is far too great a risk, and I just know you'd allow her to peek at illustrations of — of human anatomy. Simply put, Emeline, you cannot be trusted."

Emily's face reddened with indignation, her voice rose almost hysterically. "Oh, I am a dim wit. You are so right! I cannot be trusted!"

Helena sniffed in disdain. "I shall be advertising for a new governess for Fleda, one who is certain to teach her all she requires so that, when she's of age, she may make a good marriage for herself. In the meantime, *you* must stop rebelling against who you are, and remember what is expected of you." She rose from her chair, like a queen in her court, and smoothed the wrinkles in her white dress. "Perhaps it would be best for all if I further advertise for a second governess … one that could provide proper instruction for *you*."

11:00 p.m.
Hartwood Hall

"My Dear, come join us!"

In a voice warmed with drink, Adolphus called out to Emily as she tried to sneak past the music room without its occupants seeing her. Since supper she had been wandering in the garden, working off her anger and despair, and had hoped to steal off to her room without being apprehended by a member of the Lindsay family. Had she been aware that Adolphus and

Somerton — the latter newly returned from town — had been drinking and puffing on cigars in this part of the house, so close to the garden, Emily would have traversed a more secluded part of the estate. Her black mood would not tolerate idle chitchat, especially since she had already endured the evening meal with the crisp duchess and her glum daughter, their exchanges limited to praise of the beef fillets, the savoury consommé, and excellent apple-and-rum pudding.

"Come sit next to me," said Adolphus, patting the plush arm of one of the green-and-crimson-striped chairs that faced the chimneypiece and overmantel mirror. "And tell us … what can we offer you?"

Somerton sat opposite her on a sofa, his posture relaxed, his shirt open at the neck, and a foolish expression pasted upon his face. Between them, on a rosewood table, stood an impressive collection of used glasses and half-empty bottles of Madeira, port, brandy, and gin. Swirling over all was a cloud of stale air, a pungent mixture of smoke, liquor, and body odour. Almost immediately, Emily craved the sweet aroma of the garden roses and hydrangeas.

"Nothing, thank you, I'm off to bed soon."

"Off to bed!" Somerton clamoured, his eyes glittering as if with fever.

"Why it isn't even midnight, Emeline. Do have a drink with us. Could I interest you in a brandy, or shall I call for a nice red wine?"

"No, thank you."

But Adolphus, his head the only part of his body that moved, would not take no for an answer. "Then what about a nice claret-cup or ratafia?"

Emily clasped her hands on her lap, smiled as she shook her head, and tried to ignore the chamber pot and its foaming contents that rested on the floor near Adolphus's great feet.

"Father, perhaps our guest could be convinced to stay if you were to order some chocolate."

"Splendid! A pot of chocolate for Her Royal Highness!" cried Adolphus, sending the young servant, who had been fidgeting in the gloom beneath Octavius's portrait, scurrying off to the kitchen. The duke then angled his head toward Emily, knocking his powdered wig awry. "Now tell us, my dear, are you having a good time here at Hartwood?"

"Yes, thank you, I am."

"No, she's not, Father. She is *bored*."

Adolphus looked shocked. "How can one be bored at Hartwood? What about invitations to dinner parties and such?"

"There've been many," Somerton replied, "however, Mother has dismissed them all, informing the unhappy senders that Emeline must be safeguarded against exhaustion, bucks, and blackguards."

"Harrumph! My dear, you must excuse my wife. I daresay the woman covets the glory of hosting parties above life itself. She doesn't take kindly to competition, and would therefore hold it above all the women in the neighbourhood this ... this responsibility she has for you," said Adolphus, shifting about in his chair to face Emily. "Well then, in the absence of parties, are you not spending your hours writing letters and reading books?"

"I am reading, and I've written a few letters. Although I don't seem to be receiving any in return, which surprises me greatly."

"You must know, Emeline," said Somerton, his head wobbling about on his neck, as if he could not manage the weight of it, "it'll be weeks before you hear from your companions on the Atlantic."

"I am not expecting to —"

"You're not expecting a letter from your doctor friend? What's his name again?"

"His name is Leander Braden, Father," was Somerton's swift reply. "And I believe he's *more* than a friend."

"Is this doctor the reason you're reading tomes on medicine and surgery?" asked Adolphus, his head now locked into a position that enabled him to permanently fix his gaze upon his guest. "You *can* tell us! We'll not say a word to your Uncle Clarence."

Somerton raised an eyebrow at Emily. "I could almost understand if this Braden were like Sir Halford, titled, eminent, a physician to your grandfather and family; it's astounding that you would attach yourself to a ship's doctor."

Adolphus thrust his pear nose so close to Emily it almost rubbed up against her bare arm. "He is a doctor now, is he, and not just a butcher that happens to have experience with cuts of meat?"

There was such an appetite in Emily to hear her own voice speak Leander's name — to reveal his character, his decency as a human being, to explain how the man had saved her life. It was overwhelming, as if she were slowly dying of starvation. But since these two men — these voluptuaries

— spread out before her, resplendent in all their debauchery, were not worthy of such elevated intelligence, she attempted to change up the direction of the discourse. "Gentlemen, might we discuss England's progress in her war against the United States?"

"I make it a habit not to discuss such subjects with women. You're all deplorably uninformed," said Adolphus with conviction, an echo of his son's pronouncement on the green lawns of Hartwood a few days ago.

"Perhaps then, sir, you forget … I was enlightened while at sea."

"Locked away below deck with your doctor?" Somerton's lower lip rounded in a pout. "Come now, Emeline, we're most anxious to hear of your man, Braden."

Emily bristled. "For what reason? To mock me? I would have thought you'd be more interested in how I became the wife of Thomas Trevelyan."

"We shall hear all about *him* at the Old Bailey, I presume. But this Braden … well, he's a good deal more intriguing."

"Besides, Emeline, I've been assured that you'll soon be free of Trevelyan," said Adolphus, manoeuvring his port toward his lips and upsetting a large portion of it on his frilled shirt of which he took no notice.

"And, thus, free to marry again," finished off Somerton.

"I don't intend to marry again; at least, not right away."

Somerton waved his Madeira glass about in the air, quite as if he were conducting an orchestra. "Oh, yes, I forgot, you want to become a doctor."

Adolphus's pockmarked face clouded. "Forget this ridiculous notion. We've other plans for you."

Emily rounded on the duke. "What sort of plans?"

"Fa-ther!" scolded Somerton.

"But I *want* to tell Emeline of our most splendid plan, for I am certain it'll please her exceedingly," said Adolphus, much like a petulant boy.

"Drink up your port, and say nothing." Somerton sipped his own drink and closely watched Emily.

"If you're planning to marry me off to Mr. Gribble, you shall be disappointed," said Emily, looking from father to son, "for I'll drown myself first in one of the Hartwood ponds."

"Oh, no! Poor Mr. Gribble! He'll most certainly drown *himself* when you refuse his offer of marriage." Somerton helped himself to another bumper of Madeira.

"So long as he submerges himself in his own pond. I'll not have him sully the waters of Hartwood." Adolphus guffawed at his own remark for such a prolonged period, his grand body jiggling with mirth that he was soon in trouble. "Somerton! Bring me the chamber pot … quick … quickly, the pot, please."

Jumping up in horror, Emily headed straight for the door. "I shall leave you to it, sir."

"My dear! Your chocolate!" cried Adolphus behind her.

"Please have it redirected to my room," she said, without a backward glance, determined to neither see nor hear the duke relieving himself.

Passing through the colonnaded archway of the antechamber, where the air was much fresher, due in part to the garden fragrance wafting through an open window, Emily was struck with the memory of sharing a mug of beer with Biscuit, Morgan Evans, and their sundry messmates on the *Isabelle*. Why did the remembrance of that time never fail to induce an inward smile; yet the scene she had just quit left her cold, with a bad taste in her mouth?

Meeting no one, she hurried past the orangery and the sealed doors of the dressing rooms; past the breakfast room — the dining table all set and prepared for the morning's meal — and into the darkened hall where her footsteps clicked on the marble floor, echoing throughout the upper reaches of the house. Just as she was about to mount the main staircase, Somerton caught up to her, alarming her with his sudden, stealthy approach. In a surprising move, he hopped up on the first step to obstruct her way, and grinned at her, the candles in the wall sconces casting distorted shadows upon his face, giving him an insalubrious appearance. An icy chill ran down Emily's spine, feeling for a dreadful moment as if she were being assailed in the back-slums of London, or in the hold of a pitch-black ship.

"I thought your father needed your assistance," she said, her sharp tone belying her unravelling nerves.

"Father knows how to use the chamber pot."

Like a sailor who had knocked his head upon the ship's beams, he swayed before her, and soon had to lean against the wall for support. In a huff of annoyance, Emily pushed past him, not expecting the speed with which his arm shot out, grabbing the skirt of her gown and yanking her backward. The force of his impetuous action sent her stumbling and grasping for the gleaming rail of the wrought-iron balustrade.

"Let me pass," she seethed, steadying herself.

"You forgot to say *good night*."

"Good night ... sir."

He advanced toward her, assaulting her nostrils with his sour, offensive breath, and tightened his moist fingers around her bare arm. "I thought I should escort you to your room."

"I'm capable of finding my way, thank you."

"A woman is not safe walking alone at night through the halls of Hartwood."

"If you took yourself to bed, the women of Hartwood would all be quite safe."

Sickened by his breath and the nearness of his body, Emily wriggled free of his clutch. "If you don't let me pass, I shall arrange for you to join Trevelyan on the gallows."

There was a sudden transformation upon his face; his drunken expression hardened, so much so that Emily was certain he would strike her. As she recoiled, anticipating a blow, Somerton stood over her, his eyes blazing in the quivering candlelight. But as quickly as it had appeared, his dark mood vanished, and he began to laugh. Releasing her, he plunked himself down upon the stairs where he then fell into a fit of hysterics.

Emily scrambled up a few more stairs, putting distance between them, ready to flee to her room if he tried to come after her. In contempt, she gazed down at him, rolling about — half on the steps, half on the floor.

"Your Royal Highness," he said haltingly, covering his mouth with the back of his hand to smother his merriment, "you, who were *enlightened* while on the sea ... you have learned well how to handle a man who is ... good and drunk. It was my fervent wish to send you off to your bed with sweet dreams."

"Then I do not require your escort. I've only to find my pillow."

"No! It's just that ... I thought you should know —" He left off, his words hanging between them like an invisible adversary, while he began brushing off a real or imagined crust of dirt from his boots.

"Know what ... *sir*?"

"These plans we have for you —"

She tensed, waiting, praying his alcohol-laced lips would reveal all, and watched as Somerton finished up his diverting task. Finally, he threw his legs across the lower steps and his arms across his reposed body, as if preparing to spend the night on the staircase, and uplifted his smug face.

"Father thinks you'll be vastly pleased, but I think otherwise. I would suggest, Emeline, that you consider taking for yourself … a *lover*."

For a moment Emily stared at him, unable to comprehend the meaning of his words, but as soon as he renewed his drunken laughter, she turned away in disgust.

19

8:30 p.m.
(First Watch, One Bell)
Aboard HMS *Amethyst*

MORGAN SCALED THE ratlines of the futtock shrouds, careful not to overturn the two small pails — one of soup, the other of ale — swinging from his leather belt, and found Magpie huddled on the foretop, steadfastly peering through Mr. Austen's spyglass into the vast and vigorous sea.

"I swear, Magpie, if you don't rest up, that thing will stay plastered to your eye."

Lowering the glass, Magpie smiled up at Morgan, and crawled to a corner of the top's D-shaped platform to make room for him. It saddened Morgan to see the boy's blotchy face — a telltale sign of his inner turmoil. For two days now, he had stayed at his post in his quest to find Dr. Braden, Biscuit, and the others who had tried to rescue him; the only person visiting him — up until this moment — was Mr. Austen. Last evening, Captain Prickett had insisted they push on toward England, pronouncing it a waste of time, "… *searching for men who had already met their God.*" But Magpie would not give up. He had refused to abandon the platform during the nights, lashing himself to the timbers so he wouldn't roll off, thinking he might spot a lantern burning, or hear a gunshot across the water. Not one of the Amethysts working on the yards around his lofty lookout dared to tell the boy it was unlikely the skiff had been fitted out with paraphernalia such as guns and candles.

Morgan began to untie the pails at his waist. "I would've brought you some coffee, but I wasn't allowed. We're short on water 'cause a few of our scuttlebutts were stove in during the storm."

"Thank you, sir."

"Is there anything else I can get for you?"

Magpie looked hopeful. "Could ya ask Jacko to stitch me up a new pair o' shoes?"

"What happened to yours?"

"I fed 'em to the sea beasts."

"You what?"

"I didn't want 'em feedin' on me legs."

Morgan chuckled when comprehension dawned upon him. "That was clever of you. Someone, somewhere, must've told you that leather, when soaked in water, makes a good meal."

"Biscuit told me, sir."

"Well, thankfully, our Scottish cook never tried serving us lads a pot of stewed shoes."

Magpie went quiet and stared absently at the contents of his soup pail, leaving Morgan anxious for more conversation. Studying the accumulation of leaden clouds above the topgallants, he quickly said, "I'll fetch you a cape; looks like we're in for some rain."

Magpie nodded in gratitude.

"I've been meaning to ask you whatever happened to your *Isabelle* hat. I haven't seen you wearing it for a while now."

"I lost it," said Magpie gruffly, as if to curtail further inquiries on the subject.

"Oh. Well, I … I can't stay long. Mr. Austen said I could bring you your soup, so long as neither Prickett nor Bridlington see me."

Magpie peeked up at him, concern etched on his face. "If ya don't mind me askin', sir, what did they give ya?"

Raising his fingers one at a time, Morgan spelled it out for him, listing the five punishments Captain Prickett had gravely and ceremoniously heaped upon him yesterday morning in the great cabin. "No grog for a week; no more singing on deck with the lads in the evening; forfeiture of any prize money we gain on this cruise; I have to holystone the entire quarterdeck 'til we reach England; and —" he paused to display amusement in the form of a broad smile, "and never again may I stand within twenty feet of Lord Bridlington."

Magpie whistled his relief. "Oh, Mr. Evans, I were so worried they might strap ya to gratin' and give ya a hundred lashes."

"I'm lucky, Magpie, very lucky to have Mr. Austen fighting on my behalf. If Bridlington were captain, he'd have had me strung up. Why I'd be hanging here now, beside you on the yardarm, my neck all stretched, my face all blackened, my eyes bulging from their —"

Magpie quickly clapped his hands over his ears. "I can't hear it, sir. Even thinkin' they might have killed ya churns me up."

"I'm sorry." Morgan tapped the boy's thin shoulder. "Tell you what, you eat up your meal and come down the lines with me. The lads would love to hear you play your flute. It's been such awhile, and they're hankering to hear *Heart of Oak*, and that favourite of yours, the one about the grazing sheep."

"I don't have the heart fer it, sir," said Magpie. "I need to stay here."

Morgan nodded his understanding. "But you can't live on the platform forever. At least come down and sleep in your own hammock."

"I ain't goin' back to the sail room at night, sir."

"Why not?"

Morgan grew suspicious when Magpie was so long in answering. "I had a bad dream down there, sir."

"Then return to the hospital. That way you'll be with others."

"I don't like bein' called Maggot Pie."

Morgan smirked and slowly raised an upturned fist. "You know, it felt awfully good giving Bridlington a punch in the face. Maybe Mrs. Kettle needs one too."

"Ya wouldn't hit a woman, would ya, sir? Even if she's right nasty?"

"One of these days … I just might."

There was a brief brightening of Magpie's expression, but all too quickly the light left his eye and he turned toward the western horizon where, despite the gathering darkness above the ship, the sea was still drenched in evening sunshine.

"I keep thinkin' I hear Dr. Braden out there, callin' to me, tryin' to alert me to his whereabouts. And I wonder if he's feelin' cold and hungry and has to eat *his* leather shoes, and he's worried he'll never get to England to see his Em —" Magpie broke into a sob.

Morgan waited, giving the boy time to collect himself. "Come down with me, Magpie."

"I can't, sir."

"Then tell me, how much longer do you intend to stay at this?"

"'Til I find Dr. Braden, 'til I no longer hear his voice." Magpie raised the spyglass to his eye. "When he stops callin' out to me."

Midnight

THE HAUNTING CLANGS OF the ship's bell, denoting the end of the First Watch, gave Magpie a start on the foretop. Pulling the hooded cloak — the one Mr. Evans had kindly brought for him — closer still around his shivering shoulders, he lifted his face to the rain. He was chilled to the bone and in dire need of sleep, but he had to stay awake ... he had to stay alert. What if Dr. Braden was out there right now, trying to signal the ship, his ebbing voice muffled by wind and waves? Over and over again, Magpie imagined the momentous moment when the *Amethyst*'s lost skiff would at long last come into view and he would cry out, "Heave to," so loudly and with such spirit; he would afterward surely collapse in happiness. What a magnificent reunion they would all have! There would be clapping and singing and dancing, and he would pick up his flute and play the most joyous tunes he knew, and Captain Prickett would strut about the quarterdeck with his short arms hoisted high, calling for a celebratory feast, though he surely wouldn't dare insist Biscuit prepare it for the cook would be waterlogged. It was this happy image that preserved him through the long, cheerless hours of waiting.

Magpie gave his cheeks a vigorous slapping to stave off the heaviness of sleep. When the rain had first come, the topmen had been ordered up the mast to trim the fore topsail against the strengthening winds; now the footropes and yards were empty, those same men presumably asleep in their warm beds. It gave Magpie some comfort knowing he was not totally alone, that there were others moving about on the weatherdecks. At the very least, the helmsman would be standing at the wheel behind his lighted compasses in their binnacle; the Officer of the Watch would be recording the wind directions, as well as the ship's course and speed on the log board; and a poor, able seaman would be balancing in the chains, heaving the lead to make certain they were still navigating in deep water. But up here — one hundred feet up the foremast — it was a lonely, secluded place at midnight, and the sea emitted such eldritch sounds, as if, somewhere out there in the gusty darkness, a gaggle of witches was chanting over its bubbling potions. If only Morgan Evans would come for another visit, and present him with a pail of steaming coffee and a happy explanation that, despite the dearth of drinking water, an exception had been made for him.

No sooner was Magpie done wishing for Morgan than a figure appeared below in the misty gloom of the foredeck, and — to his initial delight — started up the starboard ratlines. Wiping the rain from his eye, Magpie blinked into the depths below his perch. The figure climbed awkwardly, with one hand holding a round hat to his head. He had the gait of a gangling individual, all arms and legs, and scaling the ropes seemed exhausting and unnatural to him. An icy chill crossed Magpie's neck, as if ghostly hands had touched him. This was no friend coming with coffee and companionship, in pursuit of a bit of skylarking. And that hat he was wearing … well, Magpie was certain of it … it was his own, the one he had taken from the dead, drifting sailor after the burning of the *Isabelle*.

Magpie grasped at the safety ropes that bound him to the top, incited by barbarous thoughts of being strangled by a pair of calloused hands and hurled into the sea like the fetid contents of Osmund Brockley's sick-bay bucket. No one would see, no one would know, and if anyone did hear a splash in the night they would think it nothing more than the crash of a wave. Beneath his square of oak timber — all that separated Magpie from the spectre, indefensible as a bird's eyrie — came a throaty voice, which rose up in a most dreadful declaration: "Woe and despair, woe and despair to all. The sea shall rise up and swallow the dead."

Magpie screamed at his ropes, cursing his rubbery, ineffectual fingers. His only chance for escape was fleeing down the larboard ratlines before the spectre had completed his own climb of the starboard rigging. But he had to move … now! A gurgle of laughter sent Magpie recoiling in shock, afraid to meet the blazing eyes that suddenly appeared, level with the platform. Slowly, deliberately, the spectre exposed the gruesome lineament of his face, and though obfuscated by the night, the lettering of HMS *Isabelle* embroidered across the round hat was clearly legible.

From his swollen lips there came another dark declaration. "Penitence and obscurity, and the little sailmaker shall be no more."

Feeling the ropes loosen around him, Magpie rolled away, as far as he could from his unwelcome visitor, and, in an effort to gain the larboard ratlines, grabbed two blocks of tackle. But the spectre moved quickly. Like the tongue of a lizard, one of his sinewy arms shot out, snatching up Magpie's bare foot and tugging and pumping on it gleefully, as if it were a toy. Within seconds hostile hands had closed around Magpie's leg, and he felt himself being dragged to the edge of the foretop, like a vanquished soldier from the lofty parapets of his king's castle, surely to be dropped and smashed upon the fo'c'sle. Locking his arms around the mast, Magpie squirmed and kicked with all his might, but all in vain, for the spectre's grip was vicelike, his strength overwhelming. With a violent yank, Magpie was pulled from the security of the mast's stump, his trembling fingers desperately scraping along the wooden platform, his legs soon dangling in the vast emptiness of the night air. Only a matter of seconds stood between life and a ghastly descent to his doom. Mustering his voice, he cried out for help, praying someone on watch would hear his plea. Squeezing his good eye shut, he waited for the inevitable plunge.

But it never came.

Mysteriously, the pernicious clutches let go, the spectre having turned abruptly away, vanishing from view as if something or someone had distracted him, and he was now engrossed in hurrying to deliver his reign of terror on another victim. His mutterings — now incoherent — gradually receded, becoming nothing more than an eerie echo, until, silenced completely, the gusty night resumed its fury in Magpie's ears. Breathing heavily, his chest a madhouse of palpitations, Magpie crawled back to the lubber's hole in the centre of the top where the huge mast rose up from the fore deck and, through the large cracks, peered into the rainy mists below. He could see no one on the shrouds or anywhere about on the deck. The spectre's visit seemed as fantastical as his dreams of being reunited with Dr. Braden.

Laying his head down on the cold, wet platform, Magpie wept with relief.

Sunday, August 22
Noon
At Sea

THE NIGHTS PROVED TO be so bitterly cold that the men were forced to huddle with one another to keep from perishing, but during the daylight hours, if the sun dominated the skies, their existence in the skiff was tortuous. To safeguard his freckled skin and hot head against the sun, Leander dipped his coat into the sea and wrung it out before slipping his arms into it, and then wrapped his muslin shirt around his head like a turban.

"I'd do the same, Doc, but if we've a chance o' bein' spotted I'd best keep me shock o' hair unbound," said Biscuit, reaching instead for his flask of grog. "That way we might be perceived as a burnin' vessel, and someone might come lookin'.'"

Leander's weary gaze slid past the single mast and four-sided lugsail — with which the eighteen-foot skiff had propitiously been fitted out — toward the squared-off stern where two of their three companions lay asleep, curled up and half-naked under a makeshift roof of knotted shirts and trousers, while the third, who had barely said a word since the storm, kept wetting the sail to hold the light wind. Leander was thankful that not one of them had been lost; it was already more than he could bear, this gnawing fear, this drifting around in the Atlantic, wondering if there was any chance for survival, and, if not, would they all starve or be slowly roasted to death. Admittedly, he was strangely comforted by the presence of Biscuit, as the cook seemed genuinely nonchalant about their circumstances and, having no spirit for conversation, he was content to listen to Biscuit's endless chatter, even though, after almost a week of it, the man had now taken to repeating himself and his seafaring yarns.

"When the *Isabelle* was set afire, and we lads, along with Mr. Austen, were bobbin' about, we had no food, no drink. Ach, we were a sorry lot. So I decided that won't be happenin' on the *Amethyst*, and hid a pail o' salted pork and dried beans in every boat fer this kind o' occasion. Of course, I couldn't stash the grog away."

"Why is that?"

"At night the lads on watch would sniff it out, and be sportin' grog blossoms in the mornin', the kind Mr. Austen would be sure to spot."

"Grog blossoms?"

"Ya know, when yer all flush-faced from drinkin'."

"Oh, I see."

"I grabbed nothin' prior to leavin' the sinkin' *Isabelle*, so this time I made sure we wouldna go thirsty." Biscuit helped himself to a carefully measured swig before passing off the flask to Leander, who, in turn, slid it along the boat's ribbed bottom toward the taciturn coxswain.

"I'm grateful for that which experience has taught you. It would be dire indeed if it weren't for your beans and pork, and flasks of grog. I don't think we would've survived long on handfuls of rainwater."

"Truth is, Doc, I'm always carryin' a full flask hidden in me shirt. Ya won't be tellin' that to Mr. Austen now, will ya?"

"If we're so fortunate as to see Mr. Austen once more, rest assured, I shall be as silent as a cemetery on the subject."

Biscuit winked in thanks.

"I … I've never experienced severe hunger, but the men I've known who've lived through a shipwreck, and thus met with it, tell me the stomach cramps are fierce."

"Aye, they be! When this lot's gone, ya'll know what I mean."

"I'll not think of that now."

"Best not, Doc! When the time comes, we'll draw lots."

"What for?"

"To decide which one of us we're going to eat."

"Oh! Shall we resort to cannibalism?"

"Aye, that's it!"

"And how do you propose we kill the poor victim?" Leander asked the question, drawing deep breaths to keep his stomach from heaving. "Stick his head underwater until he drowns?"

"Nay, we let 'im decide fer himself."

"How fortunate for him."

"Though 'tis best to bleed 'im, and the rest o' us drink his blood, and gorge on his flesh."

"And end up with raging insanity?"

"Won't matter at that point."

"I suppose not," said Leander in a hollow voice.

They fell quiet, Leander searching the low waves and imagining — as he had for days now — being sighted by the *Amethyst* or the *Lady Jane*, or some such ship with friendly inclinations. But the hours passed slowly, agonizingly slow, and more often than not his daydreaming mind strayed toward the sinister eventuality that either an American or French frigate would find them, and forthwith despatch them to a godforsaken prison.

He could not — would not — end his days on foreign soil, in obscurity, forgotten by all.

It wasn't long before Biscuit once again took up his chatter. "Been on the sea most of me life, seen a lot o' men drown. I keep thinkin' we all need a pair o' special-made trousers or somethin' to keep us afloat, should we have the misfortune o' bein' tossed overboard."

"Did you really see Magpie restored to the *Amethyst*?" It was a question Leander had already asked a dozen times.

"I tell ya, Doc, though I have a lazy eye, I swear to ya, the sea saw fit to take him right back to Mr. Austen. I seen the likes afore where one wave washes men overboard, and another washes them right back agin. Right astoundin', it is!"

"I do rest easier, knowing the boy is safe."

"He'll be sick with worry when he learns yer gone, Doc."

Leander frowned. "He may be more distraught to think he's lost forever his precious miniature of Emily."

Biscuit arched one of his bushy eyebrows. "*His* precious miniature, sir?"

"You see, we share it," said Leander, averting his eyes from Biscuit's leering face, "and as I was the last to have the responsibility for it, I locked it away in my writing box."

Biscuit let go a long, gurgling sigh. "Ah, she were a fine lass. All o' us loved her."

Leander could not trust himself to speak.

"Well, aside from the privateersman Prosper Burgo, that is. Emily were a bit too scrawny fer his tastes; he preferred his Meggie, his rolypoly puddin'."

Still, Leander could say nothing; his heart was too full. He could not allow himself to think of Emily at all. The pain was worse than anything he had had to endure in the skiff. And yet he could not — without giving up on life — give up hope that he might one day see her again. With his eyes following the swirling puddles of seawater racing along the bottom of the boat, he could hear Biscuit digging around in the dwindling food pail. He looked up only when the cook placed a portion of salted pork into his hands.

"Here, Doc, take a bite o' this to keep yer energy up. 'Twould taste a sight better if we'd enough freshwater to soak it properly, but no mind. Eat up and set yer eyes on the waves. We've seen a sail or two in our travels. Might be we'll see another one."

"Do you really think we might be sitting on the shipping route?"

"Might be!"

"I'm determined to believe so."

"Ah, Doc, someone's bound to spot our wee sail."

"Right!" said Leander with a firm nod of his turbaned head.

"Just hope we ain't reduced to a mound o' bleached bones when they do."

20

Monday, August 23

10:00 a.m.
Hartwood Hall

EXHAUSTED BY HER rigorous exercise, having marched around the wooded walk at least ten times before taking the gravel driveway that led to the main gate of Hartwood, Emily was only too glad to drop down upon the cool earth at the foot of a towering beech tree to rest. Gathering her skirts up around her and kicking off her silk slippers, she massaged her aching ankle, setting her sights on the insurmountable walls of stone in the hopes of seeing the magpie again. Twice now during her lonely jaunts around the estate she had spotted him, always near the main gate, and always he had given her a direct glance — a genuine indication of their kinship. Pondering her present existence, she looked up at the umbrella of branches overhead. "It would seem that the only one willing to keep your company these days is a bird," she said with a sarcastic snuffle. "But then you don't care for the human company to be found around here, do you, Emeline?"

Emily closed her eyes on the warm morning, refusing to dwell upon Somerton's behaviour on Friday evening, and his puzzling pronouncements. Already she had spent too many of her sad hours ruminating those distasteful scenes. Today she desired only to revisit the *Isabelle* and pretend she was not sitting under a tree in England, but cross-legged on the wide planks of the ship's hospital floor with Gus and Magpie and Leander around her, reading passages of Jane Austen's *Sense and Sensibility*, keenly aware of Leander's magnificent eyes and his stolen glances in her direction. The distance between them was ever widening; she could feel it. The lagging days here at Hartwood were rapidly erasing her memories of the smells and sounds and emotions of that past time, benumbing her with a forlorn sense of loss.

It wasn't long before an approaching reverberation on the road beyond the walls dispelled her musings. Opening her eyes, she watched as the gate-keeper hurried from his cottage to unlock the heavy gates and welcome a convoy of wagons that trundled past her with their loads en route to the mansion. Supplies! Always supplies! Although it was not immediately obvious what was packed away in those bags and chests and tins and boxes, Emily suspected they contained flour and sugar, haunches of meat, precious tea and candles, and perhaps even new pieces of furniture. And if allowed to inspect the wagons' loads more closely, she would surely find one filled with yards of costly fabric for Helena's maid, so that the woman might sew more unnecessary gowns for Hartwood's *royal orphan*. Emily sighed. Why couldn't a family member or a friend pass through those gates? Even the prosecuting lawyer, whose visit had been foretold by her Uncle Clarence, had not yet come to see her. Had everyone — especially those for whom she cared — forgotten her then?

Easing back against the trunk of the tree, Emily was determined to lose herself in daydreams when she noticed, at the tail end of the wagon assembly, an unfamiliar coach entering the grounds. She knew it could not belong to the duke and duchess, for earlier she had greeted the Lindsay family entering the breakfast room just as she was preparing to leave it. The duke was most disappointed that she had already taken breakfast, but did not wish to delay her in her daily ritual of walking the estate.

The closed body of the coach — a curious shade of purple — and the flanks of the two fine horses that pulled it, gleamed in the morning sun-shine, and though there was no coat of arms emblazoned upon its doors, the attending coach and footmen were fitted out in colourful liveries of lilac and yellow. Piled high upon its roof were a number of trunks, leaving Emily wondering if the passenger — or passengers — intended to partake of the duke's gracious hospitality for an extended stay. As the coach gracefully rolled passed her beech tree, she managed to glimpse a single silhouetted figure sitting erect on the seat, hands folded upon a cane, eyes looking straight ahead. With interest she followed its stately progress through the park until it had rounded a corner and was lost in a thicket of trees.

Jumping up, Emily brushed off the fallen leaves stuck to the back of her dress and looked toward the gate walls. This time her glance was rewarded, for there he was, his little feet hopping sideways atop one of the grey stones, his wing feathers an iridescence of purplish-blue.

"Hello, my friend," she called out.

Planting his feet, the magpie looked her over with his beady eyes, giving her such a lengthy, unnatural stare, Emily was certain he could read her thoughts and recite her entire turbulent history if given a voice. Laughing, she dared him to look away, but he didn't, at least not until their silent communication was broken by the sharp barking of a dog, and Fleda's voice ringing clear across the park.

"Emily! Emily, come quick!"

The magpie quit the wall and flitted toward the higher branches of his favourite mountain ash tree where he paused briefly to inspect the newcomers, unleashing an admonishing chatter before sailing off into the sky.

"What is it?" asked Emily, setting off toward Fleda.

"We have a visitor."

Emily picked up her pace. "Who has come?"

"You must hurry, and see for yourself."

1:00 p.m.

Hartwood Hall

UNTIL LUNCHEON WAS SERVED, Emily was kept in suspense. According to Fleda, the visitor had insisted upon taking a rest, a bath, a change of clothes, and being rewarded with a lavish meal to banish the dirt and weariness of the long journey. Although Emily had pumped the girl all the way back to the house, Fleda had remained smugly tight-lipped, revealing nothing further than Glenna's threat to *"hang, draw and quarter"* her if she breathed a word — the housekeeper desiring to surprise her as well. No sooner had Emily stepped into the front hall than Glenna herself, clucking disapproval, seized her elbow and steered her across the marble floor toward the staircase.

"I'll not have ya come to the table lookin' like that," she scolded.

"Like what?"

"Like yer some back-alley dweller from Tothill Fields!" Glenna paused before a hall mirror and forced Emily to look at herself. "Have ya bin sittin' on the ground? Yer dress is soiled, and, Lud … did a family o' bats make a nest o' yer hair? Go clean yerself up."

Emily managed a tone of defiance. "I'll clean up for no one but King George."

Glenna's round face reddened; her lacy cap shook. "Ya'll clean up fer this one!"

Incensed at being ordered to change and dress her hair, but in a frenzy of curiosity to know who had come to Hartwood — who it was that had succeeded in stirring up such a fuss amongst the family — Emily did as she was told. Just prior to 1:00 p.m., rather than being summoned to the parlour or music room so that she might receive a formal introduction to the guest, the butler ushered her straight to the dining room where the heavy draperies were drawn upon the hot afternoon. Wringing her hands as she made her entrance, she suddenly felt insignificant standing beneath its grand chandeliers, ornamental plastered ceiling, and myriad masterpieces fixed upon its grey-blue walls. As if on cue, everyone's glance swivelled her way, including — it seemed — the stern-looking figures in the frames, while hers eagerly sought out and fell upon the visitor. With the exception of Adolphus, who surely felt it was no longer required of him to make the effort, those seated at the elegant table rose from their chairs to greet her with a polite bow.

Praying no one had detected the lines of disappointment surely visible upon her face, Emily bowed in return. She had harboured such hopes of finding one of her uncles or aunts sitting here amongst the Lindsay family, or even the lawyer, for *he* at least, with his countless questions, would have indulged her in an afternoon of reliving her weeks on the *Isabelle*. But she must be wrong on all accounts, for never had she met a lawyer who dressed himself in such an extravagant manner as this male, middle-aged visitor standing before her.

He was attired in a quality jacket, the colour of ripened limes, cutaway at the waist with tails that nearly touched the floor. His cream-and-yellow-striped trousers were exceedingly voluminous, almost concealing his high-heeled and spurred boots, and in his waistband pocket he carried a gold watch from which dangled a fob ribbon with three seals of ivory and silver. A scarlet striped waistcoat contained his thick middle, and underneath it he wore a heavily starched frilly shirt, the collars of which rose to the height of his cheekbones. His head seemed locked between those high collars, causing Emily to wonder whether, were he not careful, they might lift up his powdered wig to reveal a scalp of scanty hair. His lips were purple and fleshy, like two rounded plum slices, and his stubby fingers — clasped comfortably on his belly — were decorated with emerald and diamond rings. Emily could not guess where the duke and duchess had made the acquaintance of such a *fop*.

With a graceful upturn of her hand, Helena's voice crackled the thick air. "Your Royal Highness, may I present my son Wetherell, the Marquess of Monroe?"

This clown in ridiculous trousers was Wetherell? An outburst of laughter threatened to take hold of Emily, and with all eyes closely watching her — especially those belonging to Somerton — she fought to quash it. Smiling sweetly, she quickly stepped toward the marquess, who didn't bother to move an inch away from his chair, to shake hands with him; his fingers looking and feeling much like floured bread dough.

"At long last I have the pleasure," he mumbled — or something to that effect — stooping theatrically to kiss her hand with his plummy lips, his eyes enlarging at the sight of her whitened scars. Upon raising himself up, he found the enormous mirror on the wall behind her and began admiring his reflection, giving his wig a tidying pat and his waistcoat a tug. There were no forthcoming inquiries after her health or that of her family, and he seemed not the least bit interested in engaging her in conversation — having found a far superior distraction in tinkering with the finely crafted seals at his waistband. Emily felt herself grow hot with embarrassment.

The Hartwood clocks bonged the hour, while those assembled in the dimly lit dining room swapped nervous glances with one another. Outside the birds chirped their August melodies, the chestnut trees soughed in the breeze, and shining through cracks in the closed draperies were ethereal strands of sunlight. The walls seemed to close upon Emily. If Helena had not had the wherewithal to instruct everyone to "Be seated," and Adolphus had not chimed in with his loud, "Splendid," Emily would have spun about on her heels and headed straight for the nearest door.

As the eldest son was now ensconced in the place of honour on his father's right, which up until this moment had been Emily's rightful place, she made her way around the table and reluctantly seated herself in the empty chair next to him. Once settled in with her linen napkin spread neatly upon her lap, she observed the family: Fleda looked miserable, Somerton was absently running a finger around the mouth of his wine glass, and Helena was sitting stiffly on the front few inches of her chair. Even Adolphus was not his usual gregarious self: he hollered like a ship's bosun for the servers to come forward with their luncheon — cold roast beef, sliced mutton, and three kinds of salad — and hollered again for them to leave the dining room at once.

A pall descended upon the room as they all ate in silence. The only one seemingly untroubled was Wetherell. Though Emily did not dare give him a direct glance, his table manners did not escape her. As the food dishes were passed his way, he generously helped himself, but did not think to pass them on to others, too eager perhaps to dig into his own meal. He ate with obvious relish, oblivious to the company around him, alternately licking his fingers and washing them in the little bowl provided for such a purpose, and then drying them on a corner of the tablecloth. And every so often he peeked at himself in the mirror, Emily fully expecting to see him blow kisses at his astonishing reflection.

Fed up with the prevalence of glumness around her, and further annoyed to find the crushing humidity had adhered her dress to the leather upholstery of her chair, Emily decided to break the silence. She turned toward Helena and, careful to use the correct styling in the presence of the *great* Marquess of Monroe, she said, "Your Grace, have you been successful in your search for a new governess?"

"I have not," Helena replied with a slow blink of her ice-blue eyes. "I shall worry about it after the ball."

Emily saw Somerton raise his chin. "Are you still interested in the position, Your Royal Highness?" he coldly asked.

"I am. I'd like nothing better."

Fleda gave her a small smile of appreciation, while, at her elbow, Wetherell whinnied in surprise, but made no comment.

There was another period of silence, broken only by Adolphus, whose large head had slumped forward upon his chest and was softly snoring.

Emily swung toward the marquess. "I understand, Lord Monroe, you live at Boodle's in St. James's Street."

"I do," he replied, his wigged head hunched over his luncheon.

"And how, sir, do you spend your days there?" Emily sensed Helena growing stiffer still on her chair, Fleda's back straightening, and Somerton's gaze growing round.

Wetherell smiled at himself in the mirror. "I eat fine meals and relish the latest gossip."

"Ah, I take it then, sir; you live a most pleasant existence."

"I do."

"And do you carry on any business in town?"

"Not if I can help it."

"I understand it is a rare occasion to have you visiting Hartwood."

"I don't like Hartwood. It's too dull, without its diversions."

"Then you intend to make St. James's Street your permanent residence?"

"I do," he grunted, heaping tomato and spinach salad onto his plate.

Emily tried her hand at levity. "And, pray, what has enticed you home this time? The prospect of a ball?"

For the first time he raised up his head and high collars. "Heavens, no! I'm far too important for such trifling affairs."

There was food on Helena's fork, but she did not carry it to her mouth, so flabbergasted did she seem by Emily's questions and her son's stinging replies. But as no one tried to stop her, and Fleda was obviously being entertained — her eyes dancing in mirth — Emily pressed on.

"What then?"

Wetherell again addressed the mirror. "I've been tempted home by the promise of good food and French wine."

"That's all?"

"For the most part."

"But surely those commodities are available to you in London." She smiled at him, though he took no notice. "And here I thought perhaps you were hoping to make my acquaintance."

"Heavens, no, Your Royal Highness, you don't interest me in the least."

Helena blanched. Somerton choked on his slice of mutton.

Undaunted, and having been assured the Lindsay's second son could still draw air, Emily continued. "Then, please, sir, enlighten me. What has enticed you home?"

Ever so slightly, Wetherell turned his head toward her. "I declare, for one so young, you are very forward in your questions."

"If I offend, then please ignore me."

"No one's ever successfully offended me!" He gave his wig a pat. "And if I wish to ignore, I shall ignore."

While Emily waited for a more satisfying answer, Adolphus's snoring grew more sonorous, and when Wetherell finally decided to enlighten her he did so in a most patronizing tone.

"You see, of all things, Your Royal Highness, I delight in gambling. I possess avidity for playing at card and dice games, and I've been known to stray from my club to the gambling hells of Jermyn Street, where often my wagers have exceeded one hundred pounds. Therefore, I agreed to leave my rooms at Boodle's *proviso quod* Father pay off my gambling debts, which I shall confess are atrociously high."

A sudden attack of giggles seized Fleda, although Emily could not be sure whether it was Wetherell's discourse or his delivery of such — complete with rolling eyes and little exaggerations of the mouth — the young girl found so amusing. Nevertheless, it served to partially obscure the shocking clatter of Helena's fork as it fell upon her plate. In his slumbering state, Adolphus shook and snorted, but was quite able to resume his nap without further perturbation.

Curious to witness Somerton's reaction, Emily gazed at him across the mountain of salad bowls and porcelain platters of meat. There was a quick movement of his head, as if he had been studying her but did not desire to be caught in the act, and to his meal he now gave his full attention. What mystified Emily was the queer, indecipherable smile tugging on the corners of his mouth.

21

Tuesday, August 24

10:00 a.m.
Winchester

GUS WAS WATCHING OVER his cousins playing at marbles when a neighbour of Aunt Sophia's wandered unexpectedly into the cobbled courtyard, announcing he was carrying a letter for Master Walby. So great was the excitement that it sent Gus into a paroxysm of coughs. His little cousins gathered around him, pushing and shoving, begging to know who it was from, but Gus firmly shooed them back to their game; he had business to conduct before there could be any reading of the letter. Being ever hopeful this day would come, he carried his three pence in his waistband pocket, and was therefore able to retrieve them straightaway, offering up the coins to the kind neighbour.

"Good Sir," he said solemnly, "I thank you for your trouble."

"Nay, Master Walby, keep your money."

Gus looked up in surprise to see the neighbour grinning down at him. "The sender saw fit to pay the postage."

Bursting into smiles he could barely contain, and grasping the letter so tightly the wind could not possibly wrest it from his fist and send it sailing over the sheep fields, Gus limped to a quiet corner of the courtyard and leaned against his aunt's whitewashed shed. The words on the letter — his very first ever — had been executed in the most magnificent script: *Master*

Augustus Walby, Midshipman, Butterfield Farm, Winchester. With trembling fingers, he carefully broke open the wax seal.

> *Bushy House*
> *Monday, August 23rd*
> *My Dear Master Walby,*
> *I am distressed to hear that so much time has gone by without you receiving a letter from my niece. I cannot fathom why she has delayed corresponding with you, for I have been informed she does nothing all day long but read books on surgery and go for lengthy walks; however, be assured that she is well and in good hands. You may write to her at the following address:*
> Hartwood Hall, Helena's Lane, Hampstead Heath, London
> *I trust you are thriving and well attended by the amiable and obedient doctor from Steventon, and that upon your complete recovery you are very much looking forward to your return to the sea.*
>
> *Your much obliged, and very sincere friend,*
> *William, Duke of Clarence.*

Gus let out a loud whoop, and hurried toward the house as fast as his strong leg and crutch could take him, fully resolved — even if it meant an extra hour or two of back-breaking chores before bedtime — to beg Aunt Sophia for a single sheet of paper and a spot of ink so he could dash off a letter forthwith to Hartwood Hall.

11:00 a.m.
Portsmouth Harbour

Trevelyan found Twitch, wrapped like an Egyptian mummy in his stolen velvet coat, in a reeking corner of the orlop deck, near the Black Holes: the poorly ventilated, damp cells below the waterline, into which prisoners were lowered for committing shipboard crimes. Twitch's chalky, skeletal face was pressed against an iron-grilled scuttle cut into the hull, so that he could draw breath and bask in its tiny slit of daylight. Inspecting the encircling gloom to make certain there were no spies listening in — English, American, or otherwise — Trevelyan dropped down on the floor beside him, and was careful to speak in subdued tones.

"I haven't crossed paths with you lately on deck."

Twitch's eyes fluttered open and narrowed as if to ascertain the identity of the speaker, but he kept his prone position on the floor. "Ain't they dragged ya off to Newgate yet?"

"I have not yet had the privilege," was Trevelyan's droll reply.

Twitch snorted. "Why then haven't ya tried to escape?"

"I've already witnessed the attempts of those who've tried and abjectly failed to flee through a hole in the hull, or hide out in the water casks carried back to shore."

"What happened to 'em?" Twitch asked with fervour.

"One drowned, his body washed up on the mud flats, the other is languishing a few feet from you in his lonely Black Hole. I believe I can hear the poor fellow sobbing as we speak."

"Ya ain't afraid of the Black Holes, are ya?"

"I can think of more agreeable places in which to pass my hours." Trevelyan changed up the subject. "So then, are you ill?"

"I'm feeble; I haven't eaten fer days."

"Have you been playing at cards and suffered the cruelties of bad luck?"

"Aye! Lost me meal rations … lost me exalted place on the gun deck … lost me trousers … lost everythin' but me coat and tricorne. Ain't givin' them up."

"When do you expect to eat next?"

"Haven't a clue. What day is it?"

"Tuesday."

"Right then, I eat again tomorrow."

Trevelyan could see that Twitch had his esteemed tricorne wrapped up in his coat, and quietly he produced a half loaf of coarse bread from the open neck of his shirt. The aroma of food instantly roused Twitch, who peered up again. "Have ya come to share yer meal with me then?"

"Why would I do that?"

"I thought maybe we was comrades forever."

"I make no man my friend."

Twitch went silent, shutting his eyes again.

"Give me your hat, and I'll give you this morsel of bread."

"Tell me first ... how did ya get yer hands on it? Did ya swindle it from the cook when he wasn't lookin'?"

"I did not! It's honest payment."

"Payment fer what?"

"Whilst you were gambling away your belongings and meat rations, I've set up classes."

One of Twitch's eyes popped open. "Classes? What! Here on the *Illustrious*?"

"Aye, classes! And thanks to one of your compatriots, we have a decent supply of ink, pens, and paper."

"What're ya teachin' at?"

"Mathematics, mainly, although there're those who have additionally pleaded for lessons in geography and reading."

"What do they want with all o' that nonsense?"

"They hope to improve their lot when they're released or exchanged."

Twitch managed a weak guffaw. "A waste o' time, I say. They might as well realize this here hulk's their home 'til the end o' time." He raised his head to sniff the bread. "It pains me to part with me tricorne, but I'm thinkin' ... if I don't eat soon, I'll perish, and I'm right dismayed thinkin' of meself as a stiffened corpse with no prospect of seein' home again." He opened the velvet coat and held out the hat.

With sang-froid Trevelyan accepted it, giving him the bread in return, and then sat back to watch with amusement as Twitch ravenously bit into the hardened lump, ripping off a big chunk of it with his broken teeth. "There's more where that came from."

Twitch's answer arrived only when he'd managed his first swallow. "Ya just said we ain't comrades."

"No, we are not, but there's something else I want from you."

"I've nothin' left to barter with."

"Oh, but you do," said Trevelyan, rising and leaving the American to lick up every last grain of his bread.

4:00 p.m.
(Afternoon Watch, Eight Bells)
Aboard HMS *Amethyst*

CLUTCHING THE SPYGLASS in one sweaty palm, Magpie knocked timidly on Captain Prickett's door. He wasn't even certain he was allowed to do such a thing, and he trembled with worry lest he be punished for taking such a liberty. It seemed everything worried him now. There was a constant anxiety at work, unrelentingly champing on his stomach; he was not the brave little sailmaker the Amethysts thought him to be. But he had to have a word with Mr. Austen, and since no musket-wielding marine was about to halt him, he took a deep breath and mastered his composure.

A servant swung the great door open, allowing Magpie to see the important men gathered around a map-strewn table, their faces as red as beets, as if they'd been at odds with one another. As soon as they realized who had come to disturb them, Captain Prickett's lower lip jut out in a show of annoyance and Bridlington's crooked nose flared violently. Next to them, Mr. Austen looked relieved, indeed grateful, as if he needed a reason to escape from the stale air, which the captain and the first lieutenant were reputed to frequently blow about.

"Pardon me, Mr. Austen, but I need to speak to ya ... in private if yer able, sir."

Mr. Austen lost no time in obliging Magpie. He collected his uniform jacket from the back of his chair, and was in the middle of excusing himself when a grumbling Prickett suddenly shouted, "One moment, sailmaker," and, upturning his jutting lip at Mr. Austen, he said, "I say we preserve our ammunition for the occasion when we have most need of it."

"Then I must ask again, sir, that you remember we're still at war with both America and France. At any time now, we may encounter hostilities. Against an enemy man-o'-war we have a chance, but these privateers, they sail swiftly and are capable of overwhelming a large ship such as ours in an instant. We *must* be ready. If we have one chance at a broadside, our aim must be accurate."

"We travel alone on this vast sea, Mr. Austen. Why we haven't even spotted the spout of a whale."

"And our little storm of a week ago," added Bridlington, lisping through his chipped teeth, his eyes sliding along the ceiling planks, "rather than throwing us off course, has nudged us nicely toward England."

"Bridlington's quite right! We're making excellent time. If these fresh winds continue, we'll be in Portsmouth in two weeks' time, perhaps less." Prickett pulled his lip in. "Mr. Austen, I wish you wouldn't worry so. Look how well our Amethysts behaved against Trevelyan and his lot."

Magpie was certain he saw a tremor pass through Mr. Austen's upper body before he wilted — just like a thirsty flower — in frustration. "How silly of me to have forgotten their superb conduct on that day. Now, if you'll excuse me." Without giving Prickett and Bridlington another glance, he hurried Magpie out of the captain's cabin and led him away from prying ears. Though his countenance was still florid and his question direct, his manner was gentle. "What's all this?"

"I don't want to rouse the lads, sir, but I've seen somethin' through yer glass. My sight ain't like Mr. Walby's — ya always said he had the keenest eyes of anyone — but I think maybe I've spotted a sail."

"Where?"

"Off the stern, comin' from the west."

Mr. Austen made a sweeping glance around him; there was a sparse scattering of men on the decks, and no one at all on the yards, most of them having gone down for their supper. "Follow me," he instructed. His gait was nonchalant, as if he was hoping to attract little attention to himself.

Arriving at the taffrail, Magpie handed him the spyglass and pointed in the general direction. For unbearably long minutes, Mr. Austen slid the glass around on the horizon, grunting now and then as he fixed his sight on various points of the sea.

Busting at the seams with hope, Magpie had to know. "Do ya think it's them, sir?"

Mr. Austen brought down the glass, keeping his eyes on the ocean. "It's too far off to know for certain."

"It's a sail then, sir, and not me 'magination?"

"'Tis," concurred the commander, snapping the glass shut. As if unaware of the expectant boy at his side, he stood still for a time, the breezes ruffling his dark hair, the afternoon sun shining fully on his face, highlighting a melancholy that was hard for Magpie to look at. When he spoke again, his voice was so hollow and suppressed that Magpie felt like an eavesdropper on his thoughts. "Perhaps it's time you steel your heart against your imagination."

"What're ya sayin', sir?"

Mr. Austen gazed down at him. "I believe you understand me, Magpie."

"I won't never lose hope, sir, if that's what yer sayin'."

"For that I am grateful." Mr. Austen placed his spyglass in Magpie's hands, drew himself up to his full height, and smiled. "Now, tell me, have you eaten today?"

"Nay, sir, I only just came off the mizzen top to tell ya what I seen."

"The mizzen? And here I thought you'd set up watch on the foretop?"

"I ... I did at first, sir," said Magpie, powerless to explain the hostile visitation Saturday evening at midnight.

"I shall have your supper sent to you straightaway, but you'll take it on the mizzen. I need you to scramble up there and keep your eye latched to that sail. Should it gain on us, you must let me know ... immediately. I'll be in my cabin."

Magpie followed Mr. Austen's eyes back to the whitish speck on the horizon. "What d'ya see, sir?"

"Even from a far distance, there's something in the aspect of a ship, and the way she sits in the waves, which reveals something of her temperament. Is she at leisure, or does she sail with purpose?"

"What are ya supposin', sir?"

"We may soon have a *chase* on our hands."

5:00 p.m.
At Sea

LEANDER STARED AT THE dead man, lying curled in a foetal position on the spiny planks of the skiff, and felt his weakened limbs coursing with dread. No one knew much about the man; why he'd barely uttered a word in the week they'd been bouncing about on the sea, barely taken a bite of salted pork or dried beans, and not one of them had been privy to his name.

"What should we do with him, Doc?" asked Biscuit, lying against the skiff's side, too exhausted to move a muscle.

Leander shot a glance at their two remaining companions, who sat huddled in the stern, anxiety etched upon their sunburned faces, their eyes hollow with hunger. How much longer could they hold on? Their flasks of rum had been drained, their food was gone, the empty pails now employed to catch the rainwater that periodically fell from the heavens. Cramps had already seized their bellies, so wrenching and relentless in their assault, Leander could think of nothing but his physical agony.

"We'll ... we'll slip him over the side, and commit him to the sea," he said in little more than a whisper.

Biscuit locked eyes with him. "Sure ya don't wanna eat him?"

A disquieting image of the unknown man's parents passed before Leander, standing together with their arms linked on some unnamed shore, the mother's long skirts blowing in the breeze, both of them staring sadly out upon the Atlantic, wondering what had become of their son. Wouldn't their pain be just as great as the searing despair his own grandparents had endured when their eldest son was lost at sea?

"Though I'd prefer a dish o' stovies meself, his flesh'll keep us goin' fer a few more days."

"He ain't even one of ours, Doctor," said one of the sailors at the stern.

"He's Yankee. He came on board with us after Trevelyan's *Serendipity* foundered," piped up the other, a strange glow working in his eyes.

The thought of carving up the dead man caused Leander's stomach to heave. "It makes no difference that he's American ... no difference at all."

Biscuit closed his eyes. "Ya'll be right sorry, Doc, 'cause in a day or two yer hunger pains will drive ya mad."

Leander believed he'd already gone mad, his mind a whirlwind of confusion and impending doom. He would sell his soul to be taken away from this skiff and its torments, away from the sight of the empty food pails and vacant eyes of the sailors, if only for an hour ... to stand upright, exercise his legs, eat to his fill, and then lay his head upon a feather pillow. Biscuit's constant chatter had been a respite from his frightening reflections, but the Scottish cook had less to say now. In his present despair, Leander's restless eyes fell upon the sailors' hands, resting upon their legs, useless with inactivity and blackened with tar, and absently he picked up one of the ropes attached to the lugsail. If he rubbed his hands over the woven yarns, it left a residue of tar upon his palms, giving him an idea. Unravelling his shirt, piled as usual like a turban upon his head, he began tearing at it, grunting as he did so and startling Biscuit.

"I didna mean fer ya to go mad this instant, Doc."

Leander said nothing and kept on, ripping a square of muslin from the tails of his shirt. Once he was satisfied with his handiwork, he set about inspecting the boat's planks, searching for the perfect splinter. Having located one he tore it off, and with its pointed end attempted to extract a blister of tar from the ropes. Meeting with success, he began to draw a letter on his patch of muslin.

"Might be best to use blood, Doc," suggested Biscuit, as if guessing Leander's intentions.

With some enthusiasm, Leander pressed on, aware the men had pitched their full concentration upon his task, as if they figured he'd come up with a brilliant strategy to save them all. But when long minutes had passed, and he'd only managed to painstakingly write one poorly executed letter, Biscuit held out his knife. Staring at its blade, glinting in the late afternoon sun, Leander hesitated.

"If ya want, ya can cut into me," said Biscuit, offering up one bare, hairy leg.

"Why not cut the dead man, Doctor? He'll be a right gusher," said one of the sailors.

"No," said Leander gravely. "When the heart stops, the blood no longer gushes. It pools in the body, predominantly in the back and in the abdomen."

"Ahhh!" said the onlookers, their faces awash with wonderment.

Biscuit placed his knife into Leander's reluctant hands and retracted his proffered leg to allow the doctor space to squat down beside the dead man. Opening up the man's shirt, Leander made a deep incision in his belly, slicing through the layers of skin and tissue until a trickle of black blood appeared. Then he dipped a fresh splinter into the small reserve of substitute ink, and set to work once more on his square of muslin, holding it up for approval upon its completion: *Aug. 24 Alive in skiff. Find us.*

Biscuit's comment was teeming with sarcasm. "Ya best add the word *please.*"

Not one of them laughed.

Leander soon lost heart. "We can wait 'til the blood dries, but we run the risk that the words will be washed away."

Biscuit raised a finger, and cried, "I got somethin' fer it!" Reaching into his trousers, he shocked Leander by pulling out a watch and fob ribbon —

items a wealthy gentleman might own, not a penniless Scottish cook. "It's the sum total o' me possessions, but here —" he gazed fondly at it before handing it off to Leander. "The watch stopped markin' time long ago, so fold yer message up in it, and snap it shut. Might keep the words from fadin', and then ya can pin the works on our dead comrade here. But take off his clothes. He don't have no more use fer 'em."

Leander nodded in agreement, and with Biscuit's assistance they stripped the dead man of his jacket and shirt, and pinned the ribbon and watch with its precious message onto his dungarees. The deed done, Leander struggled to raise himself up on his legs, which were completely bereft of strength.

"We therefore commit the earthly remains of this unknown American to the deep, looking for the general resurrection in the last day, and the life of the world to come, through our Lord Jesus Christ —" Leander stopped suddenly, unable to recall the rest from memory.

Biscuit stood up too, and supporting himself against Leander, he added what he knew of the prayer, slowly, haltingly. "Whose second comin' in glorious majesty ... the sea shall give up 'er dead. Amen."

"Amen," echoed their companions at the stern.

The effort of slipping the dead man over the side of the skiff and into the sea caused both Biscuit and Leander to collapse in exhaustion. The wind picked up and the rain came. Leander placed the unknown sailor's jacket over his head, too grief-stricken to witness the man's last journey on the waves.

22

Tuesday, August 24

8:45 p.m.
Hartwood Hall

Dressed for the evening in a cashmere shawl, for the air was cool on this night, and a green silk gown, the colour reminiscent of the long waving grasses that grew beside the Hartwood ponds, Emily flipped through the July issue of the magazine *La Belle Assemblée* with a gnawing restlessness. Helena had thrust it into her hands once they had prettily arranged themselves on the music room sofas around the elaborate chimneypiece and overmantel mirror, instructing her to enlighten herself with the latest notes on English and French fashion while they awaited the arrival of the men who had — per tradition — stayed behind in the dining room to smoke their cigars, drink their port, and speak of subjects unfit for the delicate ears of the fair sex. Having been exiled to the pianoforte in the shadow of the great, rounded window, Fleda glumly sat upon her stool, sorting through reams of sheet music, periodically shooting daggers at her mother, who sat with her back to her daughter.

"Practice your playing, Fleda, so that when Wetherell enters the room he might hear one of his favourite compositions. It would please him so."

Fleda brought her music sheets down hard upon the top of the pianoforte, and locked her thin arms across her chest. "Why should I do anything to please him?"

Helena lifted her chin to give the ceiling a serene smile. "He's your eldest brother."

"I don't give a fig!"

"You must always endeavour to maintain his favour."

"Why?" Fleda whined. "Wetherell cares not for me. Since his coming here, he hasn't spoken a single word to me."

Helena turned on her sofa cushion — though not enough to necessitate having to meet the indignant eyes of her daughter — and replied through her teeth. "In the event no suitors come begging for your hand, you may have to plead for a roof over your head, and as Wetherell will one day inherit Hartwood, he'll be the one to decide whether or not he can tolerate you living with him permanently."

"He would make me his servant."

"Yes, that is more than likely. You'd have to earn your keep somehow." Helena wagged her bejewelled hand at her daughter. "Now play! They'll soon be here."

Fleda stuck out her tongue at the back of her mother's high head of curls, beautifully arranged in a pearl-encrusted bandeau, her little display leaving Emily fighting an upsurge of laughter. With an impish smile of collusion directed at Emily, she solemnly selected a piece of music, set her little chin, and began playing — her fingers striking the keys of the instrument in a way that clearly communicated her displeasure.

"When the time comes for you to have children, Emeline, I do hope you are blessed with boys," said Helena in a lament.

Emily smiled, and set aside her magazine. "I hope to be blessed with both boys and girls."

"We women either die in childbirth or lose our figures."

"You did neither."

Helena furrowed her smooth, white brow. "No, but had I been the mistress of my fate, I would've avoided children altogether. They're a terrible nuisance, and have devoured so many hours of my life. Had I the misfortune to bear eight daughters, I surely would have wished for an early death, so that I might have been blessedly released from their vexatious management."

Emily's eyes were drawn to the portrait of Helena's forsaken eighth son; he looked so forlorn in his gilded frame. "I'm sorry you feel that way."

"Just look at Fleda! She's as skinny and brittle as a twig."

"She's just a child," whispered Emily.

"With an irascible disposition," said Helena with a dramatic toss of her head. "And she isn't in the least bit handsome."

"She has such lovely, fiery red hair."

"What benefit is the colour of one's hair if the fine strands stubbornly refuse to be arranged in curls? I fear she will never be able to wear the fashionable hairstyles of the day."

At the precise moment when Emily hoped Fleda's performance was sufficiently tempestuous to drown out her mother's shrill declarations of discontentment, Helena's voice crescendoed. "Fleda! Stop that banging on the pianoforte. Already I've a most severe headache, and I assure you Wetherell will find no pleasure in such an assault on the ivory keys."

Though Fleda eased up at once on the unfortunate instrument, Emily still detected the occasional note of musical defiance. *Poor girl*, she thought as she glanced with dissatisfaction around her, firstly at the card table — all set and ready for later entertainment — and then at the untouched tea tray upon the little rosewood table at her knees, and finally at Helena, who had just received a goblet of champagne from a servant boy. Sighing, she checked the position of the hands on the nearest clock. How soon could she quit the music room and find salvation in the garden and in the cool breezes of the night? The prospect of having to endure another hour or two with the Lindsay family left her with the simmering pains of her own headache.

Emily helped herself to a cup of tea, for the duchess, who usually did the honours, was too absorbed in the business of drinking her champagne, and did her utmost to maintain the flow of their insipid conversation. "And yet, after having so many dark-haired children, Helena, you must've been pleased to see a darling red-haired infant."

Wistfulness crept into Helena's eyes as she pensively sipped on her drink, sitting erect on the damask sofa as if someone was poking her in the back, and although Emily had as much interest in Helena Lindsay as she had in the soil of Hartwood's gardens, she found herself — for the first time — wondering about the woman's past.

"I was not at all pleased," said Helena, massaging her left temple. "It was a very dark period of my life, and the last thing I needed was to be saddled with another child. Fleda's nothing more than a daily reminder of that time."

Hearing male voices and footsteps nearing the music room, Emily knew their conversation would go no further. Swiftly, Helena set aside her champagne glass, and spread the mauve folds of her dress out around her. "Here they are at last. Prepare yourself, Emeline."

9:00 p.m.

ADOLPHUS STEPPED HEAVILY into the room, his enormous trunk careening precariously, as if one false step might send him toppling like a tree. Seeing the ladies rise from the sofas in greeting, his pockmarked face broke into a wide grin.

"Splendid! Splendid! Decant some Madeira, and bring more champagne for the ladies," he said to the servant boy, who was now standing stoically at his station near the doorway. "I'm feeling quite at leisure, and ready for a long evening of Whist."

Behind him, Wetherell pranced in, lending a dash of colour to his surroundings in his pink hunting coat and astonishingly yellow breeches, especially as he took his mincing steps next to Somerton, who was attired in shades of grey.

"If it's cards we're at, then let there be wagers," cried Wetherell, his droning voice fortified with port. "Send the child to bed, Mother, so that we may say and do as we please."

Fleda jumped up from her stool in a huff and, abandoning all her half-hearted efforts to impress Wetherell, stormed out of the room. Sadly, no one but Emily seemed particularly upset by her early exit.

Helena's hand flew to her forehead. "Dollie, I think I'll join Fleda and go to bed. I've a miserable headache, caused no doubt by her atrocious piano playing. But Emeline will gladly make up a table of four." Avoiding Emily's unhappy expression, Helena bowed to the company and slipped quietly away.

Adolphus stuffed himself into one of the chairs at the card table. "Will you feel quite safe alone with us men, Emeline?"

"I don't see why not," replied Emily, reluctantly taking the seat offered to her by Somerton. She would as soon dig a grave as play cards with these three.

"If Emeline was able to tame the men on the *Isabelle*, she has no cause to fear us, Father." The nod of Somerton's head was decidedly jaunty as he took the chair across from her.

"It's a shame you never made the acquaintance of my son, Octavius," said Adolphus, thrusting his pear-nose into Emily's face, as was his new habit now that they were sufficiently acquainted with one another. "I assure you he would've become your protector, and made certain the seamen kept away from you. By God, he could have held that despicable Trevelyan at bay."

Resistant to further discussion of Octavius, Emily responded with a sluggish smile, thankful that Wetherell, in his eagerness to begin play, desired all unrelated talk to come to an end.

"Shall we begin with a few games of Whist, and later change over to Faro?" he loudly asked, excluding Emily in his glance.

"Fine with me," said Somerton, picking up the deck of cards. "Shall we cut or draw for partners?"

"As we are already seated, Somerton, and since I'm sitting across from Father, he shall be my partner," answered Wetherell. "Besides, I never partner with a *woman*."

Emily bit her lip.

"Cut for dealer," barked Adolphus.

The young servant boy had returned with their drinks. He poured each of the men a glass of Madeira from a crystal decanter, and then handed Emily a glass of champagne. Before departing for the night, he discreetly placed a chamber pot at the foot of Adolphus's chair.

A blush of excitement suffused Wetherell's face. "What shall we wager?"

"How about Hartwood Hall?" suggested Somerton. "As poor Emeline here is homeless — no one in her family willing to take her in, you see — and I'm nothing more than a penniless, second son, should *we* win, it might come in handy."

"Heavens, no! In the event that Father doesn't take care of my debts —" Wetherell slithered a quizzical look at Adolphus "— I shall have to relinquish my fortune and estate to my debtors."

Adolphus licked the wine from his lips in appreciation of its excellence, and observed Somerton cutting the cards, giving no indication whatsoever that he had even heard his eldest son.

Emily gazed again at the clock, her mind now fixed on thoughts of her soft bed. "I'm afraid I've nothing with which to make a wager. Shall I ask Miss McCubbin to substitute for me at the table? At least she has her housekeeper's pay."

"I do not sit at cards with housekeepers," remarked Wetherell, distributing the cards as he had won dealer. "Come now, Your Royal Highness, you must have a hamper of bracelets and baubles lying around somewhere. There must be some benefit in being King George's granddaughter."

"Indeed, sir, my bedchamber is infested with such hampers, but I could not tolerate parting with my bracelets and baubles; I'd as soon part with my firstborn child."

Somerton's dark eyes rounded with mirth as he studied his cards.

"Then play well," said Wetherell, still refusing to acknowledge her with a look. "And *do* try to remember what cards have already been set down."

Emily itched for the satisfaction of punching the marquess in that purple mouth of his.

"Let's play a friendly game," said Somerton, "and not wager at all. That way we might cure you of your gambling addictions, Brother."

"If I'm to make an evening of cards, I shall have my wager."

Somerton laughed. "What can you possibly offer up when you're indebted to everyone in England?"

Wetherell paused in his card dealing to wrestle an emerald ring from one of his fat fingers, smugly tossing it onto the table. "That must be worth a farthing or two."

"That was a gift to you from Mother."

"Yes, it was, Brother," was Wetherell's disinterested reply.

With a shrug, Somerton reciprocated by producing a £25 note from somewhere on his person, arousing Adolphus, who cried out, "Splendid! Now let's get on with it. What are trumps?"

Wetherell finished dealing and turned over the last card. "Hearts and game shall be a score of two points."

As Somerton was sitting on Wetherell's left, he led the first trick, laying down a jack of Clubs. When Emily's turn came, having no clubs in her hand and hoping Wetherell — the last to lay down a card — was holding an abundance of them; she played a five of Hearts. With a stamp of his foot, Wetherell flicked a three of Clubs into the pile of cards.

"Such luck, Emeline!" gushed Adolphus. "A wonderful start."

Emily gathered up the four cards of the first trick, lay them face down near her on the table, and then led once again, this time with a queen of Diamonds — Diamonds being her longest and strongest suit. To her delight, Somerton and she successfully nabbed the next four tricks.

"I take it you played Whist regularly with the *seamen* on your ship, Your Royal Highness," muttered Wetherell before guzzling his wine.

"Indeed! I played every night in the hospital from my hammock."

"With the ship's doctor and his loblolly boys?" baited Somerton.

"Naturally!" Emily took a few sips of her champagne, though in small measure, for it would be necessary to keep a clear head. As she led the sixth trick with a new suit, she eyed Wetherell's emerald ring, its square-cut gemstone and gold band glinting in the room's candlelight. The first game was dispatched quickly, with Somerton ardently proclaiming Emily and he the winners, for they had secured five points.

Wetherell's face was flushed with indignation. "I have never played a game of Whist where the opposing team has managed five points after the first thirteen tricks. You didn't cheat, did you, Brother?"

"Would you like to explain how one successfully cheats at a game of Whist?" he asked, scooping up the emerald ring and presenting it to Emily. "It is yours, fairly won."

"Sir, it is equally yours," answered Emily, secretly hoping he would insist she keep it. "And being as it was a gift from Her Grace, perhaps you —"

Leaning over the table, Somerton closed her fingers around the prize, allowing his hand to linger on hers. "You can have it sized to fit you. As is, it'll surely fall off, for Wetherell's fingers are as fat as sausages."

"We shall play again," announced Wetherell, turning abruptly to observe his reflection in the music room window. He adjusted his wig, gave the lapels of his hunting coat a firm tug, and then twisted another ring from his hand. "This time I shall wager one of my diamonds."

Adolphus, who appeared sanguine despite being on the losing team, yelled into the darkness beyond the music room, hoping there might be a servant within earshot who would do his bidding. "Bring us more wine, and a plate of sandwiches. Ham and cheese will suffice."

"Now, Father, if you're going to partner with me, you must keep your mind sharp. I didn't expect *her* to know what she was about. Perhaps you should drink Mother's tea, and leave off the wine."

Adolphus harrumphed and filled his glass to the brim with what remained in the decanter. "Cut for dealer," he barked, opening his purse, and setting a £10 note on the table alongside Wetherell's diamond ring, and Somerton's previous wager.

Emily eyed the booty, and smiled to herself. How different the evening might have been if Helena had not retired early to bed.

2:00 a.m.

CONVULSING IN LAUGHTER against the closed door of her bedchamber, tears streaming down her cheeks, Emily was totally incapable of consideration for those whom her unrestrained gaiety might awaken at this late hour. Even if the headachy Duchess of Belmont were to scream for silence and Glenna follow up with punitive measures by impounding Emily in Hartwood's stables, she could not help herself. Bursting with energy, she kicked off her silk slippers, lifted her skirts, and raced toward the bed in her stockinged feet, leaping onto the high mattress. With a giant yelp, she sank happily into her soft quilts. What a night; culminating in two of the household servants struggling to transport an inconsolable Wetherell off to his bed, his wig upended on his head, ranting and raving about being cheated out of his jewels, and challenging Somerton "*… to a duel on the morrow.*"

Assuming a cross-legged position, Emily tossed her winnings down upon the top quilt. Somehow, Somerton and she had done the unthinkable and managed to take every single game, and now, having split the booty, she was flush with funds — nearly £50 in all — and the happy owner of a valuable emerald ring. In the jumping light of her bedside candle, she studied the gem's square-cut perfection and the delicate etchings on its broad gold band, all the while chuckling as she recalled the fury that had erupted from Wetherell's plummy lips: "Never again shall I sit at a card table with *you*!"

Gathering up her treasures, Emily held them in a tight fist to her breast and lay back upon her pillows, staring up at the embellishing knots of flowered material on the roof of her canopy, feeling the mirth slowly drain from her body. She then turned her face toward the colourful Chinoiserie wallpaper on the wall next to her; its foreign scenes and objects exciting her curiosity: villages full of round figures in comical hats, ornate pagodas, Chinese gondolas with their curling ends, and those bizarre sailing ships, traversing fictitious seas full of monsters, so very different from those she herself had once been on. Feeling more peaceful now, her eyes fell upon the precious volumes of Jane Austen's *Pride and Prejudice*, sitting next to her candle, and her smile grew wistful. Through her unshuttered window, opened a crack to allow for fresh air, the whispering darkness of Hartwood's parkland beckoned, and in the far distance a few lights still winked over the city of London. Somewhere out there, there was still life.

Curling up into a foetal position, Emily burrowed her face into her pillows, and, as she waited for sleep to come, she clutched her treasures, and dreamed of possibilities.

23

Wednesday, August 25

7:00 a.m.
(Morning Watch, Six Bells)
Aboard HMS *Amethyst*

FLY AUSTEN SUPPORTED himself against the netting of stowed hammocks on the ship's waist to follow the horizons with the spyglass he had borrowed from the sailing master — Magpie still had possession of his — trying to locate the ships the little sailmaker had first spotted the previous afternoon. Until nightfall they remained in view, never once straying from their course or attempting to gain in speed, one always lagging behind the other. Were they spies? Friends? Foes? Royal Navy? American Navy? Neutral merchantmen? Fishing vessels? At such a great distance, he simply had no idea. Consequently, he had spent a fitful night, sick with worry lest they be belligerents biding their time, and when the first light of day illuminated the sea he had hurried above deck — half-dressed in an open-necked shirt and knee breeches — to make certain they had not surreptitiously crept up on the *Amethyst* under cover of darkness. Mercifully they had not; they were nowhere to be seen. Still, Fly watched, peering into the low cloudbanks, careful not to mistake the white clouds for canvas.

"You don't mind, do you, sir?"

Hearing the youthful voice behind him, Fly lowered the glass and wheeled about to see Morgan shifting from foot to foot, his trousers rolled to his knees, a bucket of greenish water in one hand and in the other a holystone — the soft, brittle sandstone used to scour the deck; named, in part, for its resemblance to a bible.

"I was hoping to scrub the quarterdeck before breakfast, but I can come back later if you wish, sir."

"You shan't be in my way," Fly said with a smile, always pleased to engage the carpenter in conversation. "Tell me, are you shouldering your punishments well?"

"I am, sir. 'Tis nothing to scrub the decks alone — works off a bit of restlessness of the mind and body. I do miss the evening pastimes with the lads; have to keep myself cheered by humming tunes in my head. Staying clear of Lord Bridlington is the easiest part, quite painless really." Morgan frowned. "The grog on the other hand —"

"Aye! The grog! Well, it'll be restored to you come Friday."

"For that I'm thankful, sir. You've been most kind." Morgan tucked the holystone up under his arm so he could transfer the weight of the bucket to his opposite hand. "Have there been any sightings this morning, sir?"

"Nothing, but as you know all that can change in an instant." Fly held up his spyglass and gave it a playful shake. "Therefore, we must all keep a sharp lookout."

"Magpie will be up soon, sir. He said if I was to see you to let you know he'll be back on the mizzen the minute he's downed his oatmeal and ale."

"Is he still sleeping on the floor of your cabin, Mr. Evans?"

"Aye, he's done so for four nights now. First night, finding him curled up at my door, I nearly hauled off and kicked him. Mistook him for a groggy landman who'd lost his way to bed."

"Does he sleep well?"

"Cries out at times."

"But he hasn't yet told you what it was that frightened him?"

"Nay, he's revealed nothing, but then, for a little fellow, he's very proud."

"I wondered if perhaps Mrs. Kettle was trying to harm him."

"Could be, sir. He did say he didn't want to sleep in the hospital; that he hated being called Maggot Pie."

"Hmmm, and yet we all know Mrs. Kettle hasn't left her hospital cot since her run-in with the mainmast."

"If I may conjecture, sir, she's far too contented in the hospital to return to her laundry."

"I must own, Mr. Evans, were Dr. Braden with us he would've dismissed her the instant he was assured her baby was out of harm's way."

"More than likely, he would've *trundled* her out, sir!"

They shared a quiet laugh, muted at the mention of their missing friend. Fly set his chin. "You'll keep me informed of Magpie's well-being?"

"I will, sir."

When the two had parted, Fly considered returning to his cabin to change. Instead he ambled toward the stern, pausing to speak to the officers on watch, nodding to those who wished him a "Good morning." He was bounding up the steps to the poop deck when a voice cried out from way on high. Arching his back, his searching glance finally landed on the mizzentop where Magpie, already back at his station, was swinging from the topmast shrouds, his face incandescent with excitement.

"Sir! Look!" he gasped, pointing west. "It's them agin."

1:00 p.m.
(Afternoon Watch, Two Bells)

SINCE CO-OPERATION WAS FOUND wanting amongst those in charge of the *Amethyst*, Fly singlehandedly organized the ship's company for the eventuality of an encounter the moment they had eaten their dinner and left their mess tables to return to work. Contrary to Captain Prickett's sentiment, the men appeared to relish their preparatory drills and employments, filling them with much-needed pride of purpose. Standing next to Mr. McGilp at the wheel, though his foot tapped nervously against the deck, Fly's dark eyes swept the bustling decks with satisfaction. In a circle of vivid red on the ship's waist, the marines were cleaning their muskets; men were scurrying to replenish round shot in the holes of the hatchway coamings; they lugged boxes of grapeshot on deck, laid out powder horns, wads, and matches by the carronades, loaded pikes into buckets, and worked together to rig the *sauve-tête*: the blanket of netting that would protect them from the inevitable hail of splinters, spars, and blocks should it come to an all out battle. All was abuzz, all were stepping lively. Gone was the somnolence, which had hung upon the Amethysts for days like a pall, leaving Fly questioning whether Prickett had previously ordered their morning beer to be laced with a soporific drug.

Fly's gaze stopped on Lord Bridlington, whose pace on the poop deck was decidedly slower than the encircling gun crews moving like bees in a hive around the long guns, fitting them out, and rehearsing the steps involved in their loading and firing. The man was mincing about in an indolent fashion, as if he were browsing in a circulating library. At once, Fly marched toward him. "Have you nothing to do?"

Bridlington glared at him. "I don't like your tone, Mr. Austen."

"I give no apology for my tone. But given our circumstances, since you seem to be at leisure, you could round up men to clear the bulkheads of the great cabin."

"I don't take my orders from you," Bridlington whistled through the stumps of his front teeth, "for you are not yet the commander of this ship."

Fly's voice remained dead calm. "Nay, but when I am, you'd better hope the Admiralty grants you a transfer to a different ship."

Some of Bridlington's confidence fell away. "Besides … besides, Captain Prickett expressly requested we keep his cabin intact."

"Where *is* your captain?"

"In the hospital," the first lieutenant replied, hastily pushing past him to resume his stroll.

"Patience, patience," Fly cautioned, stemming his anger with thoughts of how he would have dealt with such an insubordinate on the *Isabelle*. A little shot rolling might do the trick. Wouldn't he love to see Bridlington knocked off his feet? He made his way to the forepeak, where Osmund Brockley now proudly presided over the ill and the injured. Stopping short at the bottom of the ladder, he found Prickett ensconced in a hammock, his eyes tearing up, laughing hysterically along with Meg Kettle, who lay on her side in her own bed, one arm cradling her head, her shirt indecently exposing the rounded tops of her bosom.

"The men are ready, sir."

Prickett rolled heavy eyelids toward Fly. "For what, Mr. Austen?"

"For action. We're most assuredly being followed."

"Why are you always so goosey, man? My guess is they are whalers, travelling together for safety's sake." He winked at Mrs. Kettle. "I bet I'm right, Meggie."

"I betcha are too," flirted the laundress.

"Excuse me, sir, but are you not well?"

With a long groan, Prickett dropped his head upon his pillow. "Nay! Not at all, Mr. Austen. I've such flutterings of the heart, and shifting pains in my gut, and excessive secretions in the pits of my arms. And, if that weren't enough, I'm plagued with frequent bouts of diarrhea."

Mrs. Kettle covered her mouth to titter.

Fly shot a quizzical glance at Osmund, who swiftly lowered his head to devote his full attention to the stirring and cooling of his soup. "Mr. Brockley, what are you giving him for his various complaints?"

"Laudanum, sir."

"With what?"

"He likes it taken with whiskey, sir."

When another glance at Prickett revealed the man had slipped into a stupor, Fly squeezed his eyes shut. "Mr. Brockley, I'm no doctor, but I ask that you see me before you give the captain another tincture of opium."

"Right, sir, but he won't like it. He's been beggin' fer it nonstop."

Fly rounded on Mrs. Kettle, who, without her amiable companion to amuse her, was now pretending to read a book. "Get up, and return to your chores."

"I don't want to do the launderin' no more."

"You're quite welcome to take your concern up with the captain when he's gathered his wits."

"Me back hurts so."

"Would you prefer to have the job of trapping the rats in the hold?"

Mrs. Kettle pulled an ugly face.

"We're always short of topmen. How do you think you would fare on the yards' footropes, Mrs. Kettle?"

"I don't hear no one callin' ya Captain."

"Get up at once. Do not make me call for the bosun and his rattan."

"Ya wouldn't hit a lady!"

"No, but *he* wouldn't hesitate!" Fly stood his ground until Mrs. Kettle had reluctantly flipped from her hammock.

"If I lose me babe," she squabbled, casting about for her shoes, "it'll be on account o' yer orderin' me back to hangin' laundry when I'm still sufferin' so."

"While I'm most happy to hear that you didn't lose your child, Mrs. Kettle, you should thank your stars that you've not yet lost your *head*."

Comprehending his meaning at once, Mrs. Kettle blanched as white as the *Amethyst*'s fore and aft sails. Plucking up her shoes, she hurried from the hospital with them still in her arms. Perhaps worried he too would become a recipient of Mr. Austen's wrath, Osmund slunk away and began rearranging the bottles and jars in Dr. Braden's medicine chest.

Fly stood in the middle of the hospital, his eyes blurring on Leander's writing box. *It was a mess; it was all a mess. Nothing was as it should be.* He waited until he felt more tranquil before returning to the quarterdeck, wishing he could retreat to the wardroom to drink wine rather than leading the ill-prepared Amethysts through more anxious hours.

Just as he set foot on the ladder, one of the ship's guns exploded.

1:30 p.m.
(Afternoon Watch, Three Bells)

If Fly thought chaos was reigning supreme in Dr. Braden's hospital, he was chagrined to find a smoking carronade and disorder on the poop deck.

"We was just practisin', sir; I was just leadin' the lads through the drill, and she misfired," said the gun captain, his blackened face transfixed with shock, standing there holding the gunlock's lead cover in his hand. At his feet were three of his crew: one scorched and inert, another gawping at his red, raw arms, and the third swearing profusely at a little powder monkey for stealing the buttons from his torn shirt. A fourth man sat nearby, grimacing in pain, his foot having been crushed under the recoiling weight of the gun carriage.

Exacerbating the situation was Lord Bridlington, who'd been thrown to the deck in the blast. He lay on his stomach, arms and legs spread-eagle, as if he were about to be flogged in a prone position. "They tried to kill me!" he shrieked. "There was a plot afoot to kill me!"

Ever mindful of the pain and scars of his own burns, and desiring only to get the injured down to the hospital, Fly's response was unsympathetic. "Curtail your nonsense, Mr. Bridlington."

"The very second I walked by that gun it went off. Treason! Treason, I say!" he whistled, getting up to gently strike his limbs, as if to make certain he was still all there.

"Did you lose another finger?"

Bridlington brought his hands to his face. "Noooo."

"Then you can pick yourself up, brush yourself off, and make yourself useful."

In no mood to deal with Bridlington's indignation, Fly turned away to rally volunteers. "See to these men! Easy now! Fetch the stretchers if need be! Run ahead and tell Mr. Brockley he'll soon have four more patients." Sighting Morgan's distinctive woolly thrum cap in the crowd, he pulled the carpenter aside. "Could you provide some assistance in the hospital? I fear Mr. Brockley is in way over his head. If he carries on as he has been, we'll all be devoted to laudanum when we reach England."

Morgan's fist touched his cap accordingly, and he was about to head off when he discovered Magpie at his side. Having scuttled down the mizzen the minute the ship stopped rocking, the little sailmaker had overhead Mr. Austen's request. "If ya want, sir, I'll help too. I knows somethin' o' bandages, and sand on the floor, and the like."

"I'm grateful to you, Magpie. Perhaps you could sprinkle vinegar on the floor? I believe a good disinfecting is long overdue."

Magpie nodded, recognizing the importance of his new role.

Morgan caught Fly's attention, his lips moving silently. "What about Mrs. Kettle?"

"Trundled out," he mouthed in reply.

Having cleared the accident scene, Fly rushed back to the taffrail to raise his spyglass once again. Was it his imagination? Had the ships gained on them? He gazed up at the *Amethyst*'s sails; not all of them were set. Where was the sailing master? It was imperative they stay ahead of them, at least until nightfall. He was about to call for the ship's speed, and to the captain of the tops to see to the unfurling of the gallants, when, as if in answer to their misfiring gun, there came an answer back.

A single gun boomed over the water, sending a chill through Fly. Around him, the Amethysts stopped in their tracks. Still clutching boxes and pikes and muskets and cannonballs, their eyes flew to the stern. At so far a distance, what did it mean? Was it a signal from a friend, or a signal to war?

At sea

LEANDER LIFTED HIS HEAD up, and as he listened, he nudged Biscuit, who lay slumped against him.

"Did you hear that?"

"Hear what?" grumbled Biscuit, rubbing his sleepy eyes. "I hear nothin' but me belly. I swear I swallowed two crabby old women that're scratchin' at one another's faces."

"Shhh! Listen!" whispered Leander. "Guns firing!"

"I figured it would come to this. Yer hallucinatin', Doc." Biscuit looked over at their companions, who were asleep in the skiff's stern, their mouths open as if hoping to catch a flying fish, one still grasping onto the ropes that governed their single sail. "Apparently, our mates heard nothin'."

"Wake them up! We must steer toward the guns," insisted Leander.

"Oh, nice! Folly it is then. Did ya wanna sail below their batteries, and get shot to pieces?"

"Perhaps Providence will smile on us, and we'll discover they're the guns of our countrymen."

"And what if they ain't?"

"At this point, I no longer care."

They exchanged a meaningful glance.

"Right then," whispered Biscuit. Moving nothing more than the muscles of his mouth, he barked, "You there, Helmsman!" It took a considerable amount of Biscuit's waning energy, and more than one bark to rouse the comatose sailors, as well as a few minutes of waiting before the one holding the sailing ropes looked up in anticipation. "We're settin' a new course! Tell 'im where to, Doc."

Leander felt a flutter in his belly, and a tingling in his weakening limbs. Pressing his clasped hands to his lips, he finally called out, "Due south."

24

Wednesday, August 25

2:00 p.m.
Winchester

GUS COULD HARDLY BELIEVE his ears. What was it old Dr. Braden had just said to his Aunt Sophia? He pinched himself. Was he dreaming? Hoping to hear the suggestion repeated, he fixed his shining eyes on the doctor, who sat across from him at the small oak table in the kitchen at Butterfield Farm. Begrudgingly, his aunt had prepared tea, but in doing so had mortified Gus by refusing to take out her porcelain teapot and saucers from the sideboard, using the excuse that "a country doctor such as yerself deserves, I suppose, nothing more than a clay mug and a basin of bread and butter."

Old Dr. Braden did not seem in the least bit put off by Aunt Sophia's scarcity of charm and hospitality, and, thankfully, his surprising suggestion — nay, his invitation — had served to dampen Gus's embarrassing recollection of the unfavourable beginning to his unexpected call.

"You see, I have occasion to visit a cousin in London who's long been ailing, and, I thought, as I should only be away a few days, why not take Mr. Walby with me?" He turned to smile at Gus. "Besides, I believe he has a special someone there whom he's most anxious to see again."

It took a moment for Aunt Sophia, who was bouncing her homely, ill-tempered baby on her lap, to snap shut her suspended mouth. She seemed as dumbfounded with the invitation as was Gus. "Ya mean that haughty princess what didn't have the decency to make me acquaintance on the day that fat Duke what's-his-name left Gus here?"

"She's not haughty at all, Auntie," insisted Gus.

Aunt Sophia frowned at her nephew. "Is she the one ya dashed that letter off to yesterday?"

Gus nodded with excitement.

"Well, she won't have got it yet. She won't know yer coming."

"There's nothing more pleasing than a surprise," Old Dr. Braden serenely remarked.

"And why should she stoop to receive ya at all? Yer nothing but a mid-shipmite, and a broken one at that."

"Because, Auntie, because … because we're friends," stammered Gus, wounded by her slight.

"I'm very much hopeful she'll agree to receive us both, even if she has to call off her guards and archers," said the doctor, lifting his mug to his lips and taking a generous sip, despite the fact that the tea was of poor quality and tasted quite as if Aunt Sophia had boiled it in laundry water. But he seemed content, and continued in his pleasant manner. "Mr. Walby has delighted me with stories of her warmth and compassion, and her keen sense of adventure."

"Well, I dunno," said Aunt Sophia with a toss of her head. "I never heard of a princess what had compassion fer nobody."

Old Dr. Braden winked at Gus. "I must confess that I'm most anxious to make her acquaintance."

Aunt Sophia's eyes suddenly narrowed. "Gus ain't got no money fer travelling, and no proper clothes fer visiting with a princess, even if she ain't a haughty one. And I ain't giving ya nothing fer his expenses."

"With your permission, good madam, *I* shall take care of his expenses," said the doctor, sampling his slice of buttered bread.

For a moment Aunt Sophia fell quiet, and then she began hemming and hawing, and soon she was squawking something fierce about having to take on Gus's chores, for she had no husband — the one she once had having abandoned her months ago for a *tawdry harlot* in a travelling theatre — and with so many babes underfoot, she simply could not manage more chores; and how if she were to ask the field labourers to take them on she would have to pay them extra, and this would cause her undue grief, for she had very little at her disposal, having seen no money from Gus's uncle, her seafaring, ne'er-do-well of a brother, in a crow's age.

Her tedious quibbling left Gus holding his breath. Oh, what if she refused to let him go? He was near to abandoning hope when old Dr. Braden calmly set a five-pound note upon the table, and slid it toward Aunt Sophia. The sudden change in her countenance and deportment was quite remarkable.

"Well, ya appear to be a decent sort, Doctor, so ya can take him. He's more hindrance than help 'round here anyways." She wagged a finger at him. "But I ain't putting ya up fer the night."

Old Dr. Braden bestowed a generous smile upon her. "As there are many hours of daylight remaining, the minute Mr. Walby has gathered his belongings we shall be on our way, and out of yours." He lightly tapped the palms of his hands upon the table and looked toward Gus, who sat there in a happy trance, hardly daring to believe his good luck. "Well, young sir, get a move on. Go pack your things."

Spurred to action, Gus grabbed his crutch and hobbled across the kitch-en's stone floor to the narrow passage of stairs that led to his garret room.

"Now, Doctor, if ya kin bear his sour company and that bent leg o' his," said Aunt Sophia, determined to have the last word, "yer welcome to keep him ... fer good."

2:30 p.m.
Portsmouth Harbour

THE PRISONERS DUE FOR transportation were ordered on deck — the frail ones coaxed along with the aid of the guards' musket butts — where they were to deliver up their mean hammocks and bed-sacks before being herded into rows, according to their ultimate destination. Standing before them, his boots planted in a wide stance upon a raised dais in the bow of the *Illustrious*, was the smug, slovenly lieutenant-in-command, who, in a savage voice, shouted out the place names one-at-a-time: "Dartmoor Prison in the county of Devon; Newgate Prison, London; Woolwich on the Thames, Portchester Castle, Portchester; His Britannic Majesty's Prison Ship *Brunswick* in the Medway River; His Britannic Majesty's Prison Ships *Hector* and *La Brave*, Plymouth ..."

Trevelyan was among the herded prisoners. Assessing the scenes around him, he could not help but feel encouraged; over half the ship's company of shuffling skeletons was being moved to make room for a fresh crop of incoming prisoners, newly acquired from various American prizes taken on the Atlantic. With the addition of surly English officers from shore, and their armed soldiers brought along to keep the prisoners orderly — the guards of the prison hulk evidently incapable of instilling them with confidence based on the number of recently attempted escapes — the deck was terribly overcrowded, and every so often one of the frail prisoners would collapse in the crush, crying out in painful despair. Wherever Trevelyan looked, there were sweating, stinking bodies and confusion, and the smoky air around the *Illustrious* quivered with pitiful bleats and raucous commands.

Perhaps this would be easier than he had imagined.

It was essential he stay as close as possible to Twitch, who was now able to stand thanks to a few additional loaves of bread, though the two men were careful not to speak to one another. Their last words had been communicated late in the night, when the others were asleep.

"When they find out, do ya think they'll hang me?" Twitch had whispered in fearful gulps.

"Nay, it's me they want, not you," Trevelyan had assured him, as he handed over his clothes and the final bribe of bread.

Now, as the two waited in their respective lines under the hot afternoon sun, Trevelyan gave Twitch a furtive glance. The American's countenance was a shade of sickly pale, but he was smartly outfitted in a once-fine muslin shirt, knee breeches, and wooden clogs, his convulsing infrequent and barely noticeable, looking decidedly more regal than his counterparts in their coarse yellow jackets and trousers, stamped with the initials TO for Transport Office, and those pathetic souls who wore nothing at all.

Trevelyan was clad only in his linen drawers, but in a canvas bag he carried a tricorne and a velvet coat — valuable souvenirs of his brief stay on the *Illustrious*. Initially, he had thought it wise to wear them, and then changed his mind, deciding he'd be more conspicuous *in* them than out. They would come in handy, if not now then somewhere down the road. Having overheard chatter that this would be the day for the prisoners' removal from the hulk, he had smudged his face with tar and hacked off his hair — grown long in his weeks of captivity — with the aid of scissors filched from the careless master, and zealously guarded by the prisoner who had done the filching. His oily, straw-coloured hair now stood straight up on his head, in an untamed style reminiscent of Twitch.

The lieutenant-in-command was in a foul mood. His voice was hoarse from reprimanding his guards for their bumbling organization of the prisoners; his face damp and crimson with fury at discovering, while counting, that some men had either been trampled upon somewhere on the deck, or forgotten in their Black Holes. "As you're all good-for-nothing," he yelled in exasperation, "you shall help dole out the rations of fish and bread, and then get yourselves to the aft sheds and out of my way. *I* shall do the counting myself." He crossed his arms, and set his foot to tap upon the dais while the guards, still brandishing their muskets, scurried about with the hulk's boys, handing the prisoners their pittance of food for the long journey to their next hell. When it finally came time for the lieutenant to count out the eleven prisoners bound for Newgate, and the sixty-two bound for Woolwich on the Thames, all of whom would be transported together, Trevelyan held his breath until the man was satisfied and had turned away his grumbling, red-faced attention to count the next group. Then, slowly, so as not to excite notice, he traded places with Twitch.

He kept his head down, waiting for a heavy hand to seize his arm, or a bayonet to be thrust into his buttocks. But when nothing happened, when the deck didn't erupt in pandemonium over his trickery, he dared to glance up. Two English officers and a complement of soldiers were leading the Newgate-Woolwich line of misery toward the set of wooden steps that would take them down to the floating gallery at the water's edge, and to the waiting launches that would, in turn, take them to shore.

Trevelyan felt some relief, but he could not control the trembling of his hands. He now stood in the line headed for Dartmoor Prison, which had already been checked and counted. But stories of such cruel treatment and suffering had come to those on the *Illustrious* in missives from fellow Americans holed up in that fearsome prison on its black moor that he would have no part of it. He would have to change lines again. But how, when there was no one to change with him this time?

The transportation dragged on. Trevelyan compared the sorry business to his imminent execution, only the executioner had decided to eat his lunch before carrying out his gruesome task. Perspiration rolled down his chest, his bare feet burned on the scorching timbers of the deck, his frayed nerves already made breathing difficult, but the close proximity of others pressing up against him gave him an unbearable sense of suffocation. The sun grew hotter still. The air grew increasingly fetid. And those already weakened by deprivation and want began to drop to the deck. Harassed by the English officers and their angry impatience, the lieutenant ordered the lines to move out with their escorts, even if it meant tripping over those who had fallen.

Trevelyan made his move, this time swiftly, squeezing into the bit of space left vacant by a wizened, bearded prisoner who had fortuitously fainted beside him and, most likely, passed from life. He hoped there was far too much chaos in the removal of bodies for anyone to notice the hunch-backed Thomas Trevelyan being led off the rotting decks of the *Illustrious* in his filthy drawers, away from those guards and boys and other assorted company who might recall his face.

He had managed to painfully descend the wooden stairs, and had just stepped into his designated launch — cheered at having made it this far — when nearby voices suddenly sent his pulse escalating. No more than five feet away from him was Twitch, crammed into the launch with the others headed for Newgate and Woolwich, being questioned by two English officers.

"*You* are Captain Thomas Trevelyan?" said one of them incredulously.

"I am," was Twitch's solemn answer, his shrunken body shivering.

The second officer guffawed. "Why you're just a corpuscle! You're right puny! And *you* have set all of England quaking in their beds at night?"

"We were expecting a hairy monstrosity with fangs and a serpent's tail."

They both gave Twitch's rear end a thorough inspection, but seeing nothing untoward they burst into laughter before giving him a dismissive shove. Gathering around him his dignity and his fine, loose-fitting rags, which hung from him like draperies, Twitch held his head high, and fixed his blinking gaze upon the distant town of Portsmouth. Trevelyan shot an anxious glance toward the two sentry huts on the floating gallery. Had the guards posted there overheard the jocular exchange? He kept thinking, any time now, a dozen guards would pounce upon him, shrieking obscenities, foaming at the mouth in their enthusiasm to either rip him apart or empty their bullets into his bare chest. But their attention was directed upon the slowly descending prisoners, as if they fully expected a number of them, in one last desperate attempt to escape their fate, to hurl themselves into the harbour. Trevelyan felt his shoulders droop with relief. Closing his eyes, he was able, for the first time, to draw deep breaths.

No one bothered to make inquiries about Asa Bumpus of New Bedford, who had been slated for Dartmoor Prison, and who, instead, was heading for another prison hulk, moored in the Medway River at Chatham.

5:00 p.m.
(First Dog Watch, Two Bells)
Aboard HMS *Amethyst*

CAPTAIN PRICKETT CAME hurrying onto the poop deck, his shirttails flying behind him like a billowing jib sail, his pillows having wreaked havoc upon his hair.

"Oh, Mr. Austen, I do apologize for oversleeping," he said, tucking his shirt into his stained breeches, and peeking sheepishly about at the milling Amethysts. "Now tell me why the hospital is suddenly full of men? And guns, I heard guns! What's going on?"

"Mr. Brockley didn't offer you an explanation?"

"Not at all! When I awoke he was nowhere to be found, and neither, for that matter, was Mrs. Kettle."

Fly's voice was measured in good patience, though he longed to inform the captain that the blast of guns had first rang through the air hours ago. "We are still following the movements of the two ships we spotted yesterday."

Prickett looked nervously into the distances. "Yes, yes, but who are they? And what is their business? And why are they firing their guns?"

"We've not been able to ascertain."

"Why not?"

Before giving Prickett a full accounting of the carronade accident, Fly peered down the length of the ship to see if he could spot Bridlington. If the first lieutenant were to catch sight of Prickett, raised at last from his hospital bed, he would be sure to make a beeline for the skylight — around which the two now stood — to pour forth his distorted version of the episode. When no one rushed forward to interrupt them, Fly hoped the man was safely at supper in the wardroom.

"There was only one shot fired after our accident, and we thought at first it may have been intended for us, but our deficient spyglasses can only see so far. It appears — it is my opinion — that the subsequent shots we all heard were meant for one another."

"You don't think they're in pursuit of us?" He took the glass from Fly's grasp to have a look.

"I cannot be certain of that. At times they seem to have gained on us, at others they have retreated, but always, they seem to follow our course, which makes me wonder —"

"Wonder at what, Mr. Austen?"

"Might one of them be one of ours — a ship of His Majesty's navy?"

"What if this is true?" he asked, squinting through the lens.

"Do you not think we should turn about to investigate?"

"I want no part of their business. The sooner we get home the better."

Fly's mind raced back to the decks of the *Isabelle*, to the desperate situation Captain Moreland and his loyal crew had encountered, surrounded and outgunned by three enemy ships. If only Prickett had heeded his signals for assistance on that June day. "What if they *require* our help?"

Prickett returned the glass, and then cleared and lowered his voice. "Mr. Austen, tell no one else, kind sir," — he gave a darting glance around him — "but my thinking is unclear, my eyes bleary. I have no stamina at present for an engagement of any sort."

"Even if we go back far enough so that we may have a clear view of the action. If one of our ships is in trouble we can stand to and wait, and come in if necessary."

"It'll be dark soon."

"We shall have good light until half after eight."

"Mr. Austen, I am a bundle of palpitations."

"Sir! What if it's the *Lady Jane*, and she's being chased by a privateer or an American man-o'-war?" Fly pulled his trump card. "Think of your Admiralty's orders, sir, given in Halifax."

Prickett fiddled with his straining waistband for several indecisive moments and then he looked up at Fly, his features set. "Right! We'll turn around to investigate. However, if they should both prove to be formidable foes, I'll put you in charge of handling the gun crews and getting us through it all. See that we suffer no more deaths and no more injuries, for I warrant our Mr. Brockley doesn't know what he's about." With a firm clap on Fly's arm, Prickett stomped toward the quarterdeck, bellowing with each step he took. "Pass the word for the sailing master! Where the devil has he got to? Quartermaster? What speeds have you recorded on the log board? What's our present depth? Ah, there's our master now. Good man, tell the lads to turn her around. We're going straight at 'em!"

Fly stared after him, shaking his head, not knowing whether to laugh or cry. Amidst whistles and hoots and shouts, the Amethysts worked swiftly to set a new course and tack the ship, turning her bow into the wind. For a time, Fly watched them at their various tasks, and then he walked to the taffrail and leaned upon it, fixing his thoughts upon the stern's foamy trail, which led and opened into the rolling blue vastness. "I shall never forgive you, old fellow, for abandoning me," he whispered.

It was a snuffling Magpie who finally pulled him back to the cares of the present. The little sailmaker touched his fist to his temple in a respectful salute, but his chin was trembling. "Is there a problem in the hospital?" Fly asked.

"Not at all, sir. Mr. Evans bandaged up the gunners' burns, and I done the disinfectin' like ya asked me to. I've bin on the mizzen for a bit, sir, and I was wonderin' if ya'd permit me to go out in the boats with the lads."

"The boats?" frowned Fly. "Perhaps, Magpie, sitting way up high on the top, you misunderstood. The master didn't call for the boats to be lowered. We're turning around to —"

"Beg pardon, sir," he said, his words now coming out in dry gulps. "Ya gotta know! We spotted a body floatin' in the waves, and I ... I need to see if —" He dropped his curly head on his chest, unable to finish his sentence.

25

Thursday, August 26

2:00 p.m.
Hartwood Hall

THE LIBRARY DOOR QUIETLY opened and closed. With a small shrug of annoyance, Emily twisted around on the scarlet sofa by the fireplace so that she could identify the interloper. Since her breakfast, eaten in blessed solitude, she had been hiding out, reading in the magnificent dimensions of the library under its mythically painted ceilings, surrounded by gilded and mirrored recesses and endless rows of bookshelves, her shoes off, her legs curled beneath her, and an assortment of medical tomes scattered upon the cushions beside her. But it was an old, mouldy edition of Daniel Dafoe's *The Life and Strange Surprizing Adventures of Robinson Crusoe* that she now held in her hands, having found it so absorbing and evocative that she was reluctant to tear her eyes away from its pages.

Helena sidled across the carpet toward her, as if she had come on a covert mission, and primly installed herself far from Emily, in a scarlet-silk elbow chair next to one of the great windows. She gazed out upon the verdant lawns where the gardeners were at work amongst the flowers and shrubbery. Something in her stiffened manner hinted at unpleasant business. Guessing this was neither a social visit nor an invitation to drink tea with her, Emily slipped her feet into her shoes and raised herself up on the sofa cushions.

"Mademoiselle has come back, pleading to be reinstated as Fleda's governess," Helena said, still looking out the windows.

"Oh! I did not expect her to return at all," said Emily, curious to know why the duchess felt inclined to close the door behind her in order to deliver such tedious news.

"As I made certain she could find no other employment with a *good* family, I'm not surprised in the least." Helena smiled as if she were quite pleased with herself.

"And will you reinstate her?"

"I will. But I shall be very harsh in my treatment of her from here on."

Poor Mademoiselle, thought Emily. "And how's Fleda accepting the news?"

"She made a terrible fuss, and just now had a tantrum in the schoolroom."

Emily smiled. "And have you come to inform me that you've hired a second governess for me?"

"Don't tempt me," Helena responded with a caustic roll of her eyes. "The Lord knows you require one, Emeline."

"Pray, what, precisely, do you mean by that remark?"

Helena lifted one of her dark eyebrows, as if to imply the obvious.

Setting aside *Robinson Crusoe*, Emily contemplated the duchess's severe profile. Last evening they had all dined together, the memory of which Emily found distasteful, for Wetherell and Adolphus were crapulous from their night of debauchery — their heads in their hands throughout most of the meal. Fleda had pushed her food around her plate, refusing to eat, and declaring she would never again play the pianoforte for *anyone*; and Helena had been a burgeoning storm cloud, about to unleash her rain and thunder at any moment. Only Somerton had been capable of decorum, bestowing upon Emily, every now and again, a few apologetic smiles, leaving her questioning whether he was trying to atone for past wrongs. When all six courses had been served and ingested, she was most relieved to see everyone going their separate ways — most of them to bed — for she had no desire to repeat the dramatics of the previous night.

"As the men are out, I felt this was a good time for us to have a little talk," said Helena. "I wasn't at all pleased to hear you stayed up with the men until all hours on Tuesday."

"Why is that?"

"You were unchaperoned."

"You left me with them quite willingly earlier in the evening."

"I didn't expect you to stay up with them until dawn."

"It was 2:00 when I returned to my room."

"Yes, and you proceeded to awaken the household with your hysterical laughter."

"*Most* of the household was still up with me."

"I awoke with such a fright. I was convinced a fiend had entered our midst on the first floor."

"I know for a fact there was at least one *drunken* fiend about at that late hour."

Helena admonished her remark with a withering stare before continuing. "Is this the sort of behaviour with which you conducted yourself while at sea?"

"I made a point of playing the fiend every night, and always during the Middle Watch."

"Most amusing!"

"Were you unable to sleep, worried that I was joining your husband and sons in draining your stores of Madeira? And being the light, loose woman I am, did you fancy I was flirting with your Wetherell?"

Helena's mouth had dropped open in horror, but Emily pressed on. "It is plainly evident you don't like me, Your Grace. From the moment I arrived at Hartwood your behaviour toward me has been icy at best, so much so that I've often wondered why you agreed to provide me with accommodation in the first place. I confess I'm not happy here, but I've tried to be pleasant to your family; I've tried to show my gratitude. I do not understand how I offend you so."

Helena slowly formed and enunciated her answer. "And if I can help it, you shall *never* know."

Emily's eyes flickered, so confounded she was by such a disturbing declaration. With nonchalance, Helena adjusted the collar on her gown, clasped her hands neatly upon her lap, and compressed her thin lips. "I want you to return the emerald."

Still reeling from the force of Helena's former words, Emily hesitated. "Perhaps it would be best if you take up the matter with Wetherell."

"It was a gift, you see."

"I didn't steal it from Wetherell; he gambled it away."

"*I* was the one who gave it to him."

"Then he shouldn't have been so heartless as to offer it up as a wager."

"What do you need with an emerald ring? You must have an abundance of them at Windsor."

"It was won fairly."

"I *cannot* bear the thought of you having it."

"Is there a particular sentiment attached to this ring?"

"It was given from a mother to her son on his eighteenth birthday."

"Is Wetherell your favourite son?"

Her reply was shockingly swift. "No! Somerton is."

"I'm curious; did you give your *eighth* son a ring on his eighteenth birthday? Or had he been sent to sea at that time, and was therefore out of sight and mind?"

The duchess recoiled in her chair, her posture reminiscent of the sudden change in winds, which often flattened the square sails of the *Isabelle* against her masts. "Why should you care about my *eighth* son? It was my understanding that you were not acquainted with him."

Emily was beyond caring for discretion. "I believe *Octavius* could've benefitted greatly from some of the attention you amply lavish upon your two eldest sons."

Helena grasped the arms of her chair. "Whatever does that mean?"

"If I can help it, you shall *never* know."

Helena leapt to her feet, her face as white as her summer gown. "You have kept secrets from us."

"I am no more *secretive* than you are."

"How dare you."

"You are welcome to banish me from your house; I'm quite ready to leave. Say the word and I'll have my things gathered in less than an hour. Perhaps Somerton would be so kind as to take me to town."

Helena looked down at her. "Somerton will *not* be taking you anywhere."

"Are you worried I'd knock him about the head, stuff him into a sack, and impress him into the Royal Navy?"

"I wouldn't put it past you."

"Perhaps Wetherell should be *impressed* as well. Your sons might enjoy the experience; it would give them something *useful* to do." Emily was certain she could see steam rising from Helena's elaborate crown of curls.

"You're a selfish, outspoken, ill-bred young woman."

Emily's gaze flicked upward. "Your own description, I think, though I wouldn't use the word *young*."

Helena looked like one of the boiling pots in the Hartwood kitchen, but Emily turned away from her, sickened by the stifling humidity of the room, which had enveloped her like a fur-lined pelisse. Into her consciousness crept the carefree conversation of the gardeners, and the happy songs of the chestnut trees' winged residents, awakening memories of a more tranquil world beyond the library walls. Oh, to be outside with them, seeking out her magpie, or climbing up the spreading trunk of one of those old chestnuts and hiding out upon its shady arms. She was plotting her escape when a sudden pounding upon the library door gave her a start.

"Oh, what is it now?" snapped Helena.

Glenna poked her round, glistening face into the room. "Lud! I've been knockin' for ten minutes."

"*Do* remember your station, Miss McCubbin!"

Glenna squeezed through the door, curtsied quickly, and then shot a quizzical look at Emily, mouthing the words, "*Such a rumpus!*"

"Well?" Helena asked, her eyes shut, one hand pressed to her forehead.

The old housekeeper glanced anxiously at her employer. "We have visitors, Your Grace."

"Don't tell me the Duke of Clarence is here already?"

"Nay, Your Grace. He's not expected 'til dinnertime."

"Well then, who is it?"

"An older gentleman and a lame boy."

Helena growled. "How did they get past the gatekeeper? Are they beggars? Gypsies? Send them away at once. I'll not have riffraff at my door."

"I wouldna say they're beggars," said Glenna with an uneasy peek at Emily, whose suspicion was immediately aroused.

"Have they *professed* their business?" asked Helena, standing there in all her state, a pillar of indignity.

Glenna looked flustered. "Might I've a word with ya alone, Your Grace?"

"By all means!" Helena gloated before drifting from the room with the housekeeper. "You may continue your reading, Emeline. I shall *not* disturb you again."

2:30 p.m.

EMILY HAD NO INTENTION of returning to her reading; how could anyone concentrate on *Robinson Crusoe* after such a tumult? She lingered for a few respectable minutes before leaving her books and the library to follow the women. Who was it that had come? And why had Glenna appeared so uneasy? Blazing with curiosity, she hurried after them, hoping to hear their voices whispering in collusion, or to find that Glenna had left the visitors awaiting their audience in one of the ground floor rooms. Her hopes, however, were soon dashed; her curiosity rewarded with nothing more than a series of empty rooms and secured doors.

At last, as she approached the front hall, Emily found Fleda standing in the doorway, her hair afire in a beam of afternoon sunshine that had found its way into the darkened house, her skinny arms folded and locked upon her chest, as if she were trying to intimidate someone or something. Beyond the child, out on the gravel courtyard, Helena's vocals rose up in crackling irritation. Tiptoeing toward the shelter of the nearest marble column, Emily flattened herself against it to listen in.

"I am most displeased that you were let onto the grounds. You've no business here."

A male voice, as warm as the August breeze wafting through the open door, answered her. "We shall not stay but a moment, Your Grace. If you would just allow us to extend our regards to Her Royal Highness, we would be much obliged. We've come such a long way."

"I do not permit Her Royal Highness to receive visitors with whom I am not acquainted, and, as my husband and sons are not presently at home, I ask that you leave at once."

"Of course, Your Grace." There was a lull in the conversation, and the sound of shoes shuffling upon the gravel could be heard. "Would you be so kind as to inform Her Royal Highness that we came by, and that we're lodging at the coaching inn down the road?"

"Perhaps, but as I determine who she sees, and who she does not, I can assure you she'll *not* be visiting you in the taproom of a vulgar posting-house."

At that moment a young boy spoke up, his voice panicked, as if he were terrified of being turned away. "With respect, Your — Your Grace, we don't

want to give you any trouble. Would you feel more at ease if I told you I'm
an officer of the Royal Navy?"

Helena's laughter was trenchant. "Really! An officer? Not a street urchin?"

Not to be deterred, the boy kept on. "I recently served under Captain
James Moreland on HMS *Isabelle.*"

Emily's hand flew to her mouth; the shock of joy embraced her. It was
Gus Walby, and, more than likely, his elderly doctor, the man she had seen
in Winchester, the man whom she had fancied was ...

In the doorway, Fleda relaxed her stance. "Did you know my brother?"

"I'd be happy to tell you, Miss," chirped Gus, "but I'm afraid I don't
know the name of your brother."

Helena put an end to their exchange with a rumble. "Fleda! Return
to Mademoiselle at once." She waited until her daughter had unhappily
drawn back into the shadows of the hallway. "Now then, you two, I don't
care if you're the Prince Regent and his servant, no one invited you here.
Leave quietly now, or I shall have to —"

Emily had heard quite enough. Startling Fleda, she jumped out from
behind the column, and pushing past the girl, hurried through the door
with a happy cry. "Dear Mr. Walby! How good of you to have come!"

Gus's mouth fell open, as if he hadn't quite believed in the first place
that she was actually housed within the uninviting walls of Hartwood, but
once he had gathered his wits his young face was wreathed in smiles, and he
hobbled toward her, shouting, "Em! Oh, Em!" His outburst of familiarity
sent a shiver through Helena and the gentleman at his side to leap after him
in order to place a steadying hand on his shoulder.

Unable to acknowledge the elderly gentleman — so certain she was
that he could hear the riotous pounding of her heart — Emily smiled her
warmest for Gus, and kept her eyes on the boy as she addressed the glowering Helena. "They are *my* visitors, Your Grace. If you'll not permit them to
stay, then I shall leave with them."

Helena eyed the men with disdain, her cheeks suffused with red, her lips
tightly pressed together. Finally, she levelled a stare at Emily. "They may walk
the grounds with you," she said, her voice no longer vociferous, "but they
shall not receive an invitation indoors to drink tea with *me.*" With her head
held high she slipped into the house, slamming the door behind her, and,
with Fleda at her side, took up residence at one of the hall windows to observe

them. Refusing to be put off by the duchess, Emily flew to Gus and seized his hand, the two of them talking at once in their pleasure of being reunited.

"If our coming has caused distress, Em —"

"Do not worry about the duchess! She is surly by nature." Emily stepped back to inspect Gus, unhappy to see dark circles under his eyes and that he had grown so thin. "But look at you! I swear you've gained a foot in height since I left you in Winchester. We must see to you getting fitted out with a new uniform before you return to sea. You've quite outgrown this one." Knowing the gentleman's eyes were watching her, Emily could not contain the quiver in her voice.

"Did you get my letter, Em?" Gus asked in a fit of coughing. "I sent it to you yesterday."

"Not yet! But why only yesterday, why did you wait so long to write to me? I sent *you* a note the minute I'd slept off the exhaustion of our long voyage."

"I never received it. If it hadn't been for the kindness of the Duke of Clarence, I never would've known where you were."

"Let us sort that out later, shall we?" said Emily, too elated to be discussing letters which had not arrived. She straightened before the gentleman and extended her hand, aware of having blushed as scarlet as the silk sofas in the library. "Kind sir, thank you so very much for bringing Mr. Walby to me."

Gus stood between the two of them on his crutch, beaming at one and then the other.

"Your Royal Highness," the man said, clasping her hand. "Arthur Braden is my name, and I believe … I've been told that you are acquainted with my son."

Emily finally found the courage to meet the older man's eyes, and just as she had suspected they were kind and intelligent, and the colour of the sea.

6:00 p.m.

"God Almighty, Emeline!" declared Uncle Clarence upon seeing Emily stepping lightly into the music room with a flushed-faced Fleda in tow. "Have I not taught you to be prompt for meals, especially when you're so blessed to be taking your dinner in the esteemed company of such illustrious gentlemen?"

Emily and Fleda had hastily washed and spruced up, having passed the afternoon strolling the worn paths of the estate with old Dr. Braden and Mr. Walby with no desire to part their company sooner than necessary. Arriving downstairs in their evening dress, they had discovered Somerton, Wetherell, and the latest arrival, the Duke of Clarence, assembled in the music room around the chimneypiece, enjoying a drink as they awaited both the call to dinner and the young ladies' return. Wetherell was standing apart from the others, seemingly humming a tune in his head, but it did not escape Emily's notice that Somerton had positioned himself with a clear view to the door, and had looked up the very second they appeared.

Emily bowed to the brothers, and gave her uncle a quick buss on the cheek. "I am so sorry. I quite forgot the time."

"You didn't forget I was coming."

"Not at all; however, I do understand you shall be staying with us for a few days."

"I shall be, for the duchess requires my brilliant and bluff repartee and some assistance in planning her next ball."

"I keep hearing mutterings of another ball, and yet no one has said when the great event is to be held," said Emily, looking to the brothers for an answer. Wetherell averted his head to carry on with his humming, and Somerton, although she had perceived his eyes moving over the detailing of her gown, decided it was time to consult his pocket watch. It was, therefore, left to her uncle to indulge her.

"Soon, my dear, soon," he said with a wink.

Emily grimaced. "I do hope you won't be inviting Mr. Gribble again, Uncle."

"His name ranks among the first on our guest list. If I were to exclude him from our little party he'd be insulted, and return to his country seat for good."

What a pleasing repercussion, thought Emily, deciding against sharing her sentiment with the others. She teased her uncle instead. "You shan't run off on us?"

"Only if my eldest brother calls me urgently to town on business. I must be ready at all times to heed his summons and do my duty."

"You're looking well, Emeline. Your exercise must've agreed with you," said Somerton, his rigid demeanour so similar to that of his mother.

Emily smiled to herself, thinking of old Dr. Braden and the precious hours they had shared together. It was not only the colour and contours of his eyes, which his son, Leander, had inherited from him. "Indeed! It was *most* restorative," she said, with an emphatic vivaciousness.

"I suppose," added Wetherell, dressed in another outlandish combination of colours and collars, "if one enjoys that sort of thing, tramping about the county in the society of vagabonds."

Emily swung toward him. "Really, sir, you should leave your club in St. James's Street more frequently; you might be surprised to learn that your compatriots are not all hoydens and heathens."

Wetherell's response was to crouch before the music room mirror to pinch his cheeks and articulate his complaints. "I don't like these country hours that Mother and Father keep for their meals. In town we eat dinner at 8:00, sometimes 9:00, and then enjoy a late supper after playing cards."

Uncle Clarence brought the attention back to Emily. "And how's young Mr. Walby?"

It was Fleda who piped up. "He's very well, Your Royal Highness! So affable! And he tells such stories!"

"All seamen have *such* stories to tell," he grinned. "I've quite a reputation myself as a spinner of yarns, though I'd be given the boot for recounting them in mixed company. Now tell me, Emeline, is Mr. Walby raring to return to sea?"

"The first chance he gets!"

"As what? A swabber?" asked Wetherell. "The boy is misshapen!"

"He is not! He's a midshipman," said Fleda, rising on her heels.

Wetherell made some unintelligible remark and returned to the mirror for further adjustment. Fleda looked up eagerly at Somerton. "Mr. Walby is staying at the coaching inn down the road while Dr. Braden is visiting his sick cousin. Could he stay with us, Brother? Please? I've never had a friend my own age, and he's such fun."

Deep, ugly lines furrowed Somerton's brow. "Your mother is not at all happy with you, Fleda, neglecting your lessons to spend time with this Mr. *Walby*." He finished with a darting glance at Emily.

"Mother is never happy! If I were to wear my hair in the style of Mrs. Fitzherbert and play flawless tunes on the pianoforte, she would still find fault," she lamented before grabbing Somerton's arm in earnest. "Please,

Brother? I could share my meals with him in the schoolroom, and we shall promise to stay out of sight."

Uncle Clarence leaned over to whisper in Emily's ear. "Who is this tiny witch?"

"She's a *sprite*, not a witch!"

"I don't believe I've met her before."

"You have, Uncle, I introduced you to her in my bedchamber the evening of the ball."

"Yes, yes! But who is she? I've quite forgotten."

"I shan't tell you again; she's your friends' youngest child."

Uncle Clarence looked terribly puzzled as he finished his wine, but was soon diverted by the appearance of Glenna McCubbin, who had come to inform them all that the *roast o' beef* was ready to be delivered to the table, and that the duke and duchess were awaiting their presence in the dining room. Scurrying up to the housekeeper, he groped for her hand to kiss it. "My dear Miss McCubbin! Will you do me the honour and save a dance for me at the next Hartwood ball?"

Glenna blushed with the heart-pumping surprise of securing the attentions of such an exalted gentleman. "Lud! On my arthritic ankles? And where will I be goin' when Her Grace dismisses me, and throws me out on the road to be ravished by the highwaymen?"

Wetherell had successfully pulled himself away from the mirror in time to witness the Duke of Clarence's wanton display of affection for Miss McCubbin. "There now!" he said drolly, giving Emily a rare direct glance. "If that isn't evidence that the royal apple doesn't fall far from the tree of Hanover, I don't know what is." Then, taking her by surprise, he linked arms with her to lead her to supper. As they journeyed to the dining room, he licked his lips and said, "You will play cards with us again soon, won't you, Your Royal Highness? I'm a heap of rapturous shivers just thinking about it."

26

Friday, August 27

FLY SAT OPPOSITE CAPTAIN Prickett and First Lieutenant Bridlington in the great cabin, watching the two relish their breakfast of soft-boiled eggs and bacon, his anxiety so devastating this morning that he could swallow nothing more than coffee. Behind the relaxed eaters rain pelted the galleried windows, and the mournful sea beyond abounded in bobbing whitecaps.

"I'm rapidly tiring of this chase, Mr. Austen," said Prickett, wiping his hands on his linen napkin, which, stuffed into the open neck of his shirt, resembled a coarse-looking tucker. "The men have been at their battle stations for almost two days now, and seen no action."

"Gentlemen, not all battles are fought and won in the space of an afternoon." Fly pulled his chair closer to the table. "We have the two ships in sight again this morning; they're now but a few hours away."

"Do they continue to sail close to one another?"

"Nay, there's presently a wide expanse between them."

Bridlington started fretting. "Mr. Austen, we cannot go chasing after every sail we see. How much longer must we keep this up?"

"Until we are quite certain we can be of no assistance."

"I shall be a force to be reckoned with, Mr. Austen, if they should both prove to be our friends," said Prickett, jabbing his knife in the air at him.

"At the very least, it is obvious *both* are not His Majesty's ships."

"How do you know that?"

Fly suppressed a laugh. "If they are, sir, they have a strange way of showing their regard for one another."

Prickett pursed his lips. "Yes, yes, I suppose you're right.

"Unless, of course, they have no idea who the other is, which is not unreasonable. It wouldn't be the first time ships of the same navy have inadvertently taken broadsides at one another." Fly forced a smile. "Think how overjoyed you shall feel if one of them proves to be the *Lady Jane*."

"Very well then, but you must promise me to take down our ensign and flags — at least until we know what and who we're up against."

Fly nodded in assent, not in the least surprised by the captain's request, remembering all too well the day Prickett had concealed the markers of the *Amethyst*'s country of origin from a distraught Captain Moreland.

"Oh, my goodness me!" said Prickett suddenly, as if he had just noticed he was wearing no trousers. "And what of this dead body we found yesterday? What have you discovered of him?"

It was on Fly's lips to inquire why the captain had been absent from the quarterdeck when the corpse had been brought on board. "He was one of the sailors who went with Dr. Braden and Biscuit in the skiff to rescue Magpie."

Prickett shook his head with gravity. "Then it is confirmed, Mr. Austen; your friends are lost."

"Not necessarily, sir. Several of us have examined the body. The man has not been long dead."

"But as *he* was floating in the sea, I suppose the others are as well."

Fly closed his hands around his coffee mug. "Just now we made a most astonishing discovery."

"Oh, what could be more astonishing than discovering a dead man on the sea?"

"There was a gold watch on the body, sir. Mr. Evans recognized it as belonging to Biscuit. We all thought it exceedingly odd until we opened it up and found a message on a strip of muslin."

"How extraordinary!" Bridlington exclaimed. "Did our men have a pen and ink on them when they jumped into the skiff?"

Prickett rolled his eyes at his second-in-command in such a dramatic fashion, Fly was positive the man could make a thriving second career as a thespian in pantomimes. "It was written in *blood*, using a toothpick or a splinter of wood."

"Blood!" Bridlington shrank back in his chair.

"For God's sake, what was the message?" asked Prickett.

"As of August twenty-fourth, they were alive. It ended with a plea to find them."

"Good Lord! How long can a body go without food?"

"I've known men to exceed two weeks, though they were very near death when found."

Prickett and Bridlington went quiet, trying to digest a scenario of starvation.

"With your permission, sir, I'd like to place more men on watch."

Prickett blinked at Fly until his meaning became clear. "We are *not* sailing on Lake Windermere."

"No — no we are not," was Fly's quiet reply. "Still, I feel it's not an impossibility."

9:00 a.m.
At Sea

WHEN THE RAIN LET UP, Leander tugged the sheltering jacket from his face and pulled one of the old biscuit pails toward him, elated to find it half-full of fresh water. Not certain he possessed the strength to lift it to his sunburned lips, he dipped his hands into the precious drink and brought it to his mouth, wishing it would extinguish the stabbing cramps of hunger. Squeezing his eyes shut to await their passing, he prayed — when he opened them again — he would find a school of fish squiggling in the many inches of rainwater that swirled about the skiff's bottom. But no, he found only the tangle of legs belonging to his mates, their upper bodies concealed under various articles of sodden clothing, with the exception of the coxswain, who still held the cordage of their square sail tightly in one hand, still navigating, though whether he too had died in the night Leander could not be certain. Had he been too hasty in slipping the dead sailor over the side a few days back?

Reaching around to grab hold of the gunwales, he hoisted his head up to resume the heart-wrenching business of searching for sails, cursing his lack of a telescope or a voice with which to awaken Biscuit to ask if the cook could see anything in the distances; yet search he must. Yesterday they had spotted two ships, had come close to them even — though, tragically, not close enough for the lookouts to spot their puny sail or hear their unison of desperate calls, *"Ahoy, ship, ahoy!"* And the firing of guns, which had initially led them in their direction had ceased long ago, though when exactly Leander could not recall, for his mind was muddled. How long they had been adrift he did not know; when they had tasted their last morsel of salted pork, he could not say.

Exhausted by the effort of hooking his arms over the side of the skiff, he listened to the waves nudging the hull and rested his head to remember the last time he had seen Emily. If nothing else, his memory of her was still clear and bright and tangible. The sunlight of that early July morning illumined and comforted his mind: there she was, dressed in sailors' trousers, sitting on the mizzentop of her uncle's ship, the *Impregnable*, her gold hair flying behind her like a pennant, her arm raised to wave farewell.

"You will come back to me, Emily?"

"I will, as soon as I can."

"You won't forget this poor doctor on the seas?"

"How could I forget the man that introduced me to rum and laudanum?"

"I'll be waiting, watching every sail on the horizon, for your return."

"As will I, Doctor."

He stayed in that peaceful position, no longer caring or able to lift his head to search for sails. It was a lovely memory; one he would not relinquish, even if life were to leave him.

11:00 a.m.
(Forenoon Watch, Six Bells)
Aboard HMS *Amethyst*

THE GUNS HAD RESUMED an hour ago, just as the *Amethyst* was closing in. Excitement had been mounting ever since — the men, with the exception of Lord Bridlington, were itching for a fight. For a time their voices had echoed with songs and boasts of bravado; they had even made love to Mrs. Kettle while she lumbered about taking in her laundry, the woman revelling in the men's attentions, showing off her stovepipe ankles and making

240

obscene gestures with her hips. Now, as the two ships rose up before them, they stood rooted at their stations, beads of sweat on their lips, fingers twitching on muskets and matches, cartridges of gunpowder, dirks and pikes and cutlasses; their emotions locked away in silent, watchful stares.

Fly had command of the guns on the larboard fo'c'sle and quarter-deck, although he was prepared to perform a double duty if need be, for Bridlington was doing nothing to inspire confidence. Wandering well beyond the fifteen guns under his command on the starboard side — quite as if he were afraid they might be turned upon him at any moment — the first lieutenant was bouncing a curled knuckle against his mouth, talking to himself like a lunatic. Fly held his fists firmly to his sides to keep from grabbing his hair in clumps. Striving to ignore Bridlington, he made a mental check of the *Amethyst's* preparedness, his eyes scanning decks and yards and masts and men. On the foretop, Magpie was sitting on his haunches behind the cracking fore topsail, his glass still raised in unshakeable concentration like a wooden figurehead whose painted eyes were forever fixed upon the sea. At intervals on the weatherdecks, stationed at the rails between the guns and their crews, were the men whom Fly had rounded up, equipped with a spyglass, and instructed to sound the alarm should they see any-thing out of the ordinary being borne along in the sea currents. To Morgan Evans, who now stood among them, he had quietly said: *"We shall kiss the dice, and throw them one last time."*

Captain Prickett had wriggled into his uniform, his black bicorne athwartships on his head, and was ambling along the larboard gangway, though a little shaky on his feet. With a mixture of consternation and amusement, Fly looked on as the captain periodically stooped to peer into the barrel of a carronade, or juggled a twelve-pounder in his hands, or clapped a poor, unsuspecting sailor on the back, all the while letting fly an interspersion of orders. "More damp sand is needed around this gun. Bring it at once! Those cannonballs are rusty. Take them away! They must be scraped and greased before used! You there, watch your gunpowder! I'll not have my ship blowing up today, and all of us sitting in the sea!" Beside the *Amethyst's* bell, Prickett drew himself up, robbed the sailing master of his speaking trumpet, and let his voice bellow round the decks: "Lads! You're to wait 'til we see what this ruffle is all about. I'll hang the man who screams, lights his cannon, or spews his bullets before I give the word."

Holding his hat against the wind, Prickett came toward Fly and took him aside. "Anything yet, Mr. Austen?"

"Neither ship is flying her colours."

"Damn! How dare they utilize my own form of trickery! Well, can you see anything of their hulls?"

"Not yet. There's too much smoke to give us a clear picture."

"What about their size?"

"I believe it's safe to say they are *not* men-of-war. Both are two-masted, and tacking easily, though one seems to have more guns at her disposal."

"If we cannot see their flags, how shall we discover who they are, Mr. Austen?"

Fly calmly stated the obvious. "We'll have to come in closer still, at least until we can determine something from the sails and rigging and uniforms, or —" he paused for effect "— or see the ships' names."

"Closer? What, and get caught up in their fray?"

"Aye, if necessary," said Fly, clenching his jaw. "That *was* the idea."

Prickett ran his hand over his damp brow, wiped it on his breeches, and then began expelling his breath in a most bizarre manner.

"May I get you a glass of water, sir?"

"Do not put yourself out, Mr. Austen," he said loudly, pulling at his top buttons to loosen his jacket. "I shall get it myself. Do not worry, I shan't be gone long." He handed Fly the speaking trumpet as if he were presenting his sword to a victorious enemy, and then spoke sotto voce: "When we're within range of those ships' carronades and long guns, whatever you do, kindly remember our masts were weakened in the storm." Executing a crisp about-turn, he marched toward the companionway — the thunder of convergent guns hastening his journey — and disappeared below deck.

Standing alone, Fly peered through the swirling smoke at the battling ships. They warred as if they were alone on the water, oblivious to the imposing ship-of-the-line closing in on them, ready to add her broadsides to the action. If only he could look up and see Captain Moreland striding across the quarterdeck toward him, prepared to stand and lead with him. But he could see only faces lined with anxiety, looking to him, waiting for *him* to tell them what to do. Heaving a sigh, he sought out Morgan Evans, and told him he could stand down. "Should we get involved in this fight, your services shall be needed elsewhere, presumably patching holes in our hull, or — dare I say it — in the hospital again."

Morgan collapsed his spyglass so he could bring his fist to his forehead in a salute. "Thank you, sir. I'll go collect Magpie from the top, and tell him to get below."

"Good luck with that!" Fly snickered. "But before you go, Mr. Evans, tell me first: what's your assessment of it all?"

Morgan sniffed the smoky air. "Two privateers, sir; a brig and a schooner; neither one interested in abandoning the fight, despite our approach." He looked squarely at Fly. "I can say with confidence that neither one is the *Lady Jane*."

Both men had set their sights once again on the ships when the *Amethyst*'s brooding silence was shattered by a high-pitched shriek. At first Fly thought the livestock had broken free of their stalls and found their way on deck, but when every man around him looked toward the soaring length of the foremast — including an ashen-faced Bridlington, who had come scurrying over as if the sudden squeal had shaken his brittle nerves — he shaded his face with his hand to follow their gaze. There on the foretop, Magpie was dancing a jig.

"What're you on about, Magpie?"

"Sir! I see him! He's runnin' 'round his ship, jumpin' on the bowsprit and swayin' on the capstan like he always does, doin' a great deal o' yellin', his face all hot and ruddy."

Fly looked bewildered. "Could you be more precise, Magpie?"

"Yon ship, the one what's downwind, sir, I just knows it ... it's Prosper Burgo and his Remarkables."

"Oh, God!" moaned Bridlington. "Not that pirate again and his horde of cutthroats!"

27

Friday, August 27

11:00 a.m.
Hartwood Hall

TRYING TO TEAR UNCLE CLARENCE away from his morning letter-writing had been a veritable chore for Emily, with him insisting he had to attend to his duty as Admiral of the Fleet, but when her employment of cajolery had finally been rewarded, she had insisted they meet out-of-doors, so that no one could attempt to put an ear to the wall to listen in. Uncle Clarence had pouted profusely, further insisting the weather was far too hot for him to be meandering around the grounds — being as his constitution was susceptible to bouts of asthma — and had, consequently, asked Glenna to lay out the little table in the garden with linen, crystal, and an iced pitcher of orgeat (his favourite concoction of distilled almonds and orange-flower water), so that they might enjoy Hartwood's sweet-smelling abundance of azaleas, rhododendrons, and roses, and, if possible, find relief in the shade cast by the west wall of the great house.

Sitting on the front few inches of his wrought-iron chair, his fingers spread upon his pudgy knees, Uncle Clarence looked around him with satisfaction. "This is a most excellent estate; one would be lucky indeed to live out one's years surrounded by such breathtaking beauty. Such a fine, solid house too, with every known comfort and convenience. I've had the pleasure to accompany my brother, the Regent, on several of his visits to aristocratic mansions in England, but, I declare, Emeline, there're none as nice as Hartwood."

Emily picked up the glass of orgeat her uncle had poured for her. "Are you planning to purchase Hartwood from the Duke of Belmont?"

"Well, hang me, Emeline, where did you get such a notion?"

"Seeing as you've such an affinity for the place —"

"Unless I was king, I'd never be able to afford such luxury. No, my dear, I must content myself with Bushy House for the remainder of my days, not that I'm complaining, of course, for, as you know, it suits me well."

Emily grew wistful. It was hard to think of dear Bushy House without recollecting her exuberant cousins and endearing Aunt Dora, who was not one to judge and so rarely gave offence. Following her uncle's lead, she too surveyed the grounds around her. She could see Somerton out riding alone, cantering on his blue-black horse down near the ponds, and closer by, Fleda rolling down the gentle undulation of the front lawn with her dog dancing in agitated circles around her, and Gus Walby, leaning on his crutch, laughing at her. The sound of Gus's laughter — and Fleda's, for that matter — filled her with both joy and sadness.

It was Uncle Clarence's steadfast assurances to the family that Mr. Walby was indeed an officer of the Royal Navy, and of impeccable breeding, that led Adolphus to heartily agree that the boy should be allowed to visit during the day while old Dr. Braden was attending his ailing cousin in the village, so long as he took his lessons with Fleda, and was returned to the coaching inn before Hartwood's dinner hour. Quivering in her chair at the end of the dining room table, Helena had looked like a shivering puddle-hound, but on the subject she had stayed curiously silent. And yet, throughout the deliberations, no one had said a word about extending an invitation to the old doctor to take dinner with them, the man who had so selflessly taken up a temporary guardianship of Mr. Walby. Of course, Wetherell had been too greatly distracted by the bowls of sugared almonds set before him to share *his* sublime opinions, and her uncle did not venture to suggest it, despite his initial joy at discovering the relationship between the doctor who had served on HMS *Isabelle* and the one he had retained for Gus. To Emily, it was Somerton who had given the most offense. Sitting across from her, studying her response to the conversation, there had been something telling, something festering and ruminating in his deportment, as if he were ready to pounce upon the person who even dared mention the name of Dr. Arthur Braden at the dinner table. The very recollection of it, the sheer indecency of it all, brought tears to Emily's eyes, compelling her to glance away from her uncle toward the woodland of oak and ash and beech and chestnut, which stood drooping and motionless in the heat under a blanket of dark, low-hanging clouds, like the vanquished crew of the *Isabelle* when Trevelyan had come aboard to reap his spoils.

"Now then, Emeline, before we're caught up in a downpour," said Uncle Clarence, eying the sky, "tell me why you wanted a word in private?"

Emily kept her face averted. "I'd like to leave here, as soon as possible."

Uncle Clarence choked on his beverage, coughing and sputtering before he was once again capable of finding his voice. "This is most shocking! And here I thought I'd found for you the perfect situation."

"Situation?"

"I meant to say *home*. I believe Hartwood is a perfect *home* for you."

"It is *not* my home, Uncle."

He grimaced and gulped, and continued to clear his throat. "Would a visit to see your grandmother, Queen Charlotte, ease the pain of your homesickness?"

"I've no desire to see my grandmother."

"That is good, because she's growing ever more curmudgeonly, flies into rages so easily, and suffers constant bowel complaints. My sisters have quite lost their patience, and have little desire to spend any time at all with her."

"Let me go home with you, Uncle. My best memories are of Bushy House."

Uncle Clarence heaved a heavy sigh.

Emily shot forward in her chair. "Your brother kindly gave you an allowance, which you, in turn, gave to the duchess to keep me clothed and fed. If it's money you need, could you not have that allowance transferred to you? I don't want to be a burden."

"I'm afraid you returning home with me is out of the question."

Emily's eyes blurred. "Do you not care? Is there no one who cares for me, no one who desires to see me simply because I'm *unmanageable*? Do my uncles and aunts all hope I'll quietly retire here, on this unfamiliar soil, so that they'll not have to bother again with me until I'm put into the ground?"

Uncle Clarence chuckled. "There, there! Naturally, we all care for your well-being, but at present we all have our own pressing concerns and families to maintain. And surely you cannot have forgotten that your uncles and I are all up to our necks, fighting Napoleon on the continent and the Americans on the sea. I cannot predict when I might be sent away on an urgent mission. No, my dear, I've quite enough to contend with, without having to worry about making certain *you* are dressing and behaving decently."

Emily exhaled — all she could do to resist bursting into sarcastic laughter.

Uncle Clarence laid one hand over his heart, and allowed his round eyes to rove over her curls and gown with open admiration. "My friends are thrilled to have you here at Hartwood. And see how well Helena has been able to improve you. You look quite respectable. I was appalled when we met in Bermuda; so full of despair thinking of your dear, departed parents, and what they would've thought were they to see you debased in dungarees with your hair all about you."

"Her Grace and I do *not* get along very well," Emily said flatly.

"Wot? This is news to me! I declare she loves you like a daughter." He laughed while he refilled his glass. "If there is any discord, it most certainly is in *your* court, Emeline. You must learn to get on with people, learn to hold your tongue. People don't take kindly to hearing what it is you honestly think of them. Do your family proud and behave like a true Hanover."

The first snarls of thunder rumbled over the city of London as if in harmony with Emily's suffering.

"God damn this weather," said Uncle Clarence, frowning at the accumulation of black clouds. "This has been a most wet summer. Perhaps we should head indoors."

Emily placed her hand on her uncle's upper arm as he was rising from his chair. "Uncle, where is Thomas Trevelyan?"

"Why, I believe he's imprisoned in Newgate as we speak."

"I cannot wait forever for his trial."

"Why ever not? You're *not* going anywhere, my dear. Besides, you've no say when his case shall be heard at the Old Bailey. But, mark my words, it'll be a superb spectacle, and everyone shall be clamouring for a seat to see you rise up and take the stand."

Emily rubbed her face in frustration. "And what news of my annulment?"

"Your case should prove to be a straightforward one. As far as your family is concerned, your marriage never existed in the first place. For one, Emeline, your marriage licence — if, in fact, you actually had one — is sitting at the bottom of the sea. This Mr. Humphreys, the clergyman who performed your ceremony, is more than likely a charlatan; however, since it's impossible to ascertain whether or not the man was ordained, it remains that you did not have your family's permission, and, though not necessary to make it valid, your marriage was not consummated. Then, of course, on this last point, I — ahem — I'm not certain I can believe you."

Emily waited for her anger to abate. "Then what must I wait for?"

"Official word from the Archbishop of Canterbury that your marriage is null and void."

"That's all well and good, but *when* shall I receive word?"

The jaunty tilt of his head and the curve of his smile were unnerving. "Are you anxious for it, Emeline? Have you set your cap at a new suitor?"

"Indeed! I'm waiting to pounce upon one of cousin Charlotte's many rejects."

His smile widened. "That's very good news!"

Emily shut her eyes to take a deep breath. "I'd sleep more peacefully knowing my connection with England's traitor is no more."

"Yes, yes, of course you would, my dear." Uncle Clarence suddenly fumbled for his pocket watch. "Ah, look at the time! Well now, I've enjoyed our chat immensely, but I would suggest we quickly retire to the house, otherwise the approaching storm may wash us away to the Thames River."

Emily's shoulders drooped like the branches of the trees around her, and her eyes drifted away from the garden to the dark stones of the unbroken wall, which enclosed the perimeter of Hartwood.

Noon

THOUGH EMILY HAD LONGED to hide out in her bedchamber and take refuge under the quilts while the rain fell, upon re-entering the house Uncle Clarence had steered her toward the music room, where they now lolled about with the rest of the family, awaiting their next meal. Overhead the storm was unfurling its fury, plunging the room into obscurity, provoking her uncle, who had compared the moody atmosphere to that of an ancient burial cavern, to send the servants scrambling for candles so that he could decipher the words on the pages of the book he was attempting to read. With the first flash of lightning, Somerton had ended his ride and stabled his horse; however, Fleda and Gus, being loath to return indoors, would still be outside if the downpour had not forced them to take cover. The two youngsters, who had found mutual merriment in seeing one another's hair and clothing soaking wet, were now safely sheltered in Mademoiselle's schoolroom, eating their cheese sandwiches and taking their lessons in handwriting.

Aside from the occasional remark about the inclement weather, there was an absence of conversation. Adolphus was napping on the sofa, his arms draped over his immense middle; Uncle Clarence, now that he could see properly, was delighting in his book on naval warfare; and Somerton, still in his riding costume, had planted his boots in a wide stance before the north-facing window, his hands locked behind him, seemingly transfixed by the puddles forming out on the gravel courtyard. Sitting as far away as possible from Emily, Helena had her elegant head bent over her needlework, wordlessly making her tiny stitches, although her behaviour indicated a restlessness of the mind. She kept shifting upon her chair, as if sharp stones were irritating her delicate bottom, and she started at the slightest sound — thunderclaps included — that always ended with an anxious glance at the doorway.

"Oh, *where* is Wetherell?" she finally crackled, collapsing her work onto her lap.

Somerton replied over his shoulder. "Mother, you must know, he's pondering the contents of his wardrobe in the hopes of bewitching us all with his latest fashion."

"You know, Somerton, you could lend a dash of splendour and variety to your own fashion. You choose such dreary colours, one would think you were still in mourning." She finished by throwing a significant look at Emily.

"Perhaps your *second* son does not choose to *frighten* us all," said Emily with a fraudulent smile, inducing Somerton, though he kept his back to her, to break into a series of chuckles.

Into the music room rushed Wetherell, who did not disappoint in his dress, blazing like a flambeau amidst the gloom in gloves of lavender, satin breeches of rose, a flowered waistcoat of predominant yellows and greens, and a serge spencer jacket of the brightest orange. With his hands on his waist he strutted about, as if expecting compliments to be showered upon him. He had discarded his distinguishing high collars in favour of shorter ones, which were completely hidden by his elaborately wrapped and starched cravat, and secured to his protruding middle was his fob-watch ribbon with a dangling medley of silver and gold seals. His white silk stockings were of the finest quality and decorated with yellow embroidered clocks at the ankles, and his black shoes were adorned with prodigious leather bows. Despite the fact that he was a vision of fastidious perfection — with the exception of his calf padding, for one of the pads had slipped down his leg, destroying the symmetry of his lower limbs — no one in the assembled audience uttered a single word of praise, which prompted a pouting end to his strutting and the articulation of a cold commandment. "Very well, then, all of you out. Out you go!"

Emily's hand flew to her throat as the family scrambled to obey him, not one of them questioning his motives. Without hesitation Somerton terminated his vigil at the window, and Uncle Clarence snapped his book shut to help Helena awaken and carry a light-headed Adolphus to the door. Trying to make sense of the scene, Emily stood up to follow, but Wetherell's hand shot out to stop her. "Oh, but *you* must stay, Your Royal Highness."

The last one to leave was Somerton. Grinning from ear to ear, he gave Emily a naval salute, and took great pains to quietly close the door on them, as if one small, creaking sound was bound to shatter the room's collection of porcelain and glass ornaments.

"Sit! Sit down again, Your Royal Highness," said Wetherell, pacing the area in front of the chimneypiece. He waited until she had returned to her chair, and then, stopping before her, he pulled himself up to his full height, and assumed a sober expression. Emily folded her hands on her lap, and waited for him to speak. There was a lengthy period of silence between them, though thunder shook the foundations of the house and rain fell in torrents against the tall window, obliterating all prospects of the outside world. At one point Wetherell did open his mouth, but closed it up again. Afterward, he resumed his pacing, his lips pursed in contemplation.

Emily's leg began to bounce. She felt the eyes of Octavius Lindsay staring down at her from his gilded frame, and a desperate need to leave the room. "I am guessing, sir, you're finding this subject a difficult one to raise with me."

"Quite! It is never easy for a man."

"Shall I help you say it then?"

"That would be most inappropriate, Your Royal Highness. As I am a gentleman, I must do the deed in my own way."

"Of course! Forgive me," she said, settling back in her chair.

"My mother, I'm afraid, does not like you."

Emily peered up at him. "You're right, she does not, though I'm not in any way troubled by her adverse feelings toward me."

Wetherell gave her a momentary glare while he paced. "Therefore, the arrangement shall be difficult."

"I believe you mean to say: the arrangement *is* difficult."

A second, stronger glare from him silenced her. "Father likes you enough, says you're a splendid sort of girl, but then I really don't care what anyone thinks of you. As a matter of fact, I don't particularly like you either. You are too perverse and headstrong for my tastes."

Emily could not help herself. "Now this is most troubling, sir! Would I rise in your noble esteem if I were daily to assist you in the selection of your shoes and jackets and trimmings, and agree to play cards with you every evening?"

He halted before her. "Oh, indeed, I would like that! This is great encouragement," he said, locking his hands behind him, just as Somerton had while gazing out the window. "The thing is, Your Royal Highness, I have my gambling debts, and if I don't settle them soon I shall be in a world of hurt. I may even lose possession of Hartwood when it comes to me, and this would bring shame to my family and leave my poor mother homeless, even though I don't especially give a fig. What worries me exceedingly is the thought that I may be given the toss from Boodle's, my beloved club, and if this were to happen, Your Royal Highness, I could not find a reason to live. Are you following me? Do you *understand* what I am saying?"

"No, sir! You speak in riddles! But my guess is, in a circuitous way, you're trying to ask for your emerald ring back, since you require it to assist in paying down your debts."

To this, Wetherell had no answer other than to gape at her, as if she were a snake that had fled the storm and had curled up comfortably on the music-room chair. Refusing to be put off by his rudeness, Emily continued. "Your mother spoke to me of its sentimental value; made known her unhappiness that it is now in my possession. You may have the ring back, so long as you do not ask me, in addition, to return the money I won fairly the other night. If you are the gentleman you claim to be, you'll accept this, and ask for no more."

Wetherell threw back his head to guffaw, surprising Emily that his wig did not flip off in the gesture. "Like all the members of your family, you *are* cork-brained."

Emily angled her head, and chilled her voice. "Excuse me; I do not believe I heard you correctly."

"I scoff at you for imagining I wanted the emerald back; it means nothing to me. It's true, my mother does hold an obscene sentiment for it — *what* exactly, I'm *not* at liberty to say. As my debts are exorbitant, the emerald would be nothing but a drop in a black hole."

"Then speak plainly, sir. What is it you want?"

"I want *you* to pay off my debts."

It was Emily's turn to laugh. "Do you imagine, sir, that I have a chest of gold coins stashed under my bed on the first floor, and would — in good faith — share it with a man such as yourself, one I hardly know and one who has no discipline when it comes to his addictions?"

His features hardened. "Ah, but you *shall* pay my debts."

"How so?"

"When we are married."

Emily blinked, her eyes falling first on his dark-red lips, and then plunking down on his belly. "Surely you jest! Tell me you are trifling with me."

"I do not jest, nor do I trifle."

"Sir! We have been acquainted for five days."

"If we'd met for the first time, standing up before the clergyman, it would've made little difference to me."

"Oh, but to me it would," said Emily, shaking her head with mock gravity, "for you have not yet apprised me of the secrets you hide under your powdered wigs."

Wetherell's retort was a swift one. "And you shall remain unapprised, for my wigs come to bed with me."

"I cannot think of two people more unsuited for one another."

"What does suitability have to do with anything?" Wetherell groaned, taking up his pacing again. "To me your connections and physical attractiveness alone will suffice. We shall produce at least one heir, and then you shall live here with my mother, and I shall take up residence in London. After that we need not bother with one another."

Emily's hand made its way to her mouth. Before answering, she had to trust she would not be prevailed upon by her churning stomach to spring for the duke's chamber pot. "When my annulment has been formally ratified," she said with slow enunciation, "I shall not be seeking to remarry."

Wetherell made a sucking sound with his tongue. "Your Royal Highness, a woman such as yourself, who has blemished her reputation with her reckless flight to the sea and her cavorting with Jack Tars, is fortunate indeed that a gentleman such as myself, of such *unblemished* lineage, has chosen to accept you as a wife."

"Sir, let me be clear: in order to marry, I must be a willing participant."

"That did not stop you the first time."

"I do not *want* a husband, and even if I did I would not choose *you*."

Wetherell reddened. "I have been informed that you do not have a choice in the matter."

"Informed? Informed by whom?"

"You must face reality, Your Royal Highness. You are an embarrassment to your relations; one who has no prospects. Marrying me is your only salvation, your only path to regaining any manner of respectability." He re-knotted his cravat while he delivered his final blow. "Your family has not only given their permission, they have promised that our marriage *shall* take place, and the ball my mother is planning shall be the celebratory backdrop for our upcoming nuptials."

A litany of events and innuendoes collided in Emily's head. All at once so many things, so many baffling speeches and glances and secret conversations, began to make perfect sense. She felt a flush of heat race through her veins, and her eyes strayed around the room, seeing nothing at first, not even Wetherell in his extravagant costume. Then the storm played into her thoughts. Periodic lightning threw silver-grey shadows upon the burial cavern, the rain pounded the gardens and the earth, and the subsequent thunder rattled the windowpanes. The noise was so tremendous, surely the family — were they listening at the door — would not hear if she were to leap up to slam drawers and overturn tables and smash china vases. But even this therapeutic notion could not lift her from her chair. Without warning, she was seized with a tickle of laughter, and try as she might she had no control over it. At first her laughs came in short, chuckling gulps, which shook her shoulders, and soon her whole body joined in, throwing her into complete convulsions, barely able to breathe let alone speak, and with each peek at Wetherell she helplessly slipped further and further off her chair.

Wetherell's lower lip hit the floor. In horror, he watched her unbridled display, as if he expected — any second now — to see her explode, and her severed head and limbs propelled across the room. A curious shade of purple, similar to the colour of his fine coach, overspread his face, and he began jerking his head in a strange manner, as if he were trying to rid his ears of water. But when Emily did nothing to stop her gales of laughter, or dash away the mirthful tears rolling down her face, he tugged on the hem of his jacket and headed for the door, moving so swiftly he walked over on his ankle, causing the crooked calf padding to slide further down his leg.

28

Noon
(Forenoon Watch, Eight Bells)
Aboard HMS *Amethyst*

IT WAS ALL OVER JUST past noon, at the precise moment when two of the *Amethyst's* midshipmen, bearing their sextants and quadrants, had completed their measurements of latitude and were reporting their findings to Captain Prickett and Fly Austen. The American schooner bobbed in the waves, as helpless as a toy whose owner had inflicted many imaginary battles upon her, and in doing so had shredded her sails, bloodied her crew, and charred her timbers. On either side of her, lying in the water like a pair of giant oars, lay the schooner's masts, which had come crashing down amidst great cheering from the Amethysts and the Remarkables, sending the vanquished crew scampering to escape certain death under their frightening weight.

It had been Prosper Burgo's fight from start to finish. The *Amethyst* had not fired a single shot; nevertheless, she had stood by with her colours proudly raised once more, a beacon to the privateersman and his Remarkables that a friend was in their midst. Now, abandoning their guns and stations, the Amethysts gathered at the rails to witness the aftermath, and at the sight of Prosper lowering his boats there came a second, cheerful outpouring of "Huzzah!" Of those who raised their voices, Fly was certain it was Mrs. Kettle who whooped the loudest. Dressed in her very best, she danced out in the open, waving a dainty handkerchief and yoo-hooing in the hopes that Prosper might hear her from across the watery divide. "I just knew he'd come back fer me ... I just knew it," was her effusive cry to the sailors and anyone else who cared to listen.

"Well, now, Mr. Austen, should we take her a prize?" asked Prickett, who had only recently returned to the quarterdeck, perhaps once he was assured his crew would not be entering into the fray. "Though her masts have gone by the board, her hull looks sound. We shouldn't have any difficulty taking her into Portsmouth with us."

"She is *not* our prize, sir," said Fly coldly.

"Mr. Burgo couldn't possibly succeed in taking that schooner into port. Why he hardly has enough men to man his own brig, let alone provide a prize master and crew to take command of the schooner."

"Perhaps we should ask Mr. Burgo if he requires our assistance. As the schooner is fairly his, he should have a say in the matter."

Prickett's hands found his hips. "I cannot agree, Mr. Austen! He's a damned privateer, and his brig is nothing but a bumboat!"

"That *damned* privateer once saved our lives."

"I cannot recall such a time, Mr. Austen." Prickett held his head high for a moment before surprising Fly by swooping in close to him and dropping his voice to a dramatic whisper. "I am at the end of my career. I cannot countenance returning home to my family and peers empty-handed, and having to inform the Admiralty that I have no idea what happened to the *Lady Jane*."

Fly remained aloof. "Our cruise has not ended; we may still find her."

"On that score, I hold little hope." Prickett pulled away to shout at his men. "Heave to! Heave to, lads! Lower the boats and prepare the launch for me. Oh, Mr. Weevil, there you are, my good man! Could you see to packing a basket for me, and include some good wine and good eats, won't you?"

"Shall you require my company?"

"For what purpose, Mr. Austen?"

Fly frowned. "Do you not intend to board the schooner, and interview what remains of her crew to root out Royal Navy deserters?"

Prickett made a face. "Nay, I shall leave *you* to do the honours, Mr. Austen. You may take Bridlington with you; he'll help you identify the scoundrels. I'll have no part in cleaning up the mess on that schooner. In the meantime, I plan to pay a visit to our friend, Mr. Burgo, and make certain he's amenable to our receiving a share in the prize money. And, knowing the very prospect should send her quivering with ecstasy, I shall ask Mrs. Kettle to accompany me."

1:00 p.m.

MAGPIE SAT ROCKING IN the cutter as the oarsmen raised and held their oars upright in the air and allowed the boat to bump up against the beaten hull of the American schooner. Having manoeuvred through waves littered with the wreckage of war and avoided the jagged stump of a fallen mast, they had come from the *Amethyst* to offer assistance to the Remarkables, who had already boarded the defeated vessel and taken command. In an effort to stay alert, Magpie rubbed his eye, pretending he didn't see the streams of blood oozing from the scuppers, nor the lifeless bodies in the waves whose faces were contorted in grisly expressions, laying bare their final agony on earth. How he wished Morgan Evans could have come with him, for he knew no one else on board the cutter, and no one paid him any heed. But minutes before Mr. Austen had stepped into the very first boat to push off after Captain Prickett's launch had left for the *Prosperous and Remarkable*, he had expressly asked Mr. Evans to stay with the Amethysts, saying "I would feel more at ease, for you'll know how to act should an emergency arise."

Magpie anxiously assessed the silent row of men sneering down at him from the schooner's broken side, armed with various forms of weaponry, their sunburned faces displaying hostility, and then he broke into a shaky laugh. Among them were those he recognized as Prosper Burgo's ruffians: there was the man whose nose resembled a tumorous strawberry, and beside him was the one with the missing ears, who, in turn, was standing next to the one with a mouthful of cracked teeth and a neck smeared in tattoos. And when it came his turn to climb up the schooner's side on the suspended rope ladder, Magpie no longer felt the sensation that a flock of birds were flapping their wings in his stomach.

Leaping onto the deck, and fearful lest a glance around should reveal untold horrors, Magpie's eye immediately lighted upon Mr. Austen, who had already established himself on a stool before a makeshift table near the schooner's wheel. Stretching before the commander, in a line that snaked toward the bow of the ship, were the battle-weary Americans, some blackened with smoke, others weakened by blood loss, all of them guarded by Prosper's ruffians, who had their weapons of intimidation at the ready. Sitting next to Mr. Austen, pressing a white handkerchief to his long crooked nose as if he could not tolerate the stench assaulting his nostrils, was First Lieutenant Bridlington. Magpie stepped closer to listen to them as they, one-by-one, conducted their interviews of the seamen.

"I was born a British subject, sir, but I ain't a deserter," declared one poor sailor whose shirt was slowly turning red from a gaping lesion on his neck. "I've a certificate of citizenship, and it shows I'm rightly an American, if ya'll allow me to fetch it fer ya. It's down below in me ditty bag."

Bridlington dropped the handkerchief from his face to whistle his indignation. "Oh, what will that prove? I happen to know that these so-called *certificates* are usually false and therefore invalid, and that anyone can easily purchase one for a mere dollar, even a low-born such as yourself."

Mr. Austen addressed the man with calm decency. "You have my permission to go and retrieve it."

"Fine then!" retaliated Bridlington, wagging his finger at the bleeding sailor. "But your damned certificate better provide more particulars beyond your name, and the colour of your hair and eyes. Fie! Don't we *all* have brown hair and brown eyes?"

Appropriating the white handkerchief from a sputtering Bridlington, Mr. Austen offered it to the sailor. "Hold this to your face to stop up the blood, and hurry back."

The next American in line looked like a mean boxer at the Fives Court in St. Martin's Lane. He kicked at the deck with his feet, and his fists were working at his sides, causing Magpie to wonder if he might haul off and punch Bridlington in the face, just as Mr. Evans had done. When he stated his case, he leaned in dangerously close to the first lieutenant and spoke in rough accentuated words. "Yer damn right I'm a deserter. I deserted six years ago after being whipped within an inch of my life, and I've found peace o' mind with the Americans. Ya can't blame a simple man like myself. I've been fed better, paid better, treated better, and haven't been whipped fer no cause at all."

Mr. Austen placed a restraining hand on Bridlington, who had leapt to his feet to fume, and simply nodded to two of his own men standing nearby, who came forward to lead the belligerent away to the *Amethyst's* cutter.

Magpie felt a large hand upon his shoulder, and looked up to find Prosper Burgo's jack-of-all-tradesman. "Pemberton Baker!"

"Well, if it ain't the little one-eyed sailmaker!" said Pemberton, his pudding face devoid of emotion. "Have ya come to offer yerself up fer the prize crew?"

"Oh, nay, sir, I came with the others, thinkin' ya might need me to patch up a sail or two," he said, wishing he could pluck up the courage to ask Pemberton if he'd seen Dr. Braden and Biscuit in his travels; too afraid the answer would be no. "Where's Mr. Burgo?"

Pemberton yanked his thumb across the water where the *Prosperous and Remarkable* was hove to. "He were about to join me, but yer captain came visitin' with a picnic basket o' victuals. Chose an odd time fer a visit, and he brought with him that snudge snout, Mrs. Kettle."

"Oh, Mrs. Kettle says she's goin' to marry Mr. Burgo."

There was no humour in Pemberton's laugh. "There won't be no marryin' unless she binds him up in hemp and tries starvin' him to commitment. And she won't be none too happy to learn he's been married afore — seven bloody times."

"I suppose not." Magpie ventured a shy glance around the schooner. "Do ya need me help, Pemberton?"

"Hmmm! Well now, yer too wee to help with the mendin' o' planks or jury-mastin' this wreck, but, as yer good with a needle, head aft. They could use ya there."

"What for?"

"To stitch up a couple o' hammocks."

Knowing what that involved, Magpie's mouth went as dry as a white-hot beach, and those birds in his belly tried to take flight again.

"Just worry yerself about the ones what are still intact," said Pemberton, "and keep a lookout for those what lost their heads, and miscellaneous body parts."

"What ... what do I do if I finds body parts?"

"Why ya throw 'em overboard fer the fishes."

Saturday, August 28
7:00 a.m.
(Morning Watch, Six Bells)
Aboard the *Prosperous and Remarkable*

MAGPIE HAD BEEN SHIVERING on his heap of discarded sails, his mind tortured with visions of blue lips and still, ashen faces, when he realized Mr. Austen was leaning over him.

"Sir?" he asked sleepily, his bleary eye falling for a quick second upon the ghastly row of canvas-bound corpses he'd helped to ready for their admittance to the sea.

"Mr. Evans has come to fetch us. We've been invited to breakfast with Mr. Burgo on his brig. Are you up for it?"

Magpie studied Mr. Austen's drawn face, and wondered if the commander had been able to find a bit of canvas upon which to lay his head, for well into the night Magpie had seen him questioning the Americans and simultaneously organizing the transport of the twenty-seven presumed deserters across the water to the *Amethyst*. At midnight, refusing to bed upon the schooner for fear his throat would be slashed in the night, Lord Bridlington had taken his leave, remarking to Mr. Austen as he settled into one of the returning boats: "Won't Captain Prickett be pleased with us!"

"I'd like that, sir," said Magpie, tossing aside his crude blankets.

"Then we must hurry, for Mr. Evans brings word that Captain Prickett is most anxious to be away."

The morning was cold and dreary. Magpie's teeth chattered as he sat in the *Amethyst*'s cutter, hugging his thin body in an effort to stay warm, but relieved to be away from the sadness and death on the schooner. He tried to set his mind on Emily, remembering their many pleasant conversations together on the *Isabelle*; it helped to blot out the image of the little white face of a boy his age he had had to sew into his small, canvas coffin, and the terrible realization that the cannonball he had placed at the boy's feet would drag him down to the *auld place*. Wisps of fog rolled past the cutter as the drowsy oarsmen pulled toward the *Prosperous and Remarkable*, giving a nebulous appearance to the three ships, sitting hove to in a triangular formation on the Atlantic, their hulls and masts as hallucinatory as a desert mirage. In the surrounding silence, the sound of the oars hitting the waves gave Magpie the shakes. If it weren't for the presence of Mr. Austen sitting grim-faced on his boat plank, and Morgan Evans heaving on one of the oars, Magpie would have been certain he was locked in an endless nightmare.

Prosper Burgo's howl of welcome and hearty handshake served to prop up Magpie's nerves, and the mug of coffee pressed into his hands was guzzled with gratitude and timely, for, upon following Mr. Austen and Mr. Evans into the privateersman's domain on the brig's stern, he encountered Mrs. Kettle, beaming like a child who'd been praised by her teacher for the successful completion of her sums.

The laundress darted a wry face at his dirty feet. "Have ya come to take breakfast with us? We ain't servin' up no Maggot Pie here." She cackled away, while everyone found something to sit upon.

Mr. Austen, who had an uncanny ability to ignore the existence of Mrs. Kettle, smiled warmly at Prosper. "It is astounding to find you here on this lonely patch of the sea, but we're most delighted to see you again."

Prosper sank down on a barrel, and wrapped his arm around his puffed-up woman. "I've been followin' ya since ya left Halifax. We set out the minute we got word ya was headin' back to England to fight them Yankee privateers plunderin' yer coasts. I was a bit down on me luck in the east … thought I'd better try new ground."

Magpie piped up. "But Prosper, where's yer red hull got to? We might've known ya long afore this."

Prosper snarled. "Ah, too many were comin' to know me *Prosperous and Remarkable* on account o' that bloody-red hull, so we painted her up fer a disguise." He looked over at Mr. Austen. "Just as well ya didn't recognize me right off. I didn't need yer help, leastwise from yer fat captain. What a galoot! He woulda turned his guns on me in order to claim that Yankee schooner fer himself."

"I am sorry for the visit he paid you," said Mr. Austen, accepting Prosper's offering of a coffee refill.

"He's a shack rag, yer captain; his blusterin' gave me a headache." Prosper showed some teeth. "But I did gladly accept his offerin' o' wine. Now, I've the greatest respect fer ya, Mr. Austen, as well as fer Mr. Evans here, and wee Magpie with his patched-up eye, but I ain't about to share me prize and its contraband with ya."

"We've come for no other reason than to enjoy the company of old friends, Prosper, and to take you up on your hospitality after a most difficult night."

Prosper nodded with satisfaction, planted a wet kiss on Mrs. Kettle's blooming cheek — sending her into a paroxysm of snorty giggles — and stood up to begin spooning out the breakfast. "Eat up! Then we must away, fer I don't rest easy in foggy weather."

Magpie wasn't certain his stomach could withstand the vile mash of burgoo bubbling in a copper pot on Prosper's table, nor the mouldy biscuits, which — being as they were infested with black-headed maggots — seemed to be moving about on a cracked plate. But it was a dish of yellowish muck that really put him off. Seeing him blanch, Prosper centred him out. "What? Ain't ya ever seen slush afore?"

"Slush, Prosper?"

"Aye! 'Tis the grease what floats to the top when ya boil yer salted meat. 'Tis right tasty stuff on yer biscuits. Bet ya'll never want Prickett's rancid butter agin."

But Magpie wasn't convinced. While Prosper regaled his guests with a blowy account of his subjugation of the schooner, he plucked the squirmy maggots from the biscuits, only too happy for an excuse to delay bringing breakfast to his lips.

Not an hour had slipped by when Pemberton Baker appeared before them with a message for his master, delivered with the gravest of countenances. "There's been a sightin'."

"Great Caesar's ghost! What? In fog?" barked Prosper.

"The sun's risin' burned it off."

"Another hapless Yankee schooner, travellin' alone?"

"Nay, Prosper," said Pemberton, lifting his wide, blank face a notch. "Might be wise to push off."

"We're still eatin', ya big bandicoot." Prosper's arm reached out to give Mrs. Kettle an affectionate squeeze.

As if smelling danger, Mr. Austen and Morgan Evans jumped up at once to peer out the cabin windows. When he swung around again, Mr. Austen's eyes were bright with alarm. "What is it you've seen, Pemberton?"

The jack-of-all-tradesman relayed the information as flatly as if he were commenting on the number of weevils Magpie had rescued from the biscuits. "Seven or eight sails, sir: a veritable fleet, flyin' American colours."

9:00 a.m.
(Forenoon Watch, Two Bells)

"MAKE SAIL!"

"Raise the boats!"

"Clear the decks, and beat to quarters!"

Fly's insides quivered as panic rained down upon the small triangle of ships on the sea; the relative peace of the morning shattered by the realization that the Americans were frighteningly close. Beneath his feet the *Prosperous and Remarkable* trembled with running men. Prosper himself was whirling like a waterspout, scaring and scattering his chickens on the main deck, his veins visible on his ruddy face as he cursed the imminent loss of his schooner prize and bemoaned the pandemonium that was certain to erupt the minute the defeated Americans, bolstered by the sight of the approaching fleet, decided to band together and punish his prize crew of ruffians as they attempted to flee.

Fly hurried Morgan and Magpie to the ladder down to their waiting cutter, while Prosper leaned over his rail to holler advice to his beleaguered ruffians across the distance. "Ahoy, ya bog trotters! The wind will be blowin' great guns afore long. Abandon that goddamned schooner! Swim back if ya knows how to, and if ya don't knows how, tough luck, 'cause I'm pushin' off." He quit his stomping about only long enough to bid farewell to his guests, including Mrs. Kettle, who wept loudly upon his shoulder while he forcibly fixed her into a bosun's chair. "Nay, Meggie, ya can't stay with me. I've no time fer yer clingin' and caterwaulin'. Get along now," he said, throwing off her arms and expediting the go-ahead for the Remarkables to lower her chair. Jumping back from the rail, he gave Morgan and Magpie an assuring nod and wished them both *Godspeed* as they began their descent. Once the young ones were well beyond earshot, he turned to Fly. "Haven't seen a sail fer weeks, Mr. Austen, and now the entire Yankee navy's bearin' down on us."

Facing west, Fly studied the approaching ships. "We're an hour, maybe two, ahead of them." He reached out to shake Prosper's hand. "You will stay close to us? God knows we'll need you."

"Don't ya worry none, Mr. Austen; I 'ave yer back."

The second Fly's boots hit the boat's bottom, the oarsmen pulled away. His head spinning, he sank to his seat and rubbed his arms as he observed the deteriorating scenes around him. Prosper's foretold scuffle had broken out on the schooner, the Americans beating off the ruffians with sticks of splintered wood. Rumbles and roars, and screams and shouts issued forth from her groaning timbers, even the occasional cracking of guns. Those who managed to escape the Americans' newfound fearlessness hurled themselves overboard. On the *Amethyst*, the topmen were balancing on their footropes, working madly to make sail. Captain Prickett was hopping along the gangway, flourishing a speaking trumpet, with Bridlington at his heels. Through the noise and confusion, his amplified voice sailed clearly through the air: "Mr. Austen! Do you hear me, Mr. Austen? We are in serious danger! I command you to act hastily, and return to the ship at once!"

Fly felt his hands go limp, and for a time the screams of pandemonium rolled away like the dying echoes of cannon fire. Prickett's urgent voice continued to bellow, though his words were now indistinct. The sight of Morgan, straining on the oars, his bronzed face distorted with gritty determination, caused tightness in his ribs. Crowding his mind were sorrowful recollections of his own family, waiting for him in England. Wedged in a corner of the cutter's stern, Magpie was sitting perfectly still, though twisted around on his seat. His white knuckles gripped the gunwales, and his face was fixed on something in the water. Following the boy's gaze, Fly detected a large object drifting on a point in the sea well beyond the *Prosperous and Remarkable*, and totally at odds with the direction in which they were pulling. His mind began to race. He squinted into the distance and bent his neck forward. Was it wreckage from yesterday's battle? Had one of the ships' boats gone astray? Slowly, he got to his feet, and gasped just as Magpie wheeled about to find him. Their eyes locked.

"Are you sure, Magpie?"

The little sailmaker's hands flew to his mouth; he couldn't speak, but his curly head bobbed up and down in affirmation.

29

Saturday, August 28

9:00 a.m.
Hartwood Hall

THE SHIP WRITHED ON *her side like one of Leander Braden's ailing patients. There was no one about; they had all abandoned Emily at the first crack of enemy gunfire. The empty hammocks and cots now overflowed with water, the sea pouring into the hospital through open gun ports and crashing down the ladders like swollen rivers in spring. Haemorrhaging from a wound in her shoulder, she struggled through the freezing water on her knees, trying to reach the single whale-oil lantern still burning brightly near what she hoped was the exit, hampered by her sodden gown and the razor-sharp scalpels and bone saws floating around her, cutting into her arms and legs.*

She could see him there, working in a small circle of light, crouched over his table but so far away. Try as she might, she could not make ground, for phantom arms had a tight hold on her waist, pulling her backward into dark, obscure regions of nothingness, where the walls of the ships had fallen away. She called out to him, but, too occupied with his grisly operation, he would not turn around. Captain Moreland was laid out on his table, and though already dead and waxen, Leander worked feverishly on him, slicing his gangrenous body into pieces and discarding the rotting lumps of blackened flesh into a bucket at his feet.

Reaching the ladder, Emily held on to its timbers, her body immobilized by the rushing torrent of water and the arms that stubbornly clung to her.

Beyond the ladder rungs, the sunken, derisive face of Thomas Trevelyan hung in the shadows, his deep, sonorous, disdainful laugh striking such fear in her. Looking toward Leander, she could see that he was gone now, his table and the bloated corpse of Captain Moreland all swept away from the ship by the rising water. Weeping, she fought the presence holding her down, and peering into the darkness behind her she realized it was Octavius Lindsay, his body still twitching, and nothing left of his head but a pile of gory pulp ...

Emily's eyes fluttered open to find the sheltering canopy of her bed above her, but the dreadful images of her old dream had left her engulfed in waves of nausea, and she had to raise herself up on her pillows to calm her racing heart. Beyond the bed-curtains, her room was still dark, her window draperies still pulled shut, and she could hear the rain outside, thundering to the ground. The house was silent, as if — like her nightmare — those who lived within its walls had moved on and forgotten her. Observing the clock, she chose to ignore the late morning hour, and flopped back upon her blankets, opting for more rest rather than leaving her bedchamber and risking stumbling upon the Lindsay family, whom she had not encountered since yesterday afternoon.

A faint rustling sound in the far corners of her large room dashed all attempts to slow her heartbeats. Peeking around her bed-curtains, she could see someone moving in the dim shadows, working to close up the wardrobe as quietly as possible. She contemplated calling out, to demand to know who was there, but too sickened by her dream, she could only lie still and wait and watch while the obfuscated figure tiptoed toward her door and slipped out as unobtrusively as a cat.

10:00 a.m.

EMILY TOOK A SERIES of deep breaths before entering the breakfast room. Sooner or later she had to face her hosts, though the prospect left her jittery, as if this were the day she had to stand in the witness box at the Old Bailey.

To her immense relief, only Helena and Somerton remained at the table. Their plates had been cleared away; the servants retired, but a silver coffeepot still stood between them. Given that the harsh weather had ruled out outdoor activities such as horseback riding and drinking tea in the garden, Emily had the impression that mother and son had lingered behind the others in order to discuss family affairs in private.

Upon seeing her guest, Helena resumed her usual posture of sitting on the front few inches of her chair like a bell tower, and pounced on Emily's unpunctuality. "Well, at least *one* of you decided to rise from the dead this morning."

"Where are the others?" asked Emily, attempting nonchalance as she headed toward the sideboard to select a few food items from the chafing dishes.

Somerton's reply was effervescent. "Let's see now: my father has retired to his bedchamber for a nap; your uncle has locked himself away in the library to write his morning letters; my sister is at her lessons with Mademoiselle, and completely inconsolable, for Mr. Walby cannot come by today on account of the rain, his *doctor* having forbid it; and my eldest brother has — ahem — taken to his bed."

Helena waited until Emily had seated herself at the table to pounce again. "Wetherell is a wreck."

"I'm sorry to hear of it."

"You have ruined all of his hopes."

Emily met her straight on. "Is it *his* hopes I've ruined, or *yours*?"

Helena would not answer, but Emily did not fail to notice the slight lifting of Somerton's brow. "Did you truly think I would agree to marry your son?"

"I did indeed, especially when the recipient of his most earnest proposal has no other recourse in life."

"What is behind this insistence of yours to condemn me to hell?"

Helena jabbed a ring-laden finger at Emily. "When word gets out of your refusal, I shall write to all of my friends and see to it that you never again receive another proposal of marriage, at least not from a man of quality."

"Don't exert yourself on my behalf, Your Grace." Emily glanced at Somerton, who was aimlessly running his hands over the linen tablecloth on either side of his coffee cup. "And why marry Wetherell? Why not your second son?"

Somerton looked up suddenly, biting his lower lip, his gaze steadfast, but it came as no surprise when his mother answered for him. "Because he does *not* love you."

Emily pouted. "Oh! How sad! Do you not love me, Somerton?" She watched his mouth forming a reply, but having no interest in hearing what he had to say she swung again toward Helena. "Do you mean to tell me that Wetherell does? I had no idea that love was a necessary prerequisite. Isn't it all about making favourable matches in order to gain profit or maintain a family's good standing in society? You obviously thought so when you connived to match me up with your son."

Helena eyes went flinty; her red mouth quivered. Emily allowed her to fester while she addressed Somerton, whose ears had reddened, and who had now taken to fiddling with the cuffs on his shirtsleeves. "Lord Somerton, though you may not inherit Hartwood Hall, I am certain, should *you* agree to take me off their hands, my family would see to setting you up handsomely, especially since they have unequivocally agreed to settle the marquess's gambling debts in exchange for his promise to tolerate me."

"Your — your breakfast is getting cold, Emeline," was all Somerton could say.

"How can one possibly think of eating when they've been so warmly welcomed to the breakfast table?"

Helena stroked Somerton's hand and smiled through her teeth. "I have other plans for *this* son. I couldn't bear to see him married to a harlot, not even a royal one."

There was a sharp edge to Emily's laugh. "Then I wish you well, Your Grace. You may call me whatever you like; however, since I don't recall ever meeting you before my uncle deposited me on your doorstep, I wonder at your labelling me thus, and can only guess your insult springs from the salacious stories you are wont to imagine."

"Any woman who has mixed company with a man such as Thomas Trevelyan —"

Emily rounded on Helena. "Oh! You reveal yourself! Are you acquainted with Thomas Trevelyan and his character? Has he been a guest here at Hartwood? Did you once have the pleasure of his company at a London dinner party before he betrayed his countrymen?"

Helena flushed. "No, but I —"

"I should very much like to describe your disposition, Your Grace, but as I can only do so based upon my own experience these past weeks, I shall refrain, for my description might be equally as cruel and unjust as your

description of me. For all I know, you may have done good works in a nun-
nery in the years prior to marrying His Grace." Emily leaned toward the
duchess. "Are you so perfect yourself that we — none of us — can succeed
in securing your esteem? If so, tell me this, for I'm quite curious and full of
wild imaginings on the subject."

Helena's eyes widened as she shrank back upon her chair, as if she
expected Emily to strike her across the face.

"Who is Fleda's father?"

"Emeline!" gasped Somerton. "That's quite enough."

Helena rose abruptly to her feet, her hands clenching her gown.

"Oh, Your Grace, you cannot leave! You've not yet given me an answer."

"And you shall not be receiving one," said Helena, her voice carefully
controlled. Lifting her skirts, she drifted queenly from the room.

Somerton's face was now overspread with a queer, patchy red blush.
He looked helplessly at Emily and shook his head. "You've done enough
upsetting of this family for one day."

Emily eyed him. "Your reprimand is feeble. You might as well be direct-
ing it at a child who's accidently broken her milk mug." She pushed her
chair back, momentarily irritated by its clawing upon the floorboards, and
then sighed, feeling as if she had not slept soundly in a month. "Perhaps
you don't truly comprehend the meaning of the word *upsetting*..Were I
a man, with enough power over you to determine your destiny, I would
secretly arrange a match between you and the most unappetizing woman
I've ever met — a woman who would, no doubt, repulse you to the very
core of your being — and when you balked and lamented, I wouldn't listen;
I would simply tell you that you are condemned — that you have no other
recourse in life." She bowed to him. "Good day to you, sir."

Emily had almost reached the door when Uncle Clarence came bounding in, a clutch of letters in his fist. "Where are you off to, Emeline? Come
and sit back down again," he said cheerfully, springing toward Somerton
and the breakfast table. "Is there any coffee left in the pot, Lord Somerton?
If so, would you be so kind as to pour me a drop?"

Emily dragged herself back to the table. "Uncle, please! I'm not in a
frame of mind to hear ultimatums regarding my future."

For a moment, Uncle Clarence's expression was one of confusion. "Oh!
I see what you're getting at! Well, my dear, I'm quite sure ultimatums will

come later on, once I've had time to consult my brother, the Regent, and then fashion my *wording* of them in a way which will give you clarity of mind." He sat down in Helena's empty chair, and waved his letters in the air. "These have just arrived, and as the senders are individuals of great importance, I should like you to be apprised of their contents."

10:30 a.m.

THERE WAS A GLEAM IN Uncle Clarence's eyes as he watched for the reaction from his audience of two before breaking the seal on the first letter — the one he deemed of most importance — and perusing its pages. "This one is from the office of the First Lord of the Admiralty," he announced, "written by the Right Honourable the Viscount Melville himself."

Emily pushed her cold breakfast around on her plate with a fork, and kept her eyes lowered as her uncle grunted over Lord Melville's letter. A stolen glance at Somerton was completely disconcerting, for he was wearing a silly grin, and seemed pleased that she had returned to the table, as if the unpleasant exchange with his mother had never taken place. Unable to remember when she had last eaten — not having elected to dine with the family the previous evening — she had just speared a piece of potato, and was bringing it to her waiting mouth when her uncle's ejaculations rent the air.

"God Almighty! My word! Hark'ee! This is bad news indeed!"

Emily looked up.

"What is it?" asked Somerton.

Uncle Clarence sat up a little straighter, held up his hand, and inhaled deeply. "Wait 'til I've read the others, for there's another one here from Whitehall, and one from the Transport Office." He continued to read, Emily watching in alarm as the rosy colour faded from his face and the lines on his brow deepened. When he was done, he slowly set the letters down beside his coffee cup and pulled a handkerchief from his breast pocket. Rising solemnly from his chair, he began mopping his brow, and took up pacing before the windows, occasionally pausing to watch the rain drum the gardens. It was some time before he wheeled about to face them. "Lord Somerton, would you arrange for my carriage to be brought to the door? I must away to London this morning."

"Of course," said Somerton, looking quizzically at Emily as he jumped up to ring the bell for the butler.

Her heart thumping, Emily rushed to her uncle's side. "First tell us what has transpired to cause you such dismay?" she insisted, leading him back to the table. "Is it Grandfather? Is he having hallucinations again?"

"No, my dear, it's not the king." Uncle Clarence allowed Emily to pour him another coffee and load it up with cream and sugar, although he normally drank it black. "The mail packet, the *Lady Jane*, arrived in Portsmouth the other day."

"The *Lady Jane*? Of what significance is she?"

Uncle Clarence took Emily's hands in his. "She was being escorted back to England from Halifax by your good friends on the *Amethyst*. About two weeks back, there was a horrendous storm; the seas were heavy, and the winds —"

Emily went white to the lips. She swallowed and was barely able to speak. "Please do not tell me the *Amethyst* was lost. Please —"

"The two ships were separated, and the crew of the *Lady Jane* has not seen her since. They had hoped to find her already moored in Portsmouth when they arrived home."

Emily shut her eyes and prayed under her breath. Muted by the pouring rain, she could hear Somerton's voice, giving instructions to the butler. He was standing but a few feet from where she sat, though he seemed miles away.

Uncle Clarence squeezed her hands. "There's something more I must tell you, my dear."

Emily pulled her hands from his. "No! Tell me no more!" she said in despair. "What little you have already said ... I cannot bear." She struggled to raise herself up, and began to creep toward the door like an elderly woman.

Uncle Clarence ran his handkerchief across his chin. "Emeline! You must hear this news from me. It won't be long before all of England is speaking of it."

Emily met her uncle, her eyes glistening with tears.

"It's astonishing really, and no one in the Transport Office knows how he managed to effect it — being as there were no witnesses to his deception — but on the day he was to be moved to Newgate, Thomas Trevelyan escaped from his prison hulk, and his whereabouts at this time are regrettably unknown."

30

THE *AMETHYST* DID NOT wait for them. Captain Prickett shot off the minute he realized that Fly and the others weren't coming back, but even as he set a new course for England and his sails began to billow with wind, he was still cursing into the speaking trumpet, and insisting their delay was "… intentional, insubordinate, and a veritable suicide."

On the main deck of the *Prosperous and Remarkable*, Magpie stood soldered to the larboard rail, keeping his eye on the goings-on in the water below. A glance at the retreating *Amethyst* had already sent his heart racing; he didn't dare look behind him. The thought alone of what was coming at them from the west was bad enough. Mr. Austen and Mr. Evans, along with the rest of his stranded boat-mates, were working against time to bring the skiff survivors up the side of the brig on bosun chairs. One of the four men had died, his hands stiffened around the ropes of the skiff's single sail, but Dr. Braden was alive. He was gaunt and sickly, and his voice was faint, but he was alive. The lump in Magpie's throat was so prodigious, he wasn't certain he'd ever swallow again.

Nearby, Prosper was wearing a rut in the deck's planks with his feverish pacing. His wispy curls flattened by the wind, his veins at attention on his bald pate, he ordered his ruffians — those who had successfully fled the

Americans' uprising on the schooner and had kicked their way back on the waves with the aid of anything that would float — to *"… refrain from comin' aboard 'til yas helps with the survivors."* Despite the long shadows cast by the American fleet, Prosper's voice sounded reassuringly normal. "Ya jackanapes! Ya galoot! Ya worthless plank shank! Careful there with the doctor! He's worth more than all o' yas put together!" Stunning Magpie even further, Prosper gave him a wink and a grin. "Yer a right lucky lad, sailin' on me *Prosperous and Remarkable* once again."

Magpie wasn't sure how that made him lucky, but there was no time to ponder it, for Mrs. Kettle was now thundering across the deck like a snorting bull. Along with Magpie, she'd been among the first ones hoisted up from the *Amethyst's* cutter, wailing the whole time about her *"poor wee babe,"* but now that she felt safe she grabbed hold of Prosper's wind-whipped shirttails. "Leave 'em be, Prosper! Git a move on, else we'll all be dead by noon, nothin' left o' us but bits of flesh hangin' like gory pendants from the yardarms."

"Git below, Meggie! Make yerself useful, and leave me to make the hard decisions," he said, peeling away her grasping hands.

Mr. Austen had come on board with the survivors, and had just arranged for them to be carried below for medical attention, when an eruption of gunfire rattled the western sky. It was nothing more than a bold warning from the enemy, but it unleashed a terrible, rippling wave of urgency around the brig. Mrs. Kettle, who had been running about in circles, suddenly dropped to the deck and began shrieking. High up on the masts, the Remarkables hugged the yards, bracing for a hit, while below the remaining ruffians and *Amethysts*, as if they were suddenly conscious of their vulnerability, cried out, and propelled themselves up the side of the hull.

Magpie could see the distraught men clinging to dangling ropes, and clambering over open gun ports and one another to gain the brig's deck. Morgan was still down there, fighting to maintain a foothold on whatever he could, but paralyzed by the weight of a lanky sailor, who scrabbled over him in order to climb higher, using him as if he were a fixed part of the ship.

The second burst of gunfire hit its mark, smashing one of the brig's heads to splinters on her bow. Prosper's head jerked in the direction of the schooner. "God be damned! Them schooner Yankees have gone and fired up the guns! That's it! Pemberton Baker! Where are ya, ya smellfungus?"

"Where ya normally finds me, Prosper," came the composed voice of Pemberton, his thick torso hunched over the ship's wheel.

"Beat to windward, ya lubber! We're gettin' the hell out o' here."

The topmen sprang into action with their weather braces and sheets, and lee tacks and bowlines, and in no time the *Prosperous and Remarkable* groaned and shifted and rolled into the waves, but, in doing so, upended the *Amethyst's* cutter, dumping those still within it into the cold Atlantic.

"Mr. Austen!" shouted Magpie, gesturing toward the water. "It's Mr. Evans, sir!"

Realizing at once that Morgan was not among the men on deck, Fly called for extra hands as he searched for something to throw over the side. "Here! This old sail! Hold onto it, lads, and pull with everything you've got."

Though he was now secure in the knowledge that everything would be all right with Morgan, Magpie was enthralled by the awful scenes below, where a handful of sailors still thrashed about in the ocean, frantic to reach the overturned cutter; their eyes huge with terror as the *Prosperous and Remarkable* lunged from them in her scramble to get away. Over the delirium of sobbing and bellowing and booming guns, Magpie yelled, "Sir, what about the others?"

"Come away from the rail."

"But, sir!"

"'Tis the terrible cost of war, Magpie." Mr. Austen's eyes fell unblinkingly on him, his hands covering his ears, as if to silence the distressing cries for help. For a while he stood perfectly still, and when the light returned to his eyes he gave Magpie an overly bright smile. "Let us go down to the hold to see our friends."

11:00 a.m.

Aboard HMS *Amethyst*

"Dear God in Heaven!" muttered Captain Prickett, lowering his telescope. "What shall we do?"

Overhearing Prickett, Bridlington sidled up to him at the taffrail, his glance darting about at the gun crews clustered around the carronades on the poop deck. They were all speaking in hushed voices to one another, their facial expressions a disturbing mixture of despair and disgust. Bridlington smoothed down his uniform jacket and shuddered. "We must get Mr. Austen back on board immediately, sir."

Prickett rolled his eyes. "It would be a sight easier to restore life to our former prime minister, Mr. Perceval."

Bridlington moved in closer; another inch and he would be climbing his captain's back. "What if the men rise up in mutiny?"

"With that fleet on our tail, there won't be time for thoughts of mutiny," said Prickett, running a roughened hand over his stubbly chin. "What've you done with the deserters?"

"They're locked up in the hold, but most petulant the lot of them. I don't like the look in their eyes, but then, neither do I like the look of our own men."

"Quit worrying about mutinies, and focus on maintaining your scalp this day."

Bridlington caught his breath. "You don't think those American ships are carrying Indian warriors, do you, sir? I've — I've heard such stories of what the Indians, fighting with our own men in the forests of Canada, like to do to the enemy as they are lying helpless, in agonies of pain, and breathing their last on the —" Bridlington suddenly leaned way over the taffrail, as if he were about to abandon ship, and released a withering cry. "Oh, Mr. Austen, do come back!"

Prickett grabbed him by the collar and hissed into his ear. "I command you to collect yourself."

"I am sorry, sir," whistled Bridlington, droplets of perspiration dripping down his scarlet cheeks.

"I'm putting you in charge. It's your watch. See to it those damned ships don't catch up to us before nightfall."

Bridlington's eyes popped open. "Where're you going, sir?"

"Below."

"What ... to check on the petulant deserters?"

Prickett pursed his lips and thought a moment. "Aye! Naturally! Where else would I be going?"

11:30 a.m.
(Morning Watch, Seven Bells)
Aboard the *Prosperous and Remarkable*

MAGPIE LOOKED AROUND HIM. He'd never been on Prosper's orlop deck before, but he knew that Mr. Walby had, and *his* tales of terror of being alone in the dark had haunted Magpie ever since their telling. He was relieved to have others with him. It smelled awful down here, the odours of fish and tar and decaying cheese and mouldy canvas and vermin excrement made him headachy and ill at the stomach. There was little room to move around the hempen anchor cable on the platform deck that overlooked the brig's hold, and its endless sea of barrels and casks, sunken into the shingle of the ballast, over which scurried rats trying to chew their way through the wooden staves to get at the food inside. But somehow a few cots had been rigged in the middle of it all for the three skiff survivors.

Mr. Austen and Prosper had put Magpie in charge, and, feeling as if he had suddenly grown a foot, he moved from cot to cot, bringing water to his patients' parched lips and occasionally giving them each a spoonful of oatmeal. Prosper had further handed him a jar of oily salve, instructing him to gently administer a bit of it onto their sunburned skin. In the distance there was gunfire, and every so often Magpie tensed, thinking the *Prosperous and Remarkable* might rock with a direct hit, but so far there'd been nothing beyond the initial bow strike. He gave thanks that, at the time, no one had been sitting on the heads, or the *seats of ease* as the lads called them. Magpie thought that would be a mortifying way to die, with one's trousers down around one's ankles.

Dr. Braden's eyes opened. Seeing Magpie sitting there next to his cot, he smiled. "Have our roles reversed?"

Magpie couldn't speak right away, still in disbelief that the doctor was here, so close to him. "I wanted to give ya a banquet, sir, but Prosper scolded me, and said ya couldn't handle it right off."

Dr. Braden's voice was little more than a whisper. "No, I couldn't, but then I wonder if Mr. Burgo's galley larder could provide for a true banquet."

Magpie shook his head. "I bin on board with him afore, and his victuals ain't so good. Pemberton gave me a cup o' tea once, and said he'd bin boilin' water over the same leaves fer two months. I won't suggest ya try Pemberton's tea, sir."

"I will gladly take your advice."

"But I promise, when I give ya some biscuit, I'll first pluck out the weevils and maggots."

"I am grateful to you. I've always found maggots to be somewhat cold and unpleasant, and weevils ... well, they have a bitter taste to them."

Magpie peeked over at the cots where his two other patients were asleep. He had to remind himself that Biscuit slept in one of them, being as he was so used to the Scottish cook's chatter and jokey nature. There seemed to be more streaks of white in his bushy hair and whiskers than Magpie remembered. When he turned back to Dr. Braden, Magpie found his eyes intently watching him.

"I — I don't suppose you know that I locked Emily's miniature into my writing box."

There was an ache in Magpie's chest. "I was hopin' ya might have it on ya, sir. This whole voyage ... me mind's bin so jumbled with fear ... I sometimes can't remember what she looks like." He stared at his hands. "I do remember she smelled nice, and she had fine white teeth, but her face ... it's not clear, and I git her features all mixed up in me head."

Dr. Braden exhaled quietly and, in the lantern light, Magpie thought he saw tears in his eyes.

Magpie sloped toward his cot. "Can I do anythin' more fer ya, sir?"

"You can," he whispered.

"Just name it, and I'll do it, sir."

"Take me home to England."

31

Noon
Hampstead Heath

GUS WALBY SAT ON a three-legged stool by the window in the low-beamed room he was sharing with old Dr. Braden at the coaching inn in Hampstead Heath. He cradled his chin upon an upturned hand and reflected upon the muddy road that led to Hartwood Hall. Would the rain ever let up? He wanted so badly to spend another day at the estate, taking his lessons with Fleda, for he enjoyed the girl's company — she was amusing, and never made mention of his crutch, and had such plans for their hours together — and he hoped he might catch a fleeting look at Emily, as he had yesterday when she was sitting in the garden with the Duke of Clarence, or even hear her voice through the schoolroom walls. It didn't matter that he was forbidden to mingle with Fleda's family. The duchess scared him. Why, he was quite certain she could hold her own in the society of Prosper Burgo's ruffians, although — as far as he had seen — she was still in possession of all her teeth and extremities. The morning had dragged on interminably, and the prospect of spending the rainy afternoon with a penny novel was not an enticing one. When the door suddenly squeaked opened and in walked old Dr. Braden, all soaking wet but with a gleam in his eyes, Gus grabbed for his crutch at once.

"Sir, I didn't expect you back until suppertime."

The doctor kicked off his mud-caked shoes and peeled off his cape and broad-brimmed hat, hanging them to dry on a hook beside the empty grate of the fireplace. "My cousin is expecting visitors this afternoon, so I thought maybe we could spend the rest of the day together." He disappeared behind a screen to change out of his wet clothes. "It's chilly in here, Mr. Walby. Do you have a woollen vest in your travelling case? I shan't allow that cough of yours to worsen."

"I don't, sir."

"Well then, put on your midshipman's jacket."

Gus bent over to retrieve it from the cold floor and slipped it on, thankful for its extra layer of warmth. His healthy leg began bouncing up and down, his mind travelling to fantastical places. Did the doctor have something exciting to tell him? Could he somehow have received a letter from his son on the sea? Had the Duke of Clarence sent a note, saying that he'd secured for *him* a posting on a ship as magnificent as HMS *Victory*? And if so, were they going to celebrate downstairs in the parlour with a mug of ale and another mouth-watering meal prepared by the innkeeper's wife?

Old Dr. Braden reappeared in his fresh clothes, and sank down upon one of the two narrow beds. "Mr. Walby, I must tell you: as I was making my way along the road, trying to avoid puddles — some of which, I declare, rose above my knees — a carriage passed me by, going at an alarming speed, drenching me through and through with a wall of rainwater. I wondered who it was coming down the road so quickly in this weather, but did not wonder long, for immediately following it a second carriage happened by, going at a much slower pace and stopping before me where I stood, across the road from our inn."

"Was it Emily?" asked Gus.

"No! It was a servant from Hartwood Hall, a sonsy-faced Scottish woman named Miss McCubbin."

"What did she want?"

"Catching me entirely off guard, she handed me an invitation, and announced that I was being invited to sup at the Hall tonight and that a carriage would be sent for me precisely at four o'clock."

Gus wilted; an empty monosyllable was all he could utter in reply.

"Miss McCubbin further announced that I was to bring my young friend with me."

Gus's mouth jumped open. "You're not trifling with me, are you, sir?"

"It's not in my nature to trifle, Mr. Walby! So stop looking like a fish, and let's determine what we shall wear tonight."

"Oh, but I don't have anything presentable."

The doctor raised himself from the bed. "Ah! Well, perhaps we should discuss this dilemma downstairs in the parlour where the innkeeper has a nice fire going."

"Do you think the Duke of Clarence will be at supper with us, sir?"

"I don't know. Are you hoping to see him?"

"I am, sir. I'm hoping he might bring up the subject of a new posting for me. I am feeling stronger, and would like to return to sea."

Old Doctor Braden turned around to straighten and tidy up his bed quilt, rumpled by his having sat upon it; Gus surprised at how long he lingered over his simple task, and how slow his reply was in coming. "Just as I was mounting the stairs, the innkeeper's wife told me she'd baked a bread pudding, stuffed full of raisins and walnuts, and that she desired the young Mr. Walby to sample it."

Gus forced a smile and tugged his jacket around him. The thought of a warm fire and a dish of dessert suddenly had no appeal. Hearing the rain intensify beyond the window, he looked away and stared once again at the muddy road and its ever widening pools of water.

1:00 p.m.
Hartwood Hall

EMILY WAS AT HER DESK in front of the west-facing window of her bedroom overlooking the wet, colourless gardens when Glenna McCubbin flew through the door like a newly discovered species of gigantic bird. The housekeeper was heaving with breathlessness and quaking with emotion, though Emily could not determine if it was excitement or anxiety, or a bit of both. Sliding the letter she was writing into the desk drawer, she reluctantly turned toward her former nursemaid, hoping her tear-stained face would not incite comment and inquiry. "Back again so soon, Glenna? Didn't you get what you wanted the first time around?"

Glenna redressed her lacy cap, which had gone awry during her flight up the stairs. "What d' ya mean by that, Pet?"

"Weren't you here in my room earlier this morning?"

"Nay!"

"Upon awaking, I was certain I saw you rummaging around in the wardrobe."

"Must've bin another o' yer tempestuous dreams," said Glenna, seemingly untroubled by Emily's accusation. "Nay! I've been runnin' 'round all day like Lady Fleda's dog! Why, the household's all in an uproar. My word, Pet, ya've turned Hartwood on its end. Such fireworks! Oh, my poor heart! I swear, sooner rather than later yer gonna lower me into the grave."

Emily could not help her empty gaze. "Could you save the telling of it for later? I'd like to be alone."

Glenna's face changed to a scowl. "Ya'll wither away in this room if I let ya, and since yer causin' all the fireworks, ya'll hear me out."

Sighing, Emily assumed a position of obedient attentiveness, while Glenna took a big breath for her recounting. "First off, the Duke o' Clarence upset everyone with his quick leave takin' on account o' some terrible news he'd received this mornin'; and now Lord Munroe's upset the kitchen with his insistence the cook prepare and deliver to his room all o' his favourite dishes. Lud! Half o' the ingredients canna be found this side o' London. And then, His Grace is bilious, bein' overset with stomach cramps, and he's keepin' to *his* room, and Lady Fleda's in such a dither over Mr. Walby comin' fer dinner that she's refused to heed her lessons, puttin' Mademoiselle in a fit o' tears, and —"

"Wait! Mr. Walby's coming for dinner?"

"Aye! And the old doctor as well."

"Whatever possessed Her Grace to allow them a place at her dining table?"

"Oh, Her Grace is madder than a trapped hornet about it all, so she's keepin' to *her* room."

"I don't understand —"

"Ya see, t'were Lord Somerton what done the invitin'."

Emily required a moment for reflection. "You mean Somerton's organizing a dinner party for this evening, and being unable to coerce his friends to attend, he wallowed through the mud to invite the residents of the local inn?"

"Ain't he a kind soul to be thinkin' o' your friends sittin' in the postin' house on such a dismal day?"

Emily felt a throbbing ache in her jaw.

"But there'll only be five o' yas at the table."

"How cosy!"

"Tell me, Pet, is the old doctor a married man?"

"No. His wife has passed on," Emily said coldly, longing to add that she'd died so very recently her own son had no idea his mother was gone.

"Oh!" crowed Glenna, playfully slapping her thighs. "He does have very fine eyes."

Emily shook her head in disgust. "Seeing as most of the family would prefer to keep to their rooms, why don't *you* join us tonight?"

Glenna blushed at the idea. "And give Her Grace a nervous disorder?"

"She'll not know; she'll be in bed with a cold compress on her head." Emily rose abruptly and guided Glenna toward the door. "Let's create more fireworks, shall we? In the event Captain Trevelyan comes knocking on the front door while we're eating our roasted pork and gravy, let him come in and join our little, intimate coterie."

Glenna's eyes popped out of her head. "Aren't ye the flippant one!"

Emily pushed her into the corridor and banged the door shut. She hobbled back to the writing desk, stumbling into the chair with a gasping sob; dark, lurking thoughts threatening to rear up again and overwhelm her. But the letter — she was determined to press on with it. Dabbing at her face, she dipped her quill pen into her silver inkwell and was just picking up where she'd left off when a black, fluttering shape suddenly appeared in the rain. Having found shelter from the storm, a magpie landed on the white stone ledge of her window to give his iridescent wing feathers a shiver, and turn his penetrating gaze upon her through the panes of glass.

6:30 p.m.

Gus Walby could hardly wait for the meal to be over. Fleda had promised to show him the tunnels under the Hall, which led to the kitchens and offices and storerooms. He'd never been in a tunnel before; he'd only read about them in novels, and the literary ones were always dark and dank and musty-smelling, and teeming with either murderers or ghosts. He didn't like sitting in this big music room, darkened by the enduring rain. The candlelight on their round table, as well as the candles that flickered on the sideboards and mantelpieces, radiated grotesque shadows upon the watchful visages of those in the many portraits nailed to the walls, and it didn't help that Fleda had remarked that most of those painted people were dead.

The dark-eyed man who had introduced himself only as *Somerton,* and insisted that he be addressed thus, since his family *"these days did not abide by formality,"* had been asking old Dr. Braden hundreds of questions about medical training, showing a particular interest in the studies taken by his son on the sea, and was now discussing the horrors of dysentery and consumption, subjects which not only terrified Gus, but also didn't seem suitable for dinner conversation, especially when there were ladies present. Somerton had barely glanced at Gus, let alone asked him any questions; then again it made perfect sense that such a significant gentleman, who lived in such an elegant country house, had no time or interest in an unemployed and crippled midshipman. Gus so wished the Duke of Clarence had been present. He at least might have singled him out with an inquiry after his health, and noticed how well his uniform was looking, thanks to the innkeeper's wife, who had blithely agreed to lower the hem on his pantaloons and wash off the dirty spots.

Even worse, Gus was concerned about Emily. Aside from her evident joy upon his arrival, she had said very little, had eaten very little, and seemed remote, as if her thoughts were roaming through some far-off realm. And every so often she lifted her head — her gold hair so prettily arranged and adorned with tiny blue flowers — to throw a wild-eyed glance at this Somerton man, as if she feared he might divulge a dark secret. But the very worst of all, Gus didn't like the way Somerton looked at Emily with those close-set eyes of his whenever her own were fixed upon her plate of rabbit cutlet and diced vegetables. It wasn't anything like Leander Braden's adoring, stolen glances he remembered well. To Gus, *this* man had the manners of a sailor.

Admiring the cornice of sculptured harps and the collection of instruments near the far window, Gus almost dropped his fork when Somerton recognized him at long last.

"Mr. Walby, I understand you served as a midshipman on HMS *Isabelle* under Captain James Moreland."

"I did, sir," said Gus, squaring his shoulders.

"The sinking of your ship must have been an awful ordeal."

"I wasn't on board when Trevelyan set her on fire, sir."

"Where were you at the time?"

"I had fallen from the mizzenmast, and was drifting in the ocean without my wits about me."

"Is that how you acquired your injuries?"

"Yes, sir. My injuries were bad at the time, but now it's really only my one leg that gives me any trouble."

Fleda suddenly hopped in her chair. "I forgot ... I never asked you ... I was so thrilled to have you as a playmate and show you around the grounds that I never asked you —"

"Fle-da!" said Somerton sternly, raising a finger. "You may make your inquiries, but only once I am done with mine."

Fleda acquiesced, but continued to squirm as if she were sitting upon some wondrous intelligence.

"What did your duties include, Mr. Walby?"

"Thank you for asking, sir," said Gus, injecting gravity into his voice, but finding instead that his words insisted upon tumbling out of his mouth. "I had to learn knots and splices, and the use of a sextant, and how to heave the log and to make notations on the log board. And I had to exercise at both the great guns and small arms, and sometimes ... sometimes Captain Moreland made me the Officer of the Watch on the fo'c'sle."

Fleda pulled a face. "What's a folksill?"

"It's the forecastle, the raised deck at the ship's bow," said Gus, proud to oblige with a knowledgeable reply.

"And did you keep up with your lessons in reading and writing?" asked Somerton, steeling his voice as if to warn his sister not to steer him off his course of questioning.

"Oh, yes, sir! Mr. Austen helped all of the middies with their lessons, and sometimes Mr. Lindsay, the first lieutenant, did too. But I always preferred it when Mr. Austen did the teaching."

From the corner of his eye, Gus saw Emily tense up, and old Dr. Braden ruffle his white brow.

"Why is that? Didn't you like Mr. Lindsay?"

Gus thrust out his lower lip. "Not at all, sir."

"Why not?"

"He was very unhappy and mean to us all; never had a kind word for any of the younger lads, and every chance he could he would betray us to Captain Moreland."

"For a man in his position, he wasn't the gentleman he should have been. Is that it, Mr. Walby?"

"That's it, sir! He gave Captain Moreland such grief, always questioning his authority, but toward Emily ... he was particularly unkind." Gus had hoped to secure Emily's affirmation, but the round horror in her eyes evaporated his confidence. Oh! Was she worried he was going to mention that awful episode that occurred in the *Isabelle*'s sail room? Why, he would never do that. He gave his head a slight shake to reassure her.

"Perhaps we shouldn't be speaking of someone who — I am guessing — is a relative of yours," old Dr. Braden gently interjected, his uncertain gaze moving between Somerton and Fleda.

In need of an ally, Gus turned toward Fleda, but what he saw in her expression curled his toes. Her eyes searched his, and her question was spoken so faintly it could have come from the tunnel beneath the floor. "You didn't like my brother?"

"Brother?" echoed Gus. "Mr. Octavius Lindsay was your *brother*?" His mind raced like a hounded fox. How could it be? How could he not have known? The people who owned Hartwood Hall were a duke and duchess ... old Dr. Braden had told him as much, and taken pains to instruct him in styling them as *His Grace* and *Her Grace* should he have the honour of making their acquaintance, but at no time did he recall hearing any mention of the Lindsay name, or if he had his mind must have been too frenzied with thoughts of his Hampstead Heath adventure to have paid any heed. Was the duchess, that hag who had tried to turn them away at the door, really the mother of Octavius Lindsay? And Fleda ... was she his sister? Octavius had never said anything about a sister, only that he had been his father's eighth son. He couldn't understand. If all this was true, then why — of all places — was Emily brought here to live?

Struck with such a thudding realization, desperate for answers, Gus swung toward Emily only to see that her cheeks had turned scarlet. Fleda had twisted in her chair to point at the portrait nearest to the entrance of the music room, the sight of which left Gus fighting down a rising belch. Good God! What had he done? Frightened by the loud silence, he fumbled to fill it. "Fleda! I didn't know! I'm so sorry for my insensitive remarks. Mr. Somerton, sir, had I — had I known, I would've told you about Mr. Lindsay's many good qualities and —" His words tapered off in a gulp when Emily reached for his hand under the table.

Somerton sniffed. "Since *you* were acquainted with my youngest brother, and no one else has thought it necessary to offer up any information to our grieving family —" he shot an insincere smile at Emily, "perhaps, Mr. Walby, you could tell me something of my brother's death?"

The candle flames shot higher; the food on the dinner plates was forgotten. Fleda looked at him, her green eyes huge in her small face, drained of its previous blush; old Dr. Braden looked grave, and had slipped forward upon his chair; Emily squeezed his hand tighter; and Somerton cocked his head, awaiting his answer.

"I don't know anything, sir," said Gus, his voice cracking.

"You must know something. Not all of Captain Moreland's men perished on the *Isabelle*. I understand you were reunited with those who survived. What did they tell you?"

"They — they told me nothing, sir."

"Was there an explosion?"

"I believe there might have been —"

"Was my brother one of the unlucky ones who couldn't get off in time?"

"He might have been, sir."

"Or … or was he *too* taken prisoner by Captain Thomas Trevelyan?"

Gus tugged on his sweaty collar and gazed around the table, praying for assistance or a way out.

"Ah! I see by your reaction, Mr. Walby, that you do know something. Please! Enlighten us! We're most anxious to hear what became of our brother."

Emily stood up so quickly she bumped the table, knocking over her glass of wine. Disregarding it, she rounded on Somerton, speaking in an even, eerie voice Gus had never heard her use before. "Lord Somerton, it was most generous of you to invite my friends to dinner. I'd hoped for an evening of pleasant conversation with two of the most engaging men I know, but it seems you invited our guests under false pretences."

Somerton jutted his chin out. "How so? I've asked Mr. Walby nothing but a few harmless questions."

"Asking is one thing, sir, *badgering* quite another."

Somerton's eyes slithered around the table. "Mr. Walby, did you find my manner to be in any way unctuous?"

Not understanding the meaning of that word, Gus sat there helplessly.

"Perhaps I was overly enthusiastic," Somerton chuckled, "finding your answers to be exceedingly intriguing."

"I take full responsibility," said Emily, maintaining calm. "I should've told Mr. Walby earlier of your relationship — and that of Fleda — to Lord Octavius. I regret that now, and can only put it down to my eagerness to forget about your unfortunate brother."

Somerton's eyes narrowed on her. "Has your being here at Hartwood made that impossible?"

"It has."

For a time no one said a thing. Gus felt as if the roof were teetering and about to collapse. He felt his chin trembling, but was at a loss to tame it. He heard the rain sputter outside, and the murmurs and footfalls of the servants as they went about their business in faraway rooms. When a clock began to chime, old Dr. Braden rose to his feet, his flushed features tight with embarrassment.

"Lord Somerton, I believe the time has come to say goodnight. Thank you so very much for the excellent meal. Please, I beg you, stay here with your sister to enjoy your dessert. Perhaps Emily will see us out. No need to worry about calling for the carriage; I believe the rain has let up, so Mr. Walby and I shall be quite happy to walk back to our lodgings." He bowed and sidled away from the table.

Gus wanted to die. This was not how he'd envisioned his evening at Hartwood. He knew it, he felt it in his bones; he'd never be allowed back. He'd never see the tunnels under the house, or explore the woods with Fleda, or picnic by the ponds. Refusing to let tears roll from his eyes, he blindly followed Emily and old Dr. Braden to the doorway, loathing himself for ending things this way with Fleda. Before passing into the darkness of the antechamber, he glanced back over his drooping shoulder. It gave him a pain to see such sadness in Fleda's ashen face. But something — her downturned eyes, her wilting posture, her empty stare — told him that the death of her brother was not the true source of her devastation; it seemed to him she was regretting the leaving and the loss of her newfound friend.

32

IN THE LENGTHENING SHADOWS of the day, Fly Austen and Prosper Burgo met together at the taffrail of the *Prosperous and Remarkable*, studying the movements of the American ships within their sights. With the exception of one ship, which had stopped to aid the drifting schooner, they were still frighteningly close, particularly the three smallest vessels. Being as she was lightweight, and with every stitch of her canvas flying, Prosper's brig flew like a seagull over the waves, but Fly despaired for the *Amethyst*, imagining the tumult most likely unfolding upon her decks. Prosper's brig had long surpassed her, and now — like a lumbering turtle — she had fallen behind, managing only to maintain a safe distance beyond the range of the Americans' bow chasers. Casting his eyes toward the red and purpling sky, Fly prayed for nightfall to descend upon the Atlantic.

Beside him, Prosper was gnawing on a sandwich of stale biscuit and cheese — his stores of cheese being so tough, Fly had witnessed some of the Remarkables carving buttons out of their portions of the stuff — and quaffing the contents of a cracked and chipped mug between bites, most likely to assist the food's path down his gullet. Not far from where they conferred, Meg Kettle had settled herself on an overturned tub normally reserved for the soaking of salted beef and pork. Prosper had warned her repeatedly to *"git *below,*" but she disregarded his words, choosing instead to keep him within her sights at all times, so that whenever he moved camp she would follow. But during the rare moments when her slitty eyes weren't padlocked on Prosper, she was mending a pair of his stockings, though Fly wondered why she bothered when there seemed to be more holes than wool with which to work.

"Meggie, best dump them woollies and git below to wrestle me laundry. I heard ya complainin' 'bout me greasy scarves."

"Nay, Prosper!" she hollered back. "Ya 'ave no lye soap on board, and I ain't about to wash clothes in urine and saltwater. Ain't proper fer a lady what's got a child comin'."

The wispy curls around Prosper's ears shivered when he glanced up at Fly, his tongue stuck in his cheek. "I fear yer a lofty lot, Mr. Austen. There's Meggie yowlin' 'bout no soap, and Mr. Evans askin' me fer tools I ain't never heard of, and then there's yer rumbustious Scotch cook declarin' me biscuits inferior, and insistin' we bake some up with sugar and rum. Mr. Austen, I haven't transported a bag o' sugar on these old timbers fer near a decade."

"And rum?"

Prosper raised his mug with a low chuckle. "I wouldn't think o' sailin' without plenty o' rum in me hold."

"I apologize for what may be perceived as our extravagant tastes, but I do assure you, we are all most obliged to you and give thanks that we are alive on your brig."

"Ah, but fer how long kin I keep ya that way? I ain't never had a fleet o' ships on me arse afore."

Meg Kettle's head shot up from her mending, her mouth all quivery. "What d' ya mean, Prosper?"

Prosper shushed her up with a snap of his fingers. "Now then, Mr. Austen, if only the clumsy winds would blow fresher, or a bit o' rain would fall, or a bank o' fog would come rollin' our way, we might make a bit o' headway. I'll not tolerate another hit to the heads. Already me lads are usin' buckets to do their business, and most o' them — bein' gowks and dullards — have habits o' tossin' their filth overboard ... into the wind."

"Mr. Evans will have your *seats of ease* restored to your men in no time."

"Aye, he's a good lad, your carpenter."

"The very best," smiled Fly, trying to spot Morgan's woolly thrum cap amongst the crush of Remarkables labouring on the other end of the brig.

Prosper gave Fly a thorough going over. "When did ya last take sustenance?"

"I cannot recall."

"Grog would be best, but I know ya likes to keep yer wits intact." Prosper shouted out at Pemberton Baker at the helm. "Bring Mr. Austen some coffee straightaway, ya galoot."

It astounded Fly to hear no protests from Pemberton, no justification as to why it would be more prudent to ask another to fetch coffee; the man simply handed the wheel to the nearest ruffian and lumbered off to do his duty.

"Now quit worryin' so. The *Amethyst*'ll pull through; she's got plenty o' heavy guns on her."

"I wish I could share your confidence. In order to lighten her weight, I fear her men may throw them overboard rather than use them."

"If there be any need fer load lightenin', they best keep the guns and pitch Prickett and Bridlington overboard."

As Prosper was quite solemn in his pronouncement, Fly chewed on his lip to mask his amusement.

"We'll soon be raisin' England. Might be we'll cross paths with yer Royal Navy."

"Let us hope —"

Draining the grog, Prosper flung his clay mug over the railing, and then hardened his fox-like features and spoke quietly so pricked up ears could not listen in. "Mr. Austen, ya might be me kinsman, but yer on my ship now. I kin do one o' two things: I kin either pull away from this lot and leave the *Amethyst* to make her own way, or I kin hope we make it through the night, and come first light I kin turn right 'round and blow those three smaller American ships to kingdom come. One way ya'll make it home fer sure; the other —" He gave his bony shoulders a shrug.

Fly's breathing accelerated; his eyes stung, memories suddenly flooding his mind — memories of places he loved: Steventon and Southampton, and the Isle of Wight, that rising treasure of an island with its chalky downs and snug villages, protecting his home harbour of Portsmouth. The anxious faces of his wife, his elderly mother, and his two sisters rose up poignantly before him; the chubby arms of his babies stretched toward him, clambering to reach his lap for their hugs, all of them waiting and hoping to see him just as he did them. And closer still, those cherished friends, convalescing beneath the waterline on the fusty orlop, who had placed their complete faith in his hands. Longing and despair crushed a small chamber in his chest, and he was scarcely aware that Pemberton Baker was standing before him, placing a warm mug into his hands as if offering him a sovereign's crown. Choking down the coffee, he resumed his reluctant vigil of the menacing shadows on the sea, watching the bows of the American ships pound the waves toward them, their open gunports and the great flukes of their raised anchors silhouetted against the darkening sky.

"There's only one option, Mr. Burgo," said Fly with a decisive nod, "only one I can truly countenance."

11:00 p.m.
(First Watch, Six Bells)

Worried he would disturb his slumbering patients, Magpie went about his task as soundlessly as he could, breaking down Prosper's empty barrels to make some much-needed space, and stacking the hoops and wooden staves into separate piles. He was over-tired, but his restlessness forbade sleep. Besides, there was no room to sling a fourth hammock; he would have to sit upon the slimy planking and rest his body against a lumpy sack of biscuits, which wiggled in a most unsettling manner. But there was no call for complaining; it was better to be here in the gloaming with a burning lantern than to be sitting atop the mizzen, exposed to the elements, or huddled in complete darkness on the gun deck with the Remarkables, petrified that — at any time — those American ships would overtake them and pour their arsenal of lead and iron into their small decks.

Magpie made a final check on Dr. Braden to be certain he was still breathing, and was settling in against his lumpy sack when a creaking noise stopped him cold. His eye slowly widened in the shadows; his heart galloped. He tried to convince himself it was only the pigs rooting around in the manger's straw one deck up, but if Biscuit — during one of his more lucid moments — hadn't gone and told him there was a strong possibility that Prosper had dead men buried in the shingle of his hold, his imaginings mightn't have been so dreadful. Were the mouldering corpses rising up in their shallow graves to go haunting in the dead hours of the night? Too terrified of what he might meet should he peer over the platform's edge, Magpie didn't move a muscle.

The second creak was on the ladder. Behind a pyramid of water barrels, Magpie could see an orb of light sweeping the floor, growing ever greater as whomever it was crept toward him. Oh! What if the spectre had followed him to the *Prosperous and Remarkable*?

"Who — who goes there?"

"Shhh! It's me, Magpie," whispered Morgan Evans, lifting his lantern to his face, haloing his woolly thrum cap and shaggy hair. Picking his way around the piles of staves, Morgan dropped down on the planks, pulled his legs into a cross-legged position, and presented Magpie with a wooden bowl and spoon. "Pemberton sends his compliments, and his jellied pea soup."

"Pemberton's still awake?"

"Everyone to a man is still awake — well, except for those who helped themselves earlier to Prosper's rum."

"What time is it, Mr. Evans?"

"It's just after 11:00. I heard the clang of six bells as I was making my way down to you."

"Have we given the slip to them Americans yet, sir?"

Despite the lanterns' cheerless illumination, Magpie could see his friend's face fall. "There're still three of them on our tail."

"But how can they see us? Hasn't Prosper doused all o' the lights?"

"He has! Your lantern and mine are the only two still burning at this hour. But the skies are clear; there's a full moon out, and a multitude of stars shining. They'll be able to follow our shadows through till daybreak, and then, as soon as we're able, we're going to —" Morgan stopped himself short as if he'd said too much.

But Magpie did not petition for an explanation. He didn't want to know what the Remarkables had planned. If there was going to be any boarding of ships, he just prayed Prosper wouldn't force him to join the boarding party. He wasn't sure he could handle going through all that heart-hammering action again. "Should I be makin' up me will, sir?"

"Aye," Morgan nodded, "if you have anything to bequeath."

Magpie wiggled the toes of his bare feet. "Jacko was gonna knock me up some new shoes, but I suppose I won't never get them. And ... and I lost me Mrs. Jordan blanket long ago, and Dr. Braden told me Emily's miniature is locked away in his writin' desk on the *Amethyst*." He shook his head sadly. "I don't got nothin' to will, sir."

"What about your flute?"

"Can't recall where it got to."

"Ah! Well, whatever became of your *Isabelle* hat? You didn't say."

Magpie nibbled on his lip, his glance sweeping the dark pockets of the orlop behind him. "I — I don't rightly know, sir."

"I've asked you a thousand times not to call me *sir*."

"Sorry, sir; it's on account o' me respectfulness fer ya."

Morgan offered up a sad, crooked smile, as if his mind had moved on. "I'd better get back. Mr. Austen has asked me to keep him company through the night on deck."

"That's a right honour, sir."

"It is that." Morgan held on to the sack of biscuits to assist him up from the floor. "If I don't drop asleep, I'll come to you again."

Magpie too scrambled to his feet, feeling an irksome wetness on the seat of his trousers. "And will ya be makin' a will fer yerself?"

"If I die, *you* can have my thrum cap. It's all I have to my name."

An icy chill ruffled the back of Magpie's neck. "Pemberton once told Mr. Walby that yer safer bein' with Prosper than ya are with God."

"Let's hope he's right," said Morgan.

An uneasy silence stretched between the two until Morgan suddenly reached out his right hand to shake Magpie's. "Godspeed, my friend."

When Morgan had vanished into the unknown, his footfalls and final words now silenced to memory, Magpie tried to get some rest. He kept the lantern close to his side and took comfort knowing that he was not alone, that it was Dr. Braden who rested in the gently swinging hammock by his head, but as he drifted off the echo of familiar words struck terror in his ears, bringing him back to the night with a terrible shudder. In his half-conscious state, he fought to find its source. Had it been a dream? Had it come from a vermin-plagued corner of the orlop, or from the cloaking gloom of the hold?

"*Penitence and obscurity, and the little sailmaker shall be no more.*"

33

Sunday, August 29

8:00 a.m.
Coaching Inn, Hampstead Heath

Old Dr. Braden quickly came forward when he saw who it was tucked away in the parlour alcove by the window, waiting to speak with him. "Come into the other room and sit by the fire; you'll be warmer there."

Emily stood wringing her hands and looking about, expecting the inn door to be kicked open by Somerton and a horde of mean-looking constables, eager to slap handcuffs on her and forcibly return her to Hartwood Hall. "I would prefer to stay here, sir. I don't want to risk attracting more attention. The innkeeper already gave me such glances; I fear his curiosity was getting the better of him. Perhaps I shouldn't have dressed in trousers, but it was my only hope of fleeing the Hall."

As they seated themselves on the alcove armchairs the doctor surreptitiously eyed her soiled slippers and the scarf that concealed her hair. "However did you get here?"

"I was able to secure a ride on a supply wagon," Emily said, a twinkle in her eyes. "A whole team of them descended upon Hartwood early this morning, so I —"

"On a Sunday?"

"Oh, Her Grace does not heed the days of the week, so long as she has *needs*."

Spying the innkeeper walking toward them with a tray of tea — which neither of them had ordered — Emily wilted in her chair, and was therefore grateful when the doctor leapt up to go and ward him off. Only once they had been provisioned with a cup of tea and a bowl of bread pudding, the latter compliments of the innkeeper's wife who had installed her smiling self on a nearby settee to fake absorption in the mending of a yellowing lace cap, did Emily resume her tale.

"I waited behind a tree by the gates, and while the wagons were lining up for the gatekeeper's inspection — he always inspects them on their way out, to make certain they haven't helped themselves to the Lindsay's treasures — I jumped onto the back of the very last one."

"Did the driver not question you?"

"He did! He thought me quite insolent until I told him I was a servant of the Hall, and that I'd been sacked, and could I just beg a ride with him to the inn." Emily wished her heart wasn't drumming so, knowing full well it was attributed to the closeness of *him*, and not the clandestine alteration of her whereabouts. "Is Mr. Walby still asleep?"

"He is. The poor lad cried himself to sleep at such a late hour; he may very well lie in 'til noon."

Emily was wistful. "I must get back soon, before breakfast, or else the duchess shall send out a search party, complete with hounds and muskets."

"When we're done here, I shall accompany you to the gate. I cannot have you wandering this lonely road on your own."

Emily looked up at him and for a moment said nothing, choosing instead to reflect upon the endearing similarities of physiognomy and breeding between the father and his son. "Sometimes I can scarcely believe that such good men as you and Leander exist on this earth."

He advanced and retracted one of his hands, as if he had considered, but decided against, reaching out to her. "Tell me why you've come."

Emily stared unseeing at her teacup. "To apologize for my behaviour last evening. I wasn't aware of Lord Somerton's bold interrogation of Mr. Walby until it was too late."

"There's no need for *you* to apologize. It seems to me it is Lord Somerton who needs to make amends, but not to me, to Mr. Walby. In my long life I've never witnessed such impolitic treatment of one's guest. However, if the young man has inherited his *mother's* character, rehabilitation would be hopeless." His voice fell to a whisper. "It is evident that your relationship with your host family is a strained one."

"More than I care to discuss at present. But please know my behaviour last evening was not a result of it. The truth is I feared that Lord Somerton's sudden turnabout in inviting you to dine was his selfish desire to be the one to give you the — the news." Unable to hold her cup still, she set it down, and her throat closed up as she started in on an explanation of the letter her Uncle Clarence had received, recounting the *Lady Jane's* arrival in Portsmouth, and her crew's concerns for HMS *Amethyst*. Haltingly she spoke, carefully choosing the words her tongue found so difficult to form. His full attention was hers. He sat unmoving on the edge of his chair like a statue, fear and incredulity fighting for predominance on his face, his eyes — bright at first — clouding over as he assimilated the forbidding facts.

Emily's voice faltered; her hand trembled against her mouth. "There is, of course, no tangible proof that the *Amethyst* is lost, but I — I am bracing for the worst."

A dreadful silence descended. Frozen with unhappiness and unable to meet his benumbed gaze, she was conscious of him slowly rising to his feet and drifting toward the window where the rain streaked the diamond-shaped panes. She rested her head against the side of her soft chair and listened to the shhh sound of the rain; heard laughter in the far reaches of the parlour, and closer by, the innkeeper's wife humming a lively tune. Eventually she peeked up at the bent figure by the window, her heart clenching in sympathy to see his eyes squeezed shut as if awaiting the passing of a stabbing pain. When he spoke again, little remained of his self-assuredness.

"I'll leave here this morning, and take Mr. Walby with me — Lord knows his Aunt Sophia doesn't want him — but I shall say nothing to him of this right away. I'll tell him we're going to visit my sister who lives near Portsmouth. He may like a little holiday by the sea while I — I await word."

"If only I could keep him with me."

"Even if you could, I'm afraid Mr. Walby's embarrassment is too severe to return to Hartwood at present. But *you* are more than welcome to accompany us. Eliza would be happy to offer you a room." He attempted to lessen his despair with a crack at levity. "I must warn you though: you might starve and freeze in your bed at night, for she keeps a diet of bread and cheese, and holds strict economy over her coal supply."

"Having been on the sea, Doctor, one appreciates any sort of bed and sustenance." Emily's smile failed as her eyes travelled around the snug alcove. "Thank you. I've not been outside of Hartwood since my coming here three weeks ago. I feel like a child who's been locked away in an airless schoolroom with only a surly instructress for company, and finally I've been rescued, allowed to spend the day as I please, though keenly aware that my freedom shall be short-lived. As much as I'd dearly love to be waiting there with you, I cannot accept your kind invitation." She hesitated a moment. "Perhaps, before we part, you would be so kind as to give me your sister's address."

He signalled comprehension with a nod. "Should you come to us, we'll take good care of you —" Struggling to swallow, to complete his thought, his hands fell limply at his sides, as if he didn't know what to do with them. Emily went to him. She seized his helpless hands and pressed encouragement into his knotted fingers.

"Leander is — my son is all I have left."

Leaning forward, Emily met his eyes. "Then we shall not give up hope," she whispered.

8:55 a.m.

EMILY HURRIED INTO HER bedroom, breathless with elation that she had evaded discovery; relieved that — having found the gates of Hartwood locked and barred — she had managed to clamber over the rough stone wall without incident or infliction, though the same could not be said for her unfortunate trousers. Her only wish now was to be alone, to shut out the world, but when a swift rustling movement caught her eye she stopped in her tracks.

The beautifully carved doors of the wardrobe stood wide open like a colossal mouth with its interior indecently exposed, and Emily could see that the lid of her little sea chest — shoved away in the bottom left corner — had been raised and shut again in a hurry, for a hapless shirt-sleeve had got caught up and was hanging over the side like a spent tongue. Balancing unsteadily before the scene in a pearl-grey morning dress and ribbon-trimmed cap was the duchess, holding a clutch of letters in one of her elegant hands, attempting to muster poise, despite looking like she had been caught plundering the cookie cupboard.

"Helena!" gasped Emily, tugging her scarf from her head, her damp curls dropping past her shoulders. "I'm glad to see you're no longer keeping to your room."

Helena's complexion altered, blanching first before a scarlet flush engulfed her. "Thank you."

"Were you looking for me, or —?" Emily eyed the wardrobe.

"Ah," said Helena, executing a cheerful pirouette. "Yes! I ... as a matter of fact ... yes, I was looking for you —"

"And did you think I might be hiding out in the wardrobe in amongst my gowns?"

As if stalling for time, Helena's eyes flitted senselessly around the room, but forthwith a fierce puckering of her lips accentuated the grooves around her mouth. "Do remember, I have the right to go where I please at Hartwood."

"Forgive me, but I'm unaccustomed to seeing you in this particular room; indeed, shocked to find you here at all when our last meeting was so disagreeable."

"You have only yourself to thank for that."

Emily chose to ignore her. "Have you come to make peace, and escort me to the breakfast table?"

"Certainly not!"

Emily inclined her head at the letters in Helena's hand. "Is there one addressed to me? I'm still awaiting the arrival of the letter Mr. Walby claims to have sent."

As if fearing Emily might try to pry them from her, Helena pressed the letters to her bosom. "No, there is not."

"To what then may I attribute the honour of your presence?"

Helena's eyes wandered the length of Emily's trousers, halting — growing huge with horror — on the knees, both of which had been muddied and torn open during Emily's scramble and plummet over the wall. Only once the shock of the trousers had abated did she explain herself. "I — well, I have the very *best* of news."

Emily relaxed her frown; her lips fell open as she waited. Was it possible? Did she dare hope?

"Tomorrow night the salons of Hartwood shall be opened to our friends for an evening of music and dancing."

"Tomorrow is Monday," blinked Emily in disgust.

"*My* friends seek pleasure every day of the week, and shall be overjoyed to have an excuse to wear their finest, and to make *your* better acquaintance." In a rustle of silk, Helena wheeled about to begin a critical inspection of Emily's gowns, hanging in the wardrobe. "Overcome with anxiety regarding your evening dress, I came at once to discuss possibilities, and," — she paused for an affecting smile — "to search for my white elbow gloves and pearls that I loaned you for your first Hartwood ball. I should like to wear them at our little soiree."

Emily was certain this last bit had been invented on the spot; nevertheless, fighting down the disappointment of Helena's *news*, she went to retrieve the items in the top drawer of the antique dresser near her bed. "Rather than upset yourself, why not postpone your soiree?" she asked, handing over the gloves and pearls.

There was an arrogant lift of Helena's patrician chin. "Once the decision has been made, I do not *postpone* my parties."

Emily searched the older woman's face. "Did Somerton have an opportunity to apprise you of the news my Uncle Clarence received before he left Hartwood yesterday morning in a mad dash?"

"He did."

"In light of *such* intelligence, how can you even contemplate parties?"

There was nothing in Helena's deportment to indicate the news had given her a moment's unrest. Instead, she backed away — in a hurry, it seemed, to leave at once — and arched one brow. "All the more reason to press forward with our plans."

34

9:00 a.m.
(Forenoon Watch, Two Bells)
Aboard the *Prosperous and Remarkable*

THE GUNS! THERE THEY were again. The guns!

Hemmed in by the insurmountable hulls of enemy vessels, Leander felt the skiff roll and lurch and descend. Overhead the mouths of carronades vomited grapeshot and canister, leaving wrecks in their wake as ruinous and worthless as carved up carcasses of meat. Masts tottered and moaned like stupefied giants, timbers haemorrhaged, yards and booms and ropes were left hanging in their execution, and gaunt sails endeavoured to drape the destruction.

Leander was alone in the skiff, alone on the sea. The enemy crews had abandoned ship, leaving the scorching guns to continue the warring, allowing ghostly fingers to strike the matches and light the fuses. His feet had blackened. His flesh had been worm eaten. His stomach convulsed with hunger. He groped the bottom of the food bucket only to find it was empty. Prepared to end his own fight, he lay back and clasped his hands over his heart, his failing vision falling upon a gaping, ragged wound in the side of one of the ships. There she was, untouched, smiling, sitting in her cot, the canvas curtain stirring behind her like a sentinel, protecting her where he once had. With a slight nod of her pale gold head she beckoned, and her voice came to him, a gentle sough in his ears: "Wait for me. Watch for me —"

"Dr. Braden? Sir?"

His eyelids fluttered open and he blinked, trying to identify the face at his bedside, struck down by an overpowering sense of loss when he realized it was not *her*. A dark circle had stained the skin beneath Magpie's eye, and his small sooty fingers — remnants and reminders of his days as a London climbing boy — gripped the hammock's rim, as if he were expecting a thirty-two-pounder to come crashing through the orlop wall.

"Is it the guns you fear, Magpie?"

"They haven't sounded yet, sir, but I'm waitin' fer 'em. Them ships have bin followin' us all night."

Leander remembered the explosions in his dream, but the spell of Emily's fond smile was broken, receding swiftly beyond the point of retrieval. "We're below the waterline down here," he assured the little sailmaker, noticing then that the two beds swinging nearby were empty, their occupants curiously absent. "We didn't lose them in the night, did we?"

Magpie still clutched the hammock. "Not to worry, sir. Pemberton Baker came and hauled Biscuit outta bed, mumblin' somethin' 'bout no rest fer wicked cooks, tellin' him he had to help feed the Remarkables afore Prosper went to work."

Leander frowned, attempting to make sense of the word *work*. "And what of our other friend?"

"He got hauled off too. And — and once ya've had yer oatmeal, sir, Pemberton wants ya to do up a surgery down here."

Oh, dear God!

Leander lay still, clutching his moth-eaten blanket, staring up at the water drops clinging to the beams, trying to predict which ones would give up the fight and fall.

"Are you okay, sir?"

"Yes — yes, I'm fine." With a herculean effort of willpower, he sat upright and massaged his neck as he considered the congested platforms around him. After long moments, he gave his throat a good clearing. "Right then! We'll need a few strong men to assist us. These barrels and staves must be moved somewhere out of the way, and I must have a table, and a covering sheet, and some sand, and — and a gag for the men to bite down upon. I'll require assistants, and light ... plenty of light. Bring me as many lanterns as you can find. And ask Prosper what surgical instruments he possesses on board, and if he can spare a bottle or two of rum."

Magpie acknowledged every one of his demands with a bob of his head. "And what about yer glasses, sir? Don't ya needs 'em to work on the men?"

Leander regarded him in dismay. "Long gone, I'm afraid, but see what you can find."

"I'll ask Mr. Austen and Mr. Evans to help us, sir."

"No, don't bother Mr. Austen, but do bring Mr. Evans, and a couple of Prosper's men."

"Ya gotta know, sir, most o' them are ruffians."

"We've no time to indulge in fastidiousness."

Magpie's little forehead furrowed up like a cloth of corduroy, prompting a smile from Leander. "Bring me anyone who possesses two arms and two legs."

"Sir!" With a tenacious salute, Magpie scampered off toward the ladder, though he'd scarcely made headway when Leander was forced to recall him at once.

"Before you dash off, I shall require your assistance in climbing from my bed. It might be wise to determine whether or not I'm able to stand upright on my own."

9:30 a.m.

"Sir, we're outta range!"

"Wait 'til Prosper brings us up on the wind. Fire low! Aim for their hulls! We must sink them." Fly paced the gun deck, his heart leaping in his chest. He detested being down here. Between billowing smoke and shot splash on the waves, he could barely discern who it was they were shooting at through the gun ports. His last look at the *Amethyst* had been a demoralizing one, the three smaller American vessels closing in on her like a black veil. Had he a speaking trumpet in hand, he could have roared at her seemingly incapacitated crew: "For God's sake, deploy your guns! Prickett! Bridlington! Deploy your guns … NOW!"

But he was not standing with the Amethysts, and *this* ship was not his to command; he therefore went where he was needed. The gun captains and their crews assigned to work the *Prosperous and Remarkable*'s fourteen, twenty-four-pounder carronades required supervision, someone in charge to rein in their exuberance; otherwise, he was quite sure, all would descend into anarchy. The Remarkables had fanned out in every direction around him, crouched over the guns, stripped to their waists, scarves tied to their heads to sop up sweat. Smoke-blackened hands pushed and pulled, glistening backs strained, heated voices goaded and bellowed.

"Damp the sparks! Reload!"

Overhead, Fly knew Prosper had seized the brig's wheel from Pemberton, for in the relative tranquillity between the whirring, cracking, splitting, and shrieking he could hear the privateersman's hoarse commands doled out with salty condescension. To Meg Kettle, the deafening sounds having reduced her to a blathering idiot, Prosper had previously delivered an ultimatum: "Either ya keep yer mandible glued, or I'll take an amputatin' saw to yer tongue." Being fond of her talking parts, Meg was now suitably employed in carrying canisters of gunpowder up from the hold, wheezing fiercely as if plagued with a respiratory ailment, and keeping her loads well before her in case they exploded in her face.

Before giving the next command, Fly gave a fleeting moment's thought to Leander on the orlop, working over the wounded on his thin, feeble legs, an ill-fitting pair of spectacles stuck on his nose — not the perfect prescription, though adequate perhaps — and at his side, little, loyal Magpie, a heap of nerves, his eye large and brilliant in the darkness.

"Wait for the downroll! Now! Fire!"

The direct hit smashed into an enemy's stern near her rudder, spewing deadly splinters and shards of metal. Fly caught a glimpse of the destruction before the *Prosperous and Remarkable* lunged away, and he had to steady himself as she tilted in her turn.

"To the other side, lads! Prepare the starboard guns!"

As he dashed across the width of the gun deck, Fly could see Morgan Evans and his small team of carpenters at work on a hot, jagged hole where a carronade had once stood. Their shoes slid in the blood pools where a gun crew had once rallied, making it difficult to hammer nails into their covering timbers and sheets of lead.

At the wheel, Prosper's bark echoed around the brig. "Ya fumble-fisted, bird-witted scoundrels, git these bleedin' undeads outta me way. Now ready yer weapons and I'll bring ya in closer, within pistol range."

Meg Kettle trudged up to Fly, her shirt stained with perspiration, her face dripping with exertion. She passed off her delivery of fresh powder to waiting hands, and breathlessly cried out, "Mr. Austen, I've bin up and down five times now! I'm at the end o' me rope."

Feeling no sympathy whatsoever, Fly's reaction was a cold one. "Then go help Dr. Braden, and be sure to refrain from whinging and rabble-rousing." He turned away from her, and squinted through the gun port to see the *Amethyst* cloaked in dense smoke, her topgallants and pennants shot away; however, there was little time to contemplate her fate, for a fierce tug on the brig's bow had brought her in line with yet another foe.

"Double-shot your loads, and bring her down!"

Within minutes the starboards guns were packed with their powder and shot, and levered into firing position.

"Wait for the ship's roll! Aim down at the hull. Not all together now; one at a time, if you please."

Fuses were lit. Ears were clamped. Hearts jumped.

"Fire! Fire! Fire!"

Flames licked the gun barrels. Tremors drubbed the brig's old timbers and rattled Fly's teeth. The gun crews vaulted out of the way to avoid the violent recoiling of the gun carriages, but seeing the success of their hits they quickly regrouped to cheer as the enemy foremast toppled over, taking with it cordage and sails and men, and crashing into the sea.

"Well done, lads!" shouted Fly. "Now quickly clean and reload!"

Unlike the *Amethyst*, there were eager, skilled hands working the enemies' cannons, anxious to retaliate, waiting for that precise moment, that precise hit. Prosper's gun crews were seconds from firing another broadside when part of the gun deck imploded. A hail of splinters, as sharp as razors, spewed everywhere in their ghastly search for flesh. Knocked backward by the blast, Fly tripped over a young powder monkey, and fell heavily against the sticky floor. Stunned, he lay there in pain, coughing, choking, tortured by screams that curdled the blood in his veins. A severed arm with its white porous bone exposed throbbed beside him, and a head came rolling toward him, eyes embedded in a sickening frown of surprise. Fly thrust it away and peered into the swirling grey smoke settling upon the carnage.

Among the dead and the fallen, stuck in a hideous, custard-like mass of gore, was a woolly thrum cap.

35

10:30 a.m.

Hartwood Hall

WHEN THE SUN DECIDED to gift the dwellers of Hampstead Heath with an appearance between the silvery-grey clouds, Emily embraced the opportunity to quit her room, and went in search of a portable writing desk and a bite of breakfast — coffee, jam, and a warm roll. Balancing her plunder upon her forearms like a novice juggler, she headed outside to the west garden where a damp tang had infused the morning air, such a pleasing improvement over the fusty, cloying smells of a house shuttered against the rain. Still, morning raindrops clung stubbornly to the ivy arbour, making it necessary for her to drag the little garden table out from under it; otherwise they would be sure to play games with her, and, in falling, wreak havoc upon her ink and paper.

Beyond the neat rows of flowers and shrubbery, Emily could hear wagon wheels on gravel as Helena's soiree supplies were delivered to the Hall, and a curious peek at the noise resulted in the shocking revelation that Wetherell was the acting overseer, strutting about in his ostentatious colours, full of loud praise for the merchants and their wares. Spying Emily in the garden, he bowed to her, bending over so low she feared he would be locked forever in that unfortunate position. Biting back annoyance (with the upcoming soiree), and amusement (with the personage of Lord Monroe), she poured her concentration into her letter, knowing that time was fast running out, and therefore didn't notice she had a visitor until a dog's big tail slapped up against her legs.

Fleda stood unsmiling before her, bereft of spirit, wearing the same gown she'd had on the previous evening. Noticing the girl's red-rimmed eyes, Emily hid her letter away in the desk's tiny compartment, and extended an unspoken invitation to join her by arranging a chair close to hers. She gave permission to the wagging dog to rest his head upon her lap, and tickled his furry neck while waiting for Fleda to say something.

"Had Mr. Walby been allowed to stay, do you think he'd have asked me to dance at the party?"

"Indeed, I do, so long as he felt he could dispense with his crutch!" said Emily gently.

"Although Mother would have insisted we dance somewhere other than the music room."

"Your mother could not tolerate her young daughter snatching away the guests' attention from *her*."

Fleda's cheeks warmed as she looked away over the misty south lawns toward London. "I only knew Mr. Walby a short time, but I decided — if he asked me — I would marry him."

Emily made certain she did not laugh. "I don't think your father would be agreeable to parting with you at so young an age."

"No," she said quietly, "but I would like to leave here, to see something of the world. I've never even been to London." She waved a limp hand in the direction of the fog-enshrouded city. "And there it is ... so close by."

"But you *have* been outside the walls of Hartwood."

"I've been out in the neighbourhood, if that's what you mean." Fleda leaned in toward Emily. "I am envious of you. *You* have been to sea." A dreamy expression occupied her wan features, as if her mind were running through scenes of Emily's sword-wielding days on the *Isabelle*.

"I have, and it was both a wondrous and frightening experience, but now you see I am not allowed beyond Hartwood."

"That's because your family and mine fear you will escape."

Emily snuffled. "And thus their urgency to see me safely married off to your brother?"

"But you don't want Wetherell."

"Please do not judge me if I say I'd rather be hanged alongside Thomas Trevelyan."

A humourless laugh burst from Fleda's lips. "He's not a dashing figure. Not like Mr. Walby, is he?"

"I'm afraid not."

Fleda gave Emily a sidelong glance. "But I did hope you might become my sister."

"Can we not become sisters without me marrying into your family?"

Fleda considered the notion with a tilt of her head. "I suppose so."

"Right then, now tell your elder sister why you've been crying. Is it Mr. Walby?"

"No, I cried over him last night."

"Oh, I see!" said Emily, fearing the spilled tears might have something to do with her dead brother, and the painful remarks made in the music room. But there was something in the way Fleda's chin inclined; the way in which she shyly searched Emily's face, a light springing into those green eyes, then vanishing again as quickly, as if she were weighing the wisdom of confession.

"I — I have something to tell you. I think you should know."

Emily grew alarmed. "What is it?" she whispered.

Fleda's breath came in snatches as if she'd just run a full circle around the estate. "Somerton and Mother were speaking together in the parlour. I didn't mean to, but I overheard them when I was crossing the front hall on my way upstairs. Somerton was very angry. I could hear him shouting at her, so I crept up on them, and watched through a crack in the door. Mother seemed shaken; she had her hand on her mouth, and was pacing before a sofa. I've — I've never known Somerton to be cross with Mother. *She's* the angry one. Oh, and I heard such things! Somerton said something to her about stealing *your* letter — the one from Captain Moreland — that she never should've read it, and mustn't tell the Duke of Clarence of it." Fleda looked fearful. "Was I right to tell you this?"

Emily couldn't answer immediately; incapable of thinking clearly over the beats of her heart. Is that why Helena had been in her room? Aware of its existence, had she rifled through her sea chest in search of Captain Moreland's precious letter? But if so ... why? What had she hoped to learn from it?

"Of course you were, Fleda."

The girl's bloodless lips quivered. "Somerton accused her of withhold-ing *all* of your letters. There've been letters from your aunts, one from Mrs.

Jordan and Mr. Walby, and you've received ever so many invitations to parties. And my mother … she … she kept them from you."

Emily felt lightheaded. Was Helena really capable of such cold-hearted deception? But hearing of the letters, another emotion welled up inside her as if a loved one had placed a shawl around her shoulders on a chilly morning. "There's a letter for me from Mrs. Jordan, my Aunt Dora?"

Fleda nodded. "Mother shouldn't have kept them from you."

"No, she shouldn't have."

"Somerton accused her of being obsessed, of recklessly seeking information."

Information … what information?

Emily was left bewildered, unable to construct a logical explanation. "Your mother's actions were wrong, but I hate to think of you ruining your pretty eyes over a bundle of stolen letters."

Fleda smiled sadly; a sudden breeze tossing the slender wisps of her hair across her face as she glanced away. "I was about to go. I didn't want to hear any more. I was too sad thinking of you never receiving Mr. Walby's dear letter. But I saw Somerton grab my mother's arm, and he shook her. He told her to forget the past — that she had to forget *him* — that she must never again breathe *his* name or it would lead to scandal and humiliation."

Emily's hand froze on the dog's head. She held her breath, watching tears forming on Fleda's eyelashes. "What did he mean?"

"My mother doesn't love my father."

"That's quite an accusation. How can you be sure?"

"I heard Somerton say as much." Fleda's tone rippled with emotion. "Mother loved … she loves a man named Charles DeChastain."

Emily's stomach fell away.

"And he's — he's somehow related to your husband Thomas Trevelyan."

11:30 a.m.

IT WAS NOT LONG BEFORE Mademoiselle came in search of her errant student — Fleda shocking her by going quietly, but only once Emily had promised her they would talk again later. Returning the desk to the house and hiding her letter away under her mattress, Emily then set off toward the service wing, determined to find Somerton. She knew he would either be some-where in the bewildering warren of storerooms and offices, or at the stables, saddling up his horse to dispel the disquieting clouds of his confrontation.

Recalling an earlier promise, Emily popped her head into the kitchen, delighted to find it buzzing with activity; the staff, doubled in number, scuttled about with their bowls and trays and platters as if the duchess were terrorizing them with a whip. The scene reminded Emily of the *Isabelle*, only here it was women in uniform toiling at their battle stations and not men.

Calling out "Good morning," Emily was pleased to be met with shy smiles rather than rounded eyes and frozen mouths, and further pleased to see the cook — after all the curtsies had been dispensed with — come forward to greet her.

"Would you like my help?"

"Oh! Yer Royal Highness," the woman blushed, "we wouldn't know how to behave with you walkin' amongst us."

Emily smiled. "No French Chef this time?"

"He's comin' later on with his pastries and savoury entremets."

"Did you have this many helping out at the last ball?"

"Nay, but it's not every day we've royalty amongst us. We're all aflutter with nerves."

Emily frowned. She'd been at Hartwood for weeks now. Whatever did the woman mean? But a plea for clarification was hindered by Somerton, who made a surprising — if somewhat surly — appearance at her side.

"Lord Somerton! Just the person I was looking for."

Ordering the cook back to work, Somerton took Emily's arm and hast-ily led her along a narrow corridor of closed doors, steering her into the last room on the right — his office, presumably. It was decorated in shades of twilight blue and dominated by an imposing oak desk and sash windows that viewed the front courtyard, and haphazardly affixed to the walls were ancient swords and shields and glassy-eyed hunting trophies. Repulsed by his rude behaviour, Emily refused his invitation to be seated, and watched as he installed himself in the leather armchair behind his desk with the air and authority of a banker about to unburden her of her life savings.

"What were you doing in the service wing?"

"I was hoping to don an apron and bake pies."

"Shouldn't you be primping for tomorrow?"

"I'll concern myself with *primping* an hour before the ball."

"Would you like me to collect you for the first two dances, to rescue you from Wetherell?"

"I do not need rescuing; besides, Lord Monroe's likely to choose the Whist tables over dancing."

"Are you certain of that?"

There was a suspicious flicker in his eyes, though Emily could not be certain which of her two remarks had produced it.

"As a gentleman and your friend," he said, mellowing his stern gaze, "I'll watch over you at the ball."

"My friend?" laughed Emily. "It would've been nice to have had a friend here beyond Fleda's dog and the resident magpie."

"You are speaking in past tense."

"Am I?"

Somerton looked confused. "I thought we were friends."

"Your actions toward me have been perplexing at best. At times you have shown kindness, but you've also shown an absolute disdain."

"You've read me wrong. I have no disdain for you. I only have —"

Emily lifted her chin, curious to know how he would complete his sentence, but seeing his colour change she switched the subject. "And here you are at your desk when the fawning ladies shall soon be descending upon Hartwood? Don't you have a pair of satin pumps to dust off?"

"Some of us must work. The estate does not run itself."

"And you ... not even the heir."

"No. But you've met my father and eldest brother. I'm certain it wouldn't surprise you to know that we've come close to losing the estate before."

"Was it your hope to end up your father's steward?"

"It was not."

"Didn't you want a career?"

"No. I wanted —" he hesitated. "I *want* Hartwood."

"Ah! Was the thought of me ending up mistress of your ancestral seat a repugnant one?"

Somerton eyed her as he untied and yanked off his neckcloth.

"It's not much fun, is it, Lord Somerton, wanting something you cannot have."

His gaze did not waver. "No."

"Your youngest brother wanted a career in law."

"Did he? I scarcely knew my youngest brother."

"Why do I have the impression that only Fleda was well acquainted with him?"

Somerton snickered. "Well she would have been. Octavius used to read to her, and take her riding. He even listened to her play the pianoforte, and before he left for the sea, he bought her that mutt."

Emily had trouble imagining the *Isabelle*'s first lieutenant — the one she had known — showing patience for a younger sister. "And yet, when Mr. Walby was here, you displayed a zealous interest in your brother. I didn't understand your behaviour last evening, in spite of Miss McCubbin's assertion that you are a kind soul."

Somerton's mouth went missing in a grim line. "If my brother had lost his life when the *Isabelle* was set afire, you would have said. I cannot accept waiting until the trial to hear all. And now who knows whenever *that* shall take place with Trevelyan at large."

"It came as a shock to find myself living with your family."

"Why? My father opened Hartwood to you as a favour to your uncle."

"Did he?" Emily challenged him with a sneer. "At first I thought so. It might also have made sense that your family wanted me here to provide them comfort and solace — someone who might recount their dead son's final days on his ship and delight in his memory."

"You've provided no comfort."

"No."

"Because my brother mistreated you on the *Isabelle*?"

"No, because I discovered early on that, with the exception of your little sister, none of you were genuinely in mourning. But then it was easier that way, for I didn't know how to tell a girl of eleven years how her brother had died." Feeling an enervating constriction in her chest, Emily crept toward the nearest chair and sat down, conscious of Somerton's expectant gaze boring down on her. "I had an uncle named Octavius. He too was his father's eighth son. I never met him — he died as a child — but upon his passing my grandfather was inconsolable. He believed there would be no heaven for him if he couldn't find his beloved Octavius there." Tears sprang to her eyes as her heart swelled. "I cannot understand a mother who does not love her child; therefore, I can only conclude that Helena invited me here for selfish reasons."

Somerton began shuffling papers about. "You — you never actually said why you were looking for me."

"I want my letters."

He looked up quickly, his features falsely indignant. Emily stared him down.

"If you won't get them for me, I'll go post-haste to your mother. I believe she will know where to find them."

A pall of silence settled on them like a dust cloth tossed upon the furnishings of a shuttered house. Mumbles of laughter and conversation filtered down the corridor from the kitchen, and outside in the courtyard wagon wheels grinded to a halt on the gravel driveway, inciting a series of welcoming barks from Fleda's dog. Somerton's sigh, which arrived only once he had contemplated the scenes beyond the windows, was almost inaudible. "Tell me something of my brother and I shall return what is yours."

Emily rubbed her bare arms as if a ghostly presence had suddenly aspirated its dead chill down her neck. The ugly words would have to be uttered with celerity. "He died of a gunshot wound to the head."

"What … in battle?"

"No."

Somerton blanched, melding into the beam of pale sunlight streaming across the room. "No?" he echoed, shaking his head, his eyes scudding over the jumble of objects on his desk. "Are you saying he was executed?"

Emily would not reveal the traitorous exploits of Octavius Lindsay. His family did not need to know about them — not yet anyway.

"It was self-inflicted."

His stare came back to her; incredulous and angry. "How do you know? Is this hearsay? Grist for the rumour mill? How can you be certain of this?"

"Because your brother killed himself in front of me."

36

LEANDER GAZED DOWN AT Magpie to see his small compressed mouth working against the horrors of the hospital. "Would you like to see if Mr. Austen needs your help now?"

"Are ya tryin' to send me off, sir?"

"It — it might be best."

"If it's all the same to ya, sir, I'd like to stay."

Leander moved away from his operating table and gently guided Magpie toward the ladder, as far away as was possible from the desperate, weeping wounded. He could feel the boy's thin shoulders quaking beneath his palms, and see his single eye transfixed upon the macabre wall shadows of the men huddled together in misery, mouths twisted and gasping in agony.

Leander drew himself up, his features grim. "You've worked yourself ragged these past hours."

"Ya'll need me to scatter the sand fer ya, sir."

"Perhaps you can go find yourself something to eat."

"I'm not hungry."

"Better still ... bring us both some coffee. Biscuit always has a pot on the boil."

"Send Mrs. Kettle in me stead, sir," Magpie pleaded, nodding at the laundress who was rocking back and forth on a rum cask, her eyes vacant, mouthing the words to a silent song. "I kin prepare the tar fer ya! I kin hand ya yer knives and saws and stuff when ya needs 'em."

Leander caught his breath, unable to oppose Magpie's youthful resolution. How he wished he could just lower himself into the hold, and go to sleep for days on end among the barrels and the rats and the dead bodies of Biscuit's dreadful tales. He made an adjustment to his pirated spectacles, which were determined to sit upon his nose like a heeling ship. "It's not an easy thing to watch."

"I won't vomit or nothin', sir."

"That would be most helpful."

Dragging himself back to his wretched table, Leander could sense the frightened child behind him as he examined Morgan's shattered left leg. The foot was already gone, so was most of the tibia, and what remained was mangled right up to and including the patella; he'd have to amputate above the knee. One of Prosper's ruffians who had kindly offered up his services — the one whose nose resembled a tumorous strawberry — had already administered a draught of rum and laudanum to the patient, while a second volunteer named Jim Beef, one of the Amethysts who'd scrambled aboard the *Prosperous and Remarkable* when the American ships first appeared on the sea, had a leather gag at the ready. Hardly recognizable as the intrepid carpenter, Morgan thrashed about in delirium, breathing in gulping snatches, mumbling incoherently except to ask for his sisters now and again. Clods of crusted blood and guts had lodged in his hair — someone else's, Leander assumed — and his pallid face was slick with perspiration and misshapen with pain.

Cannons and pistols and muskets still fired, but now their roar seemed muffled, as if they were mere echoes of Leander's dream. For over an hour the battle had raged on, the *Prosperous and Remarkable*'s ceaseless pitching and shuddering leaving any and all faint-hearted languishing in sickness. But she was still fighting, still afloat, and Pemberton had seen fit to abandon his post to report the news to the hospital — with sober propriety — that one of the American vessels was sinking. The men who were still conscious had cheered and clapped and raved; most had said nothing at all.

"I'll need you all to hold him down."

Magpie timidly came forward to stand beside Leander, and closed his hands around Morgan's left arm with care, as if he feared it might be afflicted too. Morgan rolled his head around and looked at Magpie, though his feverish eyes seemed fixed upon something stirring in the darkness behind him. Selecting the knife that would slice through skin and muscle and ligaments, Leander listened to the words that passed between them; their voices so whispery and husky with fear, he cursed the racket of the brig's grinding pumps.

"You'll tell them where I've been?"

"Who, sir?"

"Brangwen and Glyn; they've been wondering these past seven years."

"Didn't ya send them a letter, sir, when ya was in Bermuda?"

Morgan tried to raise his head up; his voice despairing. "What if it doesn't reach them?"

"Then ya kin tell 'em yerself, sir ... when yer better."

"They need to know I wasn't spirited away."

"What's that, sir?"

Assailed by another sweep of pain, Morgan clenched up, breathing heavily, and eased back on the table to fight it, leaving Leander to answer for him.

"It means when one is secretly taken, stolen by a gypsy or some kind of spectre."

Magpie's eye leapt across Morgan's recumbent form and landed on the volunteer, Jim Beef, where it swelled in magnitude as if the lanky man was the sort capable of spiriting children away from their mothers. But Morgan's fearful cry distracted him.

"Magpie? Are you still there?"

"I'm here, sir."

"Please stay near."

"I ain't goin' nowhere."

"You won't forget about my thrum cap, will you?"

Magpie's face began to crumple. Bereft of words, he could only touch his little fist to his temple in a salute. "Sir."

For an instant Morgan's face brightened; he tried to smile. Drawing a slow breath, he turned away to accept the leather gag, sank his teeth into it, and braced for what was to come. Stinging with tears, Magpie leaned his meagre weight upon his friend's arm and buried his head next to him on the bloody cloth. Together the older men bore down upon Morgan while Leander cut into his leg.

Noon

IN THE ABRUPT, disquieting silence, Leander plodded toward the main deck, pausing after each climb to steady himself and catch his breath, his journey taking him past the fatigued gunners, most of whom were either sleeping or slumped upon the floor, curls of acrid smoke still prowling between them and the scorching carronades, and tripping over charred planks and unrecognizable bits of the brig. Reaching his destination, Leander stared up at the severed web of rigging stays traversing the blue brilliance of the sky, astounded to find the two masts unbroken, towering over the ship like fearless, inexhaustible combatants. The sails had not fared as well, many of them depleted by black-edged holes; nonetheless, there was enough canvas left to catch the wind.

As if he were working in the security of Portsmouth Harbour, Pemberton was organizing small groups of ruffians to begin making repairs, the damage report having included an unfortunate but complete destruction of the seats of ease. At the brig's wheel, a subdued Prosper kept his eyes focused on the fore horizon, a steely determination on his fox-like features to put distance between the *Prosperous and Remarkable* and the American vessels he had failed to blow to kingdom-come.

Leander shook with relief when he spotted Fly standing alone by the starboard rail — whole, unharmed, alive — gazing back over the wake of the brig at the destruction and horror they had left behind them; his sad, slumped figure hauntingly reminiscent of Captain Moreland studying the white horizons, watching for Trevelyan.

Sensing his cautious approach, Fly moved his head slightly, but did not turn around. His voice was desolate. "If we'd continued fighting, those larger ships would've caught up and raked Prosper's stern to pieces."

"You did your best, Fly."

"Did I?"

"What more could you've done?"

"I wish I knew. The *Amethyst* — she'll be boarded, taken a prize, most likely sailed into New York Harbour under an outpouring of thunderous applause, and Prickett and Bridlington and the others — those that have not already fallen — will be herded into cold, crumbling jails and prisons. I'd prefer to be buried alive than become a prisoner of war."

Fly's hand — the one gripping the rail — was trembling, and the slackening pockets of flesh around his dark eyes gave him the aspect of a much older man.

Leander stood quietly beside him and listened.

"Such a gut-wrenching realization to discover — in the end — you are powerless and insignificant. All of your training, your exertion, your seemingly sound judgement, your extraordinary seamanship … what does it amount to when you know that, despite your efforts, this day, this season, is nothing more than the second summer of war. The fight will go on, and our lads will continue to be needlessly slaughtered, and we shall not triumph until more ships and supplies and men are redirected to America. The theatres of this war are too varied, far too vast, and Napoleon and his French Navy are slowly sucking us dry." He heaved a despairing sigh. "I am so battle and sea-weary. I — I believe I now understand Captain Moreland's need to ask for my forgiveness before he breathed his last on the blood-soaked deck of the *Isabelle*."

Biscuit slunk toward them, his head respectfully bowed, and handed off two steaming mugs and — to Leander — the additional delicacy of a slushed biscuit. As quietly as he had come, he moved away in search of others who required sustenance.

"Let us follow Prosper's lead and look off in another direction," encouraged Leander, tearing Fly away from the tragedy unfolding on the waves, and leading him to the brig's bow. "Look there! If you squint into that far-off cloud bank, I bet you'll glimpse Land's End."

"Perhaps the Isles of Scilly?"

"Whatever! We'll be home soon."

Fly finally raised his misty eyes. "Not yet forty years of age the two of us, and we're physical wrecks."

"I'm a long way from forty. You on the other hand, Mr. Austen —"

"Ah, but you're still an old wreck — an emaciated one at that. I would suggest you eat up that slushed biscuit, and try to include some meat in your diet tonight. We'll need to smarten you up if you ever hope to win the favour of a certain princess." He smiled sadly. "If not for your friendship, Lee, this cruise would have been intolerable."

The exhaustion and emotion of Leander's surgery suddenly over-whelmed him. His words caught in his throat. "And yet the cost ... my debt to you —"

The embers of life that had begun to stir in Fly's face were extinguished by alarm. "You've — you've come to tell me then that Mr. Evans has died."

Leander's fist bounced near his mouth; he could only nod.

Fly wandered the bow in agitated circles before stopping to lean against the bowsprit. His sorrowful groan sliced through Leander like the surgical knife he had just held in his hands.

"The odds were stacked against him. If only it'd just been his arm —"

"Infection? I know that's always your concern."

"No. Blood loss."

"Is there anyone ... sitting with him?" Fly whispered brokenly.

"Magpie will stay with him until we hold his funeral service."

"Bless our brave little sailmaker."

"The boy grieves as if he's lost an older brother."

"Yes," said Fly, contemplating the blue-green waves. "And I have lost a most cherished son."

Leander touched his friend's shoulder in sympathy.

"I shall not bury him in the North Sea or the Atlantic. There's a little churchyard at Wymering in Portsmouth; I shall take him there. That way he will always stay close to the sea. It may ease his sisters' minds to know where he is lying." Tears slipped from Fly's tired eyes. "It surely will ease mine."

37

Monday, August 30

8:30 p.m.
Hartwood Hall

"What's all yer tarryin' about? Everyone's waitin' downstairs fer ya!"

Emily jumped in fright when that scolding meddler, Glenna McCubbin, suddenly filled her bedroom doorway, sending her sidling toward the desk to shield the items she had arranged there. "Is Uncle Clarence here yet?"

"Nay! He'll likely arrive when the guests do."

Emily's stomach was a bunched knot of anxiety. She prayed her uncle had news — encouraging news this time. "Then what's the hurry? I haven't yet heard the expected barouches and phaetons below my window."

"Her Grace and Lord Monroe want to see yer gown."

"Lord Monroe? Since when did Wetherell become an authority on women's fashion?"

"They want to make certain ya look satisfactory."

"Satisfactory?" chirped Emily.

Glenna planted her fists on her hips to carry out her inspection. "Lud! That gown won't do."

Emily took a languid glance at herself in the mirror. "What's wrong with it?"

"White doesn't suit ya, and that absurd lace ruffle at yer neck reminds me o' my prudish Aunt Euphemia."

"This gown was made for me."

Glenna stomped toward the wardrobe. "I'll find ya somethin' more comely."

"No!" cried Emily, springing in front of her. "I am not changing. I don't mind blending with the crowds tonight."

"Well ya won't, not with all the bosoms what's sure to be on display!"

"Let Lord Monroe garner all the admiring glances tonight."

Glenna wrinkled her nose. "Have ya bin cryin' agin?"

"I'm fine," snapped Emily, detesting her note of hysteria. "Let me just affix a rose in my hair — I brought some red ones in from the garden earlier — and I'll be down shortly. I promise."

"Ya need a maid. When yer properly married, they'll see to gettin' ya one."

Itching to be rid of her, Emily did not inquire who *they* meant. "I am on pins and needles in anticipation!"

Seeing a narrowing of Glenna's eyes and realizing another lecture was about to be unleashed, Emily acted swiftly. Rushing toward her old nurse-maid, hoping to squeeze the breath from her, she embraced her, relieved — upon untangling herself — to see her face flushed with joyful surprise.

"Ya haven't given me one o' those fer a long while, Pet."

"I am sorry. I truly am."

"No need fer apologies; just make haste — *make haste*."

When a placated Glenna had at last departed, Emily blocked the door with a chair and hurried to the wardrobe to drag out the pillowcase she had stashed away on the floor behind her suspended gowns. On her knees, she took stock — one more time — to make certain she had everything she would need and everything she held dear. There, sitting atop her neatly folded sailor gear and the blue-and-white-striped dress, were Jane Austen's volumes of *Pride and Prejudice*, and the bundle of unread letters Somerton had finally relinquished to her. Captain Moreland's letter was there too, for Emily could not bear to leave it behind. Fishing inside a silk slipper, her fingers reassuringly closed around the £50 note she had won playing cards. Her glance then travelled to the desk. Propped up against her silver inkwell, addressed to the Admiralty, in care of the Duke of Clarence, was the letter in which she had written a detailed account of her experiences on HMS *Isabelle* and the USS *Serendipity*. Alongside it sat Helena's esteemed emerald ring. Smiling to herself, for there was nothing more she needed to do, she sealed up the pillowcase with a scarf.

Emily's eyes fell on her small sea chest. Her quivering hands sought the lid, lingering there, caressing the roughness of its simple wood construction. She closed her eyes to gather the sea around her like a pair of wings, her heart and senses swiftly responding. The salty tang of the Atlantic tickled her nose; its bracing spray cooled her face. Beneath her feet, the ship's timbers sighed, and overhead the billowing sails cracked and snapped in the fresh breeze. She could hear the bosun's whistle and the beating drum, Captain Moreland giving his orders and the Isabelles' heedful replies, and amidst all — like a soaring bird that heralds land — came the whispered words of Leander Braden.

"*You must know, Emeline Louisa Georgina Marie, that, above all else, I completely love and adore you.*"

A clock chimed the hour. The expected phaetons and barouches came clattering into the courtyard. Unwelcome voices rang out in cheerful greeting. Peals of piercing, high-pitched laughter floated upon the evening air. Along the corridor, heavy footfalls came marching toward her bedchamber; an impatient messenger rapped upon her door.

With a terrible grief clenching her breast, Emily banged the wardrobe shut and rose to face the night.

11:00 p.m.

WHEN THE MUSIC ROOM'S mantelpiece clock tolled the hour, Emily was certain only she was cognizant of it. Where was Uncle Clarence? He *had* hoped to attend the ball. Was he afraid to face her then? Had he received confirmation that the *Amethyst* was lost? Had Trevelyan become a lurker in the backstreets of London, and her uncle was determined to singlehandedly root him out and present his head to the Admiralty?

Emily shrank against the wall beneath the portrait of Octavius. Sitting woodenly on a cushioned stool beside her was Fleda, her dead eyes watching the dancers. In her curls and ribboned muslin of duck-egg blue, she was a forsaken figure, all but forgotten in the corner of the music room to which her mother had banished her. Unable to cheer Fleda up — for her own condition was one of restless turmoil — Emily sipped on a goblet of pink punch, her eyes on the lookout for Wetherell in his violet and sapphire suit. So much for the Whist tables! "Your Royal Highness," he had said after his fiercely critical scrutiny of her plain white gown, "I intend to dance every last cotillion and reel with you. Do not insult me by taking up with another partner." Had he forgotten she had rebuffed his ridiculous proposal of marriage? Emily shook her head and shuddered in remembrance of his dry, doughy hands, his pointed toes as he performed ballet-style steps, and the staleness of his perspiring body as they whirled around the dance floor. She would have welcomed rescuing from Somerton, but *he* was far too busy to supply her with charity, lapping up the worshipping attentions of the single ladies who had sewn him up in an impenetrable circle of bare shoulders and smiles.

Without warning, Emily's goblet was seized and dispensed with, and she was summarily dragged through the door and into the antechamber by the stout woman-friend of her Uncle Clarence, the one named Mrs. Jiggins — with the happy disposition — who had professed her notions on sailors and carnal recreation at the previous ball. Tonight the wiggly folds of her throat were constrained with pearls and her turban of pleated gauze was embellished with glittering amethysts and one very large ostrich plume.

"My dear, tell me," she said, her voice slurring with drink, "when will your uncles be arriving?"

"I believe you mean my *uncle* ... in the singular."

"Oh, do I?"

"I'm hoping Uncle Clarence will be here soon."

"Ah! And tell me," she went on, leaning in, her hot, sour breath hitting Emily's cheek, "when will His Grace be making the announcement?"

"What announcement?"

"Oh, come now, don't be coy. You know perfectly well what I'm alluding to."

Emily turned to face the woman. "I'm afraid I don't."

The woman's fingers sought her vermilion lips and then fluttered on the base of her pearl-laden neck. "Oh, you sly thing!" she laughed. "You want to surprise everyone! Do not worry yourself, for Helena told only *me* in the strictest confidence."

Emily's blazing eyes went hunting for the Duchess of Belmont, but ideas of violent revenge were cooled when Wetherell's vividness swelled before her, backing her up against a marble column.

"Ladies!"

He swept the parquet floor with an elaborate bow as if hoping to impress Emily with his prevailing ability to touch his toes, and then his fingers clamped her elbow like iron manacles. "Excuse us, Mrs. Jiggins," he grinned, "but I must away with this exquisite creature to execute a long-ways country dance."

11:30 p.m.

As soon as Emily spotted the distinctive pineapple head of her Uncle Clarence milling about in the antechamber, and before the master of ceremonies had trumpeted his arrival to the music room crowd, Emily made her graceful excuses to Wetherell — her ankle required a respite — and hurried away to pull her unsuspecting relative into the empty schoolroom.

"Uncle, please, what news?"

Having arrived later than anticipated, Uncle Clarence was in a flustered state and none too pleased. "Emeline, might we discuss all later on? It was an exhausting ride from London and I'm in need of a bowl of punch." He inclined his neck to view the glittering guests passing by the open doorway. "The ladies are quirking their eyebrows at me in their eagerness to dance."

"For one moment, Uncle, do forget the ladies."

His reply followed an edgy sigh. "It's too soon. There's nothing further to report on either the whereabouts of Trevelyan or HMS *Amethyst*. The only good piece of news is that this damned business with Trevelyan has not yet been leaked, thus, our Royal Navy has forestalled exceeding embarrassment. Oh, but your family, Emeline — the one you claim has forgotten you — has managed to secure your annulment. How fortunate you are to have royal relations, able to secure favours in the wink of an eye. Tonight you may show your gratitude and tomorrow we shall pray for Trevelyan's recapture and perhaps word of your mariner friends."

Emily broke eye contact with him, turning away, feeling as if the merry dancers had skipped and trampled upon her heart. She was scarcely responsive when a chorus of exclamations pealed through the halls and chambers beyond the schoolroom, instantaneously shushing the guests and the band's lively tune. Ball gowns swished, throats cleared and swallowed, and Emily thought she heard Helena's hysterical tweet of laughter pierce the ensuing stillness.

Uncle Clarence clapped his hands together. "Come along, Emeline. This is the moment for which we've all been waiting."

"Who has come?" she asked breathlessly.

"My brother and your uncle, the Prince Regent."

"The Regent?" Emily caught his arm, delaying him from making a dash for the door. "Why? After all this time, why has he come now?"

Uncle Clarence winked a round blue eye. "You'll not find out unless you follow me to the music room."

38

11:30 p.m.
(First Watch, Seven Bells)
Aboard the *Prosperous and Remarkable*

HAVING CLIMBED DOWN to the orlop surgery from the gun deck where Fly had slung a new hammock for him beside a restorative open port, Leander lifted his lantern in the black darkness to check on Magpie. The boy was still there, slumped over the operating table with his head resting against the side of the oak coffin that Pemberton had solemnly constructed to hold Morgan's remains. Leander set the lantern upon the table and squatted down on his haunches beside him.

"Is that you, sir?" said a sleepy voice.

"Magpie, could I convince you to come away and sleep on the gun deck?"

"I'm keepin' vigil over Mr. Evans, sir. But I ain't doin' a good job 'cause I've drifted off a few times."

"I'll find you a bed next to an open gun port."

"I promised Mr. Evans I wouldn't leave him."

Leander smiled fondly at the boy. "I don't believe any of us will be calling you the *little* sailmaker from this day forward."

Magpie raised his head higher. "Why's that, sir?"

"You've gained at least a foot on this cruise."

"Ya really think so?"

"I really do." Even in the poor lighting, Leander could see Magpie trying to secure the riffles of pride on his face.

"Do ya think Emily will notice when we go visitin' her castle?"

"It'll be the very first thing she notices."

"Yer kind to say, sir, but the way I picture it in me mind, she'll be noticin' you afore me."

Leander was relieved that Magpie could not see his eyes blurring. "You'll have to trust me on this one."

"Thank ya, sir. Ya've given me a bit o' comfort."

"But you still won't come up to the gun deck?"

"I wants Mr. Evans to know I'm a man o' me word."

Leander reached into his breast pocket, pulled something from it, and gave it to Magpie. "I had it cleaned and dried for you."

Magpie turned Morgan's woolly thrum cap over in his hands. He stared down at it and, though he tried, he could not speak. Lighting a candle so the boy would not be left in the mournful blackness, Leander crept away to contend with his own welling emotion.

Midnight

As Dr. Braden's retreating footsteps grew fainter, grief and skulking shadows threatened to engulf Magpie, and the only way he knew to fend them off was to conjure up courageous acts in which he had saved Mr. Evans from his untimely and devastating end. In one he had shielded him from the blast; in another he had given his blood to replace that which had been spilled; in yet another he had offered up his own life in exchange. Thinking he was alone and therefore at liberty to cry, he was startled by a low growl and a ghoulish head that appeared over the side of the hammock, slung across the table from him. Convinced a grave robber had come to pounce upon the departed, Magpie leapt to his bare feet.

"Ya might as well crawl inside with 'im, Maggot Pie," said Meg Kettle, "and the two o' yas can rot together."

Magpie could summon neither words nor verve to retaliate.

"Usually they toss the dead ones in the sea. I ain't never heard o' seamen entitled to a real coffin o' wood and nails, except fer Lord Nelson. Heard tell he were placed in a cask o' rum for the journey back to England after he were killed at Trafalgar."

"It were brandy," mumbled Magpie, "not rum."

"How'd ya know that?"

"The Duke o' Clarence told me."

"Fie! The Duke o' Clarence!" Mrs. Kettle playfully slapped her cheeks. "Do ya think yer gonna drink tea with yer princess and her frisky uncle when we dock? Why the castle guards will think yer a tatterdemalion come to beg fer food."

Magpie's blood began to boil. "I won't never have to beg fer food agin! I'm a sailmaker."

"Ah! Bet Mr. Austen gets rid o' ya in Portsmouth and sends ya to a workhouse or back to that mean Mr. Hardy, the one what starved ya whilst workin' on London chimneys as a climbin' boy. And I'll be wavin' ya off — and that stinking corpse — with me kerchief."

"Ya won't be able."

"Why not?"

"Mr. Austen will be cartin' ya off to Newgate Prison."

Mrs. Kettle frowned. "He wouldn't do that. I got a babe comin'."

"Ya've been right lucky 'til now."

"Prosper won't let no harm come to me."

"Prosper won't help ya, not when he learns yer a traitor."

She locked her arms on her bosom. "Who says I'm a traitor?"

Magpie's voice regained its confidence. "I saw what ya did on the *Isabelle*. I saw ya plottin' with Octavius Lindsay when he were clapped in irons fer attackin' Emily in the sail room. Ya stole her miniature and showed it to Captain Trevelyan to prove ya knew her. Ya told him where Emily was hidin' so he could take her prisoner agin, and he thanked ya by lettin' ya off the *Isabelle* afore he burned it."

"Who'll ever believe a one-eyed orphan over me what's gonna be a mother?" challenged Mrs. Kettle, a nervous hitch in her voice.

"I'll stand up in court, I will. I'll tell 'em all yer no better than Captain Trevelyan. The both o' yas turned yer backs on yer countrymen just to save yerselves. Ya'll pay! Ya'll suffer fer sellin' yerself to the devil."

Mrs. Kettle's eyes blazed. She looked like red-hot canister shot about to detonate its pistol balls. Fighting her way out of her hammock, she landed with a thud, bottom-first and cursing, on the orlop planks, but wasted no time in rolling toward the table to seize Dr. Braden's cloth-wrapped surgical instruments at the foot of Morgan's coffin. She yanked at the bundle, which made an awful clatter when it hit the floor, and after some muttering and fumbling about, she stood up and rounded on Magpie, a long, thin knife in her fist. "Maybe ya needs to be silenced up."

Magpie felt his hackles rise up. His brain went torpid as if he'd downed a mug of ale. He couldn't get to the sharpened instruments — not with Mrs. Kettle staggering over them — and there was no other weapon, nothing nearby with which to defend himself. "Ya won't never git away with it," he gulped.

She took a terrorizing step toward him, the knife's blade flashing in the candlelight. "Ain't no one down here to help ya," she spit. "Why they'll all think ya did yerself in on account o' yer legless friend."

Magpie cast around for a way out, but she had him cornered — a step or two backward and he'd tumble into the hold and be groped and smothered by Biscuit's dead men.

Think! Do something! Scream for help!

Maybe Dr. Braden was still within earshot; maybe a few sober Remarkables were asleep on neighbouring platforms. But there was no time for anything. In a wink, the knife lunged at him, came at him like a striking viper, narrowly missing his face, throwing him off balance. Magpie shielded his head with his arms, and again it struck, tearing into his shirtsleeve in its insidious search for flesh. Shock and searing pain dropped him to the planks. Someone cried out, whimpered like a wounded animal, but he didn't recognize his own cry, for a second horror had now come upon him.

Magpie cowered on the floor, his heart pounding in his throat, watching wild-eyed as a pitch-black figure soundlessly stole up behind Mrs. Kettle, uncoiled its long arms, and began waving them about near her head, giving her the hideous appearance of the serpent-haired Medusa. Its face peeped above Meg's shoulder — the features obscured in the shadows — and though Magpie was certain it did not speak, familiar words howled in his head.

"*Woe and despair to he who clings to a dead man on the sea. Hold fast, ye wretched soul.*"

Dear, God! Was the spectre Mrs. Kettle's accomplice? Did they mean to torture him to death? The laundress stepped closer, the spectre ostensibly latched to her back. Sensing doom, hoping to delay it, Magpie grasped for the candle Dr. Braden had left for him and snuffed its meagre flame. The descending darkness was so sudden and suffocating, he wondered if his tormentors had walled him up inside a monk's hole. Nay! They were still converging on him. He could smell the spectre's putrid breath. He could hear Mrs. Kettle swiping at the air, a chilling laugh following every unrewarded swing. Too scared now to move, Magpie curled up in a ball, sniffling, rocking, waiting for the knife blows that would surely find him despite the absence of light, praying it would soon be over.

After a dreadful silence, there came a strangled cry. The knife fell. It hit the oak timbers beside Magpie and spun away, finding the edge of the platform and tumbling into the ship's hold, colliding with the ballast in its echoing descent. Blinking in the dark, Magpie strained to listen over his own rasping breaths, puzzling over a gurgling sound and scuffle that played out within inches of him. Men's voices called out. Advancing footsteps pummelled the orlop beams. Darkness receded. And before long, Magpie was swimming in lantern light.

Lifting his head from his knees, he was astounded at what he saw there. The spectre had pinned Mrs. Kettle with one of his sinewy arms, restraining her futile thrashing, while one of his hands was clamped upon her throat like the shackle of an iron ball and chain. His face — Magpie could see it clearly now — was the same as the one that belonged to the silent volunteer who had stood across from him at the operating table and helped Dr. Braden tend to Morgan in his final, woeful minutes. Still holding fast to Mrs. Kettle, the man locked stares with Magpie, something akin to camaraderie evident in his savage eyes.

"Your arm is bleeding. Let me look at it."

Magpie was shaking so violently, he didn't know when he had crawled under the table, or when Dr. Braden had found him there, but he could feel the soft wool of Morgan's cap in his hands.

"Sir! Who — who's that man holdin' Mrs. Kettle?"

"That's Jim Beef, recently of the *Amethyst*."

"All this time, sir, I — I thought he were a spectre."

"Well, at times he does fancy himself Davy Jones."

"He's not a spectre, is he?"

"No he's real enough; the poor man's just a bit mad. You might recall he received a hit on the head when we encountered that American privateer near Halifax. I believe that hit exasperated his madness."

"Oh, sir, if it weren't fer him — if it weren't fer Mr. Beef, I wouldn't have a tongue no more."

"In that case we shall roundly reward him," smiled Dr. Braden. "Are you sure you're all right?"

Magpie wiped his nose with the back of his hand, comforted by the nearness of the doctor. "I am now, sir, but I ain't never bin so scared afore, and I think — I think I just lost that extra foot ya was talkin' about earlier."

39

Midnight
Hartwood Hall

FEARING HIS REASONS FOR finally gracing Hartwood with his venerated presence, Emily had no desire to greet the Regent. Consequently, upon leaving the schoolroom and seeing Uncle Clarence swallowed up by an onslaught of admirers, Emily stole off in the opposite direction. Her head down, inviting no discourse from others, she quickened her step once she was well beyond the guest-laden rooms. She had successfully reached the great staircase when her path of retreat was barricaded. Standing in such a way that suggested he had witnessed her flight across the front hall, Somerton was on the bottom step, a smile she could not read upon his lips.

To conceal her heart's deafening beats, Emily spoke with ebullience. "Lord Somerton, have you left the ladies bereft of their favourite dance partner?"

Towering over her like the locked gates of Hartwood, his eyes met hers. "There is only one lady with whom I care to dance, and I could not find her."

"If your search was a recent one, I was speaking to Uncle Clarence in the schoolroom."

"Ah!" He joined her on the marble floor. "Would you permit me to lead you back to the music room? Might I dance with you now?"

"Thank you, but — I believe you know that I broke my ankle while at sea."

"I have been apprised of it."

"Well, you see, while dancing with your brother, his foot frequently found mine, and now that particular ankle is throbbing."

"Perhaps we could request a gentle waltz."

"A daring waltz ... one in which we would dance face to face? Is it your intention to set the tongues wagging, sir?"

He stepped closer, too close. His breath, moist and rancid with drink, struck Emily's face. "I have long dreamed of placing my hands upon your waist."

"I should like to rest for a while," she replied, slanting away from him.

"Then I shall settle for a minuet and promise to speak only of the weather and the poor state of our roads."

"I shall be happy to dance that minuet ... after I lie down."

"What about the Regent? He has generously come all this way to our little party and wants to see you."

"As the Regent waited long enough to seek me out, he can be detained another half hour." Emily tried to pass, but Somerton hopped up on the stair again and outstretched his arms to block her way. "Sir! Are you going to make it a habit of accosting me on the staircase?"

His eyes openly wandered her face. "It doesn't have to be this way."

"I beg your pardon?"

"There's still time, Emeline."

Her laugh was sardonic. "For what?"

"For us."

Emily blinked at him. "Is it only when you carouse that the hardened shell of your exterior softens and makes you ridiculous?"

"I — I care about you."

"If you have felt in the least bit solicitous toward me, your method of communicating such feelings has been most irregular."

Rather than pausing to defend himself, Somerton pressed on with boyish enthusiasm. "You are, without a doubt, in need of some polishing ... and a good dose of taming, and your frivolous fantasies must be expunged and redirected, but —"

Emily felt a muscle quivering in her cheek. "But what?"

"I have ... since the first day I met you ... I have been dumbfounded by an inexplicable longing for you."

"Alarming!"

"There have been moments when I have suspected … you too are tortured by a most violent yearning for me."

"What moments? When?"

Somerton brought his face down to hers, his glittering eyes on her mouth. "One word of encouragement from you could change everything."

"I admit I do have feelings for you, Lord Somerton," said Emily, seeing the lines on his forehead shoot up in eager expectation. "But only the kind a sister would feel toward a brother — one with whom she rarely gets on." She angled her head away from his parted lips; her low voice quaking now with indignation. "You have long known my heart, sir. It has *not* changed."

His fervid expression withered and dropped away; he looked like a spoiled child, astonished that his desires had been rebuffed. A purpling flush began inching up his neck, and his eyes went flinty before they fell upon the burnished wood of the stairs. Seizing an opportunity, Emily attempted to squeeze past him, but his movements were quick and he cut off her path with his hip, pinning her against the wall. He swallowed several times, and finally lifted his eyes to her breasts. Reminded of the black, rotten, ungoverned disposition of his youngest brother, Octavius, Emily hissed at him in disgust.

"Are you now dreaming of placing your hands upon my throat?"

For an instant, he looked surprised. "No! But I *shall* happily leave you to your depraved fate."

"Somerton!"

Helena's shriek came as a shock; the woman's approach had been soundless. Surely she must have cast aside her low-heeled shoes in the whirling joy of dancing. Emily raised her chin to meet Helena's glare, aimed squarely at her before settling in a piercing blaze upon her son.

"I *asked* you to find Her Royal Highness and bring her straightaway to the music room."

"I am doing just that, Mother."

"Are you really?" Helena flapped her hand with impatience. "Well, Emeline? Come along! The Regent's first words were of you."

Caught between mother and son, Emily felt as if she were being coaxed into a cage. "Your Grace, please, I have injured my ankle and would like to rest upstairs. The night is still young, and knowing the Regent, he shall be awake, enjoying himself, until sunrise."

Helena mounted the stairs to hook her gloved arm behind Emily. "You must come along *now*."

"I shall not be a part of your plans. I have refused your son's proposal." Emily dug her toenails into the soles of her silk slippers. "Did you think that I would change my mind simply because the Regent is here to sanction the announcement?"

"Your annulment has been secured."

"Yes! And now one part of me is free of Thomas Trevelyan." Emily compelled herself to stay calm. "It has taken me a long while to understand you, Helena. Did you suppose, by inviting me to Hartwood, you could keep abreast of news on Trevelyan and thus learn first-hand of the dispersal of his stepfather's fortune? If Trevelyan is hanged, if he is dead and out of the way, does Charles DeChastain's fortune come to you? Or will it go to his daughter … Lady Fleda?"

Helena went white and grew fitful.

"I can only guess that is why you withheld and read my letters … why you stole Captain Moreland's letter from my room."

"I have no time for this nonsense. Come along. I hear them calling for you."

Somerton enclosed his slippery fingers around Emily's forearm and steered her down the stairs, hedging her further into the cage. Emily rounded on him. "I am curious. This fortune … has your mother decided that — should it come to her — she will eclipse Fleda and give it to you, so that you may do as you please and no longer have to act as a pawn to your father and eldest brother?"

Somerton remained silent, refusing to meet her wild stare.

"I shall not be humiliated in front of my guests and the Regent." Helena's cry was shrill and hysterical.

"You wouldn't have to be if you hadn't placed me in this untenable position. I will *not* marry your son."

"You have no choice," seethed Helena. "Your family will insist upon it. They will harass you until you agree." She closed her eyes to draw in breath. "By now … surely by now … you must realize you could not find for yourself a better *situation*."

Uncle Clarence stomped into the front foyer, scowling at the scene by the staircase. "What's all this? Do hurry, Emeline! The Regent is groaning. One does not keep him waiting."

Wetherell appeared beside him, steaming and frothing in his suit of violet and sapphire. He looked peevishly at Helena and whined, "Mother?"

Emily's first instinct was to bolt, but where to? She wanted to scream, but who would listen? The noose was being lowered upon her neck and it was about to tighten. She could only see her way through one solution, as revolting as it was. Resolved, saying nothing at all, looking at no one, Emily turned toward the music room and began a slow march in its direction. Surrounded on all sides by belligerents, she relived that awful day on HMS *Isabelle* when Trevelyan's American soldiers had forced her off the quarterdeck, their bayonets trained upon her back.

Assured of her coming at once, Uncle Clarence hurried on ahead to excite the crowds and speak a private word in the ear of the Regent, who immediately wheeled around to greet his long-lost niece with a smile and outstretched arms. Fighting tears, Emily made her grand entrance, hardly hearing the full announcement enunciated with enthusiasm by her Uncle Clarence. What she did grasp reverberated off the walls like a blast of bone-jarring cannon-fire.

" … the marriage of my darling niece, Princess Emeline Louisa Georgina Marie, daughter of my late brother, Henry, the Duke of Wessex, to Wetherell Lindsay, the Most Honourable the Marquess of Monroe and heir to Hartwood Hall."

As the guests' resounding applause pulsed like a headache behind Emily's eyes, Somerton turned slightly toward her. His face wore no jubilation, no gratification, no malice or mockery, but his haunting, whispered word numbed her to the core.

"Pity."

Sickened by the triumphant smile glistening on Wetherell's red lips, Emily looked straight ahead at the well-wishers about to close in on her.

4:00 a.m.
Tuesday, August 24

Emily peeked outside through an aperture in her bedroom curtains. Several vehicles were still parked on the grounds beneath her window, the footmen and horses stoically awaiting the return of their owners. At this late hour, the band was still playing and Emily could hear no signs of wearying in the animated voices of the guests who made it a tradition never to leave a ball until first light.

At 2:00 a.m. Helena had excused Emily from the ball with a politely constrained smile after hearing the doleful tale of her painful ankle, but the duchess had done so alone, there being no one else at hand to send Emily off to bed. Adolphus was out cold on a sofa; Wetherell had happily ensconced himself at the lively Whist tables; Somerton had disappeared, presumably with a young lady who was more amenable to his charms than she; and her two uncles had been latched to comely partners, far too focused on the precise execution of their dance steps to bid their niece goodnight. Half-expecting Helena to accompany her to her room, Emily was grateful to see her laughingly conveyed to the dance floor, for she had no intention of seeking sleep.

Working by candlelight, Emily drew the curtains and hurried to the wardrobe where she gathered up the pillowcase — steeling herself against the potent lure of the sea chest — and carried it to the door. On the chair she had left a pale-blue, ostrich-plumed turban and matching silk-embroidered shawl — items she had earlier selected from amongst her many gifts in the adjacent bedchamber, but had never worn. Putting them on now, she took care in disguising her hair and simple gown under folds of material. Her limbs tingling, her insides in an uproar, Emily gave the room a final sweeping glance, making sure the letter and ring were still atop the desk before she collected the pillowcase and quietly slipped away. In her breast she harboured a solitary lament for her commodious bed, knowing it would be a long while before she lay again in such luxury.

4:30 a.m.

IT WAS IMPOSSIBLE FOR Emily to take the main staircase; there were still too many guests milling about beneath its wrought-iron balustrade. Instead, she tiptoed along the first-floor corridor, through the shadowy upper hall, and past the rooms belonging to the duke and duchess, until she came to the back stairway which took her down to the far side of the ground floor, away from the principal rooms. As this stairway was hidden from public view, Emily could hear, but not see, those still hanging about the dining-room table, eating and drinking and flirting and heatedly discussing politics. Reaching the bottom step, she headed for the library, recalling the existence of an antechamber just beyond its walls with a door that opened onto the south gardens.

For some reason, the beautiful library had been overlooked on this evening. Its air was cool, unsullied with perfume and cigar smoke, and the furniture remained untouched, though someone had placed candles on the table beside the scarlet sofa, giving the large chamber a church-like atmosphere. Emily had almost gained the entrance to the small chamber when a sleepy moan pitched her heart into her mouth. Her eyes widened, fearing she had disturbed Somerton and his lady friend in their lovemaking. But no, it was Fleda whose head popped up over the sofa's curved frame.

"Who's there?" she demanded.

Emily quickly went to her, and saw that the girl had been reading her mouldy copy of Dafoe's *Robinson Crusoe*. "Shh! It's me!"

"It's dark out! Where are you going?" Fleda's eyes fell upon the pillowcase that Emily was cradling in her arms like a baby, and when she lifted them again they had grown large with alarm. "You're leaving, aren't you?"

"I am."

"If I scream," said Fleda, "you know they'll come running."

Emily nodded.

"And they'll — they'll lock you in your room."

"Yes, they will."

"Then you won't be able to leave."

"Only if they chain me to my bed and place a guard at my door."

"But you will try again."

"I will."

"The first chance you get?"

"Yes."

They eyed one another, waiting for the other one to say something more. Emily stood stock-still, clutching her bundle close to her, her lips moving soundlessly in prayer. The last thing she expected was for Fleda to begin weeping.

"Will you not stay for me?"

"Fleda, you know I cannot," Emily replied sadly. "But wherever I am, you shall always be welcome there."

"How will I know where you are?"

"I shall get word to you — somehow — I promise."

"Please tell me where you are going."

"If you think about it long enough, you'll know."

Fleda hopped off the sofa, *Robinson Crusoe* crashing to the floor, and threw herself into Emily's arms, holding on to her so tightly Emily was certain her ribs would crack. Outside, beyond the library windows, drunken laughter and the whickering of horses were telltale signs that more of the carriages were preparing to take their leave of Hartwood. Fleda suddenly bolted from Emily and hurried to the darkened windows where she scrutinized the flurry of activity on the pavement.

"I see Mrs. Jiggins stepping into her carriage. Go with her."

Emily moved closer toward the antechamber. "But the woman knows me."

"I overheard her telling Mother that she likes champagne so very much," said Fleda, smiling bravely, "she usually sleeps the entire way back to London."

"My dear little sprite," laughed Emily, gathering the girl up in one last embrace.

As she went through the door and into the night, she heard Fleda call out to her, "Godspeed, my sister."

4:45 a.m.

MRS. JIGGINS ROLLED HER head over the side of her barouche. The ostrich plume on her pleated turban had broken in half and was now dangling absurdly over her eyes.

"You say your friends left without you? Oh, you poor dear girl. With all the excitement of the Regent tonight, I daresay they left their heads behind as well. Hop in, hop in and I shall instruct my driver to take you to your home."

Mrs. Jiggins was snoring by the time her barouche clattered through the iron gates of Hartwood Hall. Smiling to herself, Emily pulled her shawl around her shoulders, nestled into the comfort of the leather seats and listened for the song of her magpie in the chestnut trees.

40

Friday, September 3

10:00 a.m.
The Brigantine Inn
Portsmouth, England

EMILY PULLED HER EYES away from the bow windows, away from the drizzling harbour and the ships and boats navigating its grey churning waters, to see Dr. Arthur Braden returning to their inglenook in the heavy-beamed parlour with a tray of tea and apple cakes. She could not help noticing the tremor in his hands as he set it down upon the scuffed tavern table next to her knees and went about filling mugs for them, nor the whisper of a sigh when he lowered himself into the Windsor chair beside hers. They sat alone in front of the inn's brick hearth, a terrible grief billowing between them, their backs to the far end of the room where a cluster of seamen had gathered around the oak bar to drink ale and tell jokes and yarns that spawned a raucous buzz in Emily's ears.

"Are you sure you're comfortable here?" asked the doctor, his head turning slightly in the direction of the men. "I assure you my sister would be happy to offer you a room. She is economical to a fault but discreet."

"Thank you kindly, but I wish to stay by the harbour."

"Perhaps I could see to your settling into a more … respectable place."

"The innkeeper here is kind and doesn't ask questions, even though her sights did linger upon my baggage when I first arrived." Emily smiled wearily. "And if my family is scouring the countryside for me, this establishment just might escape their notice; my Uncle Clarence, no doubt, expecting to find me lodging at the George, ordering up extravagant meals."

They pensively sipped their tea, neither one interested in eating the apple cakes, both too spent to attempt further conversation. When Emily's own shaky hands spilled drops of tea upon the mauve-edged skirt of her white gown, tears sprang to her eyes, reminding her of the longing she had felt earlier to don her blue-and-white-striped morning dress and stroll along the wharves in the hopes that a passing sailor might recognize it as the one the little sailmaker had sewn for her. But then hadn't the entire population of Portsmouth seen her wearing it at her disembarkation of HMS *Impregnable* a month ago? She could not take that chance.

Growing concerned for the quiet gentleman at her side, whose eyes were as empty as the hearth he gazed upon, Emily inquired after Mr. Walby. "I thought he might have come with you."

"When your note arrived at my sister's house, I came here directly while he set off for the wharves. I expect him shortly, for he is most anxious to see you." He gave Emily a sidelong glance. "For four days now, we have made our diligent inquiries at the offices of the Navy Board and questioned the crews of every single vessel moored within our midst. Mr. Walby is a remarkable young man, still brimming with hope, and reminding me daily — when my own hope is flagging — that a big ship-of-the-line would naturally take longer in arriving home than a swift-sailing mail packet."

"Yes, indeed, it would," whispered Emily. She had turned again toward the windows when a commotion brought her swiftly back. If it were not for the crutch, she might not have immediately recognized the flushed-faced midshipman who came scurrying toward them, narrowly averting a somersault on the parlour's carpet. He was so agitated he could not speak, only grin at Emily as he struggled to catch his breath.

"Mr. Walby!" Emily could sense Gus's heart thumping in its ribcage. "Did you run all the way from the wharves just to greet me?"

"Yes! No!" was all he could manage. He seized Emily's wrist and tried to pull her to her feet.

"What is it?" she asked, exchanging an incredulous stare with old Dr. Braden as she willingly jumped up, hope swelling in her breast.

"We must — we must hire a coach," he said, resting against the brick wall of the fireplace as he coughed. "We must go ... now!"

"Take a moment for yourself, Mr. Walby," said old Dr. Braden, himself rising.

"There's no time, sir. I'll tell you all in the coach."

Completely caught up in Gus's web of mysterious excitement, Emily laughed. "At the very least, tell us where we must go."

"To the church of St. Peter and St. Paul," he exhaled with another grin, "in the parish of Wymering."

Noon
Wymering, Portsmouth

LEANDER LEFT THE FRONT entrance of the church and stepped outside to find that the rain had stopped. He had been anguished, watching Mr. Evans's coffin being lowered into the ground next to the copse of yew trees; the presence of rain had only made the scene and the mourners more desolate. As he slowly walked along the churchyard path, Leander could hear Fly's hollow footsteps on the stones, but he did not turn around, thinking it best to leave his grieving friend to his silent reflections.

Magpie, who had tarried in the church, never having been in one before, awestruck by the hushed magnificence of its nave and altar, finally caught up to him. His face was tear-stained and his mouth was still fighting to withhold his tattered emotions, but seeing the new pair of shoes they had purchased that morning for the funeral looking so splendid on his small feet, Leander could not help but smile.

"Could I put it on now, sir?"

"Yes, now that we are out of the church, you may." He watched the boy pull on the woolly thrum cap, disheartened when his dark curls and eye-patch disappeared under its weight. "Here now," Leander said brightly, "if we fold up the bottom, it will sit very well on your head and you shall still be able to see."

"It doesn't fit me proper, does it, sir?"

"No, Magpie, but one day it shall."

Leander looked around for Fly. He had stopped walking to gaze back at the church, his eyes moving over its foundation of grey stone and the lichen-encrusted roof before scaling the length of the bell tower. "I should like to journey home now to be with my wife and children," he said, mumbling as if speaking only to himself. "It has been too long a time." He glanced sadly at Leander. "What about you, old fellow? Before the Admiralty tracks you down, I believe you have earned a day or two at leisure."

Leander continued along the pathway, keeping a watch out for their hired carriage, having asked the driver to return for them at noon. "Magpie and I have planned to — we are — we have —" His stumbling words died upon his lips. His eyes flickered away from his friends, over the churchyard's low fence and across the road where a yellow post-chaise had slowed down and come to a stop.

"What's wrong, sir?" asked Magpie, peering around as if something sinister were lurking behind the crumbling tombstones.

When Leander did not reply, his companions followed his expectant stare and frowned at the older gentleman who had alighted from the post-chaise and was now standing motionless beneath a stand of shivering trees, his arms at his side, his face turned in their direction.

"Do you recognize him, Lee?" asked Fly.

"Is it someone come to mourn their loved ones," Leander said, trying to make sense of what it was he was seeing, "or is it simply a ghost?"

Magpie gasped. "I hope it ain't a spectre, sir."

A smile began to play upon Leander's lips. "No! No, it's my father."

"But he ain't dead, is he, sir?"

"Not that I know of, but — I don't understand — how can this be? How would he ever have known to find me here in this lonely churchyard?" His eyes never once leaving the shadowy apparition, Leander drew toward the fence, but before he had reached the roadside, he stopped again, this time more abruptly, this time to catch his breath. A second person had stepped from the carriage — a young fair-haired woman in a white dress, whose dark eyes searched the churchyard until she had found him. Across the distance, he could hear her clear happy laughter, he could see her tremulous smile and the pink of her cheeks, but it was only when the boy at his side yelped and shouted her name that Leander realized he was not gazing upon a cruel vision.

"Oh, sir! She's come!" sobbed Magpie, reaching up for his hand. "She's come lookin' fer us!"

Leander's body shook with joy and disbelief. Tears started in his eyes. "Dear God! Emily!"

Fly came at once to his side. "Pull yourself together, old fellow."

"But it's really her."

"Yes! I can see that! But it won't do for her to see you so silly."

Leander hesitated, still worried that if he blinked, if he went to her, she would vanish in the trees, taking his father with her.

"What are you waiting for?

"Right!" laughed Leander. "How — how do I look?"

Fly snuffled. "You look like an old scarecrow."

"And you — of all people — who are privy to the true state of my woeful confidence."

Fly leaned in toward Leander and clapped him lightly on the back. "Standing a stone's throw away is solid proof that she did *not* forget her doctor on the sea. Go to her, man, and God bless you both."

They shook hands and Leander hurried off. Feeling wistful, Fly watched him go, praying his friend wouldn't stumble in his exuberance or be knocked down by a passing carriage. Only once he could see that Leander and Emily were safely in each other's arms did he turn away, taking Magpie with him.

"Oh, but sir, I was hopin' to go too!"

Fly studied the sailmaker's bandaged arm, and then — with affection — looked into his bright pleading eye. "'Tis such a wide, wide sea and all of us have come so far."

"Beg yer pardon, sir?"

Fly quickly brushed away a tear. "Nay! Not just yet, Magpie. Stay with me awhile. Let them have a private moment together." He glanced one last time at the jubilant scene across the way and smiled. "But, there now — look! Mr. Walby has come as well! Wave him over to our side of the road, and together we shall tell him of our adventures and show him the peaceful, sloping bit of greenery where Mr. Evans sleeps."

Epilogue

1:00 P.M.
On the Wharves at Portsmouth

THE CLERK LOOKED UP from his rickety desk, arranged on the docks beside the ramp that led to the decks of HMS *Expedition*. The tall prisoner standing before him was busy inspecting the ship's hull and rigging, giving him a chance to size him up as he would a haunch of salted beef in the victualling yard.

"You're an American then?"

"Yes," answered the prisoner, wavering slightly on his swollen, ulcerated feet.

"Any papers on you?"

"I have no papers."

"Ha! They never do!" harumphed the clerk. "Any belongings?"

"Anything I once owned was gambled away long ago."

"Had to sell your pantaloons for a crust of bread, eh? Ha! Not many of you Yankees manage well in our prisons. Sooner or later you enlist with us, just to get out of them. When your mates heard you were joining us, did they tie you up and flog you?"

"They did not."

The clerk squinted up the man, so unlike the others he was. In his manner of speaking, he seemed confident and he could steadily hold his gaze with those sunken eyes of his. "Right then, you just need to be registered in the muster books. Give me your name and place of birth?"

"Asa Bumpus. New Bedford, Massachusetts."

The clerk made a few scribbles in his ledger. "Well, on you go then. The purser's mate will see you get new slops once you've been shaved and bathed."

With a nod, the tall prisoner started to shuffle toward the ship's ramp, but he hesitated as if he'd forgotten something. "Might I ask when we are putting to sea?"

The clerk smiled proudly. "We sail at high tide, Mr. Bumpus."

Afterword

The majority of the characters in *Second Summer of War* are fictional; however, a few of them require a note of explanation.

THE ROYAL FAMILY: King George III and Queen Charlotte had a large family. Six daughters and seven sons lived to adulthood, including their eldest son, George, the Prince Regent (later George IV), and their third son, William, the Duke of Clarence (later William IV), both of whom appear in *Second Summer of War*. Their two youngest sons, Octavius and Alfred, died when they were young children. George III and Queen Charlotte did not have a son named Henry. In creating the fictitious father of my fictitious Emily, I bestowed upon him the title of Duke of Wessex, having borrowed it from the present Earl of Wessex, Queen Elizabeth's son Edward. I imagined Henry to have been born between the Duke of Cumberland and the Duke of Sussex, as Queen Charlotte — who was pregnant most years of her early marriage — had a window of childbearing opportunity between these two sons.

WILLIAM, DUKE OF CLARENCE: Although Emily's Uncle Clarence is not a fictitious character, the adventures he has in *Second Summer of War* are imaginary. I did, however, try my best to stay true to his personality and temperament. He was described as being loud, boorish, and impulsive, and fond of bawdy jokes, but he was also generous and good-natured. For twenty years he lived in domestic bliss with Mrs. Dora Jordan, a popular stage actress, at Bushy House, and though they were not legally married they had ten children together. He was, in fact, appointed Admiral of the Fleet by his brother the Regent in December 1811, and later, upon his brother's death, became King William IV.

FRANCIS "FLY" AUSTEN: Fly was one of Jane Austen's most beloved brothers. He enjoyed a long life and a distinguished naval career. Many of the personal details I gave to his character are true to his appearance and nature, but I did take literary licence with regard to the experiences I had him endure during the War of 1812. He did fight the Americans, but not as a commander of HMS *Isabelle* nor a "fighting" passenger on HMS *Amethyst*, and by 1813 he had long since been promoted to captain. But I like to imagine that the well-respected, intelligent, courageous, and humourous Fly Austen in *Second Summer of War* is very similar to the man that once was.

ROYAL NAVY SHIPS: Although there have been several ships known as HMS *Amethyst* and HMS *Illustrious*, the vessels and their crews in *Second Summer of War* are fictional.

The following appear in the text and warrant a word of explanation:

Page 18 — The prison on Melville Island, Halifax, housed several American prisoners of war during the War of 1812.

Page 22 — During the exchange on deck in this scene, Emily hears an unnamed officer quote lines from *The Sluggard* by Isaac Watts (1674–1748).

Page 23 — Georgiana Cavendish, the Duchess of Devonshire (1757–1806), was known for her beauty and her sense of fashion, including her elaborate hats.

Page 31 — Princess Charlotte (1796–1817) was the only child of the Prince Regent (later George IV) and his wife, Caroline of Brunswick.

Page 48 — Tom o' Bedlam was the name given to former inmates of London's Bethlem Royal Hospital (otherwise known as Bedlam), which treated those suffering from mental illness.

Page 63 — The lines of verse are taken from the eighteenth-century seamen's song *Can of Grog*.

Page 102 — Boodle's was a men's club on St. James's Street, London.

Page 122 — *An Orange and a Slice* refers to the Orange Prince of Holland and the Duke of Gloucester who were both romantically linked to Princess Charlotte in 1813.

Page 151 — Burgoo is a thick oatmeal porridge or gruel that was regular fare in a seaman's diet.

Page 166 — Ratafia was a popular fruit and almond-flavoured liqueur.

Page 167 — A buck was a young, spirited man whose interests included the pursuit of pleasure, often of a debauched nature.

Page 167 — Sir Henry Halford (1766–1844) was a royal and society physician who attended King George III from 1793 until his death in 1820.

Page 168 — The Old Bailey (aka the Central Criminal Court) was so named for the street in London on which it was built, and over the years thousands of criminal cases have been heard here. Newgate Prison once stood next to it.

Page 185 – Tothill Fields was a slum area in London known for its brothels and grog shops.

Page 186 — A fop was a man who took a great interest in his clothes, which were often extravagant and worn in the hopes of securing attention and setting a new fashion trend.

Page 197 — Stovies is a Scottish dish of stewed onions and potatoes.

Page 199 — Leander Braden and Biscuit utter a prayer that is a variation of the one commonly used when a man was buried at sea. In their case, however, they can recall neither the words nor their order.

Page 212 — Tossing a cannonball along the deck and knocking a man off his feet was called shot rolling. The crew often did this to the officers prior to carrying out a mutiny.

Page 235 — Mrs. Maria Fitzherbert (1756–1837) was a mistress of the Prince Regent. They were secretly married in 1785, but their marriage contract was an invalid one.

Page 258 — Sparring and boxing matches were a popular form of entertainment held at the Fives Court in St. Martin's Lane, London.

Page 275 — Prime Minister Spencer Perceval was assassinated on May 11, 1812.

Page 318 — Wymering Parish Church (the Church of St. Peter and St.
Paul) was founded in the twelfth century and is located in Wymering,
Portsmouth. Francis Austen was laid to rest in its churchyard upon his
death in 1865.

Acknowledgements

I WISH TO EXTEND MY sincerest appreciation and gratitude to the following individuals, whose input and excellent suggestions kept me on task, propelling me through *Second Summer of War*'s myriad stages of production: .

My cherished mentor, Anne Millyard, who entered my writing life in 2004; my respected publisher, Patrick Boyer, who believed in my work after forfeiting sleep to kindly read my first manuscript; my dear reader, Sonia Holiad, who selflessly devoted time to my nautical characters; my writing buddies, Cathy Cahill-Kuntz and Nancy Beal, whose enthusiasm sustained my own; my esteemed friend, Dr. Walter Hannah, who assisted me in my medical research; my editor, Cheryl Hawley, whose wit and professionalism made the editing process a joy, and the wonderful team at Dundurn Press — Kirk Howard, Margaret Bryant, Shannon Whibbs, Diane Young, and Allister Thompson — who imagined my front cover, made certain I achieved my literary deadlines, and, most importantly, granted me this opportunity.

I would also like to express my heartfelt thanks to my beloved family, whose love and support and encouragement have carried me through the long — sometimes stormy— months and years of creation.

‒ৎ In the Same Series ৎ‒

Come Looking for Me
Seasons of War #1
Cheryl Cooper
978-1-926577074
$24.95

A mysterious young English woman named Emily risks a crossing of the Atlantic during the War of 1812 for the promise of a new adventure in Canada. But she never arrives.

Captured by Captain Trevelyan, a man as cold-blooded as his frigate is menacing, Emily is held prisoner aboard the USS *Serendipity*. Seeking to save herself, she makes a desperate escape overboard in the midst of a raging sea battle and is rescued by the British crew of HMS *Isabelle*. Yet Emily has only exchanged one form of captivity for another, and remains in peril as England escalates its fight against the United States on the Atlantic.

On board the *Isabelle*, Emily encounters a crew of fascinating seamen and strikes up unexpected friendships, but life on a man-of-war is full of deprivations and dangers to which she is unaccustomed. Amidst heartache and tragedy at sea, she struggles to find her place among the men until a turn of events reveals her true identity. And when Trevelyan's ship once again looms on the horizon, Emily fears losing the only man she has ever loved and falling into the hands of the only man she has ever loathed.

Come Looking for Me is a rich and compelling story of love and courage, friendship and treachery, triumph and loss. With humour and poignancy, author Cheryl Cooper captures all the colour, detail, and excitement of the great ships from the golden age of sail, while bringing to life those who fought upon them. She tells a story of the bravery of the men locked in the epic, brutal struggle that was the War of 1812, and the courage of a woman who, with extraordinary determination, labours to make her own way in life and in love.

Available at your favourite bookseller

 **DUNDURN**

VISIT US AT

Dundurn.com | @dundurnpress | Facebook.com/dundurnpress | Pinterest.com/dundurnpress